WILLIA

Burma Tiger

ISBN: 1449978819
ISBN-13: 9781449978815
Library of Congress Control Number: 2009913932

DEDICATED TO:

ANG SAN SUU KYI,
The noble woman who personifies the heart
and soul of her captive Burma.

CHAPTER ONE

LONDON: 1862

Sergeant Major Michael Oliver St. John, recently placed on temporary duty from Her Majesty's Burma Military Police, tried a second time to open his sorely aching eyes to determine how long he had been unconscious this time. Although the malarial bouts were coming less frequently, the cold damp London climate compounded the misery throughout his thirty-eight-year-old body, especially his head.

After several painful attempts, he managed to focus on the alarm clock on the small table standing near his bed. At almost the same moment he was able to focus on the face of the clock, he heard the dull thuds of Big Ben in the distance announcing that it was noon in the City of London. For an instant his mind raced back to his last and most-beloved posting, Burma. He reckoned that it was the middle of the night in the small riverside village in the outskirts of Rangoon and that his Supi Yaw, his lovely Supi Yaw Lat, would be in her little bamboo bed, with several joss sticks burning near the door of her bamboo hut. He visualized Gunga, the small English Bulldog, lying across the doorway in order to protect his mistress from intruders or snakes.

The brief reverie was rudely interrupted by a pounding on the wooden door of his non-commissioned officers' barracks room. "Sergeant Major St. John, are you up and about?" a syrupy sweet voice called. "It's time to change your bed linen; and who knows what else!" the stout, pudgy woman at the door whined. Sergeant Major St. John managed to move his bare feet onto the cold, hard slate floor. It required every ounce of strength the ailing soldier could muster to place his suspenders over his aching shoulders and stand reasonably erect. He took a long drink from a glass of stale water and coughed. The mirror across the room confirmed how Sergeant Major Michael Oliver St. John truly felt. Again the pounding and again the voice, "Michael, please open up. We can't be sleeping all day now, can we?" she mewed like a cat in heat.

"No, I guess we can't," the Sergeant Major uttered as he moved toward the protective wooden barrier which kept the world and this bothersome woman out of his temporary sanctuary. He took hold of the cold brass door knob and forced his mouth into a smile. "Good morning, Mrs. O'Brien, and how are you this fine English morning?" he said sarcastically.

"Well, Sergeant Major for one thing, it's no longer morning; you have slept most of the day," she said in a scolding tone.

"Actually, Mrs. O'Brien, I have not been feeling too well these past few days. I believe I have had a touch of the jungle fever."

The meddlesome woman pushed her way into the small room holding a pile of bed linens and towels. She sniffed the air and surveyed the room looking for signs or smells of rum. "No, Mrs. O'Brian, I do my drinking at the pub, not in my room. I do not break the rules of the barracks." St. John said courteously.

Realizing that she had briefly offended the gentleman, she began to apologize profusely. "Michael, please call me

Katherine. My late husband, Clancy, God rest his soul, was taken by the rum. His last days were horrible. I don't want to see another of God's most glorious creatures tortured to death by the 'Devil's drink'."

The apology was politely accepted knowing that as soon as she changed the bed and replaced the towels, she would be gone until next week, much like a recurring nightmare.

As the large lady was moving toward the door, she stopped in front of Michael's dress uniform neatly hanging on a hanger. She carefully examined the dozen or so collection of medals hanging from the left breast. She also took occasion to notice the small red and gun-metal grey symbol of extreme valor and its framed citation reading:

"The Victoria Cross, presented to Sergeant Major Michael St. John;

For gallantry above and beyond the call of duty."

As the woman stood looking at the medal, the weary middle-aged man glanced at the mirror and wondered for a moment, "*Am I the same man who received the Victoria Cross from my queen only a few weeks ago?*" The blurry-eyed man pulled in his bulging stomach and attempted to stand a little taller. "*Yes, I am that same man, just a bit under weather. This lousy London weather is enough to bring an early demise to any man.*"

The lady once again moved toward the door. She stopped. "Michael," she mewed, "perhaps you would like to take a walk with me later this afternoon. Perhaps we could have tea in a cozy little tea shop I recently discovered." Her cheeks reddened as she waited for the soldier's answer. She coyly continued, "and perhaps we could find some mischief to take our minds off the weather."

St. John remembered back, a few days ago when she managed to cross his path as he was going for a brief walk. She sidled up to the poor man and affixed herself like a stray pup.

Before Michael could break free from the woman, she almost proposed marriage! The woman was clearly smitten and desperate for someone, anyone, to keep her company on cold English nights.

"Perhaps another time, Mrs. O'Brian, this afternoon I have an appointment with my tailor. We have matters of a spiritual nature to discuss."

Mrs. O'Brian, openly rejected, curtsied and left the room, moving on to the next soldier in the next barracks cubicle.

"Thank God for weekly chess games with Amerjit!" he whispered to himself. Amerjit was a Sikh friend and an excellent cook from the Junior Officers Barracks. Michael and Amerjit often met for a game of chess over an Indian meal in an obscure Indian restaurant called The Taj Mahal of London over in Soho.

CHAPTER TWO

RETROSPECT:

Sergeant Major Michael Oliver St. John was both the eldest son of Sergeant-Major Andrew Winston St. John and the grandson of Sergeant-Major Malcolm Fredrick St. John. He was from the British cast of warriors whose very reason for being was to protect the monarch and the realm against all enemies, real and imagined. From the day he was born, on April 15, 1824 in Bombay, India, Michael's singular ambition was to become a Sergeant-Major, as did his father and grandfather. Unfortunately during that life-long objective, no women entered his little world of war, guns, and long marches; no English women that is. And, unfortunately, no proper English soldier, especially a soldier aspiring to become a Sergeant Major, could marry a non-English woman. It simply wasn't done! This meant that the brief line of British warriors would end with him. For a brief moment, he considered Mrs. O'Brian's advances as a means of continuing his line of soldiers. The thought lasted long enough to cause his demeanor to alter from pleasant to sorely distressed.

His only brother, Arthur Wilson St. John, was a sickly child burdened with thick heavy glasses. All throughout his childhood and well into adulthood Arthur maintained his distain for guns, war, long marches and most of all, women. With the encouragement of his ever-doting mother, Arthur was lovingly directed toward the life of a clergyman—a celibate clergyman. The only item of interest in Arthur's little life was the collection of postage stamps. He had, in fact, collected the many letters his parents had received from their parents and others. He made regular rounds to the homes of family friends to collect used stamps and envelopes. It was a foolish pastime, but it did serve to maintain Arthur's interest in something other than himself and his numerous infirmities.

Michael Oliver St. John had entered the British Army a year before regulations allowed. He was tall for his age and his father, a highly decorated and well-seasoned sergeant major, convinced the regimental officer that his son was indeed "old enough" to fight for his God and his country. His father, Sergeant Major Andrew St. John, had trained his son in the sacred arts of the warrior almost from the time he could walk. Michael knew virtually every order, every bugle call, every formation, every regimental insignia in the British Army and Navy. By the time he was twelve, Michael could spin off the battle history of the British Empire along with the names of all of the kings and queens. His ability to re-enact battles with his set of beloved toy soldiers seemed uncanny. Often times, he would entertain his father's cohorts by recreating a particular battle using his toy soldiers. Like a chess game, Michael would advance, retreat, outflank and conquer toy armies. Michael's brother, Andrew, rejected all that "mean and hurtful" play in favor of books, books, and more books. Andrew's army-issue spectacles and an overprotective mother seemed to exempt him from ever pursuing the life of the soldier class. They even managed to protect him from the occasional fisticuffs incurred by most boys on the playground.

While it was understood that Michael would eventually move up through the ranks until he reached the rank of sergeant major, he began his military career like all of the other young recruits. His first stripe came sooner than his comrades, as did commendations for general service and acts of exemplary service. Michael was, as one of his commanding officers once called him, "a soldier's soldier." He had an uncanny ability to pick up local languages, not to mention the local "ways." Michael had a natural ability to gain the respect of the British soldiers as well as the native conscripts. Unlike many of his contemporaries, he dispensed respect to both black and white soldiers. And unlike many of his contemporaries, he demonstrated respect for those below him as well as above him in rank and social status.

Midway through his career, Michael was reassigned from the "troubles" in the bone-dry deserts of India to the dark, dank swamps of Burma. His commanding officer noticed deterioration in his sense of personal moral and overall self-esteem. Something extremely grave had happened to the "soldier's soldier." The transition from India and the British Army to the Royal Burma Police was hard, very hard. Oven-dry heat was replaced with the steamy hot climate of a troop ship's boiler room. Growling brown camels gave way to the shrill trumpeting of grey Burmese elephants. The ever-present death from thirst gave way to death from the jungle fever; the shaking, quaking, bone-breaking jungle fever. But, death in whatever form is always a soldier's closest companion. So what did it matter whether one died in a desert or a swamp? Dead is dead. After all, the British Empire is built on blood and bones of its soldier and sailors. God bless the soldiers and sailors!

CHAPTER THREE

BACK TO HIS QUARTERS IN LONDON

Michael poured a pitcher of water into his shaving basin and lathered his deeply furrowed face. He looked into the mirror; no, into the eyes in the mirror. He stood looking at those eyes which had seen more in his thirty-eight years than the eyes of a dozen men on the streets of London combined. He had lived more in his brief, thirty-eight years than a hundred carriage drivers, shop clerks, or desk-bound civil servants. He had crammed more adventure, pain, and noble accomplishments into his life than almost any man could even imagine. He felt a sense of pity and compassion for those carriage drivers, shop clerks, and desk-bound civil servants whose bodies and souls were chained to their respective prison walls. Hard to believe that some of those poor souls had never left the neighborhoods in which they were born and raised and would ultimately die. He, on the other hand, had been blessed with a life so full of memories that he was afraid to talk to others about his adventures. Who would believe a man with such a wealth of experiences? He chuckled to himself as he scraped the straight razor across his proud face. Michael glanced at the reflection of the Victoria Cross hanging behind him across the room. How many men have stood in the presence of Queen Victoria herself and been personally congratulated for a job well done? His eyes watered at the thought as his mind reached back to the event in the jungles of Burma which resulted in that small red and bronze medal hanging on his wall.

CHAPTER FOUR

BURMA, THE IRRAWADDY RIVER 1862

The ancient flat-bottomed paddle wheeler commandeered by the Royal Burma Police had taken a cargo of food and general supplies up the muddy Irrawaddy River to an outpost deep into the sweating Burmese jungle. For this particular excursion, Sergeant St. John had been given responsibility for the security detail while under the command of a very young, lieutenant recently arrived from London. Since the British Army and Police had put down a number of "skirmishes" as they called them, the smoke-belching paddle boats providing food and supplies for Her Majesty's enclaves far inland, could make the journey with little or no interference. However, on occasion, local warlords or desperate peasants had taken to occasional acts of river piracy in order to feed their families. Fortunately, there had been no confirmed reports of insurgents or pirates on or near the Irrawaddy for some time.

For this trip up the Irrawaddy, Sergeant St. John hand selected a detachment of twenty-four newly arrived soldiers to protect the cargo and crew. During their short time in the barracks in Rangoon, these newly arrived soldiers had grown tired of the humdrum routine of the barracks and the monotony of general police work. Sergeant St. John took delight in getting these "freshies" as they were called, into the bush and 'scratched-up a bit' as he liked to put it. He loved to watch the expression on the freshies' faces when they came round a bend in the river and encountered a herd of elephants bathing on the banks of the river. He enjoyed watching as his men as they turned green-faced as they watched a Burmese python swallowing a small deer.

Upon reaching the distant outpost at the far end of the Irrawaddy River, the cargo was off loaded by coolies and replaced with soldiers; mostly sick soldiers. Most of the sick had malaria or as the locals called it, 'jungle fever'. Some of the more unfortunate soldiers had contracted dingy fever where every bone in your body feels as if it were broken. Those less fortunate suffered from hemorrhagic fever where every bone in your body feels as if it were broken and every blood capillary in the lower arms and legs burst causing a deep purple, painful tinge to the skin. Of the forty-two men carried on board in litters, more than half were delirious with fevers well above normal. Thank God the cholera which had ravished India had not found this out post–yet! The sick were gently placed on cots situated around the deck of the paddle-wheeler. The boat's covered decks were tented with a thick netting to protect against the mosquitoes by day and the insidious flies by day. A detachment of ten soldiers from the outpost's garrison had been assigned to replace the freshies and escort the sick back to the coast. St. John wanted to see that the new freshies would get their baptism into the real and imagined terrors of the Burmese rainforests. Those who survived the life of a soldier could one day tell their grandchildren stories of the great Irrawaddy and how they survived the dark world of the Burma jungle.

After a lazy layover to take on fuel needed to feed the stomach of the ancient boat and a cargo consisting of a dozen or so unmarked wooden crates, the paddle-wheel flat boat's boilers were brought to life, its tethers loosed, it was sent on its way southward and back to civilization. Several hours travel away from the outpost, the river shallowed a bit and made a sharp bend. Sharp cliffs jutted up from the jungle floor on both sides of the great river. An unseen choir of Great Hornbills and gibbons sang their songs from the tops of trees as the floating hospital passed below. From behind a thick curtain of wild mango trees, dozens, perhaps twenty small log canoes formed a barrage of well-armed warriors across the expanse of the river. An unseen voice signaled the canoe armada to surround the slow, flat-bottomed floating ambulance.

Within seconds of rounding the bend in the shallow Irrawaddy, dozens of well armed pirates had completely surrounded the smoke-belching boat. The captain saw fit to pull an iron lever in the wheel house causing the great paddle to stop its forward rotation. One of the hand-hewn log canoes managed to position itself directly ahead of the oncoming paddle wheel boat. A man wearing only a loin cloth and a look of deadly determination and holding a long rifle supported on a bamboo tripod, squeezed the trigger. A half second later, the man holding the great wheel in the pilothouse of the big boat fell to the floor after a small lead ball scraped the fleshy part of his shoulder. For the most part, the soldiers on the boat were dashing for cover, firing shots into the water or into the trees beyond those in the canoes. The gibbons and Hornbills in the trees added to the sense of chaos with their yells and shrieks. As for the soldiers, there was little or no serious attempt to hit anyone in particular. Their only apparent objective was to find something substantial to hide behind. Several times during the initial mêlée, Sergeant St. John yelled the order to "hold fire!" He realized that the pirates, for the most part, were shooting into the air. Call it a seasoned soldier's intuition, but it appeared that their primary cause was to intimidate rather than to annihilate. The young lieutenant, standing next to the wounded pilot, attempted to grab the great wheel and prevent the boat from running aground on a shallow sand bar dangerously near the underbelly of the paddle wheeler. Another lead ball grazed the face of the young officer prompting him to relinquish his grip on the ship's wheel and flee the wheel house to safer quarters. St. John noticed the brief trickle of blood on the officer's face and reckoned that the poor fellow was out of the fight. With the young lieutenant wounded and now hiding somewhere below in the engine room, it occurred to Sergeant St. John that he was now the senior man on board. The attack seemed at first, an illogical act, as a massacre of this nature would have been fairly simple to achieve by any respectable group of desperate men. Any logical pirate would have set fire to the boat, causing its crew to abandon ship. From there, the smaller boats could have systematically dealt with each floundering soldier who had avoided drowning. It would have been a simple action. St. John also concluded in his soldier's mind that an act of this extreme nature would have most certainly brought on massive reprisals from Her Majesty's forces in the region. An act of this magnitude would be devastating to every Burmese clan in the region. Sergeant St. John quickly realized that he and his forces were outnumbered by ten to one. He also realized that he and his men were confined to a floating platform which could soon be set afire. Without question, his entire force and those he was charged with transporting safely to the hospital would soon be dead is he did not so something drastic. In assessing the situation, Sergeant St. John surmised that the pirates were intent on something other than killing a boat load of British soldiers; perhaps it was the cargo they wanted. The sergeant climbed to the pilot house railing and in his broken Burmese, he called for a cease fire. Waving his hands frantically, as several lead projectiles passed mere inches from his body, St. John managed to gain the attention of a black-robed figure in one of the canoes. The man covered in a loose black robe held up his hands and barked an order. The shooting stopped abruptly. The gibbons and the Great Hornbills also fell silent at the call. St. John also barked an order to hold fire. The teak log canoe carrying the black-robed figure floated through the acrid fog-like gunpowder smoke which now covered the surface of the river like a London fog. The black-robed figure yelled in English, "What is your intent?"

Sergeant St. John replied, "I wish to surrender the cargo of this boat. I only ask that you allow my soldiers and those who are ill to go on their way unharmed."

The man in the black robe threw back the hood covering his head, "What is your name, Englishman?"

"My name is Sergeant Michael St. John, of Her Majesty's Burma Police."

The warlord laughed, "Sergeant Michael St. John, I like you. I think I shall call you Mike."

The sergeant called back, "I don't like you, but, I will give you my cargo if you allow us to pass."

Again the warlord laughed, prompting several watching gibbons to imitate the actors before them. "Sergeant Mike, I could easily kill you and your men and then take your cargo, but because I like you, I will only take your cargo and not burn your boat."

Those on the boat breathed a sigh of relief as they lowered their rifles an inch or so. Realizing that the crisis was only slightly averted, the sergeant called out, "And what do they call you?"

The war lord laughed, "They call me Bua Tan Bo. My close friends call me Bua."

Not knowing exactly what to say at this point, Sergeant St. John announced, "Well then, I shall call you Bua Tan Bo until we become better acquainted. Then, looking at the sky, St. John continued, "By my recollection, Bua Tan Bo, it is about four o'clock in the afternoon, the time when most proper English gentlemen take tea. Might I invite you on board my boat for a cup of tea?"

Those who could understand both on the pirate's side and those aboard the ill-fated boat realized the audaciousness of this British soldier. Imagine inviting your enemy to join you in a cup of tea in the midst of a battle.

The pirate again laughed and spoke, "I would be honored to have a cup of tea with you, as your men load the cargo into my boats." The pirate gave a string of orders whereupon canoes began to move toward the stern of the silent riverboat. The sweat-soaked sergeant, too, gave a series of orders regarding hot tea, some ginger cakes, and the dozen wooden boxes to be off loaded.

As he boarded the dormant paddle wheel boat the pirate respectfully saluted the Union Jack at the stern. "Too big, too clumsy." he uttered in English.

Two whicker chairs and a small teak wood table were brought to the deck as were a silver pot of tea and a plate of ginger biscuits. St. John beckoned for his guest to be seated whereupon he took a chair across the table. From inside his black robe Bua Tan Bo pulled two hand-rolled green cigars. "Sergeant Mike, May I offer you a cigar?" the warlord asked.

St. John smiled and accepted the small token of congeniality. Bua Tan Bo then barked another order whereupon a man carrying a small animal skin shoulder bag produced a one liter bottle of a purple liquid. "Perhaps you might enjoy a dram of jungle berry wine along with your tea."

Accepting the offer, Sergeant Michael St. John passed the cigar under his nose. "Nice," he said as a nearby soldier struck a wooden match and lit both cigars. Bua Tan Bo held the two rough glasses as his servant poured the purple wine to the brim.

"Sault," Bua said.

"Sault," replied St. John. The juice was sweet and potent; the cigar was green and harsh. For Sergeant Michael St. John, the experience of indulging in a glass of wine and a cigar with the enemy, in the midst of a battle was absolutely exhilarating beyond description.

"So, Mr. Bua Tan Bo, you speak English?"

The pirate smiled, nodded then replied in English, "So, Mr. Sergeant Mike St. John, you speak Burmese?"

St. John retorted back, "And Urdu, a bit of Hindi, and, of course, some French."

Not to be outdone, Bua Tan Bo added to this little tit for tat. "And I have read over two hundred English classics, I know a bit of Greek and Latin and, I have memorized the entire King James Bible!"

St. John, realizing that he had been trumped, simply smiled and nodded his approval. Michael continued, "It is apparent that you are not from this region. Is that correct?"

"You are correct, Sergeant Mike. We are Baum People from the Banderban Hills which, as you no doubt know, mark the boundary between Burma and India. I am the son of an elder in the circle of elders. I have been sent here by the elders to retrieve the crates which you have so kindly relinquished."

Michael took another sip of wine and puff of the green cigar and leaned back in his chair. "Tell me, Mr. Bua Tan Bo, what is in the crates of such value that you are willing to bring the wrath of the British Army and quite possibly, Queen Victoria herself, down on your head?"

The warlord again laughed as he leaned forward toward the Englishman's ear. He whispered, "Rubies, Sergeant Mike, Burmese rubies. For years, your infernal British traders have been systematically robbing my people as they purchase these precious stones in return for insignificant trade items. A raw ruby, for example, worth a hundred English pounds sterling is purchased from a simple village miner for a few pennies worth of English clothe or some other worthless English trinket. These same British traders have systematically managed to prevent other traders from China and Russia from entering the region and making far more lucrative offers for our stones. The same is true for our precious Burmese jade and ivory. Because of your ridiculous laws, my people are required to trade with the British traders or trade with no one. So, Sergeant Mike St. John, at the request of my tribal elders, I am taking back my people's property from those who stolen it from them. As soon as possible, I will attempt to find a more profitable market in which to sell these stones."

Sergeant St. John blew a plume of grey smoke into the air as he pondered the situation before him. None of the soldiers on board the paddle wheel boat had dared to move during the entire drama being played out on the teakwood deck of the riverboat. With the exception of the river pirates unloading the twelve wooden boxes, no one in the canoes had moved a muscle. Rifles were still aimed at British foreheads with fingers on triggers.

Without saying a word, the English sergeant nodded and grunted, "Hmm."

"So, Bua, are we free to go?"

The warlord took note of the fact that the English soldier had now addressed him by his nickname, Bua, a name that was only to be used by those whom would be considered close friends.

Bua rose to his feet, saluted the Sergeant, thanked him for his hospitality, again saluted the Union Jack and left the flat-bottomed boat with the twelve wooden crates.

There was no spontaneous cheer, only an enormous sigh of relief, from the sweat-soaked British soldiers as the pirates disappeared back up the Irrawaddy and into the jungle. Once again, the Great Hornbills and the gibbons resumed their songs. The slightly wounded lieutenant had soiled himself and was found hiding below deck, behind the main boiler. A medic wound a half a bed sheet round the minuscule wound on his head, causing him to look like an Indian porter. The pilot was bandaged, the boilers stoked and the paddle wheel boat moved slowly down the thick, brown Irrawaddy River toward the coast of Burma.

CHAPTER FIVE

Within hours of the confrontation, the story of the battle between Bua Tan Bo and the British sergeant had reached into every ear in every sleepy village along the river and deep into its tributaries. Village runners spread the news of the battle and warned of impending retributions from the British.

The story had reached the town of Rangoon two days before the paddle wheel boat arrived. Each time the story was told by a runner and retold to a merchant and retold to civil servant, bits and pieces were added and multiplied. Bua's murderous horde grew from two dozen to several hundred or so to well over a thousand blood-thirsty cutthroats. The stories stopped just short of having Sergeant St. John walk on water or cause the Irrawaddy to part. Each time the story was told, the teller was quick to note that the culprits were foreigners from a distant place. Knowing that the British authorities would be quick to seek retribution, no one wanted to suggest this act of extreme treason was perpetrated by a local warlord or tribal leader.

As the paddlewheel boat belched to a halt at the main pier near the British Burma Police Headquarters, uniformed ranks of British officers and well dressed government officials, regaled in all their swords, feathered hats and finery, waited for Sergeant Michael St. John to appear. This was a God-send as it was seldom that anything broke the boredom of this backwater enclave. An occasion of this magnitude managed to ease the insidious monotony of the occupation of this faraway piece of the great puzzle known as the British Empire. At the request of the commandant of the garrison, a small brass band had convened behind the dignitaries which added to the festive nature of the event. In this part of the world, brass bands were included in everything from weddings to hangings, as were full uniforms, shiny silver swords and feathered hats.

Both ambulatory and bed-ridden soldiers were welcomed into the waiting arms of the small but enthusiastic crowd of soldiers, nurses, and coolies. The young lieutenant in charge of the ill-fated ship wore an enormous bandage across his head and much of his face. It was obvious to those aboard the boat that he wore the dressing more to hide his shame than to cover his wound. The poor chap managed to blend in with the sick and injured as he pretended to oversee the offloading of the passengers and crew. Sergeant Michael St. John was the last man to leave the boat. Dressed in his sweat-drenched uniform, Sergeant St. John appeared as he shyly acknowledged the applause of the crowd. Standing at the bottom of the gang plank, Lieutenant Colonel Ballentine, the colonel in charge complete with his feathered hat and sword, offered an abrupt salute which was returned by a surprised salute from the sergeant. “Sergeant Michael St. John, reporting, sir,” Michael barked.

Colonel Ballentine replied in a loud voice, for all in attendance to hear, "Shall we make that Sergeant Major St. John? Your actions in the interior have prompted me to make a well-deserved field promotion and, I might add, a possible citation for extreme bravery in the face of grave danger. For that we will have to wait until the senior staff at Whitehall receives the full reports on 'our' little adventure up in the hinterlands. Meanwhile, Sergeant Major St. John, why don't you tidy up a bit and report to my quarters at, let's say, high noon. From there, we can grab a bit of lunch and develop a full report on this dastardly incident up river."

After weeks of barracks and field rations served on tin plates, the lunch in Colonel Joseph Daniel Ballentine's handsomely appointed office was a welcome event. Unfortunately for Sergeant Major St. John, the meeting evolved from an informal luncheon into a lengthy debriefing session which lasted well into the afternoon. Every detail of the "battle" was transcribed and, in some cases, embellished in order to bring more attention to this often-times, forgotten corner of the Empire. Reality was combined and compromised with innuendo and mild hyperbole. With so little to occupy the hours of the days, and the monotony of writing empty reports, events of this nature were a godsend for a colonel in charge looking for a promotion and possible rotation back to a more comfortable billet. After several hours, a highly embellished version of the brief encounter on the Irrawaddy was put to paper. While St. John reflected on the actual event, he smiled passively at the revised version created by his commanding officer. After all, who was he to contest the contents of an official report?

Outside, three freelance writers, as well as credentialed reporters, attacked each and every man who had survived the

Battle of the Irrawaddy. The young lieutenant who had been in command during the battle was nowhere to be found for comment. When the young lieutenant was finally found, Ballentine ordered him to verify the final report. He simply nodded and agreed that the account was accurate. His signature was affixed and the report became history. Even those who were much too delirious to give a full account of the event managed to nod blind affirmations to the questions of the writers and reporters. By the time the "Battle of the Irrawaddy" had reached *The Times* of London, the story had grown to epic proportion. Sergeant Major Michael Oliver St. John had become a household name along with the likes of Genghis Khan, Attila the Hun, and Moses. But, as with so many heroes of the moment, the black and white images on the front pages of *The Times* soon faded and were replaced with new images of new heroes in Great Britain's quest to bring civilization to the darkest corners of the planet. It was noted by *The Times*, however, that Sergeant Major St. John might have been nominated for the Victoria Cross for extreme bravery in the face of grave danger.

After the dust had settled on the "Battle of the Irrawaddy," matters in Rangoon reverted back to the monotonously dull pace of an elephant plodding through the mud track of a rainforest jungle. After a well-deserved week of rest and recuperation, Colonel Ballentine, the colonel in charge of the region ordered, no, make that invited, Sergeant Major St. John to another luncheon in his headquarters' office. It was obvious that Ballentine was taking full advantage of the Sergeant Major's recent notoriety, not to mention his awareness of the man's keen leadership qualities. Here was a non-commissioned officer who truly possessed the qualities of a senior officer and a gentleman.

At precisely the stroke of eleven, Sergeant Major St. John presented himself, with his new insignia of a Sergeant Major neatly stitched to his uniform, to the aide d'camp outside the Colonel's office door. The Sergeant Major was shown into the colonel's office where he stomped his polished black boots on the teakwood floor and saluted. "Sergeant Major St. John reporting as ordered," he barked.

Colonel Ballentine returned the salute and dismissed the aide d'camp. In an almost unprecedented act, Ballentine offered the non-commissioned officer a snifter of whiskey. St. John was quietly shocked at the informality of the gesture. Michael accepted the glass of amber liquid. Ballentine raised his glass to a portrait of Queen Victoria above his desk. "God save the Queen," he toasted. Michael echoed the toast.

"My cousins make this stuff," Ballentine said. "This is private family stock. Good grog, what?"

Michael was not accustomed to gentlemen's whiskey and found it to be a bit soft. "Good, indeed!" he replied politely.

"Now, let's you and I get down to business. This Irrawaddy thing, you know the business with this Bua Tan Bo character. It seems to have caused quite a stir among the general staff. They are more than a little concerned about these renegade pirates running amuck taking whatever they please from whom ever they please. It simply can't be tolerated, can it?"

St. John was fully aware that the final account of the "Battle of the Irrawaddy" had been embellished to resemble the Battle of Thermopile and that the image and stature of Bua Tan Bo now resembled that of Genghis Khan. Michael had quietly hoped that the whole unfortunate affair would be forgotten, and he could once again return to his life of soldiering.

"Now then, Sergeant Major St. John, I want to be quite candid with you and you with me. Let us discuss the matter man-to-man so to speak or more appropriately, soldier-to-soldier."

St. John pondered that comment for a moment knowing full well that the highly decorated colonel had probably never fired a shot in anger or, at least, never at a creature not wearing antlers. "Sergeant Major, I need your honest assessment of the situation in the interior, particularly as it relates to this Bua Tan Bo fellow. He could become another thorn in our flesh much like that *mahadi* devil back some years in Khartoum, you know, Kitchener and all that. So, what's your take on this rabble-rouser?"

Michael pondered the question carefully. He knew full well that the Colonel would filter out those comments he did not want to hear and embellish those from which he might profit. Every word needed to be put in place, like a child's puzzle, before the words were spoken. If not, a false picture would be realized with detrimental consequences for those concerned.

"In my opinion, Colonel, Bua Tan Bo is not your storybook pirate but rather a man caught in a situation where his options are limited by circumstances not of his making. Bua Tan Bo is an extremely intelligent man, of the highest moral character, and totally devoted to his god and country."

Colonel Ballentine interrupted Michael in an almost belligerent tone. "Do you mean to tell me that this barbarian, this warlord, ranks in the same strata as, let's say, an officer in Her Majesty's Army?"

St. John nonchalantly nodded, "I would say so; yes, perhaps even a Colonel." While the comment was meant to offer a slight rebuff to Ballentine's ill-conceived assessment of Bua Tan Bo, the Colonel completely missed the jab.

"Go on, Sergeant Major, tell me more of this jungle prince of yours," Ballentine said.

"As a matter of fact, Colonel, Bua Tan Bo is the eldest son of a tribal elder of the Baum People in the Banderban Hills west of here. While this does not exactly qualify him as a prince, it does confer on him considerable rank among his people and other tribal groups. Added to this is his mastery of the English language and over two hundred of our literary classics. In fact, Colonel Ballentine, Bua Tan Bo has committed the entire Holy Bible to memory."

Ballentine recoiled in shock. The thought of a jungle man, a common primitive at that, being able to recite the entire Holy Bible was almost blasphemous. Ballentine was aghast at the thought of a non-Englishman being privy to two hundred volumes sacred classics exclusively reserved for the educated upper class. This was clearly a violation of the unwritten British colonialist caste system to keep the natives loyal to the Empire, but ignorant. To Ballentine and others of his station, it seemed somehow unholy, and most certainly unnatural, for the common heathen to rise to the levels of the highly civilized British officer or even a gentleman.

It pleased Michael to see the rancor rise in Ballentine's demeanor as he embellished Bua's persona and the growing fiction surrounding this primitive enigma.

"I would add, Colonel Ballentine, Bua Tan Bo has a taste for fine cigars and ferments his own personal wines. While the vintages are still somewhat unrefined, they are nonetheless quite satisfying to my untrained pallet."

Michael broke a slight smile as he noticed Colonel Ballentine ruminating on this last embellishment regarding the harsh green cigars and the potent jungle berry punch.

Attempting to regain his composure, Colonel Ballentine blurted, "Cigars, oh yes, can I offer you a cigar, Sergeant Major?" These are fresh in from Cuba."

It was absolutely unprecedented that an officer of significant rank would offer a cigar, especially a Cuban cigar to a non-commissioned officer. Ballentine lit the two cigars, refreshed the two glasses of whiskey and took a chair. Michael was keenly aware that he was being used for Ballentine's personal agenda.

"Now then, I have been authorized by higher authority to issue a warrant for this Bua Tan Bo fellow along with a significant reward for his capture or killing if it should come to that. So, Sergeant Major St. John, I would appreciate your insights as to how I might proceed in this somewhat delicate matter. Perhaps your first-hand knowledge of the subject might serve to direct my course in the prosecution of this unfortunate situation.

Sergeant Major St. John immediately realized that he was in a position to determine the course of several significant careers, not the least of which, his own. Michael savored the situation along with a sip of the whiskey. He blew a plume of white smoke toward the ceiling realizing that his words must be meticulously selected and precisely preformed.

Before he could speak, Colonel Ballentine interrupted his thoughts. "By the way, Sergeant Major, I have made a full report on your extraordinary conduct and acts of extreme bravery during that unfortunate incident on the Irrawaddy. If my superiors concur with my recommendation, you may be considered for the Victoria Cross." The message was delivered in a manner which underscored Ballentine's patronage of the promotion of this noble endeavor. If the Victoria Cross were to be bestowed on Michael, he would forever be in Ballentine's debt. And too, Ballentine was quick to note in his report, that he, Colonel Joseph Daniel Ballentine, III, was St. John's commanding officer and military mentor. In truth, it was the region's commanding brigadier stationed in Colombo,

Ceylon, who initiated the recommendation and who had solicited Ballentine's supportive inputs.

Michael duly noted the subtle implications of Ballentine's comments on his receiving the Victoria Cross. Michael rose from his chair and moved to the large map of Burma and the surrounding territories. He put his finger on the bend in the Irrawaddy River where he had encountered Bua's group of cut-throats. "Colonel Ballentine, I would suggest that I and a small detachment of hand- selected men be dispatched immediately to re-assess the situation and possibly make contact with Bua Tan Bo. Perhaps I can convince him to surrender or at least capitulate to another location more suited to his way of life. If nothing else, I can inform Bua that he is a subject of the Queen and as such, shall respect the requirements of her realm."

Having no other viable options other than an all-out military campaign, Colonel Joseph Ballentine agreed that this might just be the best possible way of handling the situation. Ballentine then lowered his voice and moved closer to Michael's ear. What do you say we keep this whole adventure between us? If we are able to bring this rogue to bear, it will be good for both of us. If his actions and attitudes are contrary to ours, we shall simply consider this mission as an intelligence-gathering effort and take further action."

In a whisper, St. John replied, "Between us it is, Colonel; between us soldiers."

Just then, a cannon at the main barracks announced high noon. After a lunch of boiled chicken, boiled potatoes, and boiled pudding, Michael took leave of his commanding officer and returned to his quarters. Behind the closed door, he addressed himself in the mirror. "Sergeant Major Michael Oliver St. John, you are the newly appointed rook in this silly game of chess on the Imperial chess board we call Burma. You are allowed to jump over other more powerful pieces and if you play your match correctly, you will be able to gain the board and save your queen." He smiled broadly, anxious to once again meet this worthy opponent somewhere deep in the Burma jungle.

CHAPTER SIX

Within a day, he selected two dozen new freshies from the ranks, commandeered the same paddlewheel boat and set out to once again confront the dreaded river pirate, Bua Tan Bo. He did not, however, request the company of the young officer who had accompanied him on his previous journey. The fresh troops were completely on edge, fearing that any moment they, too, would be overrun by the notorious Bua Tan Bo and his band of two thousand bloodthirsty cut throats. Three days journey up the rain choked Irrawaddy, he ordered the captain to beach the boat near the same spot where the infamous battle had taken place. Off in the distance he could see smoke, the kind of smoke indicating a jungle village. He ordered his men to set a guard, but not to shoot under any circumstances.

Then, alone, he trekked a mile or so through reasonably dense jungle until he encountered an elderly man cutting wild bananas. He politely introduced himself in Burmese, whereupon the old man fell to his knees in total admiration of the newly minted hero of the Irrawaddy. It was obvious that the man had heard of this hero and the embellishments which now enhanced his stature. In a most respectful manner, St. John spoke, "Sir, I would be most grateful if you were to locate Bua Tan Bo and inform him that I wish to talk with him tomorrow at this very place. I will come alone. It is extremely important that we meet together. Go!" The man abandoned his two stocks of bananas and ran off into the jungle towards the smoke.

Michael smiled at the thought of being a man of notoriety, even in this far- flung region of the Empire. He also looked forward to a meeting with his "adversary" the next day. There was something about this Bua chap which was likeable; call it a sense of integrity or perhaps simply kindred hearts.

The evening aboard the beached, paddle wheel boat was reasonably uneventful. Just before evening meal, a small group of local natives approached the boat with baskets of fruits. They placed the baskets on the beach and slowly melted back into the interior. Bananas, papayas, and other exotic fruit for which the English have no names. Wonderful! The offerings were consumed by the ship's company with great fervor and appreciation for God's keen sense of humor in the design, color and appearance of these delicacies. St. John was delighted by the token of respect offered by the locals. He smiled broadly as he consumed a hearty portion of the offering.

The following morning Sergeant Major St. John called for a general muster on the muddy sandbar of the river. With the usual pomp and ceremony of the British military even in these primitive conditions, formal roll call was observed. With a detachment of two dozen green soldiers, a senior non-commissioned officer had to maintain the strictest of discipline. Any break from ritual routine, particularly with new men, led to laziness and general laxity. And too, it was simply not British to begin the day without some sort of a ceremony. Sergeant Major St. John also realized that dozens of unseen Burmese were watching from behind trees and undergrowth. The Sergeant Major handed the next in rank, a newly appointed lance corporal, a list of tasks to be accomplished ranging from the cutting of firewood for the paddle wheeler's boiler to the catching of at least four dozen fish for the evening's meal. The last order was, in fact, a recreational activity intended to give the men a well-needed break from the heat and the newness of the tropics. "I shall return perhaps this evening or perhaps tomorrow before midday," Sergeant Major St. John said. Then came the order, "Dismissed."

Michael slung a leather rucksack on to his back, buckled the chin strap on his helmet and disappeared alone into the thick, green jungle. He knew full well that the men left behind would make every effort to thwart the authority of the lance corporal in charge by any means possible. Within an hour of retracing his steps from the previous day, he noticed the distinct smell of smoke, cigar smoke. A wide smile crossed his face. "Bua," he whispered aloud.

Thirty meters later, he discovered the source of the smoke. Bua Tan Bo was sitting on a bamboo chair in a recently cleared thicket of banana trees. Directly in front of him was a small wooden table upon which sat a chess board, with chess pieces neatly positioned. "It's about time you arrived. I have been waiting for years to play a good game of chess. I assume that you do play chess?" Bua asked as he blew a plume of cigar smoke into the jungle canopy.

"Of course, I play chess. What sort of an Englishman do you take me for?" Michael replied with as much alacrity as he could muster. Michael then looked around and asked, "Where is your army of blood-thirsty cutthroats?"

Bua laughed, "I sent them all home to their families. This gentleman is the only man left to protect me from the 'Hero of the Irrawaddy'." A small dark man emerged from behind a remaining banana tree with another chair. Bua motioned Michael to sit. Bua snapped his fingers and barked an order. The small man produced a sandalwood box containing an assortment of cigars. "These are not the best, but they do serve to keep the flies away from your face," Bua said. Michael selected one, passed it under his nose and placed it in his mouth as the servant struck a match and held it to the cigar. Michael reclined in his bamboo chair and smiled. "*This is the stuff of fantasy,*" he thought to himself. "*Being challenged to a game of chess, with a good cigar, in the midst of a distant jungle by a pirate chieftain. The only thing missing is a good gin and tonic.*"

Almost as if Bua had the power of mind reading, he asked, "Can I interest you in another glass of my homemade jungle berry wine or would you, as a proper Englishman, prefer a cup of bland, lukewarm tea?"

"A cup of tea would be nice but a tot of wine would be even nicer," Michael replied.

Bua spoke, "First Timothy five, twenty-three recommends a little wine for the stomach's sake, does it not?"

Again Bua barked an order in a language Michael did not understand. Within minutes, a proper glass of purple wine was delivered to each man.

Bua reached over to the chess board and picked up the queen. "To the Queen," he toasted.

Michael replied by picking up his queen, "To, Queen Victoria, may she live long and well. They each replaced the chess pieces on the board. Bua gestured to Michael to make the first move. Bua watched the eyes of his opponent and smiled a brief smile. Bua made a second move.

After only six moves, Bua whispered, "Fool's mate." Michael realized that he had been beaten by the oldest and simplest of school-boy moves, the fool's mate. For a seasoned chess player, this was reprehensible. Bua, choking with laughter, said, "Sometimes, my friend, the most seasoned of soldiers is defeated by the simplest of strategies. I promise not to do it again; at least the fool's mate."

"I demand a rematch!" Michael replied with some levity and drama in his voice.

"Sir, I have canceled all previous appointments for the day. I am at your disposal," Bua chortled. After two silent games, it was apparent to Michael that he was in the presence of a formidable and well-educated man. Behind the veneer of a dusty river pirate was a man of letters and high thinking.

The Southeast Asian sun had climbed to its zenith, directly overhead. Protected by an umbrella of banana and peepul trees, sharp spears of sunlight stabbed through to the dark, green ground below. The clearing where the two men sat was now directly exposed to the burning white ball in the sky above. Bua again barked an order to his servant whereupon the small man vanished into the jungle.

Moments later, the servant returned babbling in some distant language. Bua rose from his chair and invited Michael to follow him. A few meters away, at the edge of a small but swiftly moving stream, the servant had prepared a bamboo and banana leaf mat with an unbelievable assortment of fruit, smoked fish, and smoked meat. Michael's astonishment was quite apparent. Bua seemed to take great pleasure in Michael's reaction to this banquet in the bush. "Even a simple barbarian like myself, enjoys the bountiful pleasures of life," Bua said.

"Sir, with all due respect," Michael said, "I would hardly classify you as a barbarian. A rueful rouge, perhaps, but most certainly not a barbarian."

The two men took their places on woven bamboo mats on each side of the pallet of brightly colored fruit and meats. Michael spoke, "Tell me, Bua Tan Bo, exactly who are you and what is your part in this divine comedy we call life on the stage we call Burma?"

Bua continued to savor a cube of golden papaya as he pondered the question. As a vicar would take a deep breath prior to beginning a lengthy homily, Bua sucked in a full breath of humid air. "Like you, Sergeant Major Mike, I too am a player on a chess board. I move where I am compelled to move; sometimes to confound my opponent, sometimes to sacrifice for my master. I, like you, am neither a pawn nor a king but some minor minion somewhere in between. I am expendable; yet at the same time, valuable. My ultimate cause is the defeat of my master's opponent. So much for allegory."

"I am from the Baum tribe of people. Our home is west of here, between Burma and eastern India. We have lived for generations in the Banderban Hills near Chittagong. Most recently, your British missionaries have taken my people from the degenerate practices of paganism to the regenerate practice of soul winning. By and large, the Baum people are Christians and most of them of the Presbyterian persuasion. Unfortunately, this has placed us in rather difficult circumstances wedged between our Mohammedan and Hindu neighbors in India and the Buddhist in

Burmese; none of whom seem to like us. While we try to be as tolerant as possible with others and their respective beliefs, there is little, if any, reciprocity on their part. Our villages are under constant siege from one opponent or another. Many times our opponents, who hate each other, but hate us even more form unholy alliances against us simply to provide torment. Our singular objective is to maintain our tribal integrity, our recently adopted Christian faith, as well as the integrity of our ancestral domain. Our situation is much like that of the Jews and their adversaries, the Arabs. As for me personally, I am the son of an elder in my tribe. As a child, I was fortunate enough to have lived in the same village as one of your English missionaries. He and his good wife taught me to read, whereupon I availed myself of every book in their library. After having read every book in their brief collection, I traveled to the villages of other British missionaries and traders and consumed their literary collections. By the time I was ceremoniously declared a man by the Baum 'circle of elders' I had read over two hundred books. I found a fascination with both Latin and elementary Greek and managed to pick up sufficient skills to read a number of the Greek and Latin classics. I had, likewise, committed to memory the entire Old and New Testaments."

Sergeant Major St. John seemed genuinely impressed and openly awestruck. In Michael's thirty-eight years, he had met numerous men of letters but none as unique as the man sitting on the bamboo mat across from him.

Bua interrupted his discourse to sample a bit of smoked meat and fish.

Michael then asked, "What brings you to the jungles of central Burma?"

There was a brief silence as the servant filled two coconut-shell cups with a fermented jungle berry punch. "Actually, Sergeant Major Mike, I came to meet you."

Michael furrowed his brow and raised an eyebrow. "You came to meet me?"

"Well," said Bua, "not exactly to meet you but rather to confiscate the dozen boxes you were taking to Rangoon. As I mentioned before, those boxes contained over one hundred kilos of Burmese rubies, jade, and other precious stones. Those twelve boxes represented many years of work on the part of my people. The raw gem stones were intended to be sold on the open market. The proceeds from those stones would have been used to purchase guns and bullets for the ongoing war between my people and our Indian and Burmese neighbors. Unfortunately, a totally unscrupulous British trader managed to compromise the tribal elder entrusted with those stones. In a few minutes, our collection of stones, jade and ivory was sold for next to nothing. On the open market, those items would have brought several thousand pounds sterling. Your British trader gave us a mere seven hundred pounds sterling. Those items were wrongfully taken from my people, and it was my responsibility to recover them. While your paddle wheel boat was taking on the sick soldiers and of course, my cargo, I inquired about you and your crew. I could have recovered our property by setting the boat on fire, but I wanted to act in a manner which would be seen as honorable, yet effective.

At that point, Bua called for his servant. After whispering an order, the servant dashed into the bush. Several minutes later he returned with a small leather pouch. Bua, handing the pouch to Michael, said, "Here is the seven hundred pounds sterling your trader gave for our stones. Please return the original seven hundred to the trader so that no one can say that we stole the stones plus one hundred pounds for his inconvenience."

Michael took the pouch. This gesture caused Michael to consider the gravity of the situation. A fellow countryman had knowingly cheated these simple people out of a king's ransom in gem stones and jade almost without consequence. Then the victim becomes the criminal for attempting to resolve the situation and in so doing, makes full restitution to all parties harmed. *"Here is a man of true integrity,"* Michael thought to himself.

Bua spoke, "My father always said, 'Where there is no honor, there is no shame'."

"Well said," Michael acknowledged. "Where there is no shame, there is no honor."

"One more thing," Bua said, "Please extend my sincere apologies to the boat captain and the officer who were wounded in the skirmish. They will soon be handsomely compensated for their misery by my people in Rangoon. Believe me, Sergeant Mike, it was not my intent to harm anyone."

The sun was moving rapidly toward the western quadrant of the sky. A gentle rain began to fall but not from the clouds. It was common in this part of the world for a mist-like rain to fall from the thick canopy of trees at midday. While the mist did result in a slight decline in the one hundred degree heat, it gave rise to slight fog, much like a ground fog on the English moors. The human body, whether that body had been born in England or the Banderban Hills, insisted on an occasional consideration. This was no time for chess, literary topics or any other activity; this was time for an hour-long nap. Each man acknowledged the necessity for a brief respite, leaned back on the bamboo mat and thanks to ample cups of the fermented jungle berry punch, fell fast asleep.

An hour later, almost to the minute, Michael opened his eyes. Directly in front of him on the far side of the stream, stood an enormous yellow and black tiger. At first the tiger looked old and tired. It was crouched low and drinking from the stream. Michael realized that he had left his side arm hanging on the chair near the chess board. He froze, moving only his eyes. To the left was Bua Tan Bo, holding a black revolver aimed directly between the magnificent yellow eyes of the creature. Michael moved his eyes back to those of the tiger. He noticed the beast had one broken fang. "That cold water must be painful on that broken fang," he thought to himself. Then his thoughts returned to Bua, still frozen in place. Several minutes passed with neither man moving a hair. The old tiger looked the two men directly in the eyes, licked his lips and whiskers, rose slowly and walked back into the thick green jungle from whence he had come. From several meters away, Michael heard the old animal belch.

Michael then looked at Bua. "Why didn't you shoot?"

Bua replied, "Why didn't he attack? He could have killed us both, but he opted not to. He was simply doing what tigers do. I found no need to kill him for taking a cool drink on a hot afternoon. Likewise he found no need to kill one or both of us." Michael was still in a state of total amazement.

Bua's old servant heard the men talking and appeared on the scene. Bua pointed to the far side of the stream and suggested that the servant examine the mud there. The frail, old man put his head down low and saw the tiger tracks. He then sniffed the air confirming what he had seen. The servant looked at Bua Tan Bo with an expression of reverence and awe realizing that his master had taken the higher road by not killing the beast.

Another glass of jungle berry wine was consumed as the two men returned to the chess board.

Another game was well under way when Bua spoke. "You know, my friend, this region of the world is beginning to move and move in many directions. Our neighbors in Laos, Cambodia, and Indochina have been invaded by the French. India and, of course, Burma have been captured by the British. It is anyone's guess who will eventually put a ring through the nose of the great dragon, China. There is serious talk that Russia has designs on the old dragon. There are even those who suggest that the United States has acquired a taste for more colonial enterprises. Their investment in the Philippine Islands has perhaps enhanced their appetite for more land under which to fly their stars and stripes. It has been suggested that Siam might become their next acquisition. What I am saying is this; Burma is a key player in this game of four-handed chess. You and I each command an army on our little chess board here. Imagine, if you will, a much larger board with four or even more armies, all striving for each other's king. There would be alliances and broken alliances. There would be stalemates and fool's mates on all sides. I can see bishops and priests making secret alliances along with generals and warlords. Unfortunately, there are no rules in the book for this sort of game. The winner will have to be as ruthless as those who conquered by the sword and spear. The consequences will be hundreds of thousands of dead pawns on thousands of Asian chess fields. As one of those pawns, I can only hope that my people will be spared. But, as a man of some learning, I realize that no innocent ever escapes the appetite of a hungry tiger."

Michael immediately realized what Bua was referring to in his analogy and smiled a grim smile and nodded.

"Yes, old man, I am afraid you are quite correct. The tigers, lions, bears, and dragons are all on the prowl looking for whom they might devour. Unfortunately, my queen and her court with their insatiable appetites for more land to exploit and more people to dominate are never satisfied. Something to do with the divine right of kings or some rubbish like that."

"You know, Michael, in your attempt to subjugate India, you made an unholy alliance with the Gurkha people. You promised them the benefits of the Empire if they would shed their blood in the conquest of the Indian continent. In the end, they became far more loyal to your king or queen than even some of your British soldiers. Without the Gurkha soldiers and their curved knives, I seriously doubt that you would have been successful in raising your flag over that piece of the world. Now that India has been bridled like an angry elephant, you are setting about to put a leash on Burma. While the Burmese people appear to have been brought into the British fold, they quietly hate your infernal guts. They smile and curtsy but behind those beetle nut-stained smiles, there is a white hot fire burning which will someday erupt into a rather unpleasant situation."

Again, Michael realized the truth that was being forecast. Repression was always followed by rebellion and bloodshed. Pacification came through the winning of the soul, not by the intimidation of the spirit.

A long silence allowed for the words to settle. Bua moved his bishop forward. "Check!" he whispered.

Michael pondered his situation and moved his hand to his king, knocking it over sideways. "Make that check mate."

Bua smiled briefly. "Mike, you notice that it was my bishop, and not my queen which conquered your king. I might suggest that your invasion of my country and this land of Burma be undertaken by holy men such as my bishop. But rather than dispatching your priests and vicars to tame us savages, you use your holy men to provide religious respectability for your colonel minions. I would like to suggest that you consider sending ministers who truly care for the eternals souls and temporal bodies of these people you intend to subjugate. I can personally recall some of the highly dedicated missionaries who braved the primitive conditions of the Banderban Hills and overcame the spiritual and temporal powers of our witch doctors to deliver the Gospel. They truly loved our people and, often, gave their lives for us. Today, the Baum, the Naga, the Karen, and other tribal groups have been conquered by the power of a holy God and not the power of an earthly king or queen." This brief but convincing argument seemed to resonate with Michael. He responded in silence.

Michael St. John was not a religious man by any stretch of the imagination. He did, however, acknowledge a god, somewhere. He could recite the Ten Commandments, perhaps not in correct order, but close enough. Michael's current alienation from God came as a result of a situation a few years back while he was serving in India. As the senior sergeant, it was his responsibility to conduct the execution of a young British soldier who, while in a drunken state, had murdered a fellow soldier–in his sleep. This was, of course, a heinous, yet understandable, act of men who oftentimes brought their killing home with them at night. While Michael St. John had killed more men than he cared to admit in battle, the killing of this young lad, with a rope, repulsed him more than all the killings he had been responsible for on the battle field. Before the execution of this boy in a soldier's uniform, Michael had appealed to God to spare this boy's little life until he could at least die like a man on the battlefield. More than all the battlefield death reports he had written in his time as a soldier, he feared writing the death report for this lad most of all. Fortunately, the letter to the boy's next of kin, which described the circumstances of his death, would be written and signed by the commanding officer. For reasons Michael neither understand nor accepted, God did not intervene. Sergeant Michael St. John was compelled by duty and honor to carry out the execution rendering the young soldier's body lifeless and his ultimate judgment to the discretion of the Almighty. For this reason, Michael St. John felt obligated to share the guilt of this murder with the Almighty; thus the estrangement.

Michael spoke, "One of the unfortunate aspects of my culture is its impenetrable social system. We British have a caste system which goes far beyond that of the Indian society. We have our queen bees, our soldier bees and a myriad of other specialized bees, all working to protect our little colony from intruders. I am not only a soldier bee but a non-commissioned soldier bee. Under no circumstances can I be granted entry into the world of the commissioned officer soldier bee. No matter how many medals I have on my chest, no matter how many campaigns I have won, I am outranked by the simplest minded junior officer whose father happens to own a title granted by a distant king. The thought of converting the heathen of our newly conquered lands and then elevating them to an equal status is unthinkable. We want them to pray to our God, but from the back pews of the church. We want them to speak the Queen's English, but not with the pronounced accents denoting higher social rank. We want them to learn to cook our food, but not to eat at our tables. So there you have it, my friend, our missionaries and professional holy men must take care to convert the heathen to become Christians, but not Christian Englishmen."

A frown moved across Bua's face. "And where do you stand on this issue, Sergeant Major St. John?"

Michael fixed his gaze on the chess board in front of him and simply shook his head. "I don't know."

It is said that wise men often communicate best in silence. For the next ten or so minutes there was a great deal of silent communication between the soldier from the east and the soldier from the west.

Bua broke the silence. "So, Sergeant Major Mike, I have said my piece; what brings you to the jungle this time? I doubt you came for a game of chess and a glass of wine."

Michael issued a brief chuckle. "Actually, I did come for a game of chess and a glass of wine. I find this form of soldiering to be perhaps more productive than meeting you with guns and bullets on a battlefield. My commanding officer is a good man with reasonably good intentions, but like most of those in his station, he lacks the ability to see a given situation from all points of view. Most officers see the battle from a distance or from the comforts of a history book. For them, a victorious battle holds the prospect of having one's name attached to a victory. The corporals and privates see the battle from the front lines. For them, it's the thrill and terror of battle. We sergeants regard things from a very different perspective. The stripes on our sleeves and the medals on our chests indicate that we have successfully survived numerous battles, but unlike the young soldiers or the officers, we sergeants would much rather sue for peace over a game of chess and a glass of wine. So my friend, I have come to sue for peace."

Another thoughtful silence consumed the two men. Bua spoke, "If you wish to establish a working peace here in Burma, you must implement that peace through the hearts of its people, not through fear and intimidation. As I mentioned earlier in our conversation, you must win the hearts and minds of those you have conquered. If you will recall your military history, this was the strategy used by Alexander the Great. He offered those whom he conquered the choice of working with him and remaining alive or working against him and becoming dead. Now what could be simpler than that?"

"So, how do we implement this strategy of Alexander the Great in Queen Victoria's Burma?" St. John asked.

With the posing of that question, Bua realized that he had won the match. "How indeed?" Bua asked. Bua smiled and continued, "First, my friend, we create an alliance between those tribes with whom we have something in common; our faith. Most of the Burmese people are Buddhist and, therefore, somewhat fatalistic. If they die, they die. If they don't die, they continue to live. Now for the Burmese Christians, we respond to a much higher calling. While Heaven is our eventual destination, we, like you British, feel that it is our responsibility to make the world a better place. If we can capture the imaginations of the Christian leaders among the Nagas, the Karen, and the Baum, we can translate that vision into a better world for all Burmese while we are under the rule of your Queen Victoria. But in order to create this alliance of brothers, I would ask your government and your holy Church of England to send more and better qualified missionaries. The missionaries of whom I speak should be able to teach not only the Word of God, but to teach issues related to village sanitation, education, health and so on."

Bua's comments were being heard by the Englishman sitting across from him. Bua paused while he took a sip of wine.

Michael took the opportunity to speak. "So, you are suggesting that my government recruit vocational missionaries to promote improved living conditions for the Christian tribal groups? Now, if we were to take that approach, wouldn't the Buddhists or the Hindus become jealous of our intentions?"

"Good point," Bua countered, "but like the Gurkhas in India, you would at least have an alliance of Christian people rather than the current situation where virtually everyone in Burma hates your infernal British guts. And, unlike the Spanish who colonized the South Americas by using the Church to strike terror into the hearts of the people, England might use the Church to build hope in the hearts of its subjects."

Another pause as Michael pondered the comments of his friend.

"So, *quo vatus?* Where do we go?" Michael uttered.

Bua smiled. "You will go back to your commanders and suggest that you and I together journey to the various tribal groups and create an informal alliance with your government. I realize that as a conquered people, we are already subject to your government's demand. What I am talking about is a further step toward stronger support for your colonial efforts, especially when it comes to those people who continue to resist. In return, your government and your church would implement religious programs as well as social improvement projects. Everyone benefits!"

"I like it," Michael said. "I like it. I will return immediately to my headquarters and attempt to influence my Colonel's thoughts on this matter. If I were to make the suggestion that we develop an alliance of Christian tribal groups, nothing would become of it. If I were to inform him that it was your idea, he would flat out reject it. On the other hand, if I can manipulate the concept into his thoughts, it will become his idea and it will be sent on for higher consideration."

Michael looked at the sun. He figured that it was about four in the afternoon. If he left now, he could be back to the boat in an hour and on his way back to Rangoon by evening. "Bua, my friend, how may I contact you in the future? I can't be running up here every time I want a glass of wine, a cigar and a game of chess."

Bua replied, "There is a tea and spice shop in the main bazaar called the Green Frog Spice Shop. One of my people owns the shop and he can transmit messages both from me and to me. Aside from being a spice dealer, the proprietor is a writer of letters for the illiterate. In fact, Mike, I may come to Rangoon for a visit soon. If I do make the journey, he will bring you a message at your barracks."

The two men shook hands. Michael turned and walked toward the river. Just before moving into the jungle, Michael turned back toward Bua. "Bua, was there truly a tiger or was that a dream?"

"It is like many dangers of life; perhaps it was real, perhaps it was merely a figment of our mutual imaginations," Bua said philosophically. Both men smiled stoically and went their respective ways.

Michael moved quickly through the lush green foliage with a sense of extreme urgency in his soul. His entire life had been spent taking orders from his superiors and then implementing those orders to his subordinates. This new and exciting turn of events now put him in the position of making decisions and possibly impacting the course of history. The thought of recommending a strategy for the ultimate pacification of specific

Burmese tribal groups to his superiors gave him a bold surge of self-confidence. It could be done and he could do it.

As Michael reached the edge of the forest where he could smell the river, he heard men shouting and laughing–in English. Emerging from the green curtain he saw virtually every man in his detachment, in the close company of a Burmese man. They were fishing. Some were using simple hand lines while others had fashioned long bamboo poles. On the shore was a large woven bamboo basket filled with an assortment of strange-looking fish. The event seemed to weld together the two races of men in a common endeavor. A British soldier and a Burmese fellow hooked another fish as Sergeant Major St. John approached. Together, they held up the flapping fish and announced that this was the largest fish caught yet. St. John smiled briefly as he noticed the bond between men. Looking at the sun, he called for the lance corporal. "Lance corporal, assemble the men at once."

The young lance corporal yelled an order to assemble which abruptly doused the levity among his men. The soldiers dropped their lines and poles and immediately assembled in two lines. The Burmese congregated in a group near the river and watched to see what the hero of the "Battle of the Irrawaddy" would do next. One-half of Sergeant Major St. John's mind and heart told him to forgo his departure until after a fire could be built and the catch of fish prepared for a small feast. The other half, recalling the British military's stand on not fraternizing with the locals, pushed him toward moving out at once. A brief silence overtook the scene on the banks of the river. For a moment he recalled Bua's comments regarding Alexander the Great's strategy of not only fraternization, but assimilation with those he had conquered. If he were going to present a plan to win the hearts and minds of the Burmese people to his superiors, might he not begin with a little beach party? The long moment of consideration was over. Sergeant Major Michael St. John called out in Burmese, "Gentlemen, would you care to join us for dinner this evening?" The Burmese were totally stunned at the invitation. Smiles spread across each brown face. "Corporal, build a cooking fire. Make ready for a meal." Tight smiles spread across each British soldier's face as they continued to stand at attention.

Sergeant Major barked the order "Dismissed!" whereupon each man on the beach dashed off to gather wood or gut a fish. Several Burmese ran off into the jungle, returning with baskets of papaya, bananas, and other exotic fruits. Eventually, a very old village head man of the group of Burmese made his appearance on the beach. For the next few hours, there were speeches, toasts of jungle berry wine and a general sense of levity seldom encountered between the captives and the captors. Well into the event, several roasted pigs and goats from the nearby village were introduced to the circle of men. Gradually, the number of Burmese sitting around the fire grew. Michael noticed small groups of his soldiers attempting to communicate using hand signals with Burmese. Soldiers were comparing their tattoos with those of Burmese tattoos. Several soldiers had traded handmade native knives for their army issue knives. A strong sense of kindred spirit could be seen and felt as the food was consumed and the glow of the fire warmed the heart of those around it. "*Perhaps, Alexander was correct.*" Michael thought to himself.

The trip back to Rangoon was relatively uneventful. It was apparent, however, that soldiers aboard the paddlewheel boat had developed a new and greater regard for Sergeant Major St. John. He had won the hearts of his men by a simple act of kindness and mutual respect. The journey gave Michael an opportunity to develop a strong argument for Bua's proposal of pacification. The difficult part was the presentation of historical facts, current facts, and the consequences of future actions. Presenting a plan to Colonel Ballentine would be simple. The problem, however, involved causing Ballentine to think it was his plan all along. After all, a sergeant major does not give advice to a colonel.

CHAPTER SEVEN

About twenty miles from the Rangoon military dock, Michael gave the pilot of the boat an order to cut to half speed. At the current speed, the boat would arrive somewhere around four o'clock. If he could delay their arrival by at least an hour, any face-to-face meeting with Ballentine could be postponed until the following morning.

Before "lights out," the story of the grand beach party had been told and retold throughout the Rangoon barracks. Some soldiers even thought to invent a number of Burmese dancing girls and other similarly off-color stories which often occupy the mind of lonesome soldiers. Sergeant Major Michael St. John had become quite the talk of the town.

The following morning, Sergeant Major St. John presented himself at Colonel Ballentine's office at precisely nine o'clock. Rather than a glass of whiskey, Ballentine offered Michael a cup of tea. The Sergeant Major realized that this situation had grown into something more than a simple skirmish. It was now an obsession. Michael sensed that Ballentine's interest had become personal. He seemed deeply offended that this savage had disrupted the tranquility of his region of responsibility and, more significantly, this non-English jungle man had intruded into a world reserved for high-cast Englishmen. Michael felt uneasy in exposing Bua or his intentions to the Colonel.

"So, Sergeant Major, how was your trip?" Ballentine squired.

"It was rather uneventful, other than for the fact that I was able to meet with this Bua Tan Bo fellow."

Ballentine's eyebrows rose as he uttered "hmm." "Tell me more," he continued.

"It appears that a British gem merchant had virtually cheated a whole tribe of Baum people out of a king's ransom of raw rubies. It was simply Bua Tan Bo's intention to retrieve stones, compensating the merchant for his loss and to then sell them in a more liberal market."

Michael produced a wad of bank notes and indicated that he would personally locate the merchant and "repay" the debt. Colonel Ballentine issued another "hmm" nodded, and said nothing.

"Tell me, Sergeant Major, what do you make of this Bua Tan Bo of yours? Do you believe that he might be a threat to the peace here in Burma? Does he command sufficient forces to be considered a security risk? Do you think he presents an immediate challenge to my authority and to that of the Crown?"

Michael paused for several seconds, knowing that this answer and how he presented it could impact this insecure little man's response to a potentially constructive situation. "Let me put it this way, Colonel. While Bua Tan Bo and I were meeting in the up-country jungle, my very life was threatened by a tiger. Bua Tan Bo chose to allow the tiger to live rather than take a shot which might have killed it or might have simply angered it. Here, too, we have a situation where you could opt to confront this man and his people, or you could choose to allow the moment to pass. It is my personal opinion, as a soldier, that this man and his people could become a tremendous asset to your cause and to that of the Empire. As you will recall Colonel, the Gurkhas of Nepal became the Empire's strongest allies in its Indian conflict."

Ballentine, slowly pacing around his office puffing on a cigar, pondered Michael's words as one would ponder a battle plan. *"If I do this, then this will happen. If I do that, something else will happen."* Michael thought to himself.

Michael could see that Ballentine was taking this thing seriously. He could also see that there were darker thoughts being passed from one side of Ballentine's brain to the other.

Ballentine then asked, "What would happen, Sergeant Major St. John, if I were to take a force of men into this pirate's lair and simply wipe him out?"

Michael frowned, "Like the tiger, you may kill him with one shot between the eyes. On the other hand, you might miss. There are few animals more dangerous than a wounded tiger."

Again Ballentine issued one of his many, "hmms."

Michael did not like the way things were moving; not at all.

After another pause, Michael pondered the next move in this little game of chess - the Alexander the Great move. "Colonel Ballentine, you are no doubt familiar with the brief history of Alexander the Great. Please correct me if I am wrong, but didn't he employ a strategy of community pacification as a primary battle tactic?"

Ballentine nodded in agreement.

"It is my understanding that he presented an option to his opponents before, during, and after a battle that if they would simply surrender and join him in his campaign, their lives would be spared and that their leaders would be included into his occupation forces rather than be eliminated."

Again Ballentine nodded in agreement.

"Sir, if you were to employ the tactics and the philosophy of Alexander starting with Bua Tan Bo, I would suggest that you could and would bring most of Burma under your direct submission."

Ballentine issued several more "hmms." Go on, Sergeant Major, tell me more of these observations of yours. You seem to be making some sense."

Michael smiled to himself and thought. *"The strategy is working. Now I have to work on his personal ego."*

Michael continued, "Now then, if you were to arrange a meeting with Bua Tan Bo, formally accept his apology for the little incident on the Irrawaddy and perhaps chastise the scoundrel who cheated the Baum people out of their emeralds, you might even consider making a bit of theater out of the event by forcing the errant gem dealer to openly apologize, receive back his money plus the one hundred pounds extra and be done with it. Then, you would publicly announce that similar unscrupulous practices involving cheating natives would no longer be tolerated. Needless to say, you would become a bit of a local hero. Of course, we all know that this sort of under-the-table dealing will continue but the proclamation would look good in public."

"In the long run, Colonel, it costs you nothing and you quite possibly gain a bit more respect from the natives." Ballentine smiled at the comment.

Michael realized that this first step in his strategy was working. "Once we have settled the 'Irrawaddy thing', we can move on another of Alexander's concepts. I would suggest that you send a personal envoy to each of the Christian tribal groups in Burma and solicit their prayers and general support for the Christian Empire of Queen Victoria. Along with their prayerful support, we might also negotiate for their support in other areas of social and political concerns. In return for this support, we might arrange with a number of missionary societies to send missionaries and educators to their respective regions."

Ballentine, for the first time in quite a while, spoke, "Missionaries? Why missionaries?"

"It is obvious that we British have very little in common with these natives. However, the one thing we do have in common is our adherence with the Holy Scriptures. In the eyes of the Christian natives, we are all brothers. This is, of course, a matter of contention between us British and the natives. But, to capitalize on this single commonality might be the key to enlisting them like we did with the Gurkhas. And too, Colonel, there is no way that we will ever be able to civilize the Hindus, the Mohammedans, or the Buddhists; they are simply too primitive."

Michael looked sideways at the pacing colonel. He was smiling a sinister smile. "Sergeant Major St. John, I think we are on to something here. If I can affiliate the major Christian tribal groups into a single silent force, perhaps they can become the colonial-support people we need to ultimately bring civilization to this horrid place. And if I can arrange several dozen, no, make that at least a hundred missionaries, I can work toward the elevation of their status within the Burmese culture."

Michael held back an approving smile. "You know, Colonel, if the general staff were to hear about your concept to employ the strategy of Alexander the Great, I wouldn't be at all surprised if there might be a knighthood in your future. Anyone can launch an all-out campaign, kill every man, woman and child, but only a true genius can win the hearts of the enemy with affection–like Alexander."

Colonel Ballentine could almost feel the Sword of State touching his shoulder. "So, Sergeant Major St. John, how do you suggest that we proceed in this matter?"

Sergeant Major Michael St. John now realized that the chess game was on. For a long, hard minute, he stopped to ask himself the critical question, *"Which side am I on? Do I support my Queen and country, or do I favor these little brown savages who make their homes in the bush?"* A second thought brought the answer closer to his liking. *"Am I supporting this pompous colonel in his bid to make a name for himself, or am I supporting an effort to bring Bua into a position of authority where he can create an alliance between those little brown people with whom we British Christians have at least one common thread."* His silent assessment continued, *"Even if I can't bring about a checkmate on one side or the other, I might be able to cause a stalemate where neither party wins nor loses the game."*

St. John's thoughts returned to the question at hand, *"How do you suggest we proceed in this matter?"* St. John moved to the map on the wall. "Colonel, I suggest that you send a communiqué to Bua Tan Bo asking him to come to Rangoon in order that he might publicly apologize for his rash actions on the Irrawaddy. On behalf of the Crown, you will then extend the benevolent forgiveness of Her Majesty's government. Along with that act of forgiveness, you will require Bua Tan Bo to devote his energies to promoting peace and prosperity among the Burmese people. Then, you will invite the elders of the major Christian tribal groups to convene at Bua Tan Bo's village in the Banderban Hills."

Ballentine interrupted the comments. "If I were to single out the Christian tribal groups, the Buddhist and Mohammedan people would certainly suspect our intentions to form a counter alliance. After all, Sergeant Major, the Buddhist and Mohammedans would have much to lose if the Christian tribes were to align with us."

A serious frown moved across St. John's face as if to say, "*You are correct Colonel; I hadn't thought of that.*"

At that point, the plan became Ballentine's. Ballentine continued with total ownership of the scheme. "Sergeant Major St. John, I want you to personally draft a communiqué to Bua Tan Bo, inviting him to Rangoon for a meeting. Offer him my personal protection to him and his entourage during this visit. I will sign the communiqué, and you will see that it is conveyed to Bua Tan Bo. Then find the rascal who bought the rubies and get him in here. I will give him a brief slap on the back side and send him back to do what he does. He, too, will be under my protection. I would like all this to take place within a fortnight. Sergeant Major, I am putting you on administrative leave so that you are free to come and go as you see fit. Take whatever steps you feel necessary to make this thing happen. During Bua Tan Bo's visit, we can discuss the details of a summit meeting, perhaps at his village."

St. John very much liked the way this game was unfolding. Now it was St. John's turn to once again make a move. "Colonel, if I may make a suggestion?"

"Of course, Sergeant Major St. John, I would appreciate any suggestions you might offer."

"Colonel, I would suggest that you allow Bua Tan Bo to suggest the concept of an alliance among the Christian tribal groups. If you were to present the idea, he might see an attempt on our side to bring these tribal groups under some sort of domination. On the other hand, if he were to see the opportunity for an alliance as a developmental component, I think he would be more supportive. And too, Colonel, it would become his idea, not yours."

"I couldn't agree more, Sergeant Major, I couldn't agree more!" Ballentine boomed as if the whole brilliant plan had been conceived and borne in his head. Ballentine looked again at the portrait of Queen Victoria on the wall above his desk. Once again, he could almost feel the Sword of State on his shoulder.

St. John could see the entire game as if he were a chess master observing a game between two novices. "Colonel, allow me to add another thought to your plan. In India, we were able to bring the Gurkhas alongside by elevating their tribal group to an extraordinary military level. We, likewise, gave their people preference when selecting senior non-commissioned officers. If you were to offer preferential commissions to tribal groups aligning with your plan, I believe you would find far more support than you would find from either Buddhist or Mohammedan junior officers. Loyalty is not a value in either of these cultures while it is a supreme value amongst Christian tribes."

"Brilliant!" Ballentine barked, as he filled two whisky glasses. "To Bua Tan Bo," Ballentine toasted.

"To Bua Tan Bo," St. John replied with a brief smile.

CHAPTER EIGHT

St. John left Ballentine's office, changed into more casual dress and went directly to the Green Frog Spice Shop in the main bazaar. An old man with thick spectacles was sitting in front of a typing machine pecking out a letter for a female client. The old man pointed to a chair inside the shop. "Please sir, take a seat, and I will be with you as soon as I finish this young lady's letter."

As Michael's eyes adjusted to the darkness of the spice shop and to the myriad of fragrances coming from the hundreds of trays of spices, a rather handsome lady offered him a glass of cool tea with lemon.

Michael could identify many of the spices from India but many from Siam, he could not. The fragrances evoked dozens or even hundreds of places Michael had been in his career. While most British soldiers and colonial people detested "native" fare, Michael delighted on curries and sauces of unknown origin. How odd, he often thought, "The British Empire owned most of the world's spice-producing regions, but used only salt and pepper in its limited assortment of consumable foods. On rare occasions, an Englishman would sample a native fruit or perhaps a well-cooked vegetable and pronounce it edible. Even rice was considered suspect and used only when potatoes were not available.

After a cup of cool tea and a refill, the old man collected his fee for the correspondence and turned his attention to the British gentleman waiting inside his shop. "Sergeant Major St. John, I was told that you would be visiting me. How pleased I am to meet you," the old man said extending his hand toward Michael. This was a test. British gentlemen did not shake hands with "natives."

Michael extended his hand toward the elderly man. "The pleasure is mine," Michael said with utmost sincerity.

Michael noticed at the rear of the shop, a series of pictures hung high on the wall. Two were of an old man and an old woman. The others were images of Queen Victoria and Jesus. Seeing that Michael was focused on the images, the old man spoke, "My parents, my queen, and my King."

Michael immediately took a liking to the old man.

"My name, sir, is one you cannot pronounce nor remember. So if it please you, sir, you may call me James. I am the cousin of your good friend Bua Tan Bo. Actually, all Baum people are cousins of one another. No one wishes to marry with us except the members of our extended family. In that regard, we are much like your royal family. No one will have us except for other members of the family."

James had offered this little jab at European royalty to let the British gentleman know that he was not just another ignorant market vendor. And, too, he wanted to see if there would be any negative reaction to his little jab at British royalty.

Michael smiled and nodded. "All too true. When our royals look into their mirrors, all they see is themselves. They do not see the people who make them who they are."

The old man seemed satisfied that the Englishman sitting with him was sufficiently flexible in his attitude to allow for disagreement and opinion.

Michael went on. "Like your royal family, ours is made from the same meat and bone."

James continued, "Sir, do you have a correspondence for our mutual friend, Bua Tan Bo?"

"Yes, it is urgent and extremely important. How soon can it be delivered?"

James replied, "We have access to a telegraph station a few miles from where Bua Tan Bo currently resides. I can have the message in his hands this afternoon if you like."

Michael smiled, "Here's the message. 'Please come at once. The chess game has begun. Bring sufficient support personnel as worthy of a 'prince' of the Baum people. I will meet you and make formal introductions to the regional commanding officer. Sign it, Sergeant Major Mike."

The old man looked at the clock on the wall. "Sir, if you excuse me, I will personally take the message to the telegraph office and see that it is sent at once."

Michael rose from his chair and extended his hand toward the old man. "I look forward to another cup of tea soon."

The old man was pleased, extremely pleased, to have met a British gentleman who actually extended his hand in what seemed like a true gesture of friendship. Before leaving the spice shop, the old man turned and whispered, "Sergeant Major, the cook of your colonel is lurking across the alley. It appears that he is watching you."

St. John nodded. As he left the spice shop, he noticed the familiar face of the Colonel's cook pretending to talk with a nearby shop owner. As St. John moved away, the cook followed. *"So,"* he thought, *"Ballentine wants to keep an eye on me. Let's play for a while."* For the next two hours, Sergeant Major St. John moved throughout the bazaar, sitting talking with various vendors and even a beggar or two. Not wanting the game to end, Michael walked a brief distance to a pub frequented by low-class Brits and upper class Burmans as well. He took a stool near the door where he could keep an eye on the spying cook standing in the street. Michael smiled to himself knowing that the hour for preparation of the evening meal at Colonel Ballentine's residence was well passed and that Ballentine might be dining on cold soup and dry bread tonight.

Michael hadn't finished his first pint of warm beer when someone in the pub recognized him. "It's Sergeant Major St. John of the Battle of the Irrawaddy." For the next three hours, one pub patron after another had to buy the hero a pint for his service to God and country. Well before midnight Michael moved slowly in the general direction of the barracks. On occasion, he would turn his head and spot the colonel's cook. "*Poor Colonel Ballentine*," he thought, "*poor chap had to go to bed hungry tonight.*"

CHAPTER NINE

For the first time in many years, Sergeant Major Michael St. John slept through the wake-up bugle call. He smiled to himself and went back to a well-deserved sleep. St. John's sleep was interrupted by a gentle tapping on the door of his quarters. "Who is it and what do you want?" he barked.

A small voice answered, "A telegram for Sergeant Major Mike."

St. John leapt from his bed, opened the door and grabbed the telegram from the small Burman boy standing before him. He tore the envelope open and read the text. "Will arrive next Wednesday. Meet at Green Frog, four o'clock. Ten men in my group. Regards, Bua."

St. John tossed the boy a coin and closed the door. He shaved, dressed and walked abruptly to the Colonel Ballentine's office. Ballentine was delighted with the telegram. "*What's this Sergeant Mike thing?*" he queried. "*Oh, never mind, the heathen probably can't spell Michael.*"

Ballentine savored the telegram as if it were a summons from the Queen. "So the Pirate of the Irrawaddy is coming to my office to beg for forgiveness, is he?"

St. John replied, "Yes, Colonel, he and his men will be here next Wednesday. The first step of your strategy is working. Once he is here, you can make your next move: the alliance of Christian tribal groups."

Ballentine gazed lovingly at the portrait of Queen Victoria.

St. John spoke, "Colonel, if I may offer a suggestion?"

"Why, yes, of course. I value your advice very much in this matter. After all, you seem to be a man of the people," Ballentine stated, making a blind reference to St. John's previous evening activities.

St. John caught the comment and silently thanked the colonel's cook for his diligence. "I would suggest that you host a small dinner reception for Bua Tan Bo and his entourage," Michael said.

Colonel Ballentine looked surprised and somewhat perplexed. "A reception, a dinner?" he queried.

"Thou preparest a banquet in the presence of my enemies," the Holy Book says. "When the history books are compiled and the chapter on this portion of British Empire is mentioned, it shall be said that, 'Ballentine of Burma' once prepared a banquet table for his archenemy, Bua Tan Bo, Pirate of the Irrawaddy. And, in so doing, won the hearts and minds of the Christian tribes of Burma.

"Ballentine of Burma?" Colonel Ballentine uttered quietly. "Ballentine of Burma!"

"Colonel, I would also like to suggest that this little reception you will be holding should include a dozen or so journalists and their photographers. You could then express the underlying theme of your administration in this area. "Win their hearts and their minds; their loyalties will then follow."

Again Ballentine looked at the portrait above his desk. "I like it! By Jove, I like it! Sergeant Major St. John, what do you think about inviting the diplomatic corps?"

St. John stood and moved toward the map on the wall, "Colonel, as you well know, the Germans, the French, and most assuredly, the Americans would love to get a hold of this Bua Tan Bo fellow. If they were to have access to him, no telling what deals they might formulate."

"Quite right! Those bloody Americans, they want to be everyone's friend," Ballentine recanted. "Yes, Sergeant Major, let's just keep this little fellow for ourselves. If you would be good enough to sit with my aid d'camp and draw up a list of invitees, I would be most grateful."

Within the hour, the list was completed. Included on the list were British military officers, British journalists, senior British merchants, and six representatives of various Christian denominational groups and missionary societies working in the region. While Sergeant St. John was not a particularly religious man and did not particularly like the professional holy men, including his brother, with whom he had come in contact, he felt that these men might support his efforts in the long run.

CHAPTER TEN

The days prior to the meeting between Bua Tan Bo, the notorious river pirate and 'Ballentine of Burma' were filled with details. It was St. John's intention to set the stage for a drama which would hopefully benefit the British Empire and the Burmese people. It would be necessary to create some illusions like a good magician. At several points, Michael had to stop and distinguish between illusion and deception. Illusion, yes; deception, no. Deception fell into the category of treason against one's country. Illusion, on the other hand, created something which might be, rather than something which is.

Michael made several visits to the Green Frog for a cup of cool tea. Each visit was made by a different and more circuitous route. Each time he noticed the familiar face of the Colonel's cook. Each time he managed to find his way into the front door of a shop and out the back door. It was indeed a game. On one occasion he asked James to locate a tailor capable of creating the most elegant costumes in the Baum tradition. James laughed as he informed Sergeant Major Mike, as James now called him, that the Baum were simple mountain people and that they didn't have elaborate ceremonial costumes.

"James, it is extremely important that my people see the Baum and other mountain tribal groups as somewhat sophisticated and reasonably well dressed. In my culture, you can take the lowliest peasant, dress him in fine raiment, and present him in court as a nobleman. As long as he keeps his mouth shut, a beggar can pass as a baron. I can take any rabble in the marketplace, dress him in an officer's uniform and he becomes an officer. Appearance is everything in my culture. I want Bua Tan Bo and his men to look like the Wise Men who visited the Christ child. If they look wise, they will be treated as wise. If they look like a bunch of river pirates, they will be treated like river pirates. We must create the illusion of wise men."

James smiled and agreed. "I will find you a tailor and commission him to make costumes for our visitors."

"One more thing, James, Bua served me a wine; I believe he called it jungle berry wine. Do you know anything about this?"

"Know anything about jungle berry wine? I make it right here in my shop," the old man retorted with a huge smile. I purchase baskets of this wild fruit from villagers who wish to earn a few coins when they come to town."

"Can you put several liters in glass bottles and have it ready for our little party?" St. John asked.

The old man nodded. "I must warn you, Sergeant Major Mike, my jungle berry wine contains more alcohol than your English gentlemen's wine. When we kill an ox, we give the animal a liter or two of the wine to knock him out before we cut his throat."

St. John replied, "I thought you Baum people were Christian. How come the strong drink?"

Again, the old man smiled, "In the Bible, the First Book of Timothy, chapter five, verse twenty-three states, *'Be not a drinker of water only but, take a little wine for the stomach's sake.'*

We Baums seem to have a lot of stomach trouble." Both men laughed as the bond grew stronger.

For the first time in his military career, Michael St. John felt different. He was no longer a simple staff sergeant responsible for a unit of men looking out for an unpolished boot or a wrinkled uniform. He was no longer a simple pawn moved by some unseen hand. He was now a silent advocate sitting off to the side of the board quietly whispering moves to the two players. St. John felt a sense of power in his new position, a power which he much use wisely and in the best interest of his country.

Michael had ordered himself a new dress uniform for the reception from his favorite Indian tailor. It was extremely uncommon for a non-commissioned officer to be invited to a full-dress affair. A full-dress uniform for a sergeant major required some degree of creativity on the part of the Indian tailor. Michael even bought a new pair of the finest boots to be found in all Rangoon.

Wednesday, shortly after lunch, the small boy who had delivered Bua's first telegram, appeared in St. John's barracks doorway. The boy, dressed in a turban and a purple gown, barked his message, "Mr. Bua Tan Bo is here. He wants you to please come to this place now."

The boy handed over a page of paper with a map on it and smiled as St. John tossed him another coin. Michael spoke in Burmese, "You tell Mr. Bua Tan Bo that I will come within the hour. Now go."

CHAPTER ELEVEN

The boy ran off and Michael put on his tunic. Just outside the barracks, Sergeant Major St. John hailed a horse-drawn carriage standing on the opposite side of the cobblestone street. He handed the driver the map and sat back, feeling somewhat like an ambassador about to present his credentials to a foreign potentate. After about a forty-minute drive through the muddy streets of Rangoon, the carriage pulled into a walled compound with several small pavilions. He ordered the carriage driver to wait. In one of the teakwood pavilions, he saw Bua Tan Bo and his men standing on low wooden stools while an Indian tailor and his assistants sewed and hemmed various exotic garments. "Mike, come over here please! What is going on? Why must we wear these silly costumes? Brother James tells me you want us to look like the Wise Men in the Bible. Is this true?"

Michael simply smiled, "Something like that. After all, you are a Baum 'prince' and these are your courtiers. You must at least look like something other than a gang of ruffians. Bua, this meeting tomorrow is probably the most important event in the history of your people. If you can succeed in convincing

Colonel Ballentine that you are both a man of power and a man of peace, we can avert some extremely ugly relations between our two people. Unfortunately, we are the conquerors and you are the conquered. If we can assume the thoughts of Alexander the Great, you can at least live as men and not as slaves."

"Michael, tell me about this Colonel Ballentine. What are his weak points and what must I avoid?"

"First of all, Bua, be who you are. You are at least Ballentine's equal, if not his superior. His weak point is his enormous ego. He wishes to become 'Ballentine of Burma' and possibly knighted by the Queen for his extraordinary work here in Southeast Asia. If he can be moved to create an alliance between the various Christian tribal groups and those groups be convinced to swear total loyalty to the Queen, he could claim responsibility. I truly believe that such an alliance would be beneficial to both our interests in light of the quiet opposition we are feeling from the Buddhist and the Mohammedans. Ballentine is going to attempt to persuade you to solicit the support of the Christian tribal leaders. If you agree, he will assume that it was his persuasion that brought it about. I strongly suggest that you refuse the idea until he makes some serious concessions."

"What sort of concession, Mike?"

"I suggest that you request several dozen missionaries with strong interest in agricultural, medical, and educational projects. With their support and backing, you would most certainly be able to develop a school system, a network of clinics, and some sort of agricultural market. I would also suggest that you ask for a number of preferential positions in the Burmese police force. This will give you a significant political leg up in protecting the general population against enemies, foreign and domestic."

"Mike, this is well above my station in life. I am the son of an elder, not an elder. What happens if I agree to something my elders do not like? What then?"

Michael smiled. "I have one move I wish to make. I will suggest to Colonel Ballentine that you and I travel to your village and talk with your elders and the elders from the other Christian tribes. I feel certain that you and I together would be able to convince the elders that they and their people will benefit from the concept. It would be critical that we keep this meeting secret. If the Buddhist and the Mohammedans were to hear of it, I am certain they would attempt to disrupt it. They would, no doubt, see that an alliance between the Christian and the British would not be in their best interest." Bua silently agreed.

Michael went on, "In fact, I will send the information out that there will be a meeting between the Christians and the British somewhere over in the Three Pagoda Pass area near the eastern frontier with Siam. This will, hopefully, send them packing in the opposite direction. Meanwhile, we will be meeting in the northwest."

Michael noticed that the Indian tailor was nearing completion on the costumes for Bua's men. He also noticed that James was not included in the costume party. "My dear James, come here this instant!" Michael ordered.

"And why, may I ask, are you not in costume? After all, you will be making the introductions tomorrow in Colonel Ballentine's office."

James reacted with shock. "Me? I am not good with words. I cannot be a part of this thing."

"My friend, you are already a part of this thing. Tomorrow you will be acting as the Lord Chamberlin for the Baum People. Tailor, make this man a costume worthy of a Lord Chamberlin complete with neck chain and staff." By midnight the pavilion looked something like the Globe Theater, complete with actors, costumes, and prompters. Rehearsal after rehearsal was held until everyone knew his part in the little charade. Michael then remembered the coachman waiting outside the compound. "James, quickly fetch the coachman outside in the street. I need to talk with him."

Soon, the coachman rubbing his sleepy eyes appeared. "Sir," Michael ordered, "tell me your name."

The toothless old man answered with a name which Michael could neither understand nor repeat. It sounded something like Gabooreale1.

Michael responded, "Sir, I shall call you Gabriel, like the Archangel Gabriel."

The old man laughed, "Yes, Gabriel will do nicely, sir."

"Gabriel, I want six coaches each with a driver and a footman. I want them dressed in their finest clothing and each wearing a hat, turban or something appropriate to their profession. I want the horses bathed and the coaches clean. I shall pay you and the other coachmen handsomely upon completion of the day's event. I want these coaches to arrive here at the compound at exactly two o'clock. We will allow for one hour to drive to the headquarters, three to four hours for the evening's events and then back to this compound."

Again he addressed James, who was now festooned in a silk gown with several strands of gold chord draped over his sagging shoulders, "James, do you have some sort of old sword or long knife?"

James thought for a minute and ordered one of his children to fetch an old sword from inside the house. Within minutes an old cutlass was produced. "Tailor, I want you to transform this piece of junk into the Baum Sword of State. Wrap some gold chord around it, give it a coat of polish and buff up the scabbard. Tomorrow, Prince Bua Tan Bo, you will surrender the Baum Sword of State to Colonel Ballentine as a token of your high esteem for his most generous act of clemency. Then, Brother James here shall suggest a toast to her Majesty the Queen of England. At that point, you will call for the bottles of jungle berry wine to be brought out for the toast. After the toast to the Queen, I shall call for a toast to the tribal elders of the Baum people. Then, I will call for a toast to Colonel Ballentine and to Bua. If all goes well by the completion of the ceremonies, everyone should be just a bit tipsy. From there, we can negotiate.

A slight mist began to fall around midnight. The fragrance of the night- blooming jasmine filled the warm moist Burmese air. The kerosene lantern cast magic shadows against the compound's wall, much like a traditional shadow puppet theater. Two of the members of James' family began playing traditional musical instruments. One of Bua's men found a wash tub and entered with his drumming. This, of course, called for a glass or two of jungle berry wine. Within minutes, the men in the pavilion were doing what men everywhere do before a great battle–they enjoyed themselves by dancing. Even Sergeant Major Michael and the infamous river pirate, Bua Tan Bo, found themselves dancing to the strange chords of the music. Even the carriage driver found his part in the slow but joyous dance. It was good.

CHAPTER TWELVE

The following morning Sergeant Major St. John found himself in his bed, not knowing exactly how he got there. Thanks to his most recent dancing partner, Gabriel the carriage driver, he had been neatly tucked into bed with his boots and trousers placed at the foot of the bed. The alarm clock showed nine thirty. He leapt from his bed only to fall back when his eyes went black. After a few deep breaths and a considerably more cautious approach to the day, Michael rose and dressed himself. Not wishing to don his newly tailored dress uniform, he dressed in his fatigues. He called out for the barracks orderly, "Bring me a pot of very strong tea and a tray of biscuits." Before the tea arrived, St. John went outside to where the fire barrel stood. He removed the lid and plunged his head under water for as long as he could. After several baptisms, the throbbing in his head subsided, but only slightly.

A pot of tea later, the potential for gastric eruption in his belly was almost gone. He silently cursed that jungle berry wine and the demons which reside within it.

Another pot of tea and a tray of biscuits later, Sergeant Major Michael St. John stood before Colonel Ballentine's aid d'camp, a Lieutenant Pepper. Here was a young man obviously born into a wealthy family who desperately needed military experience in order to move into his father's family shoes. And what better way to gain that experience, to serve as a secretary to an officer whose only military combat was on some rugby pitch at Oxford. The list of invited guests was carefully examined. The floor plan consisting of small numbers indicating who was to stand where was scrutinized. Then speeches of both Colonel Ballentine and Bua Tan Bo were sanitized of any language which might cause offense or confusion. St. John did make one significant amendment to Bua's speech. Where Colonel Ballentine's name was mentioned, Michael wrote, Colonel 'Ballentine of Burma', hoping this moniker would find its way into a history book somewhere or perhaps a London newspaper.

Lieutenant Pepper smiled at the addition. "Quite right!" he muttered.

At two o'clock the military band along with a few recruits from the Burmese community, were assembled on the parade grounds in front of the unit headquarters. A large Union Jack dominated the sky above. Invited guests began arriving in carriages and on horseback. The journalists and their photographers began setting up their tripods near the primary platform. A series of green carpets had been arranged from the point at which carriages discharged their passengers leading to the dais. A single red carpet has been laid from the headquarters entry door to the dais.

Thirty minutes before the set arrival time of Bua Tan Bo and his party, St. John got an idea which brought a huge smile to his face. He marched quick step to the office of one of his few friends, a sergeant who played the bagpipes. Ten minutes later, the sergeant, dressed in kilts and full regalia, stood curbside with his pipes ready to play an escort.

At exactly three o'clock, all heads in the assembly turned to see what looked like the procession of an Indian wedding: six horse-drawn carriages, completely festooned with flowers, ribbons, and bells with drivers and footmen in high colorful turbans. Those in the crowd didn't know whether to laugh or fall prostrate on the ground. The first carriage carried Bua Tan Bo. With his "sword of state" tucked in his cummerbund and a turban of sorts covering most of his head, he dismounted the carriage as would an Indian maharaja. The piper saluted smartly and filled his bag with air. With all the pomp of the opening of Parliament, the piper led the princely potentate and his entire entourage down the green carpet to where Colonel Joseph Ballentine III stood like Julius Caesar awaiting the surrender of Attila the Hun. Flash powder went off like lightning as cameras clicked from all directions. The band leader stood silent, not knowing when or even if to play. Colonel Ballentine looked over at St. John and gave him a brief smile and wink. Obviously, he liked the bit of ornamentation of the piper. The procession of each separate member of Bua Tan Bo's entourage was complete. Standing next to Bua was James, holding a staff, much like Moses before Pharaoh. In a loud but frail voice, James spoke, "Your Excellency, Colonel Ballentine, distinguished guests, and honorable soldiers. It is my high honor to present to you, Bua Tan Bo, humble subject of Her Majesty's Government in Burma. Bua Tan Bo bowed slightly as Colonel Ballentine offered a slow and somewhat perfunctory salute.

Lieutenant Pepper then nodded to the band director whereupon the Queen's anthem was played. With that out of the way, the speeches and counter speeches could be given. James handed Bua a copy of his speech which he began to deliver in the clearest and most succinct English pronunciation. This was duly noted by the journalists. When he arrived at the sentence which contained the words, 'Ballentine of Burma', his voice exaggerated just enough to cause the journalists to make note of the newly coined moniker. St. John noticed a slight smile on Ballentine's face. With the brief speech given, Bua Tan Bo took the neatly dressed sword from his waist band and handed it to Colonel Ballentine who accepted it as if it were indeed a "sword of state."

Then it was the Colonel's turn to make amends. Within the contents of his dissertation were several subtle scoldings for the horrific battle on the Irrawaddy. Then there were several quotes from the Bible related to forgiveness and brotherly love. "And, in conclusion," Ballentine droned, "I would ask that the merchant who brought this unfortunate issue to a critical state come forward and receive his just compensation for the booty taken from him. Likewise, I would consider it well within the context of British tradition for both parties to shake hands and be done with it."

The offending gemstone merchant accepted an envelope containing his money, plus one hundred pounds. Bua Tan Bo offered his hand as the camera clicked and the flash powder flashed. Colonel Ballentine, with Bua's sword still in his hand, had managed to take a position between the two in order that the photographs would record this event with him standing like King Solomon resolving yet another human conflict. All in all, it was not a bad speech. Ballentine was quietly ecstatic. If this didn't bring a knighthood, nothing would. Again and again, he glanced at St. John with a reassuring look.

As scripted, James called for a toast to the queen. Ballentine placed his arm around Bua Tan Bo as the entourage followed into the great room of the headquarters building. Several crates of the jungle berry wine were brought in by the coach drivers and their footmen. Glasses were found, filled and lifted toward the portrait of Queen Victoria. "To Her Imperial Highness, Queen Victoria," James crooned.

Ballentine sniffed the wine, then tasted it. He took the entire glass in one gulp. "Jolly good!" he whispered to St. John.

Then St. John announced another toast, "To Bua Tan Bo, friend of the British Empire." Another round of the purple liquid and more comments on its bouquet. Then another toast to the tribal elders of the Baum People was called for and then to the leaders of the Karen and so on. Within an hour, several dozen notables had been toasted and several dozen bottles of jungle berry wine were now coursing through the veins of all those present. Well, almost all those present. St. John and Bua's entourage managed to forgo any significant consumption of the pleasant toxin. Even most of the clergymen present found it rude and unforgiving to refuse to toast the Queen and the rest of those toasted.

A light buffet was announced at the courtyard behind the headquarters. English delicacies like boiled beef, boiled potatoes, boiled cabbage, and boiled kidneys were consumed in great quantity by the British. The Baum people, on the other hand, managed to nibble on cups full of rice, tomato sauce and some fruit which had not as yet been boiled to a paste.

"Ballentine of Burma" was in his glory. Several of the journalists had regained sufficient sobriety to jot down and outline his Alexander the Great strategy. He referenced his intimate knowledge of Burma and its people even though he had never even once left the environs of Rangoon. He was able to rattle off numerous tribal groups, geographic phenomena, and several species of animals. The semi-intoxicated journalists were enthralled with Ballentine of Burma's overall assessment of Burma and its issues. "I will let you in on a little secret, gentlemen, I plan to hold a meeting where the leaders of the various Christian tribal groups will come together and consider a formal pact with Her Majesty's Government. Even though we hold total governance over these simple people, we would, nonetheless, welcome a formal declaration of assistance and unity between them and us."

One of the reporters asked, "Sir, when and where do you plan this conclave?"

With a wry smile, Ballentine replied, "That, gentleman, must be kept a secret. There are those who would not like to see such an alliance take place."

Like a cramp from having eaten a rotten fig, Ballentine realized that he had far exceeded his authority in making these and previous statements. The thought of his superiors or even, heaven forbid, the Vice-Roy reading about this new strategy of Her Majesty's Government coming from the mouth of a mere colonial colonel left him weak. Realizing that he had just communicated his plan for subjugation of the Burmese people to the world's press, he caught St. John's eye. Motioning St. John to his side, he whispered, "We must talk. Now."

Behind the closed door of Ballentine's office, he confessed his dilemma and fear of falling before he had even had a chance to rise. As the jungle berry began to wear off, Colonel Ballentine's demeanor sunk to an all-time low. For St. John, this was good.

Ballentine looked at the portrait of the Queen as if he were praying to her, "How can we deal with this unfortunate turn of events?"

St. John seized the opportunity. "Sir, there is an old Asian proverb, '*Noble is the man who seizes an opportunity rather than he who asks if he may seize it*'." In other words, sir, it is better to apologize for taking an action if things go wrong, than to ask permission and lose the opportunity. I suggest that you outline your thoughts and send them immediately to your superiors. Borrow what credibility you can from history books and, of course, the Bible. I will have a chat with the gentlemen from the press and persuade them to support your thoughts."

Ballentine issued another of his frequent "hmms."

"Yes, Sergeant Major, have a chat with the press people and see what you can do."

"If I may make a suggestion, Colonel Ballentine, four of the six journalists have applied to become members of your Rangoon Gentlemen's Club. I might suggest that you support and promote their membership as soon as possible."

"Excellent idea, Sergeant Major, excellent," Ballentine retorted.

Seeing Ballentine's mood begin to change, St. John decided to make his next move. "Colonel, may I suggest that we invite Bua Tan Bo in for a little chat; just the three of us?"

Again another "hmm."

Outside the Colonel's office, the reception was going well. Because of the fact that all Baum people speak fluent English, reporters, clergymen and others had managed to engage them in meaningful conversation. Reporters were taking notes on cultural issues, clergymen were discussing points of doctrine, and others were extracting information regarding the exploitation of natural resources. Bua was talking with a missionary regarding the translation of Bibles into local dialects when Michael interrupted. "Excuse me, your Excellency," Michael said as he pretended to bow to Bua. "Colonel Ballentine requests your presence in his office."

With the door closed, Colonel Ballentine offered Bua Tan Bo a cigar from his humidor. Bua passed the cigar under his nose. "Cuban!" he remarked.

Ballentine then offered a cigar to St. John who took a match from the desk and lit all three cigars. Almost in unison, the three men exhaled plumes of blue smoke skyward. "Nice. Mild," whispered Bua.

Ballentine gestured to the two chairs in front of his desk, "Gentlemen, if you will take a seat, we can move a little closer to our objectives here."

Ballentine took his seat behind his desk, looking very much like a judge at a court marshal. "Now then," he began addressing Bua Tan Bo, "my Sergeant Major St. John told me of an incident wherein a tiger had taken you two unawares and that the tiger had it in his power to attack and kill both of you, had he wished. Then, Bua Tan Bo, I was told that you managed to acquire a gun and aim it directly at the beast's forehead. Then I was told that you opted not to shoot and the tiger opted not to attack. You then went your separate ways, all parties unharmed. Perhaps someday, you may encounter that same tiger when he is not as benevolent, and he will kill you. Likewise, you may come upon that tiger and decide that his skin would make a stunning rug in front of your fireplace. Now then, Mr. Bua Tan Bo, in my right hand desk drawer I keep a loaded pistol. At this very moment I have the right and the authority to take that pistol and shoot you between the eyes. After all, you did commit piracy against a vessel of the Queen. But, like you with your tiger, I opt not to put a bullet between your eyes and eliminate the problem forever. Instead, I prefer to let you live in hopes of allowing you to help me make a better world, beginning with Burma."

Both St. John and Bua were absolutely stunned at the Colonel's comments. St. John thought, "*The audacity of this pompous peacock*."

Bua's thoughts traveled in a different direction. "Colonel Ballentine, with all due respect, when I handed you the sword earlier this afternoon, I could have just as easily pulled the sword from its scabbard and cut your head off. I would, of course, have been killed by your troops, but your blood and mine would have mingled in the mud of the parade grounds. Then the blood of your people and my people would soon mingle on the battlegrounds throughout Burma. No, Colonel, your actions were not predicated on benevolence; they were based on the simple question, 'what happens if I miss and simply wound the beast?' In killing me, you would simply inflame an already tenuous situation. By letting me live and placating me and my people, you stand to possibly prosper in your attempt to pacify Burma. With us on your side, you may win. Without us, you will be defeated."

Both Ballentine and St. John sat speechless as the young man's words echoed in their minds. Ballentine's attempt at a check had been met with a countercheck. The game was on!

Ballentine broke the frozen moment with a wide British smile. "So, my friend, Bua Tan Bo, let's get on with the future and leave the ugly things of the past in the past. Together, you and I can build an empire. Let us think of ourselves as the British lion and Burmese tiger. While definitely not from the same litter, we are nonetheless large and wily cats, looking for food and an occasional adventure."

In an attempt to mitigate the silliness of Ballentine's pathetic retreat, St. John rose from his chair and moved toward the map on the wall. "Gentlemen, allow me to direct our attention toward the primary objective of this moment - the Christian tribal groups."

In order to regain a bit of authority, Colonel Ballentine acquiesced, "Please carry on, Sergeant Major St. John; carry on."

"As we are all keenly aware, the forces of Her Majesty the Queen have managed to subjugate most of India and much of Burma. Unfortunately, placing our names on a paper map does not necessarily mean we are in control of the country on which our name appears. Such is the case with Burma. We own it but we do not necessarily control it. Our objective here and now is to move closer to managing this piece of God's creation and bring it and its subjects firmly into the British Empire."

Both Bua and Ballentine nodded in agreement as they each blew plumes of cigar smoke towards the ceiling.

St. John continued, "If we fail to achieve this objective, Burma will fall to the French, the Russians, or God forbid, the Americans. And if all that fails, Burma will fall into absolute chaos. It is, therefore, incumbent of us to bring these people under the protection of the Empire."

"Quite right," Ballentine boomed as he slapped Bua Tan Bo on the back.

"Now, Sergeant Major St. John, if you could relate our discussions regarding the achievement of this objective to our good friend, Bua Tan Bo," Ballentine blathered.

St. John and Bua exchanged slight smiles as they both realized that the chessboard was theirs for the taking.

St. John began, "Our primary objective is to meet with the elders of the Baum people in the Banderban Hills, here, pointing to the region east of Chittagong. Bua and I are reasonably certain that we can achieve their participation and, possibly, leadership in bringing the other Christian groups to bear. Colonel Ballentine has suggested that you and I take a small detachment and go to your people as soon as possible. The Colonel also strongly insists on the utmost secrecy of this mission."

Actually, Ballentine was completely unaware of St. John's plans but nodded in staunch agreement as if he were.

St. John continued, "Then, once we have the support of the Baum people, we can draft a general doctrine in code, of course, and disseminate it to the leaders of the Christian tribes. I suspect this would require a month or perhaps six weeks for a general consensus. In order to facilitate our need for direct and rapid communication, I would need a sufficient budget to select, train, and transport a number of intelligence operatives capable of sending and receiving coded messages over the telegraph wires. This will eliminate the necessity for long- distance couriers. I would add that we would also use the telegraph system to send out dozens of false messages in the event that the Mohammedans or the Buddhists should become involved. I strongly suspect they will. Are there any questions?"

St. John looked directly at Bua as if to say, "It's your move; make it a good one!"

Bua took a long drag on his dwindling cigar and exhaled. "Tell me, Colonel Ballentine, why should we Christians align with you British? Once we clasp hands on this campaign, we incur even more persecution from the Buddhists and Mohammedans. We will be adding to our own misery. What could you offer as compensation for this alliance?"

Ballentine looked directly at St. John as if to say, "Say something, do something!"

St. John smiled, "Bua, Colonel Ballentine and I have discussed this matter more in terms of the benefits to the Christian tribes. For one, we would request more Christian missionaries be sent from the Church of England and some of its peripheral missionary societies. Included in those missionaries, we would ask for educators, medical personnel, and perhaps, agricultural experts. This sort of impact would lead to superiority in most aspect of your lives. Your people and the people in other Christian areas would become as the Holy Book puts it, *'A city on a hill cannot be hid.'* You and other Christian tribes would become examples of progress under the support of the Empire. Eventually, your people could, *'beat their swords into plow shares and their spears into pruning hooks'."* Ballentine smiled with a silly grin and nodded profusely.

Bua nodded with his hand on his chin as if he were stroking the chin whiskers which had not yet grown. Bua spoke, "Colonel, there is one thing I wish to add to this mix. Once we have taken the step across the line into the British Empire, we will be putting ourselves at great risk. I would like to suggest, no, let's make that a requirement." He pondered the moment and selected his words which would be critical to the long-term welfare of thousands of people. I would require that a significant number of our people be allowed into the British Burma Police and at significant ranks."

Now it was Ballentine's turn to stroke his chin. Not knowing exactly how to respond, Ballentine again looked at St. John.

St. John looked long and hard at Ballentine who was beginning to sweat profusely. St. John spoke, "Bua Tan Bo, are you aware of the Indian tribal group called the Gurkhas?"

Bua nodded. St. John continued cautiously, "Colonel Ballentine has mentioned the possibility of asking for a special detachment of Gurkhas to assist in the policing of some of our more troubled tribal areas. I might suggest that he expand that concept even a bit further. I would suggest that he enlist a small detachment of Gurkhas under the leadership of a British officer and train police units made up from the various Christian tribal groups. This would serve to ensure localized stability, again, under the direct leadership of British officers. You would, in essence, have your own police force to deal with local matters and to a broader extent, serve to protect your respective interests. I must make myself totally clear; like our friends the Gurkhas, your loyalty must at all times be directed toward the Empire and not some local potentate or warlord. Any infraction of that underlying premise would be considered treason in its highest and ugliest form."

For a long minute each of the three men pondered what had been said, what would be said, and what would happen if the proposal were rejected by anyone on either side.

Ballentine tried to project this concept into the dozens of generals and politicians above him. What would they think and, more importantly, what would they think of him? If the concept was to be approved and it failed, his career would be over. On the other hand, if it were to be successful at least for the moment, his knighthood would be assured.

Bua's thoughts ran in the direction of his elders, particularly his father. For generations, the Baum people had managed to remain more or less independent of their long list of conquerors. While bending their knee to the reigning king, emperor, or warlord, they managed to keep their heads held reasonably high. Would they accept this absorption into the British system, or would they opt to ignore the inevitable and hope that the problem would simply go away. Perhaps the Baum and other Christian groups could exist like the Gurkhas.

"We have a situation where plans have been expressed publicly and now we must bring those plans to fruition," Ballentine said emphatically.

St. John could see that Ballentine was clearly in a corner. Good! It would now fall to Bua and St. John to find a way out of that corner.

"Colonel, I would like to suggest that Prince Bua Tan Bo and I travel to his tribal center and meet with his elders. I believe that we can convince these wise men to accept your proposal for an alliance. Once that agreement is achieved, we can ask that envoys be sent to the other Christian tribal leaders in other parts of the country. Then, a very secret conclave can be convened somewhere where the Buddhist and the Mohammedans won't suspect. I believe that we can bring at least five of the seven groups into a loose alliance if we act now."

Bua spoke up. "Colonel Ballentine, as you well know we Burmese are not happy about being brought under the rule of the British. You neither like us nor respect us as equals or even as near equals. But as you also know, in the past we have found ourselves under the dominance of other more ruthless rulers than your Queen Victoria. The Chinese, for example, treated our people like cattle to be milked whenever they wanted milk and slaughtered whenever they wanted meat. Likewise, the Moguls of India considered us as maggots feeding on the carcass of their empire. We could easily find ourselves under the rule of the French who would use us as work slaves like they are doing in Indochina. All in all, you British are the least of all the current evils. With that being said, we need to get on with the situations as it stands today and let tomorrow happen as it will.

Ballentine uttered yet another "hmm." He then refocused on the map.

"Sergeant Major St. John, I am relieving you of your regimental duties and assigning you as a 'special police agent' answerable to me. I am assigning you and a selected detachment of men to a special police unit. This unit shall operate in secret and shall have access to whatever resources you deem necessary to achieve our objectives. The objectives were, of course, the formation of an alliance between the Christian tribal groups and Her Majesty's government. This special unit shall remain in effect not to exceed one year."

Then turning to Bua Tan Bo, Ballentine continued, "Sir, I hereby extend the protection of Her Majesty's government to you for the duration of this campaign. Sergeant Major

St. John, you are to afford all protection and convenience to Bua Tan Bo. Is that understood?"

St. John, realizing that his plan had been more than successful, snapped to attention, saluted, and barked, "Yes sir!"

Bua Tan Bo bowed and issued a gesture of placing his hands together and touching his forehead in reverent submission. He then issued the same gesture to the painting of Queen Victoria on the wall above Ballentine's desk. In Ballentine's mind, this sealed the pact.

St. John, in a quiet glance toward Bua, raised his eyebrow slightly and issued a very brief smile indicating that the performance was magnificent and the game was on.

Colonel Ballentine motioned the two toward the door. "Let's join the group outside and sample a bit more of my cook's rack of mutton and your vintage wine."

Bua's men had totally ingratiated themselves with the gentlemen of the press as well as those from the clergy. Several of the British businessmen had struck up impromptu business deals with members of the Baum group. One merchant struck a deal with James for one hundred barrels of the now famous, jungle berry wine. Two slightly intoxicated gentlemen had to be restrained as they each sought to act as agent for the Baum's cash of rubies. Each promised the highest and most honest representation for the rights to search out honest buyers. Each was answered with a gentle smile and a waggle of the head indicating a polite, 'no thank you'.

At precisely four o'clock, Sergeant Major St. John suggested that evening was drawing near and that the Baum delegation needed to be returning to their quarters. Actually, the Baum delegation was having the time of their individual and collective lives and didn't want to return to quarters. Bua bid a formal farewell to each of the guests with a final handshake with St. John. St. John whispered, "I will see you tomorrow at your compound."

Colonel Ballentine stood on the steps of his headquarters triumphantly smiling as if had just negotiated a major peace treaty between the British Empire and all the kingdoms of Asia.

Sergeant Major St. John moved toward the still grinning colonel and spoke, "Well done Sir, very well done."

Ballentine simply uttered, "hmm."

St. John then suggested that they break for a brief respite and resume drafting documents supporting recommendations yet to be made to the regional command. "What say we meet in your office at five o'clock?"

Rather than accept an appointment from a subordinate, Ballentine replied, "Shall we make that six o'clock, Sergeant Major?"

"Six o'clock it is, Sir," St. John said in a slightly subservient tone.

CHAPTER THIRTEEN

St. John realized that his work had just begun. The rest of the afternoon and evening would need to be spent drafting detailed documents to the commanding brigadier in the region. Each word had to be carefully crafted in order to convey just enough information, but not too much detail. Every word had to be void of innuendo except where some ambiguity was necessary in order to blur some unpleasant aspect of reality. The document had to be specific but ambiguous. If the document were to be forwarded to the office of the Vice Roy and possibly on to Whitehall, it had to contain the rhetoric of politicians, not simply the jargon of soldiers. And if it should find its way to the halls of parliament, it needed to be decorated with an ornate vocabulary sufficient to confuse and confound any politician who would dare to oppose it. The document had to convey the urgency of action at a time when the empire was on the true brink of domination of Burma. St. John's mind pondered these thoughts as he disengaged from the last of the event's participants. He was struck by an absolutely brilliant thought. To give the document an aura of almost divine magnitude, he would suggest that it be entitled "*The Ballentine Doctrine for Burma.*"

St. John moved off toward his barracks. En route, he passed the quarters of Sergeant Andrew McMillan, the piper whose bagpipes added just the right flavor to the afternoon's event. "Andy, I almost broke into tears as you escorted the 'Maharaja of the Banderban Hills to meet his Excellency Colonel Ballentine. It was perfect!"

"Michael," the Scot whispered as he drew St. John into his quarters, "what's going on here? I know the Baum People and I know they don't dress like that. What's the story?"

St. John plunked down in a leather and teakwood chair in McMillan's small apartment. He unbuttoned his dress tunic, took out a green cigar from his inner pocket and lit up.

"Andy, give me your word that you will not repeat a word of what I am about to tell you, and I will bring you into one of the greatest games of chess in all of Asia."

Andy nodded, "You have my word as a Scot."

"You can't do better than that," St. John replied. For the next hour he unrolled the events of the Battle of the Irrawaddy, the meeting in the jungle, and the recent event at Colonel Ballentine's headquarters. He likewise laid out his thoughts on the pacification of Burma and how the British Empire would be the ultimate benefactor of the plan. Several times he interjected his concern about his loyalty to the crown and to his country. Andrew McMillan listened silently as his comrade in arms attempted to re-examine each of the events which had taken place and those yet to happen. At one point McMillan began to see himself as a 'father confessor' listening to the catharsis of a man who was intent on his actions but confused about his intentions. After about an hour of painting word pictures, Michael St. John rested his case.

McMillan said nothing. He instead rose up from his chair and poured two cups of strong afternoon tea. Handing one cup to St. John, he began his rebuttal. "The only thing I can say is this. I would give all the medals on my chest to be a part of your little chess game. As far as going beyond your station in life and in particular, the Army, don't give that a second thought. In this case, you are far more intelligent than our commanding officer. As long as he gets the final salute, you do what you can to bring honor, glory, and respect to your queen. In fact, Sergeant Major St. John, I have heard rumors that you might soon be coming face-to-face with Her Majesty. The business about the Victoria Cross has been whispered about recently."

St. John frowned at the mentioned of the Cross. "I am quite happy with my service medals, thank you. And as far as becoming a part of this little chess game, consider yourself in. Colonel Ballentine has given me permission to select my men for a very secret journey to the Banderban Hills and a meeting with the elders of the Baum Tribe."

Andrew McMillan's two hundred and thirty pounds of bone and flesh leapt into the air as he grabbed Sergeant Major Michael St. John around the chest and gave him a rib-crushing bear hug.

"I am absolutely sick to my bones of marching these 'freshies' around, while waiting for a fight in some backwater village," Andy said.

Michael again sat down. "Andy, the first order of business is to select a crew of twelve of the best men we can find. I want at least two who are signalmen, at least two medics, and two supply men. For the rest, I want men who can get along well with the locals; no troublemakers. And, most importantly, I want a cook who can make use of local supplies. No boiled beef or boiled potatoes on the march. If any of the men have problems with local foods, leave them behind. I want men who can fit in with the locals."

Andy replied, "Aye."

Michael looked Andy straight in the face and in a most serious manner said, "Any man who can eat a haggis, is capable of eating absolutely anything. So, I will assume that you will not have problems with the fare on the march."

McMillan's serious expression then exploded into laughter.

"One more thing, Sergeant McMillan. I want you to bring those bagpipes of yours. They would be just the thing in the event of an encounter with a hungry tiger or errant ghost."

"Yes, Sergeant Major," Andy responded with a firm salute.

St. John rose from his chair and moved toward the door. "Sergeant McMillan," he said extending his hand toward the beaming Scot, "I feel good about this mission, very good."

For the first time in many years Michael St. John felt unusually enthusiastic, even euphoric, about a mission. Before Michael reached the door, McMillan stopped him. "Michael, are you a religious man?" he asked.

St. John stood looking directly into the eyes of the man. "Not really. I believe in a god, but right now, he and I are not on speaking terms."

McMillan picked up a well-worn Bible from off his nightstand and flipped it open to the middle. He began to read, "Commit your way unto the Lord and He will give you the desires of your heart."

The big Scot attempted to read St. John's face. Not wanting to reveal his 'issue' with God, Michael simply said, "Alright, if you say so."

McMillan frowned, "It is God who says so. I would suggest that we take his advice."

St. John nodded in silent agreement. "All right," he said. "Consider it done. With that, St. John left the quarters and moved toward his own.

With the door closed Michael looked into his shaving mirror. "All right, God, let's try it your way."

CHAPTER FOURTEEN

The next four hours were devoted to crafting a primary document which St. John frequently referred to as the Ballentine Doctrine. Each word was carefully weighed and considered for its meaning and response from those who would read it. It had to be firm and resolute while at the same time allowing for some degree of flexibility or even compromise. It had to reflect the opinion and first-hand information of the commander in the field while at the same time meeting the concerns of politicians and an occasional fool. Colonel Ballentine's mastery of the English language blended with St. John's propensity toward hyperbole made for a tapestry of words which created a picture of what was and what might be for the region of Burma. A final draft was inscribed on linen paper signed by Colonel Ballentine and sealed into a courier pouch for transmittal to the next ship going to India.

Ballentine and St. John sat back in their respective chairs and made one last toast with their teacups to the portrait of the Queen on the wall.

Ballentine spoke, "You know, Sergeant Major St. John, you would have made a bloody fine officer. Sorry you weren't born into the right family. If this little doctrine of mine is approved by the higher ups and we get the signal to proceed, well I don't mind saying so, but I would like to have you working with me to make it happen."

St. John forced a smile at the comment and at Ballentine's unconscious sense of hubris. *"My little doctrine indeed!"* he thought to himself. *"This pompous little man couldn't organize a cockfight by himself."*

For the first time in his life, Michael St. John felt the sharp pain of class discrimination–British class discrimination. For an instant, he truly knew what the lower casts of India felt like when in the presence of the higher class. Michael was a better soldier and perhaps a better man than this pompous little man who wore the uniform of a colonel instead of a sergeant major. "I would be honored to work with you, Colonel Ballentine," St. John said almost sincerely.

Looking at his heirloom pocket watch, Ballentine suggested that they call it a day and turn in.

~

CHAPTER FIFTEEN

St. John's sleep was populated with shiny-eyed tigers, animated people dressed in turbans and flowing silk robes. Several times in the night he awoke and wondered if this whole business of the Battle of the Irrawaddy, Bua Tan Bo, and the Ballentine Doctrine was just a part of a long and strange dream. He checked the temperature on his forehead to see if he might be having a bout of his recurring malaria. The whole thing was a bit too bizarre for a common soldier in Her Majesty's British military.

Michael managed to sleep thorough the bugler's first call but not McMillan's persistent pounding on his door. "It is the foolish who seldom see the sun rise," McMillan called out. "Wake up and say 'good morning' to God," he continued.

Andrew McMillan's bearded face was stretched into the widest smile he could muster while Michael St. John looked as if he had been pummeled by bandits and left for dead.

Michael spoke, "I would rather be fighting heathens in the deserts of India than playing patty-cake with officers and politicians. At least with the heathens, you can simply shoot them and be rid of them. With the officers and politicians, one has to curtsy and smile politely, but not too politely lest one might be seen as insubordinate, or worst of all, low class.

It was several seconds before St. John noticed that McMillan was holding a tray covered with a tea towel. He sniffed the air. Coffee. "Don't stand there like a door-to-door peddler. Come in, man."

McMillan put the tray on the small wooden table and pulled back the towel. "If we are going into the Banderban Hills, you will have to learn to drink coffee and drink it strong," he said. Six lumps of sugar and a half cup of cream rendered the black liquid potable, almost pleasant. On a plate lay a half dozen fresh biscuits, orange marmalade, and a dozen rashers of thick bacon.

McMillan watched a smile move slowly across St. John's face. "The cook in the officers' mess hall is a friend of mine. After yesterday's great event, I thought you deserved something a bit better than the usual boiled oatmeal, tea and biscuits."

St. John noticed that there were two plates, two coffee cups and two silver settings. "Won't you join me?" Michael said almost jokingly.

"It would be an honor, Sergeant Major St. John," Andrew replied, almost jokingly. Before taking his first bite, Andrew bowed his head and uttered a brief prayer. Michael politely followed suit.

Breakfast over, McMillan opened a brown manila folder marked CONFIDENTIAL. McMillan's tone of voice changed from casual to military. "Sergeant Major, I have taken the liberty of listing down the names of men I know to be reliable and well suited to their jobs. These are men whom I trust with my life."

Sergeant Major St. John opened the envelope and began to peruse the names and profiles. As he made mental notes on the names before him, Sergeant McMillan spoke, "Sergeant Major, if I may make a suggestion. . ."

St. John nodded, realizing that this man was well into the operation, as was he. "Please do," he responded respectfully. "I value your insights in this operation."

"Sergeant Major, if we are to approach our objective as a military unit, the opposition will certainly notice our presence. If, on the other hand, we approach our objective, let us say, as a corps of engineers with the objective of building a rail line from Chittagong to Rangoon, we might attract less attention."

St. John was immediately impressed with McMillan's sense of creativity and innovation. "I like it!' he said. "Yes, I like the idea very much."

McMillan smiled through his thick red beard. "I thought you might," he said. "That is why I have recommended men who might appear a bit less military. I have also included two chaps who are well trained in field medical aid."

McMillan could clearly see that St. John was pleased with his perception of the operation and the details necessary for its successful outcome. It became openly apparent that St. John's disposition for the larger picture was to be well complemented by McMillan's attention to detail.

For the next four hours, the two men filled page after page of notes, supply lists, and time tables. At the top of each page, McMillan would print in large letters CONFIDENTIAL.

After a brief lunch of bully beef and boiled potatoes, the two men continued with the final draft of a comprehensive plan while at the same time being somewhat circumspect. It was important that people like Colonel Ballentine and others like him knew the plan, but not the details of the plan. It was well known within the military and civilian government that information was an extremely valuable commodity to those who were not pleased with the British invaders.

Addressing this issue of information leakage, McMillan filled two pages of paper with information and details regarding a decoy operation in the eastern region of Burma, near the Siamese frontier. This information would be leaked through a number of sources in McMillan's circle of native friends. If all went according to plan, the decoy information would find its way into the hands of one of the Mohammadan priests or Buddhist antagonist groups. And if all truly went well, the small group of "engineers" could slip quietly off to the west, without being noticed.

By evening, the plan was complete; at least as complete as St. John and McMillan could make it. The next major obstacle was to get it approved by Colonel Ballentine without too many points of interference.

It was time for the evening meal when both men began to feel the true gravity of the task before them. It seemed truly strange that they, non-commissioned officers, should be planning an operation without a senior officer being involved. It also seemed odd that these two military men would soon be packing their uniforms away in favor of civilian clothes.

As the two men walked toward the mess hall, Sergeant Major St. John suggested that the men selected for the mission be furloughed from their respective units and moved to a special pre-operation camp somewhere out of the neighborhood. From that point, they could spend time getting to know each other before making the final break. This time together could also allow for a "civilianization," as McMillan called it. It would be difficult but necessary for those involved in the engineering team to address each other by their civilian names, not by their military ranks.

After the evening meal, St. John and McMillan agreed to pass the plan by Bua Tan Bo before going any further.

CHAPTER SIXTEEN

Outside the main gate of the barracks compound the two found Gabriel fast asleep in his coach. McMillan quietly reached over and plucked up the buggy whip and tickled the nose of the sleeping man. Finally, Gabriel woke up.

The old man jumped to his feet and issued a salute worthy of a British conscript. Standing at attention, the old man barked, "Sir, where can this unworthy Burman carriage deliver a most worthy English soldier?"

St. John and McMillan grabbed the old man as if he were a close friend and lifted him to his seat above the carriage. St. John spoke, "My good friend, Gabriel, your performance in our little comic opera was magnificent, absolutely magnificent! I shall most certainly see that you are given the news clippings of your ceremonial delivery of the Baum prince."

McMillan repeated the congratulatory comments with considerable embellishment. The old man beamed with pride as he and the two British sergeants climbed into the carriage. "Take us to Bua Tan Bo's compound. And, Gabriel, take us in a route where no one can follow us."

An hour later the carriage arrived at the rear gate of the compound. St. John instructed Gabriel to return in three hours.

One of James' many children answered the bell at the rear gate and led the two into the dining area of the compound. Bua Tan Bo, James, and the entire group of actors were sitting at a low wooden table filled with rice and various curries. Bua leapt to his feet. "Michael!" he shouted. "It is wonderful, brilliant, Shakespeare could not have written a better script himself."

Bua noticed the large bearded man standing next to Michael. His demeanor changed abruptly.

Michael noticed the chill and responded. "Bua Tan Bo, it is my extreme pleasure to introduce you to Sergeant Andrew McMillan, a true friend and comrade in arms."

Cautiously, Bua extended his hand toward the man. Bua's side glance toward Michael posed the question, *"Who is this man and why is he here?"*

Michael spoke, "Bua, don't you remember? This is the man who played the bagpipes at your most royal procession."

Again, Bua looked at Michael as if to say, *"So? He played the bagpipes. Why is he here?"*

"Bua, I suggest that we discuss this and other matters in private. There are too many ears in too many places." Bua Tan Bo offered apologies to his group and led the way to a small room inside one of the buildings in the compound. He lit a match and then a kerosene lamp. The three men took stools around a small wooden table.

"Now then, Bua, I have personally selected Sergeant McMillan to serve as my adjutant in our mission to the Banderban Hills. I fully trust this man, both his experience and his wisdom."

Bua was clearly unhappy by the inclusion of another individual in this critical project. Bua focused on Michael's comment and asked McMillan, "Sir, where does your wisdom come from?"

Sergeant Andrew McMillan answered without so much as a pause. "Sir, fear of the Lord is the beginning of wisdom, and what wisdom I do have comes from the Almighty." Bua Tan Bo's countenance changed abruptly with Andrew's answer.

"Any man who acknowledges God as his source of wisdom is, indeed, wise. It is the fool who attributes wisdom to himself."

McMillan replied, "There is an old Scottish saying, '*It takes a wise man to recognize a wise man*'."

Bua extended his hand toward McMillan. McMillan then spoke, "And Mr. Bua Tan Bo, from whence cometh thy wisdom?"

Bua replied, "What little wisdom attributed to me comes fully from God who made me. It was also my God who made me to know that without Him I am a fool like those who profess to be wise."

Michael stood there silently hoping that neither man would question him about the source of his wisdom. The encounter was brief, but in a culture where a man's integrity is paramount, the dialogue between the two strangers was sufficient to move to the next step of the relationship.

Bua ordered a pot of strong tea and a plate of fruit. For the next three hours, the three men discussed the plan before them. Every detail was scrutinized for possible error or oversight. A full complement of survey equipment was drafted as was a food ration. Medical supplies were checked and rechecked. Both decoy and actual messages were written for transmission to Chittagong and points east toward the Siam frontier. A list of code words were written down which would eventually distinguish decoy transmission from the real.

The Burmese moon was full and high in the sky when the three men emerged from the small room. McMillan held the leather letter case containing the written documents tightly under his arm as if it were his bagpipes. Bua then called out for his three Baum men who would be accompanying the team to their destination in the Banderban Hills. A brief introduction was made as the two British soldiers stood by the rear gate.

CHAPTER SEVENTEEN

The following morning, Sergeant Major St. John and Sergeant McMillan requested and received a brief meeting with Colonel Ballentine. Without going into any significant detail, St. John presented a brief outline of the operation to the Banderban Hills. It had been determined that an overland march would most certainly attract too much attention and that travel by coastal steamer would be preferable. On the day chosen for departure, a detachment of British military would be dispatched in an eastwardly direction, supposedly to the Siamese frontier. St. John did mention that Gabriel, the carriage driver and his fellows, would be spreading false information within the community as to the nature and destination of the operation.

After sufficient information had been communicated to Colonel Ballentine, St. John placed a drafted outline of the points of discussion he and Bua Tan Bo would be carrying to the elders of the Baum people. Each point was followed with advantages and consequences.

During the entire conversation, Ballentine's utterances consisted of a single word, "Hmmm," which was followed with a nodding of his head. Unbeknownst to Sergeant Major

St. John and Sergeant McMillan, Colonel Ballentine had received a message from the Brigadier in command of the region, telling him to proceed with caution. Further, it had been stated that should the plan be successful, sanction would be granted by general staff. If, on the other hand, problems arose in execution of the plan, the general staff would disavow any knowledge or support of the plan.

With the final item on the list being read, St. John asked, "Colonel, are there any questions?"

For a full minute, if not two, Ballentine pretended to ponder the plan. At last he spoke, "No, Sergeant Major St. John, I think we have approached every contingency with as much diligence as necessary. I must say, you have thus far exceeded my expectations on this matter. I can only hope that my expectations will be exceeded even further with our little plan's completion."

St. John glanced sideways at McMillan with an expression that was meant to say, "*Our little plan!?*"

"So, Sergeant Major, when do you plan to leave for Chittagong?" Ballentine asked as he stared lovingly at the portrait of Queen Victoria.

St. John replied, "One week from today. That will give us time to garner our basic supplies here and telegraph Chittagong for the rest. That will also give your detachment bound for the Siam frontier sufficient lead time for the march."

It was McMillan's turn to enter the conversation. "Colonel, if you would be so good as to sign and send this message to the commanding officer of the garrison at Chittagong, we can forward a list of supplies we will need for the survey expedition."

McMillan handed Ballentine a two-page list of items which the colonel only glanced at before scratching his signature at the top and bottom. Ballentine then called for his aide and ordered the telegram be sent. With that, the game was on.

As the two sergeants left Colonel Ballentine's office, they noticed the Colonel's cook chatting with the aide d'camp. St. John alerted McMillan to the presence of the cook.

St. John spoke in a voice which would ensure the cook heard every word. "Sergeant McMillan, it is imperative that this march to the Three Pagoda Pass be completed with all diligence. We must convince the Christian tribes to sign on to our plan."

McMillan, seeing St. John's intent, responded, "I believe the tribal leaders along the Burma-Siam frontier can be persuaded to align with us without too many concessions."

St. John replied, "Sergeant, have a full complement ready to march one week from today. If all goes well, we can be at Three Pagoda Pass in a week."

With that, the two sergeants left the room. The cook smiled silently and left the building as well.

CHAPTER EIGHTEEN

In a dimly lit Buddhist temple south of the city, Colonel Ballentine's cook sat legs folded under him while he recited, word for word, the conversation between the two British sergeants. The man in the saffron robe sitting beneath a large brass statue of Buddha listened intently. Without saying a word, the monk nodded. He then reached inside his robe and retrieved a small leather pouch. The cook bowed his head and, with both hands, received the bag of coins.

As the cook moved back into the night toward his master's residence, he passed a drinking establishment and acquiesced to the enticement of a heavily painted young woman. Although a devout Buddhist, he rationalized that the young woman was in need of money, as was the keeper of the establishment. An hour later, he atoned for his sins by leaving several coins on the table.

Word of the march to the Siamese frontier spread through the Rangoon region faster than food poisoning from a pot of spoiled chicken rice. Like a lump of yeast in a bowl of bread flour, Gabriel and his cohorts managed to pass the word of the operation and its objective to all carriage passengers. Even the local newspaper made mention of a very secret operation taking place in the near future.

When asked for confirmation by several members of the press, two of whom the Colonel sponsored into the gentlemen's club, Colonel Ballentine simply acknowledged that he wanted to take a walk about and assess the state of the country; nothing more, nothing less. When asked if he was planning to meet with Christian tribal leaders, he responded that he was hoping to meet with tribal leaders of all aspects. Once the good colonel began talking to the men from the press, the words seemed to flow as fast at the whisky he was consuming. Soon, the campaign grew from a simple walk about to a full-scale public relations effort on behalf of Her Majesty's government and, of course, the Ballentine doctrine. Between the intoxicated ramblings of Colonel Ballentine and the imaginations of the journalists, the project had taken on the magnitude of a conquest; a conquest of light over darkness, of good over evil, of happiness over sorrow and so on. The expectations of this campaign had gone from clandestine to absurdly public.

When at last the ramblings of Colonel Joseph Daniel Ballentine III were found in print, both Ballentine and St. John were not happy. Somehow in the midst of all the brandy and blather, Ballentine agreed to allow three journalists and their respective cameramen to accompany the campaign to the Three Pagoda Pass. To complicate matters further, several prominent English business entrepreneurs requested to be included in the long march to the Siamese frontier. Within three days of the leaks, Ballentine's entourage had grown from slightly less than one hundred soldiers to somewhere around one hundred and twenty souls all totaled. Immediately, Ballentine blamed St. John for planting such an elaborate scheme complete with multiple themes. St. John silently blamed Ballentine for firing off his mouth like an overloaded cannon. With two days left before St. John's silent expedition was to quietly leave to the west and Ballentine's crusade for the east, all details had been attended to—at least on St. John's side of the ledger. The expectations of both had increased considerably.

The day of the long march to the eastern edge of Her Majesty's Burmese domain had begun with all the pomp and ceremony Ballentine's subordinates could muster. Drummers were placed immediately behind the color guard. Behind them Ballentine was mounted on his rarely ridden white stallion. Immediately behind Ballentine were two wagons carrying the press people and their cameramen. The supply wagons and the foot soldiers followed. The long line of British conquerors moved from the headquarters through the city's main street and into the western environs of Rangoon. Barely outside the outskirts of Rangoon, Colonel Ballentine called a halt and made camp for the night.

CHAPTER NINETEEN

At the headquarters of the Royal Burma Police, Rangoon Barracks, a dozen soldiers dressed in civilian clothing and two sergeants also dressed in civilian clothing, silently left the compound where they found numerous horse- drawn carriages waiting. Gabriel smiled as his charges, Sergeant Major St. John, and Sergeant McMillan tossed their bags into the carriage and pulled the folded canopy over the top of the carriage.

An hour later all carriages had delivered their respective charges to a seldom-used pier near the principal rice warehouses. A small, covered steamboat was waiting. With all fourteen men and their gear aboard, the boat silently slipped into the dark waters of the morning.

Slightly more than an hour later, the small water taxi pulled alongside a motionless coastal steamer. A well-weathered captain, apparently of Lebanese origin, welcomed his charges aboard. In the main cabin, St. John and McMillan found Bua Tan Bo and his three Baum cohorts sipping tea. Bua spoke, "We arrived about two hours ago, long before the sun rose. I am certain no one has noticed our departure. For the duration of our trip, I would suggest that you call me Gop; that is the

Siamese word for frog. We would not want the captain or his crew telling their story about hosting the infamous warlord, Bua Tan Bo, now would we?"

The men were shown to their cabins, two men to a compartment. It had been agreed that all military titles and military responses were to be totally avoided. St. John was to be addressed as Professor St. John, Licensed Civil Engineer. McMillan was to be addressed simply as Mr. McMillan. All others were to be addressed by their given names.

∾

CHAPTER TWENTY

CHITTAGONG, ON THE BAY OF BENGAL

The three-day cruise to Chittagong was reasonably uneventful. Each afternoon, the monsoon rains came and went with little or no consequence. While St. John studied the maps of the Banderban Hills district, McMillan studied his well-worn Bible.

Well before the captain announced the ship's arrival at Chittagong, the smell and fetid garbage floating on the sea, proclaimed the proximity of civilization. The smoke from a thousand cooking fires combined with the stench of raw sewage being dumped into the Bay of Bengal was sufficient to alert even the most insensitive of men to the level of civilization they were about to encounter.

The coastal steamer was made fast, the captain thanked and the fourteen Englishmen and their porters were quietly escorted through the dismal streets of Chittagong to the British garrison. Upon arrival, the young officer in charge of the escort invited Professor St. John and Mr. McMillan to their quarters. He then indicated that the "porters" could sleep in the servant's quarters some distance away. St. John immediately indicated that the porters would be lodged with the main group and would likewise take their meals with the main group. While the young officer appeared to be somewhat incensed with St. John's countermand of his instruction, he nonetheless, let it go. "Civilians!" he quietly snorted to himself. "The next thing you know, they will be marrying our women. Bloody heathens!"

It had been discussed prior to leaving Rangoon, that Bua Tan Bo should remain as anonymous as possible. It was actually his suggestion that he be seen as a simple porter hired by the expedition. Because of his status within the Baum community, someone might recognize him and assume the railroad survey expedition was simple a ruse and that other plans were in the making. Bua went as far as to insist that he not be introduced to anyone, including any official of the British military. It was noted that the cook of Colonel Ballentine was thought to be a spy, not only for Colonel Ballentine, but anyone who would pay for any and all information he could garner.

The major in charge of the Chittagong garrison almost immediately recognized McMillan as the group entered his office. St. John realized that the covert nature of the mission could be compromised if this commanding officer could not be convinced that he was mistaken. Before St. John could mentally formulate an explanation or a diversion, McMillan rose to the occasion. "Major, I get this frequently when I am in these parts. My twin brother, Andrew F. McMillan, is a sergeant in Her Majesty's armed forces. I, on the other hand, am Andrew S. McMillan. Our father wanted to name his first son after his favorite uncle, Andrew McMillan, but when he found that he had twin sons, he named us both after our esteemed uncle. Our middle initial denotes 'F' for First and 'S' for Second. In fact, Andrew and I met up last week while I was in Rangoon. I, too, would be serving my queen if it were not for my slightly irregular heartbeat. So, Major, rather than focusing my attention down the barrel of a rifle, I must be satisfied with focusing attention down the tube of a survey transit.

Major Winston Somerset, commanding officer of the Chittagong garrison, seemed satisfied with the explanation as was St. John. McMillan focused a broad smile toward Michael as if to say, "*How was that?*"

"So, Professor St. John, as I understand it, you are hoping to find a route for a rail system over the Banderban Hills, through the jungles of Burma, and into the swamps of Rangoon?" Somerset asked.

"That about sums it up, Major. While this project is not imminent, Her Majesty's government would like to have topographical details of the region on file. Perhaps sometime in the near future, an actual rail system might be considered. We want to keep this operation hush-hush so as not to invite unwarranted speculation as to where we might wish to set up depots and the like. So, Major, if you could keep this little project between us, we would be very appreciative."

McMillan then added, "We are also aware that there are some groups of people in the region who would not like to see any more British incursion into their tribal lands. They might see a rail system as being counterproductive to their cultural and religious tenets. We, on the other hand, see a rail system as promoting logging, mining, and a wide assortment of other enterprises. And let's not forget the military consideration. Whole detachments of troops could be moved by rail instead of elephant trail. But, as I said, there are some groups of people who shun progress in favor of tradition."

Major Somerset, much like Colonel Ballentine, issued a slight, "Hmm." at McMillan's commentary.

St. John waited before bringing the conversation to a conclusion. "Our team plans to move out in two days. We have our porters and a guide we found who knows the area. All we will need are the horses and pack mules and the fresh supplies Colonel Ballentine requested in his telegram. With that, we will be out of your hair before you know it."

Major Somerset issued another "Hmm."

It was apparent that "Professor" St. John's presence in the region was an inconvenience for the Major. It was also obvious from the lack of conversation that the quiet balance of nature was not quite as it should be. Usually, visitors were welcomed with a bit more conversation and exchange of information than Major Somerset had provided. There was an uneasiness which seemed to hang in the air like stale cigar smoke.

St. John's team, including the "natives" were escorted to their quarters where they were to stay until their departure. A high mud brick wall surrounded the compound blocking out the horrific squalor of abject poverty. Unfortunately, the high wall did not block out the smell emanating from a large patch of vacant land adjacent to the compound; vacant except for the occupants of a Mohammedan cemetery.

McMillan spotted a water tower at the far end of the compound. They raced toward the tower. Like two gibbon apes, they climbed to the small wooden platform surrounding the tank at the top. To the west, spread the Bay of Bengal. To the north and south, were labyrinths of mud brick huts, walls, and mosques. To the east, was their objective–the Banderban Hills. As they stood high above the compound, Bua Tan Bo called up from below. "What are you chaps up to?"

McMillan replied, "Join us."

With a bit more caution, Bua made his way to the platform. Looking to the east, he spoke, "That, gentlemen, is my home."

McMillan asked, "Bua, is it possible to see this tower from any point in or near your village?"

Bua replied, "I remember as a child, we could see the great Chittagong warehouse fire from our village. With a pair of your best field glasses or perhaps a small telescope, you could see quite well."

McMillan thought for a few seconds. "Michael, I would suggest that we attempt to set up a heliograph between this tower and a high point near the village. This would allow us to communicate by way of this new Morse Code."

St. John thought for a moment and replied, "Explain!"

"By using the sun's reflection onto a large mirror we could send messages back and forth much like the navy lads aboard ship. This would give us direct communication without having to use runners or wire telegraph lines. I would suggest that we talk with Major Somerset and request that he assign a signalman to this task," Andrew said.

"I like it," replied St. John. "Great idea!"

Somewhat reluctantly, Major Somerset had invited St. John and McMillan to dine with him in his private quarters. It was obvious that the Major was uneasy about something or another. Nonetheless, the meal was not too unpleasant, nor was the wine or even the after-dinner brandy. St. John thought for a moment that they should, perhaps, tell the Major that they, too, were military and explain the nature of the operation. Realizing that they were outranked, St. John opted to maintain the illusion of being civilian engineers.

As the brandy snifters became increasingly more empty, Major Somerset made no attempt to prolong the evening with a polite refill. With the last drop of brandy, Somerset raised his glass to the portrait of Queen Victoria, and said, "To Her Imperial Majesty, the Queen." With that, he bid his two guests a good night.

Michael and Andrew moved casually back toward the barracks. Both men noticed an uneasy feeling in the personality and attitude of the compound and those who occupied it. Something was not quite right here.

"Michael," Andrew said, "what say we find the command sergeant's quarters and have a chat. Perhaps we can ascertain why Major Somerset seems to be walking on pins and needles."

"Right you are, Andrew, right you are," replied Michael.

A sentry pointed the way to Senior Sergeant Robert Roberts' quarters.

After a brief introduction, the two civil engineers were invited into the Spartan room Roberts called home. It was immediately obvious from the first word Roberts uttered that he, too, was a Scot. After a bit of chit-chat about the Roberts family, the two sons of Scotland were like brothers. Two cups of tea were offered and accepted. It was St. John who noticed the open Bible on the night table next to the sergeant's bed.

"Well, another man of the Word," McMillan uttered attempting to redirect the conversation toward yet another point of commonality.

"Yes, in this God forsaken place with all these Mohammedan heathen running all about, one must fortify one's soul at every occasion."

McMillan, looked directly at St. John as if to ask, "Should we bring Roberts into this?"

St. John, thinking the very same thought, nodded. St. John then spoke, "Sergeant Roberts, we need to make you privy to some rather secret information. We would ask that you keep this information between us and no one else. Not even your commanding officer is to know the intent of our operation."

Robert Roberts took a deep breath and replied, "Gentlemen, I am a man under authority. I do what I am commanded to do. I am loyal to my regiment and my Queen and none other. If you are involved in anything which is contrary to the welfare of my country or Queen, I will not only have to ask you to leave immediately, but I shall bring this conversation to the attention of Major Somerset."

McMillan realized the corner they were in and the corner they would be putting Roberts in if they were to subvert the authority of his commanding officer in any way.

Both McMillan and St. John looked at each other and issued a perfunctory "Hmm."

St. John spoke, "Well you see, Sergeant Roberts, McMillan and I are both non-commissioned officers in Her Majesty's military services. In fact, McMillan here is a sergeant and I, a sergeant major."

Roberts interrupted, "Don't tell me you are Sergeant Major Michael St. John of the Battle of Irrawaddy!"

St. John smiled and nodded, "The same."

Roberts stiffened as if in the presence of a saint.

St. John continued, "As a result of that Irrawaddy thing, Sergeant McMillan and I are on a secret assignment to take care of some unfinished business."

McMillan entered the conversation. "You see, Sergeant Roberts, due to the nature of our assignment, no one, not even your commanding officer, has knowledge of our identity or nature of our visit here. They must be made to believe that we are, indeed, here to survey for a rail system.

St. John came back, "I am sure you know, Sergeant Roberts, that there are forces which would like to see the Empire fail as well as any and all attempts at progress. For this reason, we must know if there are specific individuals or groups of individuals, in this region who we might wish to consider as enemies or potential adversaries."

Roberts pondered the situation for a quiet minute. "Gentlemen, as you may have noticed, there is a cloud hanging over the Chittagong barracks. Major Somerset is a fine man and a fine officer. In fact, he is one of the finest officers I have served under. Unfortunately, there exists a situation which placed Major Somerset in a very difficult position. There is a local bandit who calls himself the Prince. He claims to be the descendent of some very serious Mohammedan folks as well as some Hindu royalty. The truth of the matter is that he is simply a bandit with a large imagination. Because of his claim to royalty and considerable holiness, the locals dare not touch him. This, coupled with the fact that he professes to have the power to cast horrific spells on people if they oppose him, insulates him from opposition. Oddly enough, when people offer opposition, bad luck seems to follow almost immediately. When he and his band of renegades rob a village, the villagers simply report that they offered appropriate sacrifices for protection. Major Somerset has attempted to mitigate the situation, but the people in this area are afraid to levy any offenses against the Prince. Thus, the rascal runs free to rob and plunder as he wishes.

On the other hand, the people are unhappy with the British forces for not bringing the protection they promised. Then, to make matters even worse, if Major Somerset reports this situation to his superiors, they will expect him to launch a full military campaign to apprehend this Prince. If British forces are moved against the Prince, both he and the people will accuse the British of religious oppression and all Hell breaks loose.

Both St. John and McMillan looked at each other and issued another "Hmm."

Roberts continued, "And to make matters even worse, these rascals are now coming into Chittagong and robbing stores and markets–in broad daylight."

McMillan spoke, "Do you know where these rogues are living?"

Roberts replied, "Oh yes, we know exactly were they live–about thirty kilometers from here. They even have their own temples, both Hindu and Mohammedan. The Prince has even gone so far as to erect a Buddhist shrine in the event any followers of Buddha should seek asylum among his band. This rascal has made provisions for every contingency. The only thing lacking is a Christian chapel."

St. John then spoke, "What about the villages up in the Banderban Hills? Are they impacted by this Prince and his rabble?"

Roberts answered, "No, they are off limits. It seems the Baum folks in the hills raise pigs which are completely taboo to both Mohammedans and Hindus. Many of the pigs are left to run wild in and around the Baum villages. If a Mohammedan or Hindu even step on pig dropping, they are out of business for eternity. Any person who is contaminated by pig blood, meat, fat, or feces is off limits. All the soap in the empire can't remove the curse. Anything to do with swine is poison for these people."

McMillan's face broadened into a huge smile. "Michael, are you thinking what I am thinking?" Michael's face also grew into a wide, wicked grin. Finally, Roberts caught on.

"Sergeant Roberts, by chance is this village anywhere near our route to the Banderban Hills?"

"Yes," Roberts replied, "in fact it is quite near a bridge crossing you chaps will be taking. Just after the bridge, you will turn north toward the hills. The main Baum village is about ten kilometers up the road. The Prince's enclave is located in a narrow gorge along the river to the south about five kilometers."

It was clear from the expressions on St. John and McMillan's face that serious mischief was in the works.

St. John spoke. "Tell me more about the Baum and the Prince's folks, Sergeant."

Roberts continued. "Well, you know the bridge I mentioned? The Prince's people claim ownership of that bridge and all who cross it are expected to pay a duty on all goods coming or going. Because the Baum people use a barter system of buying and selling, they seldom have money. The Prince has taken advantage of this by requiring that they pay their "taxes" in the form of coffee beans and cashew nuts. He equates one kilo of beans or nuts as equal to one rupee. The Prince then sells the nuts and beans to export merchants for ten rupees a kilo.

McMillan then asked, "Why can't the Baum people sell their coffee and cashews to the same merchants?

Roberts continued, "The merchants buying coffee and cashews are located down river from the village the Prince controls. No one except for him can follow the river road to that port town. He has a virtual stranglehold on the market. While this situation is clearly illegal, the Prince manages to get away with it anyhow. Unfortunately, when Major Somerset and his troops inquire about the situation, the Baum folks and others are silent. They fear reprisals from the Prince. They are also afraid of his magic. He simply closes the bridge and there is no going to market."

St. John brought the conversation back to details which Sergeant Roberts might, if he wished, attend to. First of all, Roberts was formally asked if he wished to participate in the operation. If not, nothing would be said either way. If, on the other hand, he did wish to enter in this little adventure, he would be asked to swear an oath of secrecy which, in no way, compromised his allegiance to Queen or country.

One detail which was discussed was that of setting up a heliograph on the water tower and providing a signalman to send and receive messages from the hills. Sergeant Roberts made a mental note of the task and indicated that a large mirror could be found in the local bazaar.

Somewhere around midnight, the three soldiers brought their conversation to an end. Before leaving Sergeant Robert's quarters, McMillan asked Roberts to pick up his Bible and open to Psalm chapter 37, verse six.

Roberts politely complied and began to read, '. . .if you will commit your way unto the Lord, the Lord will give you the desires of your heart."

McMillan spoke, "Well?" The two others responded with a firm, "Amen!"

The following day, all supplies and equipment were assembled in one of the empty warehouses. The dozen or so pack animals along with the riding horses were examined, curried and fed. That morning, Sergeant Roberts mentioned to several native grooms that an expedition of British civil servants was being sent into the Banderban Hills. This would allay any rumors of conquest or problems in the region–just a simple survey project. At St. John's request, Bua Tan Bo dispatched one of his men to ride to his village to notify the elders of the arrival of this group. The rider was given several coins in the event he was stopped by the Prince's men and required tribute money.

Much of the day was spent setting up the heliograph system on the water tower. Two signalmen were briefed on its use, and a list of instructions was written down. There was also a list of code words to be used for transmittal to and from Rangoon, in particular, to the Green Frog Tea Shop. The code words were simple phrases with secret meanings.

Reveille sounded and the day began with a brief but adequate breakfast. Horses were saddled, pack animals loaded and farewells made. Sergeant Roberts quietly passed a small paper bag to McMillan. "Sweets for the children–kids up in the hills love candy, you know," he said.

∾

CHAPTER TWENTY-ONE

EAST OF RANGOON

Lieutenant Colonel Joseph Ballentine's caravan had progressed with all the momentum of a tired tortoise. The first day out, three pack animals bolted from the march when startled by shouting villagers. Although the villagers were shouting the praises of the Queen, they knew full well that their chants would frighten the animals, possibly allowing them to capture and conceal the animals and their loads. The second day was spoiled by Colonel Ballentine's unfortunate bout with what was jokingly called, "Burmese belly." The unfortunate Colonel had ordered the improvisation of a portable latrine; that is to say, a small tent capable of being erected at a moment's notice. Four bearers were given the task of carrying the canvas structure and erecting it as required by the Colonel.

While Colonel Ballentine was the only unfortunate to show symptoms of the Burmese belly, the medical officer strongly suggested that the campaign be aborted in favor of more favorable conditions. He surmised that it might just be the onset of the dreaded cholera. It was also announced to the men that

Colonel Ballentine had received an intelligence report indicating that a bridge had been washed out by monsoon rains and that the march would be made sometime later, perhaps in the dry season. The news brought secret smiles to the faces of foot soldiers and cavalry soldiers already travel weary from the short march, barely out of sight of Rangoon.

As the long line of quietly elated British soldiers returned toward the comforts of their barracks, there was more cheering by village folk and several more pack animals irretrievably lost. On several occasions, Colonel Ballentine was overheard to say, "These bloody heathen really do love the queen!"

CHAPTER TWENTY-TWO

THREE PAGODA PASS – SIAMESE FRONTIER .

A day later, in a small dilapidated Buddhist temple near the Three Pagoda Pass, a dozen or so Burmans sat around an iron fire pot considering the news of Colonel Ballentine's retreat. Three of the men were wrapped in dirty saffron robes with shaved heads. Four others were clearly followers of the Prophet Mohammad, while two others were holy men of some unnamed religion. However distant from one another in philosophy, all those around the fire pot had one thing in common–they hated the British and their hunger for Burma's resources. Upon hearing the rumors about Colonel Ballentine's episode with an extreme intestinal disorder, one of the monks suggested that the word be spread regarding the outbreak of cholera among the British soldiers. If there was anything that would put the public into a panic, it was the threat of the dreaded cholera. A Mohammadan then suggested that the story be sent out that every spot where the Colonel erected his portable latrine be considered a source of cholera. He suggested that the simple folk would believe this story and cause such a fuss that Colonel

Ballentine would be blamed for any and all illnesses or death along his unfortunate march route.

As the fire pot smoldered on into the night, questions were expressed as to why Ballentine was going to the Three Pagoda Pass. Ballentine's cook had indicated that the mission was to pacify contrary tribal groups and resolve old feuds. There was even mention of a possible amalgamation of Christian tribal groups into some sort of alliance. This thought truly disturbed those around the fire.

One mullah stated in a fiery tone, "This must be avoided at all costs. If the Christians or their sympathizers ever side with the British, things will not go well for our cause." This statement seemed to unify all those around the fire pot.

Another monk then spoke, "I suggest that we carefully and quietly watch the goings-on in and around the Christian villages. If there is anything unusual happening, we need to know about it." Again, there was unanimous agreement. The monk continued, "I shall send a message to all Buddhist monks, asking them to take note of any unusual activities among the Christians."

The mullah agreed and promised the same action. The animist holy men nodded in agreement. Within a week, the words of the mullah and monk had spread like cholera throughout the region. Fortunately, several of the Christian leaders in the area had also heard the message.

CHAPTER TWENTY-THREE

CHITTAGONG:

The file of men, horses, and several carts were in line and ready to march when Major Somerset called St. John and McMillan aside for a quiet conversation. Although Major Somerset had strongly suggested that a complement of British soldiers be sent to advise and protect Her Majesty's civil servants, St. John declined. Polite warnings were again issued regarding possible encounters with local bandits or incidents of civil disorder. McMillan assured Somerset that they would take every precaution to see that any unpleasantries were avoided.

McMillan then spoke. "Major, I can clearly see that our welfare is of significant concern to you. For that we are truly grateful. I am told that you have a Sergeant Roberts who I understand knows the region and the people quite well. If I might suggest, sir, Sergeant Roberts might serve as a satisfactory compromise."

McMillan looked at St. John to see if there was any indication of an error in judgment. There was none.

Somerset smiled and yelled out, "Sergeant Roberts, report at once!"

Within seconds, Sergeant Roberts snapped to attention in front of the Major. "Roberts, I am sending you as a personal escort for this expedition. You will be responsible for protecting and advising these gentlemen, but you will be answerable to me. Is that clear?"

Roberts barked out, "Yes, sir!" Robert's eyes moved ever so slightly to his right where he caught the wink from McMillan.

Major Somerset then barked, "Roberts, you have exactly five minutes to grab your field gear and stand present."

Roberts returned in four minutes, ready to mount a waiting horse.

The column moved slowly through the fetid and stinking streets of Chittagong toward the Banderban hills in the smoky distance. Not even in Rangoon or Calcutta had St. John seen such squalor and poverty. Lepers by the dozens seemed to congregate at every intersection, hoping to incite sympathy even from those as destitute as they. Although it was against the law to beg from British soldiers or British subjects, beggars held out their pathetic hands just in case one of these civilized human beings might just have a twinge of compassion.

McMillan broke ranks and spurred his horse next to Roberts. Handing over the sack of candy, he said, "Why don't you toss a few pieces of candy to the children here?"

Roberts took the bag, stuffed it into his saddle bag and said, "My friend, if I were to toss even a single piece of candy to a child, that child would be mobbed and possibly killed for that single piece of candy. These people are absolutely destitute. They have become like dogs. If you give a bone to one dog, all the other dogs will turn on it and fight over the bone until the last living dog has it. Sad, but true."

McMillan shook his head and focused straight ahead. Two hours later, the column had reached the edge of town where the dense labyrinth of mud-brick buildings gave way to small farms with bamboo huts. The dense smoke from thousands of cooking fires seemed to follow the column toward the hills. Well out of sight of the last signs of the city, Bua Tan Bo broke his simple disguise of a hired porter and nudged his horse up to where St. John and McMillan rode. For the first time since leaving Rangoon, Bua spoke directly to St. John. "Michael, I would suggest that we plan on making camp at the bridge at the base of the hills. This will give the Prince an opportunity to make a polite visit to our camp and have a little chat. This will allow us to assess his resources and he, ours. From a point of peaceful confrontation, we can provide him with bits of information or misinformation we should wish to convey. Who knows, we might be able to mitigate any unfortunate situations which might arise later on.

Roberts noticed the brown-skinned porter talking directly with an Englishman. He spurred his horse up to where he, too, was riding abreast of St. John. "St. John, if I might ask, what is this fellow doing riding next to you? Doesn't he know his place?"

St. John held up his hand before any more damage could be done. "Sergeant Roberts, allow me to introduce you to Bua Tan Bo, son of one of the Baum elders we are going to meet."

It was obvious the damage had been done. It was also obvious that Bua was going to take full advantage of any and all attempts to rectify the offense.

Roberts apologized profoundly and extended his hand toward the offended party. St. John clearly saw that Bua was playing Roberts for his offense.

He spoke, "Sergeant Roberts, Bua Tan Bo here has committed to memory the entire Bible. He especially recalls the part about forgiveness."

Bua gave St. John a harsh stare which almost immediately transformed into a grin. "I forgive you, Brother Roberts," he said as he intentionally dropped the title of sergeant.

Both Roberts and St. John thought to themselves, "*Brother Roberts?*"

Roberts, not to be outdone, replied, "Thank you, Brother Bua."

Roberts and St. John looked at each other with a look of befuddlement.

By late afternoon, the column arrived at the river which divided the lowlands from the Banderban Hills. As anticipated, three horsemen were waiting at the bridge. As the column approached, Bua Tan Bo sank back to the rear ranks along with the carts and covered his head and face with a dirty rag.

St. John gave the order to make camp on the west side of the bridge. He knew that the three horsemen were there to collect a tribute for the Prince. If the column were to delay their crossing until the following morning, the horsemen would either have to make camp or return to their village. As the camp was set, one of the horsemen departed downstream toward his unseen village.

Roberts suggested that the Prince might be provoked to send more horsemen and thus incite a confrontation requiring a military response. McMillan agreed in part, but suggested that any sort of confrontation would lead to a far more serious response than the Prince would wish. As the camp settled into their blankets, two sets of night sentries watched each other from across a narrow bridge.

∾

CHAPTER TWENTY-FOUR

The sun rose late in the morning at the base of the Banderban Hills. As the thin morning fog rose from the river gorge, thirty or so men could be seen on the far side of the bridge. The British camp had been alerted to the presence of a force of men with unknown intentions on the opposite side of the river. Sergeant Roberts strapped on his cartridge belt, chambered a round and placed his helmet on his head.

A voice from the other side called out, "Sergeant Roberts, how nice to see you again."

Roberts whispered in a quiet tone, "It's the Prince. He and I go back a ways."

St. John and McMillan finished buttoning their tunics as if they were about to be visited by local civil servant.

Again, the Prince called out, "Sergeant Roberts, perhaps you would be so kind as to introduce me to your colleagues. Let me invite you and your friends to a humble breakfast on this side of my bridge."

St. John moved back to where Bua Tan Bo was standing shrouded under a blanket. "Bua, what's your advice in this matter? Do we sit down for breakfast tea with this rascal, or do we simply ignore him and move on?"

Bua spoke, "I believe it was your man, the Duke of Wellington, who prior to the Battle of Waterloo, said, 'know your enemy.' If that be the case, I would suggest a cup of tea. If you were to refuse, it would cause him to lose face in front of his men and his hatred of you British would intensify all the more. Once again, my friend, if we were to go back to our game of chess, you could be seen setting up a classic fool's mate. Make the Prince think that you regard him as a force to contend with. We can also let him know that the British Empire could make him a prince or a pauper. He is a power to contend with, but as with Alexander the Great, a power can either be compromised or crushed like a bug."

"Good thought," uttered St. John, "tea and biscuits it is."

St. John moved toward the bridge just as the morning fog lifted altogether.

"Sir," he shouted, "we should be delighted to join you for breakfast." With that, St. John, McMillan, and Roberts walked three abreast across the river. A fire had been set with a small goat on a spit slung between two rocks. A pot of very strong tea was boiling next to the fire. A kettle of rice along with a pot of curry sauce had been placed on a mat near the fire.

The Prince was a short man draped in a full-length robe. He wore a twisted black-rag turban topped with a cap indicating that he had made the required pilgrimage to Mecca. On his delicate hands were jeweled rings of every color. The dagger tucked in his waistband was clearly a work of art replete with more jewels than found on his hands. It was, however, obvious to a reasonably trained eye that these jewels were not even closely related to real gem stones. Perhaps they were carved off some carousel pony found in a carnival. The Prince's beard was thick and reasonably well groomed. Upon closer examination, it was obvious that he had used boot black to enhance his beard thus adding to his fearsome appearance. Again, it was obvious to those sitting near him that he had darkened his eye sockets with some sort of powder. The small bump on his forehead indicated that he prayed with great fervor banging his forehead upon the ground each time he bowed toward Mecca.

The Englishmen were invited to sit upon dried goat skins placed around the eating pallet. Before any food or drink was offered, the Prince commanded that a washing bowel and towel be brought. Each man purified his hands and face in order to comply with Mohammedan etiquette. In order to counter the Prince's little ceremony, McMillan bowed his head and offered a prayer, "Father for what we are about to receive, make us truly grateful."

McMillan smiled at the Prince as if to say, "Touché."

The roasted goat was well received by all around the table as was the rice and sauce. Several toasts of the highly sweetened tea were made by the Prince including one toast for Allah, one for Queen Victoria, and one for each of the Englishmen sitting around the table. Oddly enough, no one thought to make a toast to the Prince. The sun was beginning to rise higher in the sky as St. John suggested that the group needed to be moving on toward their objective.

Before anyone could move, the Prince spoke, "Gentlemen, it has come to my attention that your government has intentions of building a railroad system through my domain including across my bridge. As you may well know, it was my ancestors who built this bridge and brought this area under the responsibility of my family. If this be the case, gentlemen, I will most certainly need to be taken into consideration."

Roberts, St. John, and McMillan all looked briefly at each other. After a brief pause, it was St. John who offered the rebuttal. "Sir, with all due respect, we acknowledge your position as head of your clan and, in fact, your claim to have settled this region. However, I must remind you of one extremely significant matter which you seem to have overlooked. This land and all land currently known as India and Burma is part and parcel property of Her Imperial Majesty, Queen Victoria. Any claims otherwise are tantamount to treason."

The Prince's eyes became red and large. He looked as if he had been slapped, by a woman at that.

St. John continued, "However, as it was with Alexander the Great, enemies and adversaries can remain hostile to the crown and be severely dealt with, or they can subjugate themselves to their new and benevolent rulers. History clearly shows that those who came up against Alexander's forces quickly capitulated in favor of an alliance. Those who were foolish enough to resist were removed from the history books all together. Unfortunately for you and your people, you have the choice of becoming loyal subjects of Her Majesty's government, or face tens of thousands of British soldiers here on your little bridge."

It was obvious that the Prince was furious and had lost face in the presence of those who had just witnessed St. John's proclamation.

It was McMillan's turn to speak. "Sir, as a point of information, if this railroad project is to happen, and I believe it will, your occupancy of this crossing point might prove to be more beneficial than you think. If we build our railroad, we will most certainly construct a major bridge for our trains. This would render your little bridge useless. On the other hand, you might consider building a small town, complete with fuel and water services, for our locomotives. Plus you may wish to include food services for passengers and other assorted travel amenities. An enterprise such as this would provide far more income than the meager revenues from this paltry bridge.

The Prince's eyes narrowed as if he were looking into the future. A slight smile replaced the scowl previously seen. "You know, my friend that is a wonderful idea. Yes, a wonderful idea."

With that, breakfast was over. The Englishmen thanked their host and slowly walked back across the bridge to where the main body of the squad was anxiously waiting. The order was given to march whereupon the column moved, unimpeded, across the narrow stone bridge. The Prince waved as the column moved up the trail toward the Banderban Hills.

CHAPTER TWENTY-FIVE

BAUM VILLAGE – BANDERBAN HILL – EAST OF CHITTAGONG

Several hundred meters up the trail out of earshot of the Prince, the three sergeants burst into laughter. Their comments about the Prince and his fiefdom provided sufficient amusement for the next few kilometers. They had gone approximately three kilometers when they heard the drum. It was a deep, hollow sound which echoed off the ever-rising hills. A few hundred meters beyond where the banana trees began to grow, voices could be heard along with the deep base voice of the drum. Bua Tan Bo broke ranks and raced his horse to the front of the line. "They are singing the welcome song. The drum is telling us that we are welcome to enter the hills," Bua announced. Bua then rode well head of the group with his head thrown back and his arms spread wide. The voices became louder as did the drum as the column moved closer. The tempo of the drum became faster as the column drew near the first mountain village. Coming around a bend in the trail was something the Englishmen never expected to see. There, at the end of the dirt road, was a red brick road. Aligned on both sides were men, women, and children dressed in their finest clothing and all waving branches of crimson bougainvillea. Children tossed bougainvillea blossom onto the brick road as the westerners approached. This was a total contradiction to the rubbish-clogged streets of Chittagong.

Somewhere in the distance a female voice was singing out a chant followed by a choir of those lining the road. Several smaller drums entered the symphony as did a number of bamboo flutes. Alexander the Great could not have been received with more tasteful ceremony. A congregation of old men in brightly colored jackets stood in front of a red-brick arch denoting the entrance to the village. It was beautiful and totally unlike anything they had seen in the lowlands.

As the horsemen and those on carts dismounted, throngs of children ran to place flower garlands around the necks of the visitors. Bua Tan Bo walked up the brick path to where the elders stood and bowed reverently. One old man held up his hand whereupon the drums and singing stopped.

Bua Tan Bo turned to the Englishmen and beckoned them to come. Reaching the assembly of elders, Bua, in the most pronounced English, introduced each man to the elders, beginning with his father, Elder Simon. The welcome was more than sincere. One of the elders gave an order for cups of jungle berry juice for the travelers. St. John immediately recognized the fluid and warned the others, "One cup, no more!"

After repetitious hand shakings with what seemed like a thousand hands, one of the elders ordered the drums and singing begin again. Moving through the red-brick arches of the village, the Englishmen notice the sweet smell of roasting meat, pork to be exact. Nowhere in the lowlands of Chittagong nor in the regions surrounding Rangoon could pork be had. Not only did the smell of roasting pork perfume the air, so did the pungent aroma of ginger and pineapple sauce.

St. John's order that no one consume more than one cup of the jungle berry juice almost immediately gave way to a diplomatic acquiescence. One cup soon became many cups. By the time the sun had set into the Bay of Bengal off in the distance, and the roasted pig declared ready to eat, all English participants of the village welcome party were thoroughly intoxicated.

The pork and its accompanying pineapple ginger sauce were magnificent. The papaya, fresh bananas, and other jungle fruits provided a feast not seen by any of the Englishmen in years, if at all. Several times during the feast, the Brits were heard to say, "Why can't the British learn to cook like this? After all, we do own most of the spice-producing regions in the world."

To settle the rich pork and assorted condiments, a huge pot of black, very black, coffee was brought to the table. A young woman dressed in a beautifully hand-woven skirt poured cups of the black substance along with thick cream and sugar. Almost immediately after taking a single sip of the brew, heart rhythms began to increase. More logs were added to the fire. Once again, the drums began to beat; this time a dozen or so. Villagers, some young and some not so young, began to dance around the fire. Several ladies, some young and some not so young, invited the Englishmen to dance. Before long, both the alcohol and the caffeine had impacted the Englishmen's judgment as well as coordination. The dancing was fun, but reckless.

It was well into the night when McMillan announced that he would take leave and return in a moment. Soon, McMillan reappeared with his bagpipes under his arm. Without warning, he blew and squeezed out the first frightening sounds. Many of the older men had heard the pipes when the British Army was marching around the countryside. Some people covered their ears while other savored the new sound like one would savor a new food. Roberts, seeing the opportunity, took one of the drums from a villager and began to accompany McMillan as he marched around the campfire. Bua Tan Bo nudged St. John, "Michael, this event will be repeated in Baum history for centuries." When McMillan began to play Amazing Grace, every Baum immediately broke into song. Before the fire died away, Amazing Grace had been played and sung at least a dozen times. A good time was being had by all.

The following morning was not so pleasant. While the Baum people were not the least affected by the jungle juice, the Englishmen were laid low. Heads pounded almost as loud and hard as the drums the night before. Once again strong, almost toxic black coffee was administered in massive doses to ease the pain. By noon, the evil spirits which plagued the Brits had been lessened.

One-by-one, the Englishmen left the confines of their small bamboo hut and explored the village and its environs. Unlike the villages in the lowlands, there was no refuse on the ground, no piles of litter, no open sewers. Proper latrines were set in various places far from huts or water sources. All refuse was placed in bamboo troughs where several dozen pigs would almost immediately consume it. The waste from the swine was then channeled into holding ponds where it was dried and used for plant fertilizer.

Water cisterns had been built on flowing streams with bamboo pipes transporting water to small fields of pineapple plants and potatoes. Huts were surrounded by coffee trees and cashew trees to provide protection from the morning and afternoon sun. It was as perfect a village setting as it could possibly be. The village was in stark contrast to the settlements in the lowlands.

McMillan, Roberts, and St. John walked down a red-brick path to a flattened hilltop which overlooked the whole Chittagong basin below. Far in the distance, through the thick acrid smoke of a thousand cooking fires, one could make out the walled compound where they had slept several nights before. It seemed so tiny and so insignificant.

Shortly, Bua Tan Bo joined the three men as they stood overlooking the lowlands below and the great Bay of Bengal beyond.

He spoke, "After our noon meal, we can talk. The elders know the nature of our visit and the subject of our conversation. As far as I can tell, they are in full agreement with your plan. We must, however, become more specific in the consequences of our actions. You see, our elders try to determine how change, any change will affect those to be born two and three generations hence. You westerners, on the other hand, consider the present perhaps more than you should.

Roberts then spoke, "Perhaps I need to be informed a bit more as to this plan you are talking about." Both St. John and McMillan agreed. For the next hour the plan and the details of the plan were put forth, including the unfortunate encounter with the notorious pirate, Bua Tan Bo on the Irrawaddy. When St. John mentioned the part of the plan which included bringing more missionaries to the region, Roberts was ecstatic.

"I have prayed to God Almighty, since arriving in this god-forsaken outpost that He would provide missionaries who were interested in a man's body as well as his soul," he said.

An hour later, the three Englishmen were introduced to the elders of the Baum people. Rather than continue the charade, Bua Tan Bo introduced St. John as Sergeant Major Michael St. John and Andrew McMillan as Sergeant McMillan. Bua had also given the elders his version of the Battle on the Irrawaddy. They were amused and impressed.

Roberts was well known to the elders and highly respected for his sense of piety and fair play. For three hours the details of the plan were discussed in deep earnest. Several times Bua Tan Bo found himself playing referee between two points of controversy. Several times it was Bua Tan Bo who negotiated an acceptable resolution to a particular point of confusion or controversy. Many times during the conversation, Bua Tan Bo's father would look at his son and smile silently. There was no denying that the old man was immensely proud of his son. It was also obvious that the other elders were impressed with the young man's ability to see critical issues from both the Baum side and from the British side. It was also quite apparent that Bua Tan Bo could see well into the future when dealing with conditional issues. At no point in the discussions did he appear to sell out his people in favor of their captors. Bua Tan Bo was seen by both parties as a true diplomat and patriot to both his people and the Empire.

That evening, after a less sumptuous dinner than the previous evening, the three English sergeants and Bua Tan Bo retired to their hut where they amended the documents which had come to be known as the Ballentine Doctrine. Points of ambiguity were defined and clarified. Specific resolutions were drafted providing for a specialized security force which was to closely resemble the Gurkhas forces of Nepal. Roberts indicated that he had personally served with the Gurkhas and was tremendously impressed with both their loyalty and their fighting skill. Roberts implied that if such a unit of Baum soldiers were to be created, he would be most honored to serve as an advisor. St. John made a mental note of this.

The following morning, Bua and the three Englishmen met with the group of elders for one final look at documents. Within minutes, the accord was approved. A dozen athletic young men compete with woven backpacks were summoned to the elders. Each was given a series of verbal messages and destinations. Each message was simplified into a paragraph.

We, the elders of the Baum people, invite a representative of your tribe, clan, or village to a meeting. The discussion will involve our response to an offer made by the British government to align ourselves with the British. In return, many benefits will be forthcoming. As there are those who would wish to do us harm, the meeting is to be held most secret. Our time will be at the next full moon. With God as our witness, we encourage you to meet with us and discuss the matter further.

Each of the runners was blessed and sent on his way. Bua Tan Bo indicated that each runner would run to a specific village and deliver the message. From there, several other runners would be sent to more villages. Within the span of a few days, all Baum and aligned villages would receive the message.

McMillan summoned the two signalmen and ordered them to make the heliograph ready to send a message to the water tower in Chittagong. The coded message read as follows:

We have arrived successfully at the first village. The trip went well. We enjoyed a cordial meeting with a fellow calling himself the Prince.

In his office in the Chittagong barracks, Major read the communiqué and smiled. *"So,"* he thought to himself, *"they had breakfast with the Prince."* The heliograph message continued, "I would request a telegram be sent to Rangoon to a man called James. His address is The Green Frog located at the main bazaar."

Major Somerset finished reading the message, and then ordered that St. John's message be sent on to Rangoon as soon as possible.

The message for James read:

"Thank you for the excellent tea. It has provided satisfactory relief for my stomach ailments.

Regards, St. John."

If the outcome of the meeting with the Baum elders had been fruitless, the message would have read:

The tea which you sold me has failed to correct my stomach ailments.

Regards, St. John."

A third message indicating a less than enthusiastic response would have read:

"The tea which you sold me has not as yet proven successful in the treatment of my stomach ailments.

Regards, St. John."

The latter message would have postponed the conclave in the Banderban Hills by at least one full month, if not longer.

The implication of the message was to initiate the process of notifying all Christian tribal leaders in the north and eastern part of Burma that a secret conclave was going to take place in the Banderban Hills on the day of the next full moon.

CHAPTER TWENTY-SIX

RANGOON:

A telegraph messenger arrived at the Green Frog Tea Shop. James opened the telegram and read the message. A huge smile crossed his face. Immediately, he summoned a rickshaw and ordered the puller to take him to the telegraph office. From there, the message went out to dozens of small villages. From those villages, more runners were dispatched with the message of the conclave. Within five days, every Christian tribal leader had been informed about the meeting. Some simply shook their heads and ignored the information as they had done so many times before. Some, on the other hand, packed their bags and left quietly for the west.

CHAPTER TWENTY-SEVEN

THE BANDERBAN HILLS

With the preliminary work on the Ballentine Doctrine completed, the men on the survey expedition busied themselves with small tasks and building projects around the village. One of the unique factors about the Baum village was its small red brick-making industry. A source for red-brick clay had been found about one kilometer from the village. Several kilns were dug into the mountain side and reasonably large quantities of red-brick were made. These items were then laid down as roads and path. When asked about using brick for buildings, villagers indicated that bamboo houses and bamboo huts were, in fact, far more comfortable. And too, when the great cyclones came from off the Bay of Bengal, bamboo huts simply blew down. Brick houses would collapse, causing injury to their occupants.

It was Sergeant Roberts who suggested to several of the elders that they consider building a permanent brick church on the point overlooking the Bay of Bengal. One of the elders then motioned for Roberts to follow him to the point. Upon arriving, the old man looked around a full three hundred and sixty degrees. He spoke, "Brother Roberts, if we were to build a church like you English, we would block out all of the beauty of this place and replace it with walls and a roof. We would much rather gaze at God's creation than man's creation."

Roberts, seeing the wisdom of the old man's comments, burst into laughter. "My brother, in many places we build churches to block out the ugliness around us. Here that would be a sin. You are right."

Another elder then spoke up, "Brother Roberts, we have seen the churches and cathedrals you and those from your world have built. Not only do they cost enormous amounts of money to build, but they eventually become monuments to those who built them. Granted, some are indeed awe-inspiring, but do they truly magnify our God? I think not." Roberts nodded silently.

Another elder then took up the lesson. "And if Christ himself were to visit one of these monumental structures with its clergy adorned in princely regalia, would He feel comfortable? Again, I think not. It is my understanding that He was most comfortable on a hillside or next to the sea. While all of the pretty ornamentation and elaborate ceremonies of the church are pleasing to those sitting on the rough-hewn pews or on the gold-gilded thrones, I rather doubt the God, to whom they are addressing their worship, is impressed. I would prefer to think that He would much rather have a conversation with His children, let us say, on a mountaintop like this one upon which we are standing." By this time, tears were welling up in Robert's eyes.

Seeing the opportunity at hand, one of the elders suggested that they take a few minutes sitting on the light green ground cover, and "talk to God." They all sat and all quietly talked–to God. Almost two hours later, Roberts noticed that he was now alone.

Bua Tan Bo and Michael St. John had taken several long walks around the mountains. St. John had focused his interest on the hundreds of coffee and cashew trees growing in arbitrary places. After a day and a goodly number of kilometers, St. John had counted one hundred and twenty-three coffee trees and one hundred and four cashew trees. He noticed hundreds of banana, papaya, and other fruits growing along the fertile mountain sides. At several places along the trails, St. John would engage villagers regarding their livelihoods. Most villagers had several sources of income ranging from textile weaving to pottery making, to pork production and so on. He noted that this lifestyle was totally contrary to those living in the lowlands. Everyone had a job. Bua explained that every member of the community had a role to play in the survival of the clan. Each member was valuable for his or her contribution to the overall community. Everyone enjoys the dignity of work and the respect which comes from a job well done. Respect and personal integrity are considered as paramount and above all respect for God. "His respect and love for us is taught from the very day one is born into our community. Our law is simple, the Ten Commandments. We even love those who hate us; like the Prince," said Bua.

The afternoon sun was moving closer to the Bay of Bengal in the west. Michael and Bua were nearing the village when they noticed Roberts and McMillan. Both sergeants had their shirts off and both were wearing kilts. Around them were several dozen young men. St. John noticed Roberts pick up a woven rope with a woven hemp basket at the far end. The rope measured about two meters from handle to basket. In the basket was a large round rock, roughly the size of a pumpkin. He began to swing the rock round and round before letting it fly far into a field. Roberts ordered two lads to fetch the object and leave a marker where it landed. It was then McMillan's turn to swing the rock and let it fly. It landed a good two meters beyond the marker where Robert's rock had landed. Several more times the two Scots tossed the small boulder before letting some of the young men have a try. Several managed to get the rock off the ground but failed to make it fly more than a meter in any direction. Here was another story which would be told around Baum campfires for generations.

The group, including the two kilt-wearing Scots, returned to the village in time for the evening meal. As rice was being dished out, a man came running up the brick road. The man was bruised and bloodied, but coherent. Bua and his father were called over to the injured man. They bent down to listen to his message. Both Bua and his father were clearly shaken.

Bua came over to where St. John was sitting. "Something terrible has happened. Supi Yaw Law Lat, my sister has been kidnapped by the Prince. It appears that she and her assistant were heading back from a visit to another village when the Prince's men overpowered them and took her to their camp."

St. John called out for Roberts and McMillan to come immediately. Within a few minutes a large crowed had formed around the injured man and those dealing with the issue. St. John then began asking questions, "Bua, why would this fool take your sister hostage when he knows there will be a response; possibly a strong response?"

Bua replied, "I can only assume that he wants to test us and see just how far we will go to get her back. He might propose a ransom or possibly concessions related to the railroad. Who knows? The man is mad."

Roberts entered the conversation. "If word of this gets back to Major Somerset, he will be compelled to bring a force of men and settle the matter with guns. We must do everything possible to prevent an armed confrontation. This would quite possibly ignite a regional uprising. The Prince knows this and will use it to his advantage. I suggest that we deal with the matter ourselves."

There was a tense silence. St. John spoke, "Alright Sergeant Roberts, how would you suggest that we deal with this madman?"

Roberts smiled broadly. "The Prince's camp is located in a gorge approximately five kilometers south of the bridge we crossed getting here. I have been to his camp and I know the layout. His tents are pitched on the west bank of the river, with a sheer cliff rising straight up on the east side. The cliff is somewhere around two hundred meters high. It is virtually impossible to descend the cliff without being detected, or for that matter, killed. It would, however, be possible to launch projectiles down on the camp from the top of the cliff."

McMillan then spoke, "You may be correct, Sergeant Roberts, but we must first concern ourselves with the safety of Bua's sister."

Looking McMillan straight in the eye, Roberts asked, "Sergeant McMillan, what is the only thing that a Mohammedan or a Hindu is terrified of?"

Both St. John and McMillan replied at the same time. "Pigs!"

St. John spoke, "Sergeant Roberts are you suggesting that we toss pigs over the cliff onto the Prince's camp?"

McMillan spoke, "Just how do you propose that we throw a fifty kilo pig over the side of a cliff?"

Roberts replied, "In little pieces." Roberts stood there smiling as mental images of pieces of pork were tossed onto the Prince's camp. All those standing in the tight little circle began to laugh hysterically.

Roberts again spoke, "If we take and butcher the piggies, collect their blood and body parts, we can place them on those clay pots I see around the village. We then attach ropes to each pot, much like the baskets McMillan were using this afternoon in our little game of highland hammer throwing. Both McMillan and I will then toss the pots high into the air and over the cliff onto the Prince's camp. Once they see that pig heads, guts, and other assorted parts are raining down from heaven, they will depart down river as fast as their little limbs will carry them."

It seemed almost a joke as those standing around the circle absorbed the thought. Bua Tan Bo then added, "Let's take this one step further. The Prince and his followers are extremely superstitious. If I were to go into the Prince's camp, alone, and demand that my sister be returned immediately, the Prince would think I was mad. Then, like Moses standing before Pharaoh, I would demand that he release my sister or I would call down a curse from the skies. At that point, you gentlemen would then launch dozens of pig bombs on those standing below. Once the Prince and his followers realized that they were about to be eternally contaminated, they would head south, down river. And too, their camp would be forever unclean. I would then grab my sister and make our escape. With the exception of one or two unfortunates who might bear the full impact of a pig bomb, no one would be hurt or killed. "

The concept seemed almost too audacious to be taken seriously. Killing a bunch of pigs, collecting their blood and body parts into clay pots and tossing them on an enemy below?

"Only a Scot could think of a battle tactic like this," St. John thought to himself.

Elder Simon then spoke. "Sergeant Roberts, I believe your plan might work. If we make any attempt to ransom my daughter back, it will only lead to more and more kidnappings. Looking at our options right now, it is the only plan we have."

Roberts looked at his pocket watch. "It is seven o'clock. I would suggest that we round up two dozen or so pigs, all the clay pots we can find and make ready to march toward the point of confrontation. I would add that Her Majesty's government will be happy to pay the cost of the pigs." St. John nodded in agreement.

Roberts asked, "Bua, exactly how far is the point above the river?"

Bua indicated that it was five kilometers over some very high hills. Roberts then said, "If McMillan and I, along with a group of your men, leave now, we can set up a staging area back away from the cliff. There, we can butcher the pigs and make ready the clay pots. Bua, you and Sergeant Major St. John should arrange to be at the Prince's camp at exactly six o'clock. This would put the sun directly in the eyes of the poor devils below the cliff. I would guess that most of the Prince's men would be involved in morning prayers and mostly in one place. If you were to enter the camp from the north and make your little speech, asking God to rain down curses on the evildoers, we would then proceed to launch our pig bombs from the high cliffs. Once the folks below realize that pig heads, pig guts, and of course, pig blood was raining down from the sky, they will move and move very fast. At that point, you will grab your sister and proceed up river as fast as you can. From there, it should be an easy ride home."

Each man standing in the circle looked at each other as if this were a joke or at least a comedy play. No one moved. Roberts then looked at St. John, "Well Sergeant Major St. John, are we on or are we not?"

St. John, looking as if he had been slapped, stiffened and spoke. "Bua, tell your people to round up two dozen pigs and the pots. Have them ready to move out in one hour."

The game was on. Pigs were tethered on leashes, water jars were emptied, and woven ropes were quickly gathered. In an hour's time some forty men were assembled at the base of the hill. Bua's father asked all to bow their heads as he commended this task to God Almighty and asked that no one be hurt or killed – except for the pigs, of course.

The small army of men and pigs moved up and over hills which separated the Baum village from the Prince's camp. Several of the Baum men were sent on ahead to locate a staging area where the pig could be butchered and the pig bombs could be assembled.

Somewhere around two o'clock in the morning, the line of men arrived at the designated staging area. The site was located in a boulder garden approximately one kilometer from the edge of the cliff. Roberts gave the order to begin butchering the pigs and placing the heads, and all assorted pieces in the pots, along with ample quantities of blood. One of the young men then suggested that they save the long intestines to drape across the trail in and out of the camp area. This would prevent the Prince's men from returning to collect their belongings after the raid. "Great idea!" Roberts whispered.

Roberts asked one of the Baum men to take him and McMillan to the edge of the cliff so that he might have an idea of what to expect. They crept on their bellies toward the edge of the cliff like three silent lizards. It was just as Bua described. A long narrow cut in the earth with a river flowing down the middle of it. The Prince's camp was situated in a wide spot along the shallow river. They could clearly see several torch-lit guard posts around the camp, including a significant posting at the north end of the camp.

Roberts moved back about five meters from the edge, where he could not be seen from below when standing. He then determined the exact direction of the main entry point to the camp, the primary concentration of tents, and the horse corral at the western end of the camp. He then determined which of the tents was that of the Prince. He assumed that was where Bua's sister was being held. Roberts then placed small stones indicating the direction of each of his targets.

McMillan spoke in a whisper, "It looks good to me. Just imagine what those poor devils will say when they reach civilization, "The Christian God rained down pig guts on us poor defenseless souls just because we kidnapped one of their women."

Roberts replied, "Just think what our superiors will say when they find out that we won a battle without firing a single shot."

The men crept back to the staging area where every pig had been dismembered and neatly packed into clay water pots. There were forty or so pots, each with a two-meter rope attached. The Baum men were busy tying loops at the end of each rope to make handles. Long ropes of intestines were piled in baskets ready to taken below as barriers against any thoughts of returning.

∾

CHAPTER TWENTY-EIGHT

On the road below, just out of sight of the bridge, Bua Tan Bo and Sergeant Major St. John waited on horseback for his pocket watch to indicate the proper time to move. A third horse, complete with saddle, followed on a tether. They both knew that the Prince would have several men at the bridge. They also rightly suspected that those men would act as escorts into the Prince's camp. They were correct on both accounts. Three heavily armed horsemen were waiting. Bua and St. John rode into the three, simply ignoring them. The three horsemen followed all the way into the camp.

Bua and St. John dismounted and moved toward a small circle of robed men sitting on the ground. Bua recognized the Prince immediately.

The Prince smiled and spoke, "Gentlemen, please sit and take some breakfast. We have much to talk about."

Neither Bua nor St. John acknowledged the invitation. Bua spoke, "Sir, I believe you are holding my sister against her will. I would ask that you relinquish her immediately."

The Prince smiled again, "Gentlemen, I merely invited your sister to visit my camp so that she might tend one of my men. It seems the poor man has come down with an unfortunate case of tetanus. I am hoping your sister can help him. That's all; nothing more. When she has finished, I shall happily return her to your village."

Bua did not return the smile. "Sir," he said most respectfully, "I understand that you claim to possess certain powers over nature." The Prince nodded in agreement.

"I too possess the powers of my God. Unless you relinquish my sister at once, I shall call down a curse on you and your men unlike any you have ever seen."

The Prince raised his eyebrow to the top of his forehead and uttered, "Well then, let us see your mighty powers."

With that, Bua Tan Bo raised his arms above his head and called out in a loud and clear voice, "Almighty and Everlasting God, show these unbelievers that they cannot laugh in your face and malign your mighty name. This man, like the Pharaoh of Moses time, chooses to play games with you. Rain down a curse on these people and this place." The Prince smiled a cautious smile and gazed skyward.

At the top of the cliff, a Baum lookout had been situated in place where he could see and hear all that was going on below. As he saw Bua Tan Bo's arms raise skyward, he signaled McMillan and Roberts who were standing several meters back from the cliff, each with a pig bomb ready to launch. At the signal, each Scot swung the pork laden pot around and around, letting it go in the direction of the northern guard post. Everyone on the ground below froze as they saw the unidentified objects descend down upon them. The first, then the second pot burst open revealing the head of pig. The gasp was clearly audible from every member of the Prince's small army. The pig bombs landed only a few meters from the guard post, splashing ample amounts of blood on several of the guards. The guards dropped their weapon and dashed toward the river, throwing themselves into the current. Too late; eternally contaminated and eternally dammed. Within seconds two more pig bombs hit the ground, this time closer to the group of the now standing men. Bua Tan Bo remained with his arms and his head raised skyward as St. John continued to stare directly at the Prince. Within the scope of a minute, ten more pig bombs landed in and around the camp, each time coming closer to the Prince and his people. Finally, one clay pot landed directly on the camp fire, exploding in all directions. Without exception, all those standing around the fire, including the Prince fled toward the south end of the gorge and into the river.

McMillan and Roberts took time out from their launching to peek over the rim of the cliff. Below, they could see each and every man running at top speed toward the exit of the camp. None of the panicked men even bothered to run for the horses. Nor did any man run to a tent to collect his possessions. Each and every one was yelling as if they were imploring this God of Bua to stop the rain of terror.

McMillan then suggested that they launch the remaining pig bombs into the river and onto the road. This would most certainly prevent any further attempts at returning to the camp. After another ten or so pig bombs were tossed into the river and their contents loose to float downstream, McMillan and Roberts returned to the staging area and the congratulations of all those who participated in the great battle.

With the Prince and his men no longer anywhere near the camp, Bua called out, "Supi Yaw Lat!" A voice came from inside the largest tent in the cluster of tents. St. John and Bua ran to the tent and found the lady bound, hand and foot.

As soon as the lady was untied, she excused herself, "I must see to my patient in the next tent."

St. John looked at Bua with a puzzled look. Bua then explained, "My sister is, well, sort of a doctor in this area. While she is not a formal doctor, she nonetheless has all the qualifications of a physician. Like me, Supi Yaw Lat read all the books and committed them to memory. She has, in fact, worked with the British doctors in the hospital in Chittagong. If it were not for the fact that she is a Baum and a woman, she could easily pass the examination for general practice and quite possibly surgery. But, you English have determined that neither a woman nor a non-white can possess the title of doctor."

St. John stood there for several minutes trying to take in all that had happened, including the information about Bua's sister.

Shortly, Supi Yaw Lat returned to where Bua and St. John were standing.

"The patient is dead. There was nothing I could do without proper medication. Even with proper medical attention, I strongly doubt the man would have lived anyhow; tetanus."

Supi Yaw Lat then acknowledged Michael St. John. She extended her hand in his direction. St. John was completely transfixed on the beautiful woman standing before him. Her long, shiny black hair was pulled back into a neat bun bound by a ribbon. While she was somewhat wrinkled from her night in captivity, she was nonetheless quite beautiful and handsomely attired.

The only words he could utter were, "Sergeant Major Michael St. John, Queens Burma Police."

Bua, seeing the expression on St. John's face, spoke, "My sister is named after one of Burma's most beautiful queens, Queen Supi Yaw Lat. Her nickname is Supi Yaw." St. John could do nothing but nod his head.

Supi Yaw then spoke, "Would you gentlemen excuse me for a few minutes. I need to freshen up a bit." The tall slim woman walked through the scattered pig heads and assorted body parts to the edge of the river. She slowly washed her face and pushed her shiny black hair back into a bun.

Michael too did a bit of tidying up.

As she returned, she spoke, "Let's get out of here before they try to come back."

Bua replied, "Sister, I don't think they or any of their kind will ever come to this place again. We shall see that the story of God's wrath being rained down reaches all villages in the region."

Bua, Supi Yaw, and Michael mounted their horses and proceeded north toward the Baum village. The lady was allowed to ride ahead so as to exempt her from the trail dust. Michael never once took his eyes off the lady ahead of him. Bua took notice of this.

From the edge of the high cliff above the "battleground," the last of the Prince's people could be seen running frantically along the riverside trying to avoid several pig heads floating nearby. McMillan then ordered the men with him to fetch the pig intestines for a final *coup d'grace*. A rock was placed in the end of each intestine and tied off. Then it would be swung around and around until it had gained sufficient momentum to be launched into the river gorge. Within minutes the walls of the gorge, as well as all the shrubbery below were festooned with long ribbons of pig guts. No Mohammedan would ever trespass this place again. Ever!

CHAPTER TWENTY-NINE

Bua, his sister, and St. John were met by villagers a few kilometers from the Baum village. Within the span of one kilometer, the big drum began to pound, announcing the arrival of the trio. Again the red-brick path was lined with villagers, all throwing bougainvillea blossoms. Everyone was embraced and congratulated on a successful "battle."

At almost the same moment, McMillan, Roberts, and the small army of Baum men entered the village from behind a grove of banana trees. Again, a cheer went up as the story of the battle went round the villagers. Laughter pervaded the joyful celebration.

At the brick arches, the elders, including Bua and Supi Yaw's father greeted the victors. Again, the old man asked that all present bow their heads. This time his prayer was more in the form of an "oath of silence." He asked that each and every person who knew of or took part in the great battle would keep its origins and implementation an eternal secret. He wished that the rain of pig bombs be attributed to God Almighty and not to the imaginations of men. We must allow all those who hear the tale of the great battle to understand that it was God Almighty who implemented the act. It was to be seen as an "act of God." All those in attendance agreed with a solemn, "Amen."

Michael St. John's eyes followed Supi Yaw as she and her family walked toward their hut. Again, Bua noticed St. John's eyes and the confused look on his face.

McMillan and Roberts walked toward St. John. "What do you say we order up a basin of hot water? After a night's work like the one we just put in, I think a soldier deserves a good bath," Roberts said.

Several wooden cloth-dying vats were cleaned and filled with hot water. For the next hour the three soldiers soaked in the glory of the hot soapy water and the narrative of the battle from multiple perspectives.

Roberts spoke, "Michael, tell us more about this little lady you rescued from the clutches of the evil wizard."

"Just you never mind this little lady. She's not to be discussed in a bathhouse full of carnal-minded men. She is a lady; probably the only one in this whole bloody part of the world."

McMillan and Roberts looked at each other, "Oww, I think Sergeant Major Michael St. John has found a lady friend."

Michael launched a bar of handmade soap at Roberts' head. "Gentlemen, that will be enough of that sort of talk," St. John ordered.

An hour later all three British soldiers were thoroughly scrubbed, neatly trimmed, and properly dressed for another banquet. It was noted that this banquet included far fewer pigs on the roast than did the first banquet. Someone suggested that they needed to conserve their remaining pigs for the great conclave coming with the next full moon.

While there was a shortage of roasted pork, there was an abundance of the infamous jungle berry juice. And with multiple toasts to the brave men who participated in the battle which did not happen, spirits quickly rose. Drums were pounded, songs were sung, and eventually someone called for a playing of the pipes. With little hesitancy, McMillan produced his bagpipes and began with the first of many renditions of *Amazing Grace*. Well into his fourth or fifth or possibly sixth goblet of jungle berry juice, Sergeant Roberts demonstrated his version of the *Scottish Sword Dance*. After three encores, several Baum villagers rose to the occasion and gave a decent imitation of the sword dance.

Midway into the evening, Supi Yaw, beautifully adorned in a colorful brocade skirt and jacket entered the group and took a seat next to her father. Bua noticed her as she looked sideways to where St. John was seated. He also noticed St. John returning the glance. There was no question; these two were attracted to one another, strongly attracted.

The evening concluded as the fire tuned to embers. One-by-one, each person retired to their respective hut. It was good! God was good and Sergeant Major Michael St. John felt confused about the feelings going on inside; very confused.

By ten o'clock the next morning, the drums were pounding. Unfortunately, these were not the Baum drums, but those inside Michael St. John's head. He had never before felt pain like this, even when he had been struck on the side of his skull by a glancing bullet. Roberts and McMillan knew there was something more than a simple hangover when they found St. John still in his cot at ten thirty. Roberts bent down and placed his hand on St. John's forehead. "The man is burning up!" he announced.

Roberts summoned Bua to come double quick. Within minutes Bua and several elders arrived at the small bamboo hut. As they looked down on their friend and colleague, he began to shake violently. Sweat began to pour from his brow in quick ripples. Bua ordered, "Fetch Supi Yaw at once!"

Supi Yaw arrived within minutes of being summoned, took one look at the man lying on the cot and announced, "Malaria."

Although Michael St. John was entering into the realm of delirium, he recognized the face of the woman kneeling over him. For a moment the pain in his head became unimportant. He focused every ounce of his attention on the majestic woman looking into his eyes. As she touched his burning forehead, he moaned, but not a moan of pain. For the first time in his entire life, he had encountered a woman who. . .before he was able to conclude that thought, he lapsed into the murky state of delirium.

The village elders formed a circle around the bamboo hut and began to pray. Shortly, the circle grew to include all members of the community, including McMillan and Roberts. Roberts then fetched his Bible, opening it to the Book of James, Chapter five. He quoted, "'*If anyone among you is sick, let him call for the elders. They shall anoint the sick person with oil, pray for him, and the sick man shall be healed.*' In the stead of this fallen friend and by the command of this Holy Book, I am calling for the elders to anoint this man with oil and pray for his recovery." The elders responded with a unanimous "Amen." Someone then brought a small bowl of cooking oil whereupon each elder dipped his finger into the bowl. Then, passing in line past the prostrate man, they added their small quantity of oil to his forehead and uttered a prayer for complete recovery.

One hallucination after another collided in a nightmare of pig guts, grinning Mohammedans, river pirates, and pain.

Violent tremors racked his body for hours on end, causing him to quake like a tree branch caught in a typhoon. St. John had watched, many times, as men simply died from bouts of malarial far less severe than this.

The siege in his body and brain continued for three days and three nights. All the while Supi Yaw attempted to administer small quantities of herbal medication made by one of the elders. The second day, she dispatched a runner to the hospital at Chittagong to fetch a supply of quinine and any other medicines they could spare.

Well into the forth day, the quinine began to work. St. John's temperature began to move downward. Unfortunately for Michael, the unseen demons which had entered his body also impacted his liver. A predominant yellow or jaundiced hue crept through his body indicating that the malaria had caused his liver to shut down. Supi Yaw explained that a person contracting malaria either died or recuperated. A person with hepatitis or jaundice, could languish for months or even years before recuperation. Even after complete recuperation, a relapse or recurrence of the insidious disease was almost always fatal. She further explained that there was no way to determine if the secondary jaundice was actual hepatitis or simply a result of the malaria doing damage to the liver. Time would tell.

Several times during times of hallucination and nightmare, St. John revealed events from his past. One in particular involved the hanging of a young British soldier in India, a hanging over which St. John anguished loudly. His primary lament involved long and painful dialogues between himself and God. *"Why did this young, foolish English boy have to die at the end of a rope and utter disgrace? Why did Sergeant St. John have to place the noose around the boy's neck and pull the deadly lever? Why did he have to spend three sleepless nights writing a letter to the boy's parents explaining that their son had killed a sleeping comrade? Why didn't a loving God intervene in this malaise of tragedies compounded by more useless tragedies?*

Many times during Michael's multiple confessions, Supi Yaw attempted to act as "confessor" and absolve the guilt and pain from his soul. She tried to justify the madness of war and the weakness of the men who are sacrificed on the altar of the empire. On one or two occasions, Supi Yaw privately abdicated her role as Michael's defense counsel and assumed the role of prosecuting counsel. She too silently confronted the same demons her delirious patient was battling. She too asked, *"Why, God do you allow good and innocent people to suffer and die when there are so many evil people prospering in a world where justice is said to prevail?"* Moreover, she asked, *"Why, she, a fully competent medical practitioner with all of the qualifications of a male medial doctor could not be granted the title of doctor?"* No answers came.

The fourth day Michael St. John's fever broke. He had lost somewhere around three kilos in body weight. His unshaven face was gaunt and his skin and eyes still showed the yellow bile from the disease. He craved water and oddly enough, pineapple juice.

The runner Supi Yaw had sent to Chittagong to get medicine two days before had brought back a telegram which had been received by Major Somerset. Both McMillan and Roberts had read the telegram. They, along with Bua Tan Bo, entered Michael's hut just as he was attempting to stand up for the first time in four days. One of Supi Yaw's male helpers was trying, with a great deal of difficulty, to lift him to his feet. McMillan handed St. John the telegram. It simply said, "I am happy to hear that the tea I gave you has helped your stomach problems."

Upon reading the message, Michael laughed and crumpled back onto the bamboo cot. "My stomach indeed!" he uttered

McMillan spoke, "The message indicates that James has received your message and that he has transmitted it out to the tribes. The game is on."

St. John managed to sit up on the edge of his cot. "Roberts, what is the date today?"

Roberts gave the date, the time of day, and the weather and their immediate location as point of reference.

St. John spoke, "We need to make a calendar of events. We must have everything in order for the conclave. I want sufficient food supplies brought up from Chittagong. We must see that there are sufficient accommodations for those attending."

Bua stopped him. "Michael, my people have been through these tribal meetings many times before. This is nothing new for us. Please allow our elders to deal with the event. You must reserve your strength for the implementation of the plan once it has been considered and approved."

Supi Yaw entered the hut, "Sergeant Major St. John, you might outrank me in some circles, sir, but in this circle, I am giving the orders. My immediate orders are that you remain in or near your cot and do little more than eat, drink, and sleep. Judging from the color of your eyes and skin, I would say that your liver is in extremely bad shape. That factor, coupled with the inordinate quantity of jungle berry juice you consumed prior to your malarial attack has put you at great risk of a complicated recovery. I can say with some certainty that you stand an eighty percent chance of recovery if you mind my orders. On the other hand, if you don't and you suffer a relapse, I can almost guarantee that you will be meeting your maker well before your time. The choice is yours Sergeant Major."

Michael looked at Roberts and McMillan and smiled his resignation. Supi Yaw looked at St. John and said, "Good! Now, time for a bath. You smell like a rotten sock."

For the next few days, Michael's condition improved in slight increments. His appetite for fresh pineapple and lean meat began to clear his skin pigment, not to mention restoring some of the body weight he had lost. Brief walks around the hut and in the full sunshine seemed to restore his physical stamina. While resting, Supi Yaw would read from many of Bua's books. On occasion she would read aloud some of her medical books and journals. While the medical topics were completely foreign to Michael's frame of reference, he nonetheless appreciated the attention of this beautiful woman.

One evening, after a meal, Supi Yaw returned from her hut with a small banjo-like instrument. Made from a turtle shell and the leg bone of a water buffalo, she stroked the horse-hair strings into strange and wonderful sounds. In a mellow alto tone, she sang words of her own creation; words hidden deep in her heart. While Michael could not comprehend the words, he perceived these words to involve her deep affection for her mountains, her flowers, and her way of life in the Banderban Hills. When she would end a song, he would plead for another until he fell into a deep sleep. As Michael slept, Supi Yaw would place her hand on his forehead, telling herself that she was simply checking her patient's temperature. In actuality, she was caressing the forehead of a man, of whom she was becoming quite fond. On occasion she would catch herself looking at this British soldier, this foreign conqueror of her people and wonder silently, if she could ever bring herself to regard him as a friend or possibly even more than a friend.

In these long moments of silence Supi Yaw would delve deeply into her motive to live the life she had chosen. Like her elder brother, Bua Tan Bo, she too had devoted herself to absorbing every piece of knowledge available on the subject of medicine and the human condition. As a young girl, she begged her parents to allow her to work as a floor sweeper in the English hospital in Chittagong. When she wasn't cleaning, she was reading a "borrowed" medical book from the shelves of the hospital's library. Other times she would arrange her schedule to be "cleaning" in the same ward or lecture room where a visiting physician would be giving a lecture or lesson. Because of her familiarity with medical procedures, she was eventually enlisted as a nurse's aide, complete with a starched uniform and cap. Eventually, she managed to work her way into the hospital's operating theater as a support nurse, handling surgical implements. In her mind's eye, she could perform almost any operation necessary to save a person's life.

Numerous members of the senior medial staff soon recognized Supi Yaw's superior intellect and knowledge of the secrets of healing. Unfortunately, she was, in fact, a woman and a woman of color. This totally excluded her from any and all forms of professional recognition. She was considered somewhat of an extraordinary anomaly. She was blessed with an extreme intellect and unique skills, but cursed by her gender and race. On numerous occasions, British doctors would cautiously ask her advice on difficult cases. Generally, without relinquishing any of their "God-given" authority, they would give serious consideration to Supi Yaw's counsel. If the facts were known, many British subjects were alive and well due to Supi Yaw's "advice."

Within the context of her tribal community, she was again considered an anomaly. Unlike every Baum girl every created, her aspirations were not those of becoming a wife and a mother. When the topic of marriage arose in her family, she stated that God had indeed called her to become a doctor and heal people. If she were to become a wife, her call to healing would be impossible.

Much the same as Supi Yaw, Bua Tan Bo opted not to take one of the dozens of Baum girls who fancied him as a husband. When asked about his intentions, he replied that the Apostle Paul strongly urged that a true follower of Christ remain celibate. The responsibilities of a husband would interfere with his teaching the word of God throughout the Banderban Hills.

While Bua and Supi Yaw's father was extremely proud of his two children, he was disappointed that neither of his children fit into the traditional fabric of Baum culture. Bua Tan Bo would never become an elder, no matter how pious or industrious he became. Baum elders were required to be the fathers of exemplary children and honorable wives before they could be considered to the rank of elder. And too, the old man quietly lamented the absence of grandchildren who would carry on his family name and reputation.

A week had passed since Michael St. John's near fatal encounter with malaria had begun. Each day saw slight improvements in his recuperation. Those nearest to him and his situation attributed this to the care and encouragement of Supi Yaw.

CHAPTER THIRTY

It was Sunday afternoon, during the lunch break of the morning to night church service when the signalman looking after the heliograph came running to find McMillan and Roberts. A message had been received from the water tower in the Chittagong barracks. The message had been written down on a piece of paper after the signalmen confirmed and reconfirmed the signal from below. The two Scots looked at each other with an expression of absolute consternation. Roberts spoke, "What in heaven's name are we to do now?"

McMillan replied, "This can't happen; it can't happen now."

Bua Tan Bo noticed the conversation between the two soldiers and the alarm in their faces. Bua immediately made for the two. "What is the problem?" he demanded. Rather than attempt to reply to his concern, Roberts simply handed Bua the paper on which the message was written. It read:

Her Imperial Majesty, Queen Victoria, Regent of the British Empire and Empress of India, summons one, Sergeant Major Michael Oliver St. John of Her Majesty's Burma Police to immediately embark on the next available form of transport to London. Upon arrival, Sergeant Major Michael Oliver St. John shall, with all diligence, present himself before Her Imperial Majesty, whereupon Sergeant Major Michael Oliver St. John shall be presented with Empire's highest military order, the Victoria Cross for Gallantry. All military and civil support is to be afforded Sergeant Major Michael Oliver St. John and an entourage of his requirement in responding to this royal command from Her Imperial Majesty. Done this day, in the name and by the command of Her Imperial Majesty, Victoria, Regina Rex.

The three men simply stood, speechless as the words of the message penetrated their minds like water seeping into a loaf of bread. McMillan spoke, "This can't be happening. Not now."

Roberts continued, "Michael must be here to complete the plan. Without him, the plan will fail."

Bua then spoke, "Michael can't possibly travel to London, and he's seriously ill; a voyage would surely kill him."

McMillan spoke, "This is a direct order from the Queen herself! There is no way, dead or alive a British soldier would or could disobey a command from Queen Victoria. Even Almighty God regards this woman with caution."

Roberts spoke, "We must take this to Sergeant Major St. John immediately. To do anything else would constitute a breach in response to authority and dereliction of a direct order."

The three men walked silently to St. John's hut. Michael was asleep while Supi Yaw and one of her assistants were occupied with household matters.

"Excuse me, sister, we have an urgent matter which I am afraid involves you as well," Bua said. He handed Supi Yaw the message. As she read, and re-read the letter, her face hardened. She looked at Michael; then read the message once again.

"Well, I suppose there's no use in attempting to persuade Her Majesty that her beloved sergeant Major is dangerously ill and that a voyage of this nature would more than likely result in him receiving his little medal posthumously. So, I suppose we must make haste to bundle him up, cart him to Chittagong and get him off to London," she said in a tone of complete resignation. "The Queen calls!"

Just then, Michael woke from one of his many naps. Seeing the faces of those standing around his cot, he knew something was not quite as it should be.

Supi Yaw spoke, "Michael, it looks as though your beloved Queen Victoria has heard of your exploits over on the Irrawaddy against the notorious bandit, Bua Tan Bo. It seems that she wants to give you a little token of her appreciation."

She then handed Michael the message. He read the message. For three or four long minutes, there was silence except for the distant beating of the drum indicating that church was about to continue. Michael spoke, "This can't be happening. This has got to be another of my many hallucinations. I simply can't drop everything and go running off to have tea with the Queen." Looking at Roberts, he continued, "Why can't Her Imperial Majesty simply put the little medal in a box and send it to me if she truly thinks that I deserve the silly thing?"

All of this conversation was futile and everyone knew it. An order, no, make that a command from the Queen was just that; a command from the Queen. No mortal in the realm would even consider refusing a royal command.

Supi Yaw spoke, "I and one of my assistants shall accompany Michael to London. Allowing him to go without any form of medical support would almost certainly result in a relapse and death." Bua made an effort to speak. "Brother," she said, "don't try to dissuade me. The message stated quite clearly, that he is entitled to bring 'an entourage of his requirement.' Under the circumstances, that most certainly means a qualified medical person."

She then looked directly at Michael. "Sergeant Major St. John, do you agree?"

Michael looked plaintively at his three colleagues and nodded, "Yes, I think that would be acceptable."

Supi Yaw then addressed Bua with all the authority she could muster. "Brother, I want a wagon, with a cot in the box and all the mattresses we can find made ready to travel at first light tomorrow morning. If we move at a steady pace, we can make Chittagong hospital by late evening. From there, a day or two of rest and then we can board the next ship bound for London. If the weather holds good, the Sergeant Major could enjoy a relaxing recuperation aboard ship. In fact, I strongly believe the salt air would aid in his recuperation."

Bua immediately sent for his father who was praising the Lord for all he was worth. The old man reluctantly left the congregation and came to where Bua, Supi Yaw and the Englishmen were huddled. The situation was carefully explained to the old man. The Elder Simon pondered the news and spoke, "Supi Yaw, I will grant you permission to accompany Sergeant Major St. John if and only if your brother accompanies you. After all, you are a single woman and in our culture, a single woman cannot be seen running off to London with an unmarried British soldier."

Bua was shocked. "Father, I must be here for the conclave. I must participate in the discussions."

Bua's father smiled, "My son, being that you are not an elder, you may not even be present in the conclave, much less speak."

Bua again appeared shocked, "Father, I am a part of this thing. If it is to be successful, I must be a part of it."

The old man replied, “Please, my son, allow me and the others of our various tribes to take some part in this plan. Any plan which depends on the inputs or ideas of one young man, must be a very weak plan indeed. Please allow us to discuss the past, present, and future of this thing you call, the Ballentine Doctrine. After all, we are not a collection of old fools.” Bua realized the wisdom in his father’s words and the arrogance of his own words. The old man continued, “Under the circumstances, I believe that you might provide even more influence for our cause by accompanying Sergeant Major St. John to see his Queen. You might present a truer picture of the situation here in Asia than either the Sergeant Major or other British opinions. You may have an opportunity to present yourself as a well-educated and well-mannered Baum gentleman. If you will recall your western history books, you might remember an American Indian lady named Pocahontas who was presented to the English court as proper lady. As a result of her visit, the monarch and those who received this Pocahontas altered their opinion of the American Indian race. I can only hope that you might have the same opportunity to present yourself and our cause to those in authority. If the British could only see us as civilized people, like themselves, we may have a better advantage in achieving our objectives in bringing about the benefits of this thing you call ‘The Ballentine Doctrine’.”

All those present, including Bua Tan Bo, recognized the true wisdom in the old man’s comments. Bua smiled as he bowed his head in reverence toward his father.

The following morning, the sky grew pink in the east. The village elders stood around the wagon and several horses which were loaded and about to move down the mountain road to Chittagong. Michael St. John was neatly tucked into a well-padded cot in the back of the wagon. A second smaller wagon was loaded with several woven bamboo suitcases containing Supi Yaw's and Bua Tan Bo's clothing and personal possessions. Also included were beautifully woven blankets, skirts, and carved objects to be used as gifts where needed.

Bua's father called for a prayer of commitment. Everyone knelt as the old man offered a prayer of protection, wisdom, and safe return. Slowly, the caravan moved off into the morning mist. Sergeants Roberts and McMillan remained behind in the Baum village.

Roberts ordered his signalman to send a heliograph message informing Major Somerset that Sergeant Major St. John and his party were in route and would be arriving sometime early evening.

CHAPTER THIRTY-ONE

CHITTIGONG BARRACKS

The telegram from the High Command regarding 'Sergeant Major Michael St. John's being the recipient of the Victoria Cross both confused and perplexed Major Somerset. Why was he not told that Dr. St. John was, in fact, Sergeant Major St. John of the Royal Burma Police? It was extraordinary that a subordinate member of the military should be passed off as a covert operative to a superior officer without his knowledge. While slightly offended by the ruse, Somerset nonetheless acknowledged the high achievement of the Sergeant Major and put aside any thought of offense. An honor guard was sent to the outskirts of Chittagong to await the caravan's arrival and provide a hero's escort to the barracks.

Upon arrival at the barracks, a local military tailor immediately took Sergeant Major St. John's present measurements. Within hours a full-dress uniform had been sewn, complete with stripes and insignias. Several other less formal uniforms were likewise stitched together and decorated with proper ribbons and buttons.

Major Somerset was more than cordial to the invalid Sergeant Major. A private dinner in the Major's quarters was arranged with St. John being the only invited guest. Without attempting to pry the details of his mission, Somerset nonetheless tried to inquire about the events of the past weeks in the Banderban Hills. Without breaking his oath of secrecy between himself and Colonel Ballentine, Michael managed to outline the broad concept of cooperation among the various tribal groups who were seen as sympathetic to the objectives of the Empire. As much as possible, Sergeant Major St. John managed to elude the specific details of the big plan. Somerset seemed content with the explanation.

Whenever possible, Michael attempted to direct the conversation with Somerset to more mundane subjects. While it was unusual for a non-commissioned officer like Michael to openly converse with a commissioned officer, he took full advantage of the informal relationship which had developed. Michael spent as much time as he could asking Somerset about his career, his thoughts on the world situation, and his feelings about things in general. Somerset seemed to find the relationship somewhat relaxing. On several occasion, Somerset thought to himself, *"How could such an intelligent man be found in the ranks of the enlisted personnel? This man thinks like an officer."*

Late in the evening, when Major Somerset broached the topic of the Prince, St. John smiled broadly. Somerset indicated that rumors had come from Cox Bazaar, some kilometers to the south of Chittagong, that the Prince and his men had been attacked by demons and devils. There was mention of a sorcerer who waved his hands in the air and caused a rain of swine entrails. There were even reports of the Prince's men cutting off their own limbs which had been contaminated by swine blood. The locals have even named the river valley, "the

Valley of the Damned." "Sergeant Major St. John, what do you know about these rumors?"

"Sir, while I have taken an oath of secrecy along with those who participated in the event, you as the senior officer in this region, do have a legitimate reason to know what transpired with our mutual friend, the Prince. St. John then unfolded the story, detail by detail. With all the theater of a village storyteller, St. John described each and every facet of the campaign so that Somerset might savor the full impact of the "battle." When it came to the part where pig guts and pig heads were raining down from heaven, Major Somerset totally abandoned his formal British demeanor and became hysterical with laughter. St. John created images of the Prince and his band of rogues stumbling down river, dodging flying and floating pig parts. St. John saw the deep impact this event had on the Major. With the Prince out of the picture, many of Major Somerset's unsolvable problems were resolved.

The following morning, a London bound sailing steamer loaded with hard wood raised anchor with Sergeant Major Michael St. John, Bua Tan Bo, and Supi Yaw safely aboard. Michael's baggage consisted of a single traveling case, containing his newly made uniforms and a few personal items. Bua and Supi Yaw's baggage consisted of six large traveling cases, each filled with books and gifts. The ship's captain, while somewhat irritated at not being allowed to sail on the tide, welcomed the trio aboard as if they were royalty. There were a dozen or so other passengers already aboard.

Before the ship left sight of land, the ship's signal officer mentioned a heliograph message received from somewhere in the distant Banderban Hills. It read, "*Bon voyage Dr. St. John and party. We are praying for you.*"

CHAPTER THIRTY-TWO

While the trade winds were reasonably fair, the captain ordered the steam boilers to be lit. Between the constant smell of wood smoke and rocking of the ship, Michael, Bua, and Supi Yaw were to be found frequently vomiting over the side or in a basin. Eventually, Supi Yaw convinced the captain of the ship to find a cabin or storage bin where, at least Michael could find relief from the smoke. Unfortunately for Michael, the farther away from the center of the ship one goes, the more up-and-down, side-to-side motion is experienced. After several days in his forward quarters, the jaundice in Michael's skin began to disappear, as did his elevated temperature. Supi Yaw was delighted to see that Michael did not have the symptoms of classic hepatitis, but rather, a secondary infection of the liver resulting from the malaria.

The captain announced that the ship was currently sailing between the southern tip of India and the island of Ceylon. He suggested that if all went well, they would be rounding the Horn of Africa in a week or so. The passengers on board finally vomited their last vomit and began to eat and drink as they should. Michael found himself actually asking for small meals between the regularly scheduled breakfast, lunch, tea, and dinner. His hunger indicated a strong desire to return to life rather than a sleepy surrender to the comforts of death. At Supi Yaw's insistence, Michael was required to walk the entire perimeter of the ship, beginning with one tour and adding another for each day at sea. Within a few days of being at sea, most of the other passengers were accompanying Michael and Supi Yaw on their daily regimen. Most days after the promenade, Michael would engage Bua in several games of chess as others watched silently. Supi Yaw occupied herself with the contents of every book she had brought in her travel cases. The volumes ranged from such titles as *Survey of Tropical Medicine* to *Surgical Techniques of the Thoracic Surgeon*. Many times while her focus was on the page of a book, her fingers were moving as if she were drawing a scalpel through the flesh of an imaginary patient. On other occasions she would stare into the ocean as she attempted to assess a series of hypothetical symptoms and conclude a formal diagnosis.

On more than one occasion, other passengers would beg her attention in order to present a symptom or condition. In almost every situation, she would politely listen to the inquiring person and explain the nature of the symptoms and then suggest a possible answer to their inquiry. She would always preface her comments by telling the person that she was merely a medical practitioner and not a formal medical doctor.

By the time the ship had reached the Horn of Africa, almost every passenger, and in some cases members of the crew, had sought the advice of Supi Yaw. Some even addressed her affectionately as "Doctor" Supi Yaw. The ship was now heading north toward the equator. Winds were favorable and the weather good. The officer on watch notified the captain that a whaler was almost dead ahead flying a universal distress flag immediately below its American flag. The captain ordered the helmsman to bring the ship alongside the whaler. The captain hailed the whaler, "What troubles you?"

The reply came, "Our captain has had an accident and is in desperate need of medical attention. Do you have a ship's doctor aboard?"

The steamer captain called back, "No, but we do have someone on board who might be able to assist." The captain sent for Supi Yaw who arrived on the bridge within minutes.

The captain then called out over the loud hailer, "What is the nature of the problem?"

The whaler's first officer replied back, "Our captain has a severely broken and mangled leg. I fear that gangrene has set in. He is not conscious and I fear he is done for."

The steamer captain looked at Supi Yaw. "Madam, is there anything you can do in this matter?"

By this time, Bua Tan Bo joined her on the bridge. "Captain, if I could examine the man, I could determine the extent of his injuries and possibly render help. Either I must go to him or he must come to me."

The captain then called out to the whaler, "Can your man be transported to our vessel without doing him further harm?"

The officer on the whaler replied, "I believe he is too far gone to risk a transfer."

Supi Yaw then responded, "Then I must go to him. Captain, could you garner all of the medical supplies I might need for a possible amputation?"

The captain looked shocked at the woman's request. "Amputation?"

She replied, "If we are talking about a mangled leg and possible gangrene, we have few options. Without the assets of a hospital or certified surgeons, our options are limited to me."

The captain looked at Bua. "Well, Captain, what are you waiting for?"

The captain ordered the helmsman to maintain a course parallel to that of the whaler. He then ordered a long boat be lowered and a line be made ready to bring the lady and her supplies across the narrow span of ocean which separated the two ships.

Bua informed the captain that he too would be accompanying Supi Yaw. The captain nodded in agreement. By this time, everyone on the ship was at the side rails, watching as the small, long boat cross from the steamer to the whaler. Michael St. John too watched as the magnificent woman boarded the pitching ship, followed by Bua and two sailors. Two duffels filled with medical supplies were hoisted from the long boat.

Below deck of the whaler, the smell of rotting flesh was almost toxic. Barrels of whale oil mixed with the stench of whale meat permeated every breath of air. Inside the captain's cabin, another smell filled the stale, dank air; it was the smell of rotten cheese. Immediately, Supi Yaw knew the odor–gangrene. A heavily bearded man lay on a bunk, moaning incoherently. Several of the whaler's crew stood near with lanterns and desperate expressions. Unlike those standing near the injured man, Supi Yaw did not flinch when she pulled back the blood-soaked sheet covering the man's lower body. She ordered a lantern and examined the man's leg.

Supi Yaw ordered Bua to fetch a basin of boiled water and the duffel bags of medical supplies. On a nearby table, she arranged what supplies she felt necessary for what must be done.

The first officer, still not fully aware of what a female was doing in the place of a doctor, asked, "Do you think the captain can be saved?"

She answered, "I have seen injuries much worse than this and the patient recovered. I have also seen cases much less severe than this and the patient died. I will do my best."

Supi Yaw determined that the man's foot, ankle and part of his lower leg was crushed beyond repair. The flesh was black and stank beyond belief.

The boiling water arrived and was placed in a wash basin. Supi Yaw carefully cleaned the area around the knee where she determined that she would amputate. Both Supi Yaw and Bua tied cloths around their noses and mouth to prevent the stench of rotting flesh from distracting them further.

Those whalers, who were well accustomed to the blood and gore of their trade, looked away as Supi Yaw began to cut through the skin, muscle and blood vessels of the unconscious man on the bunk. She had seen amputations before, many times before. She knew the procedure for tying off blood vessels and tying down muscles before they could retract back up into the leg. Within an hour, the rotten lower leg was thrown into the sea, stitches sewn into the remaining flesh, and the remaining part of the leg wrapped with clean bandages.

Two hours later, Supi Yaw was satisfied that the man, barring infection or further complications, would indeed live. She asked the first officer to prepare a litter whereby the injured captain could be transferred to the steamer for transport to the next port of call. The first officer then placed the captain's hat on his head and gave the order for the ailing man to be evacuated to the steamer. Several sailors grabbed up some of the captain's belonging and stuffed them into a sea bag to be transported along with him.

Four hours after first sighting the whaler, the steamship pulled away from the whaler with its one-legged captain aboard.

As Supi Yaw arrived back aboard the steamer, still covered with blood, all passengers and crew alike applauded the lady doctor. The captain offered a smart salute as did Michael St. John.

For the next two days, Supi Yaw tended to the ailing captain with virtually every ounce of her professional and human ability. Several vials of morphine had been located in a locked medicine cabinet and administered. The second day of convalescence, the captain regained consciousness. Heavily dosed with morphine, the captain took the news of his missing leg with a rueful smile. "That's one of the perils of my trade," he said.

On the third day, the recuperating captain was brought on deck to "bathe in the fresh air and sunlight" as Supi Yaw put it. She arranged his lounge next to that of Michael St. John. After Michael's first walk about the deck, he took his seat next to the one-legged man. "Bad luck," Michael said to the man.

"Perhaps not," the American said. "Perhaps not," he said with a grin. "Did you see that woman, the one who cut off my leg? She's a beaut. I would very much like to bag that little lady and take her home to cook my soup."

St. John's silent response to this bearded brute was absolute rage. Michael spoke, "She is the daughter of a Burmese head hunter chieftain. She is off to see the Queen. If you were to even touch that lady, her brother would happily take your head and who knows what else."

With that, all thoughts or comments about the lady ended abruptly. This was Michael's first encounter with an American. While he was not particularly impressed with the man's manners nor his level of educated conversation, he did engage him in lengthy conversation about this country of America. Michael had heard the stories about the red Indians and the Wild West, but he knew very little about the concept of equality of all those calling themselves Americans.

St. John became fascinated with the idea that a society could function without a royal family to oversee every aspect of social life. This seemed exciting to him.

The steamer's next port of call was the Canary Islands. Upon docking, the steamship's captain and Supi Yaw consulted with local medical personnel and determined that it would be far more advantageous for the American captain to proceed on to England where medical facilities were superior to those on the small island. Fuel and stores were taken on for the final voyage to England. During the brief time in the port of Santa Cruz, all passengers opted to go ashore for a visit. Bua insisted that Supi Yaw and Michael go along for a day at the beach.

Sitting on a cargo tarp borrowed from the ship, Michael watched Supi Yaw and Bua as they walked along the surf. He felt better, mind, soul, and body than he had in years. For an instant, his thought returned to the American sea captain who had mentioned "bagging" that little woman and taking her home to cook his soup. His nostrils flared at the thought of Supi Yaw falling into the clutches of a boorish slob like the American whaler. There was no denying it; Michael had developed strong, very strong, affections for Supi Yaw.

As he watched the majestically beautiful woman stroll, ankle-deep in the Atlantic waves, he wondered about the possibility of marriage to this magnificent creature. He looked at his hands; they were shaking. He, a well-seasoned soldier, was completely frightened at the mere thought of taking a woman to be his wife. Supi Yaw noticed Michael watching her and waved. Michael returned the wave and smiled. He then looked at himself, introspectively. What did he have to offer this well-accomplished woman? Nothing! He was a soldier, skilled at killing. She, on the other hand, was a noble woman skilled in the arts of healing. Except for a few pounds of soldier's pay or pension each month and a pretty medal to hang on a tunic, Michael had nothing to offer. Any serious relationship would serve to demean this woman and deprive her of her calling. And too, colonial Englishmen who took "native" wives were considered to have become desperate for a woman and "gone native." They were, for the most part, excluded from English society. Likewise, the native women who married Englishmen were ostracized from their own families and considered cultural bastards. The internal battle waged silently while Michael considered the beautiful woman collecting seashells a few meters away from him. Finally, Michael concluded that he had indeed fallen in love with Supi Yaw. He painfully concluded that his love was, in fact, great enough to allow her to remain free of the encumbrances of a formal relationship. He also resolved within himself that no attempt would be made to use this woman to satisfy any selfish desire or personal aspiration. He would love her as she is and make no attempt to own her or to change her in any way. He concluded that the highest form of love was respect.

The ship's whistle sounded in the distance indicating that it was time for all passengers and crew to return to the ship at once. Two hours later, all hands and passengers were accounted for. Several passengers transiting to South America had left the ship and would wait for the next vessel westward bound. Michael was a bit disappointed that the decision had been made to take the American captain on to England. He silently plotted how to occupy as much of the American's time as he could so as to prevent any contact with Supi Yaw. Oddly enough, the more time Michael spent with the one-legged captain, the more he grew to like him. Even Bua found himself listening to stories of the Wild West, the Mississippi River, Buffalo Bill and stories of "gold in them thar hills." The American was likable – that was, as long as he kept a distance from Supi Yaw.

Depending on the wind and current conditions, the ship was scheduled to make a direct run to England. Michael's physical condition had improved considerably. In fact, he felt better than he had in many years. Silently, he attributed this to the congenial company in which he was travelling. And too, a professional soldier is never at ease. There is either an enemy to confront or an officer to salute. For the first time in his life, he had neither. He even failed to come to attention when in the presence of the ship's captain. The journey from Burma had allowed Michael and Bua to spend considerable time in polite conversation about various subjects: politics, life in general, and of course, religion. On one particular afternoon, over a game of chess, the subject was religion. Supi Yaw's shadow moved over the board as both men broke their concentration of the game. She asked if she could watch. Both men acknowledged her by standing and offered her a chair. Once again, the conversation began where it left off. "Why does God allow good people to suffer and bad people to prosper?"

Bua presented his thesis that evil was the result of the devil and good was the influence of God. The balance or imbalance determined the condition of the world. After an hour of quoting Holy Scripture and renowned philosophers, it was determined that the balance between good and evil in any society was actually determined by the balance of good and evil within the individuals in that community. Much like a disease, evil was contagious and easily caught. Goodness, on the other hand, had to be sought out and cultivated; thus the need for a disciplined religious system. This then "forced" people to be good and promote goodness.

Supi Yaw asked if she might pose a question regarding the influence of God in a neutral situation. She posed her question,

"If God is all-powerful and has preeminence over this person we call Satan, why would Satan be given equal authority in, what you Christians call 'the Kingdom of God'? The reigning sovereign, not some foreign power, has dominion over the specific kingdom. And too, if this reigning sovereign is totally benevolent, why would He allow His subjects to be influenced by this 'killer of men's souls'"?

Bua and Michael looked at each other, each waiting for the other to respond. No answer came. Supi Yaw then continued, "I know that there are no answers to these questions on this side of what you call 'heaven'. There always seems to be a point at which theologians and philosophers simply throw their hands in the air and say, 'Who can know the mind of God?' That pretty much takes care of the question."

Again, Bua and Michael looked at each other and remained silent. Not wanting to let the opportunity escape, Supi Yaw posed yet another question. "Bua, as you know, I too have read the Bible many times; perhaps not as many times as you. The one question which frequently crosses my mind is, if the Bible is the Word of God, why did He select such a primitive language with which to convey His word? When you examine the text, you find ambiguities in matters of eternal consequence. The Catholics read the words one way and the Protestants read them another. Why did He use parchment or clay? Why did He not proclaim His word to many tribes and in many forms? According to you, God presented His word to the Hebrews who, during the course of history, rejected it. Then the gentiles took the teachings and rejected the Jews. Now the British own God's word and attempt to force it upon people like us. Then, after we have accepted this British religion, the British refuse to allow us to worship in the same sanctuary. While they teach that all men are equal in the sight of God, they insist that we natives remain outside their churches or simply attend special services for natives. I, myself, have attempted to attend the services at the church at Chittagong only to be asked to take a seat on the front steps or perhaps outside next to a window. Even at funerals for a British person, we natives were not allowed to participate. We had to remain in the background. There seems to be two levels of Christians in God's Kingdom, British Christians and brown Christians'?"

Supi Yaw's comments had struck a nerve deep in Michael's soul. While he fully realized the truth of Supi Yaw's comments, he had never truly realized the hypocrisy of that truth. He had no answers; only an enormous sense of guilt in light of this brilliant woman's indictment.

Bua opened his mouth to respond. Michael held up his hand and whispered, "Forgive me! For God's sake, forgive me."

Supi Yaw smiled and touched Michael's hand. "You are forgiven."

With that, she left. Nothing more was said, either by Michael or Bua. Both simply pondered the words and thoughts which had transpired over the chess board.

CHAPTER THIRTY-THREE

LONDON

The ship found its way to its designated dock. A military unit, complete with yet another small brass band was waiting to escort Sergeant Major Michael St. John to his temporary quarters. As the gangplank was put in place, the officer in charge ordered the band to begin its perfunctory ceremony. Sergeant Major Michael St. John, attired in one of his new uniforms, proceeded down the gangway to the officer in charge. Salutes were exchanged and perfunctory introductions made. Supi Yaw was dressed in a beautiful Indian-style sari with a hand-woven shawl of the Baum tradition. Bua Tan Bo was dressed in a robe similar to the one he had made for the ceremony at Rangoon. Three reporters and their respective photographers were on hand to take pictures for tomorrow's newspapers. After a bit of chit-chat, St. John was shown to a carriage with Bua and Supi Yaw entering a second carriage. Four mounted soldiers provided escort through the cobblestone streets of London. It had been eighteen years since St. John had seen London. He was amazed at the wealth and development of the city. Although he was British, this seemed like a foreign country. Because of the notoriety he had received in the British press, many along the route recognized him and waved their hats. Those in military uniform offered a snappy salute as he drove past. The drive though London streets took somewhere around an hour. In that time, Michael realized that he was indeed a foreigner in a foreign land.

In the carriage behind, Bua and Supi Yaw sat in a dignified manner, trying not to show their fear of this strange place. In the distance, the chimes of Big Ben announced twelve o'clock. The carriages and the horsemen entered the stone gates of a military barracks for junior officers and came to a stop. Another honor guard came to attention as Sergeant Major Michael St. John emerged from the open carriage. An officer dressed in an overly decorated uniform, complete with feathered hat, extended his hand to St. John who first saluted and then extended his hand. Michael looked over to Bua and Supi Yaw and beckoned them over to where he was standing. The befeathered officer began to speak in an overly theatrical British dialect which gave Michael the impression that this chap had never been outside London. "Sergeant Major St. John, on behalf of her Imperial Majesty the Queen, it is my pleasure to afford you and your party all comforts and accommodations you might require during your stay here in London. Her Imperial Majesty has requested your attendance at court the day after tomorrow, ten o'clock in the morning. Thereupon, you shall have bestowed upon you, the Victoria Cross for Gallantry. Until that time, I and my good offices are at your disposal. Tomorrow evening, several members of the High Command have arranged a small reception for you and your party. You shall be collected at precisely eighteen hundred hours. Until that time, you may rest, or if you wish, venture out into the streets of London. Her Majesty has made several carriages available along with escorts if you should wish to venture out.

St. John was escorted to a small well-appointed suite within the junior officer's barracks while Supi Yaw and Bua were shown to less formal guest quarters. Luncheon was served in a small private dining room. While the service was exemplary, the food was not. Boiled beef, boiled potatoes, boiled pudding, and weak tea. For a country which owned virtually every spice in the known world and the country from which it came, the British could not tolerate anything stronger than salt and pepper. Bua asked one of the table servants for a bottle of vinegar to deaden the taste of the boiled beef. St. John asked, "How would you like to see the British Museum or perhaps the Tower of London?"

Bua and Supi Yaw whispered among themselves. "Michael," Bua said, "I would love to visit the book vendors, and Supi Yaw would like to visit the medical supplies vendors."

Michael was surprised. "You mean you don't want to see the British Museum?"

"Perhaps later," Supi Yaw smiled. "Father has given each of us a considerable sum of money, and we simply want to look into books and medical instruments." Michael shrugged his shoulders and smiled.

It had occurred to Michael during his malarial episode back in Burma that he needed to make some attempt to reunite with his brother the vicar. Michael had not seen or communicated with his brother since receiving the letter announcing the death of Michael's mother. The letter was utilitarian in that it simply stated the facts of her passing and a brief homily regarding the disposition of her eternal soul. It was cold and perfunctory with absolutely no sense of loss or consolation. Michael's reply to that letter did at least offer a brief eulogy on the dear woman's influence on him as a child.

∾

CHAPTER THIRTY-FOUR

Michael availed himself of the one of the Queen's carriages and ordered the driver to take him to the last-known address of his brother, Vicar Andrew Douglas St. John. It was a small stone church near the outskirts of London. A small well-kept cottage was hidden at the rear of the primary church building. Michael spotted a man in the adjacent cottage bending over a hoe. The slightly balding man wore a clerical collar and thick glasses. Michael called out, "Andrew, Andrew St. John?"

The man straightened and regarded Michael. "Michael, is that you?" he asked. The two men stopped short of each other. The emotions churning inside Michael wanted to grab hold of his brother, his only living relative, the only person who shared any of his past. He desperately wanted to hug the little man.

Andrew St. John simply extended his hand. "I read about your exploits in the TIMES. Congratulations." Andrew even seemed to be oblivious to the Sergeant Major's stripes and the numerous battle ribbons on his brother's full-dress uniform.

There was a long silence as the two men struggled for something two strangers might say to each other. For an Englishman, when there is nothing to say, the only thing to say is, "Can I offer you a cup of tea?"

Michael pondered the invitation for a minute. "I would love a cup of tea, Andrew, but I really must be getting back to my quarters. They are expecting me."

Andrew smiled politely, "So good of you to have come. Please stop by when you have some time to chat."

"I will do that," Michael said as he realized that in spite of the many letters back and forth, any relationship with this little man had died years and years ago. As he turned to go, Michael called back. "Andrew, where did you bury Mother and Father?"

Andrew pointed, "They are both over there, in the church yard; back corner on the right."

Michael nodded and moved toward the church cemetery. Within minutes he found the stone markers indicating that his mother and father were indeed below this sod. Michael turned around to see his brother return to his gardening as Michael issued a silent greeting to his parents. He felt an enormous sadness, none like he had ever experienced before. Not only did he not have a mother and father, but he no longer had a brother.

The journey back to the barracks was empty. The expectations of finding a long-lost brother had been completely dashed. The ultimate realization that his father and mother were indeed dead finally struck home. From time to time during the trip through the streets of London, he would try to imagine good times at play with his brother or events with his parents which brought him some happiness. None came. At one intersection, an old soldier recognized Michael in the carriage and saluted smartly. "*At least I have my brothers-in-arms*," he whispered to himself.

CHAPTER THIRTY-FIVE

Upon his return to the barracks, he found Bua and Supi Yaw happily going through packages of books and medical instruments. Like children at Christmas, they unwrapped their newly acquired treasures as if each were a complete surprise. Supi Yaw was particularly enthralled with her new set of glass hypodermic needles. Bua was well into a volume on the biography of Alexander the Great. Michael felt a warm surge upon seeing his friends thoroughly enjoying themselves. He shook his head at the thought of being happy over something like hypodermic needles.

Bua asked Michael, "And what adventure did you undertake this afternoon?"

Michael simply smiled and said, "I went to see my brother." The empty expression on his face eliminated any doubt that the visit was not a subject for further discussion.

Both Bua and Supi Yaw felt the sadness in Michael's eyes. Bua then changed the subject. "Michael, you really should rehearse your forthcoming audience with the Queen. You can't simply walk into the palace, greet the Queen, and take your medal, now can you?"

Michael smiled, "I am told that we shall receive a course in court courtesy tomorrow morning."

Supi Yaw looked directly at Michael, "What do you mean, we, Michael? You are the one being honored, not us. We have no place in this event."

Michael's smile widened even further. "My dear friends, my summons to court included a consort of my choosing. Generally, this would include members of my immediate family. In this case, I am considering you, Supi Yaw and Bua Tan Bo, as members of my family. After all, if it were not for you two, I would not be here."

Bua spoke, "But what about your brother?"

Michael replied, "What about my brother?"

Supi Yaw, in a state of near panic said, "Michael, you can't drag two savages from the hills of Burma into Queen Victoria's court. She would be most offended, and you would more than likely be tossed out on your ear."

Michael replied, "If that be the case, then so be it. Your names are on the list of invitees. And that's that!"

Fortunately for Supi Yaw and Bua, Bua had brought along a flask of jungle berry juice. This purple potion provided a sufficient level of sleep-inducing intoxication so that all three enjoyed a good night's rest.

The following morning, breakfast was served followed by an introduction to several members of the Queen's household. Instructions were given on every aspect of the presentation, from the carriage ride to the palace, to the entry into the appropriate ceremonial hall. After an hour or so spent in practicing formal bowing, curtsying, and wiping of one's drippy nose should the necessity arise, the three were ready to run for the nearest boat bound for home. Then came a brief lunch of sandwiches and fruit. Another extremely stuffy instructor of courtly craft tutored the three on items of conversation, in the event Her Majesty should direct a comment their way. He insisted, "One must never initiate a conversation with Her Majesty; nor should one ask Her Majesty a question. One must only speak when spoken to, and one must never express any sort of emotional exchange." The list of "one must" and "one must not" went on for what seemed like forever.

Then the courtier asked, "Are there any questions?"

Michael looked at the stuffy little man and said, "No sir, I think we fully understand our place in this little performance."

The little man raised an eyebrow and replied in an extremely condescending tone, "Sergeant Major, it is a rare privilege to come into the presence of the Queen. I suggest that you and your friends here consider the gravity of your 'performance' as you put it."

Michael simply nodded. "*Thank God for English tea time*," Michael thought to himself as the prickly little courtier excused himself just as the clock on the wall struck four.

"Until tomorrow," the little man chirped.

A steward announced that the wife of one of the many generals was hosting high tea in a nearby pavilion. The steward escorted the trio out of the barracks hall and into a courtyard where a sparkling white pavilion was located. A dozen or more women dressed in frilly dresses were congregated around several tables filled with tea and tea cakes. One of the ladies came forward and introduced herself as General So-And-So's wife. For the next fifteen minutes, each frilly-frocked lady in the group was introduced as another General Somebody-or-Another's wife. The tea was flat, the cakes were dull and the conversation was mind numbing. Each of the ladies in the frilly frocks had to comment on Supi Yaw's beautifully hand-stitched silk skirt and brocaded jacket. Supi Yaw thought to herself, *"Even though they love to look at these items, not one of these silly women would be caught dead wearing them."*

One of the ladies eventually conjured the courage to ask, "Sergeant Major St. John, please tell us about this horrible battle on the Irrawaddy and this awful pirate fellow you subdued."

The lady's comment was followed by a chorus of "Oh yes, Sergeant Major St. John, please do tell us of the great battle."

St. John smiled at Bua who was dressed in a fashionable Indian-style suit and Panama hat.

"Well ladies," he began with a most serious expression on his face. "Our boat was innocently making its way down the Irrawaddy River when out of nowhere this fellow, Bua Tan Bo, and his band of cutthroats blocked our progress. Then with guns and swords drawn. . . " Michael stopped short. The ladies were silent, waiting for the next words to describe the impending bloodbath.

Then Michael said, "Bua Tan Bo, why don't you tell the ladies what happened next." Every eye in the pavilion moved from Michael to the dark-skinned man standing several feet away from Sergeant Major St. John. There were gasps and expressions of shock.

The hostess then asked, "Sergeant Major St. John, do you mean to tell us that this is the blood-thirsty pirate who confronted you and our forces on the Irrawaddy?"

Michael looked at Supi Yaw and smiled. Polite panic moved through the group of women as several moved back away from the brown man in the white Indian suit.

Michael continued, "And this is his sister, the daughter of a tribal elder in the mountains of western Burma. She is, in fact, a medical doctor." Another round of shock passed through the assembly.

Supi Yaw politely and in the most precise English spoke, "Actually, Sergeant Major St. John is not exactly correct.

I am a medical practitioner, but unfortunately do not carry the credentials of a medical doctor." There was absolute silence in the pavilion.

Finally Michael spoke, "Bua Tan Bo, would you mind continuing with the story of the infamous 'Battle of the Irrawaddy?"

"With pleasure," he replied. For the next thirty minutes, Bua gave a highly dramatized and exaggerated narrative of the confrontation. He concluded his version of this little piece of history with a brief sermon on how this unfortunate incident was actually divinely ordained. It provided an opportunity to bring both he and Sergeant Major St. John together in order that a peaceful alliance between men of good will could be forged. Bua went on for some time suggesting how the heathens who had been transformed by Christianity could become vital elements in Her Majesty's Empire. It was actually Bua's intention that these ladies might relate the subject of his little speech to their respective husbands over breakfast. This certainly wouldn't hurt their efforts in promoting the "Ballentine Doctrine" he thought.

Throughout his monologue Bua quoted scripture after scripture verse supporting his various points. On occasion, Michael glanced over at Supi Yaw and silently nodded his agreement of the lesson that was being taught. At last, Bua concluded his little homily by asking if there were any questions.

The ladies were absolutely captivated by Bua. One lady directed a question, not to Bua but to Supi Yaw. "My dear, could you tell us how you came to be a medical practitioner? After all, most women these days are well satisfied to be wives and mothers." Another lady then picked up on the opportunity to inform Supi Yaw that England was indeed a small country whose political and intellectual strength had allowed it to subjugate much of the primitive world. With Great Britain's empire expanding with each passing day, many more people would be needed to support the administration of the Empire. She reasoned emphatically that if women were more concerned with pursuing 'male' professions, they would not have the time, the inclination or the opportunity to provide more servants of the Crown and its administration of the realm.

Supi Yaw noticed the overt criticism of her pursuit of a profession, while at the same time realizing the interest in a woman who had broken away from tradition. She, like Bua, expressed herself in the most eloquent English she could speak. Each comment was delivered in a slow, methodical meter so as to give the impression that she, a Baum woman, was as equally educated as those in the audience. She told about begging her parents to allow her to spend weeks at a time sweeping floors at the Chittagong hospital. She told about finding a corner in an operating theater during surgeries and procedures. Then at night, she would slip into the unlocked hospital library and read medical books until the matron stumbled upon the child slumped over an open book. She spoke about the chastisement of several doctors who strongly opposed a native and particularly a native woman showing interest in the manly art of medicine.

Supi Yaw spoke about the many hundreds of trips into remote villages in the Banderban Hills to serve those who were either too poor or too sick to come to the hospital in Chittagong. She told about the hundreds of babies delivered by her and dozens of midwives she had trained.

The women in the frilly dresses were both entranced by this native woman while at the same time fearful that their roles in polite society might someday be challenged by these new ideas of equality between men and women, natives and Englishmen.

The hostess eventually thanked everyone for attending and dismissed the guests to return to their polite little lives.

The hostess then addressed St. John, Bua, and Supi Yaw. "I understand that you are being hosted at a reception this evening. I suggest that you get a bit to eat and quite possibly catch a short nap. These events can be quite taxing you know."

On the way back to their quarters, Supi Yaw suggested that she not attend the reception. She reasoned that the reception was a man's event and she might be seen as in interference. She also indicated that she was tired and needed to rest. St. John reluctantly agreed as he left her at the door of her quarters. Michael and Bua agreed to meet in the barrack's dining room at seventeen hundred hours. Michael noted to Bua that seventeen hundred hours meant five o'clock in civilian language.

Michael went to his quarters where he took pen and paper and listed an agenda of items he wanted to informally discuss at the reception. This was probably the only opportunity in his entire life to discuss the items on his mind with members of the British High Command. In fact, it was probably the only opportunity in his life to even see the members of the British Military Senior Staff. For a few hours, he would have direct conversations with generals, admirals, knights of the realm and who knows who else. He needed to prepare his mind and his thoughts. For some completely unknown reason, Sergeant Major Michael St. John dropped to his knees, folded his hands, and began to speak with the God he hardly knew.

He began with some of the formal and liturgical language he had known as a boy. After a few formal introductions and high-sounding phrases, he dropped into the words coming from his heart. "God, you and I are not always on good terms. This I admit openly is my fault. My sins and imperfections are far too great to even approach you for any consideration. I would, however, like to ask that you guide my words and those of my good friend Bua when we are in conversation with these powerful men tonight. There is an enormous amount of good which can come from this meeting if only Bua and I can convince these powerful people that the way to expand the British Empire and your kingdom is through works of charity and words which demonstrate brotherhood and true Christian benevolence. Words alone are like bullets. Words and works give hope and promise to those who fear and hate us. And if I might be personal for a moment, I would ask that you might make some arrangement so that this magnificent woman you have apparently placed in my path, might somehow, well, - you know." With that, Michael stood, addressed himself in the full-length mirror and left the room.

In Bua's small room, he too was on his knees reciting a similar prayer for wisdom and honesty. He too added a brief petition that his friend, Michael, and his sister might somehow enter into a more formal relationship in accordance with their strong sense of mutual affection.

Supi Yaw was flat on her back sound asleep.

CHAPTER THIRTY-SIX

At the appointed time, a carriage arrived complete with escort and conveyed Sergeant Major St. John and Bua Tan Bo to the officers' club. It was clearly obvious that many of the officers were well into their second, third, or even fourth gin and tonic of the evening. The uniforms worn by those in attendance looked more like costumes at a Mardi Gras party than a senior officers corps. Gold braid, shiny buttons, and every sort of stripe, star or crown were sewn onto every uniform in the room. Long rows of medals bedecked the chests of mustached old men, many of whom had never seen a shot fired in anger. One particular gold-bedecked general raised his glass in the direction of Sergeant Major Michael Oliver St. John, soon-to-be recipient of the Victoria Cross for Gallantry. This was followed by dozens of echoed responses. Michael shyly acknowledged the toasts and thought to himself, *"How unusual for these senior officers to even be seen in the company of a non-commissioned officer like myself. How odd indeed?"*

The general, obviously impacted by the gin and tonics coursing through his bloodstream, then approached Bua Tan Bo. "So, this is the infamous river pirate who brought this whole incident to pass. Hmm!"

Every eye in the room focused on the little brown man in the white suit. Bua smiled and spoke, breaking the uncomfortable silence. "A pirate is a pirate if he is not on your side. Your famous Captain Henry Morgan was a pirate until he swore allegiance to the British Crown. At that point, he became a patriot. I am here today to swear allegiance to the crown which now overshadows my country. So I suppose that makes me a patriot." At that point, Bua reached for a glass of brandy in a silver tray, raised it to a portrait of the Queen and said in a loud voice, "Long live her Imperial Majesty Queen Victoria!" All responded to the toast.

One-by-one, those in the room realized the significance of the little brown man's comments. Someone called out, "A toast to another patriot, hopefully more a friend of the Crown than our Captain Morgan." Laughter enveloped the room as another round of fire water was consumed.

While both Michael and Bua held glasses of whiskey, they purposely avoided ingesting any liquor which might impair their judgment in any way. One false word or careless comment could have a profound impact on their primary objectives. And too, Michael recalled the warnings from Supi Yaw regarding the effects of alcohol on his delicate liver.

Michael and Bua soon found themselves in smaller groups of senior officers answering questions and giving opinions on matters well above their stations. One general asked Bua to relate the situation regarding some fellow calling himself "the Prince." Bua thought for a moment, like a chess player before a critical move. "Well, you see gentlemen, there is this chap who sees himself as savior of the people. He has created his own legend, claiming kinship to Mohammad and to various other religious figures. I am surprised that he has not claimed kinship to Jesus Christ as well. Actually, he is somewhat of a fraud in that his true motives are to get rich at the expense of his people. In any case, a certain Major Somerset, commanding officer of the Chittagong garrison has seen fit to neutralize this rascal by allowing him to run free, ultimately incurring the ire of the people whom he clamed to support. It was the Prince's intent that Somerset take aggressive action against him and his men, thus inciting more and greater dissatisfaction with the British. Instead, Somerset turned a blind eye, allowing nature to take its course. Nature did take its course. Under the leadership of Major Somerset and Sergeant Major St. John, Sergeant Roberts, and Sergeant McMillan, the Prince and his people were reduced to comic figures and run out of town."

Another general then asked, "What is all this about pig entrails falling from the sky?"

"Gentlemen," he began in all earnest, "due to the sensitivity of this operation, those who participated in the 'battle' and those were ultimately affected by its outcome, swore an oath to maintain the details of the event as a secret. However, being that you gentlemen are, in fact, responsible for the ultimate welfare of those in the region, I will trust your personal integrity with the utmost secrecy of the operation. If the Prince were to ever realize that this was not an act of God, but rather a silly idea conceived by a couple of British sergeants, he would not be happy. Bua smiled and began telling the story, complete with all the drama and theater he could muster. All those standing in his circle were enthralled with the antics and the description of the "Battle of the Pigs."

One general mentioned to another, "Let's check on this Somerset fellow. Sounds like a good man. Perhaps a promotion or a commendation should be put in the works."

The other general replied, "I shall also look into these two chaps, McMillan and Roberts."

In St. John's circle, the topic of the Gurkha forces had been brought up. St. John took the opportunity to relate his first-hand knowledge of the Gurkhas and their fierce loyalty to the Empire. He then suggested that a similar force might be forged from those tribes following the Christian religion. The payback for this extremely risky enterprise would come in the form of higher levels of social development within those regions participating in plan. St. John then broached an actual plan. While some had heard of this obscure movement some called "the Ballentine Doctrine," most were occupied with other regions of the globe and other political issues. St. John elaborated on the major issues of the doctrine, starting with the concept of Alexander the Great's method of pacification versus all-out conquest.

Several generals commented among themselves, that this Sergeant Major is an extremely bright fellow – for an enlisted man. While there was general consensus that St. John's rationale seemed logical and worthy of consideration, most of those present were preoccupied with agendas of their own. St. John sensed a mild consensus, but also realized a slight apathy to the plan. Michael then decided to take the conversation to an entirely new level. He determined to stoke the fire of his topic with international politics. He went on, "Those of us who are intimately involved in the mud and muck of Burma are keenly aware of the fact that the Americans, French, and Russians are very interested in making significant inroads into Burma. As you gentlemen know, the French have taken Vietnam, Laos, Cambodia, and have designs on Siam. Likewise, the Americans have taken the Philippines, and they too have a keen interest in adding Siam to their list of colonies. If the British Empire does not firmly establish itself in the hearts and minds of the people, we could lose Burma. Colonization does not simply involve planting one's flag on someone else's property and calling it home. Like Alexander the Great, we must win the hearts and minds of the people we subjugate."

One general shouted out, "Here, here!" This was followed by a brief applause and a few more quiet comments about "how could an enlisted man have this level of insight?"

By midnight, most of those in the hall were much too sleepy, intoxicated, or both to carry on a reasonable conversation. St. John mentioned to the general standing next to him that he had a rather important appointment with the Queen the next morning and that he needed to excuse himself and get some rest. "After all, one does not have an audience with the Queen every day – at least not a Sergeant Major." The general laughed and escorted St. John and Bua to a waiting carriage.

The London air was cold and damp. The trip back to the barracks was brief. "Well Michael," Bua said, "did we accomplish what we came all this way for?"

Michael replied, "My friend, talk is cheap. We shall see."

Bua added, "I did give credit for the little skirmish with the Prince to Major Somerset. I figured that he might become more sympathetic to our cause if he were to receive a promotion as a result of our involvement."

"Good move, Bua. Somerset is a good man. If he receives a promotion, I will see to it that a little bird mentions that it was you who caused it to happen."

Both men fell asleep within minutes of hitting their respective pillows. In another part of the vast building, Supi Yaw was dreaming of her beloved Banderban Hills.

This particular morning came earlier than most. Several valets and other assorted servants arrived at each door with instructions to dress, quaff, and make ready each participant in this morning's royal audience. A new brilliantly polished pair of boots were delivered to Michael, compliments of his regimental senior officer. Bua received a newly tailored suit and top hat as well as a new pair of patent-leather shoes. A barber trimmed and shaved the men while down the hall, a hair dresser placed every hair on Supi Yaw's head in correct order. While several dresses were offered, Supi Yaw firmly but politely opted for one of her home-made traditional skirts and jackets. An informal breakfast consisting of tea, cakes, and cut fruit was consumed between shavings, combings, and dustings. By eight o'clock, the three looked like characters from a Mozart opera waiting for the curtain to rise at the London Opera. Two coaches complete with escorts were waiting outside the barracks. Michael was openly agitated with the fact that Bua and Supi Yaw had to take a second carriage. But, not wanting to make an issue of this obvious act of British discrimination, he quietly apologized to Bua and Supi Yaw. They both graciously ignored the offense and accepted Michael's regret.

The streets to Buckingham Palace were lined with people going to work. For most, a carriage full of diplomats, foreign dignitaries, or others wearing funny costumes were an everyday event. Heroes, on the other hand, afforded a bit more notoriety, especially from military men or oddly enough, policemen. Most stopped, came to attention and offered a salute to Sergeant Major Michael St. John, 'Hero of the Irrawaddy'. Michael acknowledged them with a salute and a warm smile directed toward a "brother in arms." As for the two brown people in the second carriage, they were regarded with curiosity and a slight nod or tip of the hat.

~

CHAPTER THIRTY-SEVEN

The carriage entered the gate of Buckingham Palace, a place Michael had only seen once while on home leave to bury his father. The Queen's guards came to attention and offered a smart "order arms" salute. The corporal in charge of the escort loudly announced the arrival of Sergeant Major Michael Oliver St. John to see the Queen. No mention was made of Bua Tan Bo or Supi Yaw. Several other carriages could be seen delivering their charges to a small side door of the palace. Dozens of costumed court functionaries scurried around placing those invited to see the Queen. Each group was again tutored on proper forms of entry, proper responses to any response the Queen might or might not make. They were instructed to never, no never turn their backs on the Queen – for any reason. If they were feeling faint, they should simply move back to where they might find a chair or someone to assist them, but under no circumstances were they to turn their back to Her Imperial Majesty.

Another escort consisting of more strange little people dressed in strange little costumes led Michael, Bua and Supi Yaw down several enormous corridors cluttered with huge paintings of strange-looking people dressed in strange-looking costumes. Michael recognized several as former sovereigns and history book people; the Duke of This and the Earl of That. Prince-So-And-So and Princess Such-And-Such. It reminded Michael of some of the Hindu temples he had visited with their hundreds of deities carved into the walls.

One of the costumed courtiers whispered to Michael, "The Lord Chamberlin will announce you. Wait here until you are summoned."

From inside an enormous room, Michael could hear someone speaking what he thought to be Italian. This was followed by a translation into English. Something to do with a place called Ethiopia.

At last, a man holding a very large and very ornate staff acknowledged Michael. "Sergeant Major Michael Oliver St. John?"

"That would be me, sir," Michael responded with utmost respect.

The Lord Chamberlin then acknowledged Bua Tan Bo and Supi Yaw. "I bid you welcome to Her Imperial Majesty's Court. I trust that you have all been instructed as to court protocol?"

Michael responded, "We have Lord Chamberlin."

"Excellent. Please follow me; Sergeant Major St. John first, then Supi Yaw followed by Bua Tan Bo."

At the center of the room was a throne upon which sat a large well- covered lady. Upon her head was a small crown. The Lord Chamberlin stopped in front of the lady sitting on the throne. "Your Imperial Majesty, it is my pleasure to present Sergeant Major Michael Oliver St. John of Her Majesty's Burma Police. He has been summoned here by Your Majesty to receive the Victoria Cross for Gallantry. I am also pleased to introduce his escort, Mr. Bua Tan Bo, as well as Miss Supi Yaw Lat of the Baum Tribe in Western Burma." Bua bowed properly and Supi Yaw curtsied as instructed.

Queen Victoria moved her right hand from off the arm of the throne whereupon a small box was handed to her. She spoke, "Sergeant Major St. John come forward please and receive this token of our extreme gratitude for service to the Crown above and beyond the call of duty. Your actions bring credit to your family and your Queen."

With that, Michael took three steps forward, extended his hand and received the small box. He then took three steps backward, bowed and along with Bua and Supi Yaw, followed the Lord Chamberlin out the door.

Michael regarded one of the great clocks on the wall. "That took less than three minutes. It took us more than a month to get here, all for three minutes," he said.

Just as they were about to follow another collection of costumed courtiers, the Lord Chamberlin sent someone running after the trio. "Please wait, sir," the costumed man said. "The Lord Chamberlin wishes to speak with you further."

They waited approximately thirty minutes before the Lord Chamberlin reappeared.

He wore a polite but dignified smile. "Sergeant Major St. John, it is my pleasure to inform you that Her Imperial Majesty has extended an invitation to you and to your consorts to join her in a private luncheon."

Michael looked as though he had been struck by lightning. He then looked at Bua and Supi Yaw. Unable to speak, Supi Yaw smiled. "Michael, now do you think the trip was worth it?"

The Lord Chamberlin then summoned several costumed courtiers and instructed them to escort the trio to the Queen's private dining room.

As they waited for the Queen, Supi Yaw asked to see the medal in the small box. Michael had all but forgotten the item. He handed the box to Supi Yaw who removed it from its place and neatly pinned it on Michael's uniform. She then stepped back, placed her hands together and moved them to her forehead in a gesture of extreme respect. Bua repeated the gesture, bowing low as he did it.

An enormous sense of elation surged through Michael's body as he realized the true expression of respect coming from these two very dear friends. Supi Yaw's eyes conveyed yet another emotion which Michael returned. Bua noticed the unspoken words.

The Queen entered the dining room, seemingly exhausted from her part in the morning's performances. She plunked down in a large overstuffed chair and beckoned her guests to be seated. "Would you care for a cup of tea or perhaps coffee before we partake of lunch?" she asked.

Michael indicated that he would enjoy a cup of coffee. Bua and Supi Yaw nodded in agreement.

"Now that that's over, perhaps we can enjoy a few minutes of private conversation. Now then, Sergeant Major St. John, I have read the newspaper accounts of your daring encounter with this river pirate fellow; would you be so kind as to relate the story as it truly happened?" The Queen said in a polite but commanding tone.

Once again, Michael related the story, including the private conversations between himself and Bua Tan Bo during the event. He then followed with the narrative of how he and Bua met sometime later in the jungle and discussed their situation further. Michael even mentioned the incident about the tiger. "So there you have it, Your Majesty. The true and untarnished version of the 'Battle of the Irrawaddy'," he said.

The Queen laughed a deep, guttural laugh. She finally regained her composure and spoke, "I think it is fair to say that your medal should have been given for extreme gallantry and unusual wisdom. Most soldiers in your position might have simply trusted in the use of force which would have led to the unnecessary deaths of dozens of soldiers. I should say that wisdom prevailed, not to mention bravery."

Michael blushed as he looked at Supi Yaw. "Thank you, Your Majesty. Your comments are worth far more than this little medal," Michael said.

Then turning her attention to Bua Tan Bo, the Queen asked, "Now sir, tell me about yourself. I am told that you are the son of one of the tribal leaders in the mountains in Burma."

Bua began by telling of his early education at the foot of British missionaries. Bua, of course, mentioned that he had memorized the entire King James Bible and was quite familiar with the doctrines of several current denominations. The Queen acknowledged her amazement with a raised eyebrow and a nod of her head. He then went on to explain his desire for the introduction of more missionaries into his region, particularly educational and developmental missionaries. The Queen seemed genuinely impressed with his comments, interrupting on occasion for points of clarification.

At one point, the Queen reached for a small bell and rang it. A secretary entered the room whereupon she gave in instruction. "We would like Mr. Bua Tan Bo to meet with the Archbishop of Canterbury and the heads of as many mission societies as we can assemble. We would like this meeting to take place as soon as possible. The subject of conversation shall be the implementation of a significant mission development program within the Burmese communities."

Bua was obviously stunned at the Queen's instruction. The Queen continued, "And you Miss Supi Yaw Lat, we understand that you had the unfortunate opportunity to amputate the leg of an American sea captain? Is this true?"

Supi Yaw's heart skipped several beats. "Yes Your Majesty, I did perform an amputation, but it was preformed aboard an American vessel."

The Queen again laughed, "No my dear, I am not questioning your legal standing or unlicensed medical practices. I am merely interested in your medical skills. I am told that you possess the qualities of a qualified physician, but hold no license or diploma in any medical sciences. In fact, my Foreign Secretary has received a formal note from the American ambassador thanking our medical personnel, that being you, for giving assistance to an American citizen in distress." Supi Yaw smiled. "Miss Supi Yaw Lat, perhaps you could fill me in on how you came to this specialized knowledge?"

Now it was Supi Yaw's turn to give a brief autobiography. She included stories about how she read virtually every medical book in the Chittagong hospital and every medical journal she could find. She told of the many minor and some not-so-minor operations she had performed in the mountain villages of the Banderban Hills. She concluded her comments with a polite, but forceful, criticism of the British medical system and its refusal to allow women, in particular native women, into the ranks of legitimate medical practice. She suggested that she would be happy to sit for formal medical license any time, any place." The Queen simply smiled at this comment.

The steward announced politely that lunch was served. The Queen and her guests moved to the table where they were each seated by a uniformed waiter. Michael again commented to himself, "*More bland English food. I would give anything for a plate of rice and Indian curry.*"

Once again, the Queen carried the conversation. "Sergeant Major St. John, as with most of our national heroes, we have taken the liberty of delving into your family history. My secretary has informed me that your ancestry contains some rather notable persons. I have received information that one of your illustrious ancestors was, in fact, Oliver St. John, Chief Justice of Common Pleas under Oliver Cromwell. And then there was Henry St. John Viscount of Bolingbroke who became Secretary of War in 1704." Michael sat with his fork half way to his mouth–totally stunned at what the Queen was saying. "Were you aware of your pedigree, Sergeant Major St. John?"

"No, Your Majesty, this is the first time I have heard of this," Michael said.

The Queen continued, "With you permission, Sergeant Major, I would like to look further into your lineage and see if there might possibly be a vacant title you might wish to claim. After all, a gentleman of your qualities might do well to obtain a title. And of course, with a title might come a commission as an officer. With your permission, I should be happy to pursue any such efforts on your behalf."

A million thoughts raced through Michael's head as he considered this newly reported information. Still, the fork was poised between his plate and his mouth.

Supi Yaw spoke up. "Michael, perhaps you might like to think about this issue when you have had time to digest the thought and the bite on your fork."

Again the Queen laughed a deep, rumbling laugh. "Yes, of course, Sergeant Major, think about and communicate your feelings back to my secretary," the Queen said.

The Queen rose from her chair as did her guests. "Please, let us move to the drawing room for tea."

As the Queen led the way, a small English Bulldog scurried across the floor. One of the stewards politely chased the pup but was unable to catch it before it became obvious to the Queen. Before the steward could apologize and retrieve the dog, the pup ran to Sergeant Major St. John's new boot and lifted his leg. St. John neither moved nor indicated disgust. The Queen, however, was aghast. Before the Queen could regain her composure and order the servant to catch the dog, Michael reached down and picked the pup up in his arms. The dog licked Michael's face as the servant attempted to take the dog. "No, never mind, Your Majesty, most of my best friends are dogs." Another servant, seeing the near calamity, rushed in with a towel and wiped Michael's boot and the puddle on the royal floor. The Queen was clearly upset with the incident. Michael spoke, "Please Your Majesty the little fellow meant no offense. My father taught me to never take offense when none was intended. This poor mutt was only doing what poor mutts do. Like tigers.

The Queen laughed again and spoke, "Sergeant Major St. John, I would consider it a favor if you were to take your 'friend' as a remembrance of this meeting. It is my gift to you. He was an unwelcome gift from a cousin. As yet, I have not given him a name."

Michael held the dog up before his face. "Your Majesty, I think I have a name. His face reminds me of a truly great man I once served with in India. He was a regimental beastie, a water bearer. He was one of the finest men I have ever known. His name was Gunga Din. I shall call him Gunga."

The Queen replied, "Then Gunga it is."

After a cup of tea, and more discussion of topics related to Burma, the Queen asked if Sergeant Major St. John and Bua would be good enough to step outside and allow her and Supi Yaw to "talk girl talk."

The two men politely excused themselves, keeping in mind that they, including Gunga, were not to turn their backs on the monarch as they left the room.

Queen Victoria motioned her several servants in attendance to leave the room. For the next twenty minutes, the two women, one a native medical practitioner and one a Queen of half of the world discussed one of the Queen's personal issues. The Queen suggested that her personal physicians were indeed competent, but insensitive to a number of issues which she needed to discuss with an educated and sympathetic woman. For the most part, these issues were not so much matters of the body but matters of the heart.

Supi Yaw was escorted to the carriage where Michael, Bua, and Gunga were waiting. Bua asked, "And what did you and the Queen talk about?"

Supi Yaw answered with a slight smile, "It is not proper to discuss one's patients with those who are not qualified."

Michael looked at Bua. Both smiled at the enormous significance of this event–Supi Yaw Lat ministering to the Queen of the British Empire!

The ride through the streets of London was, for the most part silent. Bua and Supi Yaw ruminated over the entire event, recounting every minute and every word with the world's most powerful woman. Michael, on the other hand, focused one hundred percent of his attentions on the small boxy English Bulldog sitting on his lap. Both Bua and Supi Yaw were silently amazed that a man of St. John's stature and disposition should fall madly in love with a dog. Here was a man who fought for his country and killed people doing it. Here was a man who addressed this tiny beast as if it were an equal. Perhaps it was the dog who had first regarded this uniformed human as his equal. In either case, the man and the beast were content to make strange noises at each other while expressing mutual affections. Neither Bua nor Supi Yaw had seen this side of Michael St. John before. They looked at each other and smiled approvingly.

CHAPTER THIRTY-EIGHT

The coach arrived at the barracks. Two guards at the front door post moved toward the carriage to open the door and assist Supi Yaw to the sidewalk. One of the guards spoke, "Sir, I regret to inform you that dogs are not allowed in the barracks. Perhaps we can find a place near the horses. The other guard then noticed the small collar around the dog's neck which bore Queen Victoria's royal emblem upon it. The guard's eyes opened wide, "Under the circumstances, Sir, I think we will be able to find a suitable basket for the little fellow in a corner of the kitchen."

"Thank you, corporal, that would do nicely," Michael replied.

Supi Yaw opened the door to her room where she found a formal envelope waiting on a silver tray. The envelope contained a red wax seal and her name beautifully inscribed. At the top of the envelope was a small American flag.

After a meeting with the Queen of Great Britain, what else could possibly happen to this Burmese mountain woman?

Supi Yaw carefully opened the envelope and removed the letter inside. It read:

Greetings:

It has come to my attention that a certain Captain Jonathan Carter, citizen of the United States of America had encountered an unfortunate accident while pursuing his duties on the high seas. I was further informed that through your medical knowledge and experience, you came to the assistance of this unfortunate man and in so doing, saved his life. My sources tell me that you were required to make a mid-ocean transfer of both yourself and ultimately the stricken captain. This action did, in fact, constitute direct risk to your life and those who assisted you. As representative of the United States government I would very much appreciate an opportunity to personally express our gratitude for your actions. Therefore, I would consider it an honor to host you and your colleagues at an informal luncheon at my residence. If you are available, I would ask that you confirm with my currier. I would look forward to meeting you and your associates tomorrow at twelve o'clock.

Supi Yaw read the note several times in disbelief. Looking into a full-sized mirror, she whispered to herself, "What is going on here?"

Supi Yaw went down the stairway to Bua's quarters. Showing the note to Bua, she said, "We need to take this to Michael immediately. I don't know what to make of this."

Michael answered the door in his tee shirt and britches. In the background Bua could see the small dog playing on the bed. Bua handed Michael the note. Michael read the note and smiled. "Hmm, looks like the Yanks want in on the deal."

Bua looked at Supi Yaw. He spoke, "What is that supposed to mean?"

Michael replied, "We all know that the Americans would like to find any points of entry into Burma. There is no way that the British government will allow for formal entry, so there must be a point of informal entry. If the Americans could identify influential individuals or groups of individuals, they could invite themselves to the party so to speak. Of course, Her Majesty's government would not be happy if the Americans were to be invited."

Bua smiled, "So, if your people at the Foreign Office and the Military High Command were to receive information that the Yanks are up to something, they might be inclined to take a greater interest in our cause."

Michael replied with a broader smile and a wink. "The chess game is becoming more interesting. If we are not careful, we could have a game of three-handed chess."

Before the conversation could go any further, a soldier, clad in yet another uniform, bedecked with gold braid, shiny buttons, and all sorts of doo-dads, snapped to attention next to Bua and Supi Yaw. He extended a note to Sergeant Major Michael St. John and waited as Michael read the note.

"This is from General Wallace. He wants to see me at once. Please don't do anything until I return. It won't hurt the American ambassador's man to wait a bit longer."

Michael handed the small dog to Bua and said, "Gunga needs a walk and something to eat. Would you be good enough to see to him?"

Bua thought to himself, "*Me, a 'prince' of the Baum People playing nursemaid to a mutt?*"

Bua took the dog and handed it off to Supi Yaw who cradled it affectionately. She recalled an old Chinese proverb, "If you show respect to a man's dog, you will receive the man's respect."

Within minutes of having received the note from General Wallace, Sergeant Major St. John was on his way to the General's office. He did, however, dash into his quarters and grab a copy of the Ballentine Doctrine and stuff it into his tunic. Without waiting, even for a minute, St. John was ushered into the General's presence. Like most of the offices Michael had seen during his brief stay in this rarified air of the British hierarchy, General Wallace's walls were adorned with larger-than-life-sized portraits of generals, admirals, and costumed courtiers. There was no question that this General Wallace had indeed earned his position in the system. A number of battle flags, swords, and other souvenirs of battle adorned the walls and bookcases. Sergeant Major Michael St. John seemed honestly impressed with the man rising from his chair to shake his hand. Michael was somewhat perplexed when he offered a salute when the General offered his hand. Michael took the man's hand and gave it a firm but polite shake.

The General who was a small thin man with a tightly trimmed military moustache spoke, "Any man who rightly earns the Victoria Cross is to be saluted"–which he did. Once again, Sergeant Major Michael St. John returned the salute.

The General continued, "Please Sergeant Major, have a seat." Michael sat abruptly. Then, the unthinkable happened; the General offered Michael a brandy. Michael thought for a moment, "*It is unheard of for a general officer to drink with a non-commissioned officer, no matter what medals were pinned to his tunic.*

He thought for a minute. "*Something is going on here. They are playing a chess game of their own.*"

The next fifteen minutes or so were devoted to idle chit-chat. Then the General asked Michael about his plans for the future. Michael was shocked at the question. "*No British soldier ever makes his own plans. Plans are made by his superiors for him. From the moment of enlistment to the moment of retirement, someone tells him what he will be doing and where he will be doing it.*" "Well, General, the only plans I have at this moment are to have lunch with the American ambassador tomorrow; if that is permissible."

The General jumped to his feet. "What, you are having lunch with whom?" Michael went on to explain the business with Supi Yaw and the American sea captain. He was intent on mentioning Queen Victoria's reference to the event as well.

The General moved to the window of his office. "Hmm" was heard several times as the General attempted to assess this bit of information. "So, the Yanks want into the game, do they?" the General whispered aloud. General Wallace looked directly at Sergeant Major St. John. "Ordinarily, we would absolutely forbid any direct contact between a non-commissioned officer and a foreign diplomat. No telling what might come of it." Michael was silently offended by the comment. "However, in this case, I think we might find it to our advantage to have you and your Supi Yaw and Bua friends, guiding the American ship of state to, shall we say, another port."

Michael rose to his feet. "Permission to speak, General?" Michael asked.

"Yes, of course Sergeant Major, I would like to get your inputs on this matter," Wallace replied.

Michael walked to an enormous map on the wall, picked up a pointer and began speaking. In actuality, he had no idea of what he was going to say. He did however, utter the words, *"Lord, if you can hear me, let my words be your words."*

For the next fifteen minutes, Sergeant Major Michael O. St. John recited a history of the Indian sub-continent. He then went on to give an outline of the Burmese situation before and after the British involvement. He placed particular emphasis on the spiritual conquest of Burma opposed to that of the Indian populace. He was quick to point out that many of the animist tribes and those not embracing Buddhism or the Mohammedan faith were quick to accept the Christian faith. Moving his pointer over to Siam and French Indochina, he repeated his theme of spiritual conquest through well-organized evangelistic effort, particularly on the part of the Catholics.

"Now then, General, with Burma we have a vacuum of sorts. Thus far, our efforts to convert the Burmese people have been slight at best. Our churches have been established in major cities for British citizens. The natives, be they Christian or merely interested in the message of the Bible, are found waiting outside near church windows or in 'special native services' in bamboo huts."

The General nodded reluctantly and then spoke, "Sergeant Major, I think you are on to something."

St. John then reached into his tunic and pulled out the four-page document, now somewhat moist from sweat. He placed the document on the table. "General, there are some concepts contained within this document which I believe you will find beneficial to the cause of the Empire."

General Wallace spent the next few minutes reading the four pages.

The General then pressed a button on his desk. Within two seconds, an orderly entered the room and snapped to a formal salute. The General uttered an order to the soldier, "Please ask Generals Pool and Smith-Clyde to join us at once."

Several minutes later the two junior generals were ushered into Wallace's office. Introductions were made all around. Both generals could not help but notice the small medal on the Sergeant Major's chest. Both commented on the events related to this insignificant piece of metal attached to a ribbon. Every officer in the British military coveted this tiny trinket even more than some of the diamond-encrusted royal orders which cluttered the chests of "noblemen" and those who had never fired a shot in anger. While it was to be envied by all who served the Queen and the Empire, the singular man wearing it was to be honored. Both generals offered a salute which was humbly returned by Sergeant Major St. John.

General Wallace handed the document to the two men who read each page carefully. Wallace continued, "Now then, Sergeant Major St. John, tell these gentlemen what you have told me. I would add that it is always somewhat of a surprise when we hear actual first-hand reports of the business of the Empire. All too often our field officers tend to fancy themselves as authors of historical fiction. A five-minute skirmish in the bush of India can be reported in one hundred pages of prose combined with occasional poetry. And needless to say, the author often times presents himself as the hero of the battle." St. John simply smiled with the realization that the General's words were unfortunately true.

For the next two hours, the Ballentine Doctrine was mentioned and discussed. After some time, one of the generals made a comment which caught St. John off guard. "Sergeant Major St. John, I personally know this chap, Ballentine. He and I served together on a number of occasions. I can say quite honestly, this man is not qualified to write this document. To put it politely, Colonel Ballentine is somewhat of an idiot in officer's clothing. The only reason he keeps his posting is because of his family. I would add that his kinsmen have gone so far as to, quietly mind you, ask the High Command to keep him as far away from the family business as possible."

The three generals in the room smirked at the unfortunate truth. St. John wanted to smirk but it would be seen, in his eyes, as insubordination. To lessen the stress of the last comment, General Wallace offered the other two generals a brandy and refilled Michael's class. Then came the perfunctory toast to the Queen.

Wiping the drops of amber liquid from his mustache, General Wallace looked directly into St. John's eyes and asked, "Sergeant Major, did you pen this so called, Ballentine Doctrine?"

Michael's head was becoming a bit light. He wanted to smile, no make that a laugh. He settled for a chuckle and spoke. "General, I feel just like a school boy caught cheating in school. Yes, I, Bua Tan Bo, and the two sergeants with whom I am working devised the document." The three generals laughed aloud.

"But!" St. John injected, "Colonel Ballentine did peruse the document and gave it his blessing. So, I suppose he can be considered a part of its creation."

General Wallace removed his smile and replaced it with a stern look. "Gentlemen, I like what is presented here. I would very much like to see it translated from mere words into deeds and actions in Burma."

He continued, "I am particularly impressed with Sergeant Major St. John's attention to history, particularly the business about Alexander the Great. From this day forth, I would like the plan to carry the moniker, *Opus Britannia - Burma*. This will remove the fly from the ointment and possibly give it a chance of succeeding."

The comments were followed by the usual "Hmm" from the two generals.

"General Wallace, if I might add something here," St. John interjected. "I would strongly suggest that we include Bua Tan Bo in any further discussion. After all, it is he who will ultimately carry the weight of this plan, should it come to pass." Another round of "Hmms."

"Quite right," Wallace replied. "I would suggest that we pull together one or two others, with current knowledge of our situation in that part of the world and meet with this Bua Tan Bo fellow. I understand he is quite bright."

St. John nodded, "Quite bright, General."

St. John was taken back to his quarters where he encountered Bua having a cup of tea and talking with a gentleman wearing a clerical collar. The man was introduced as the Archbishop of Canterbury's personal secretary.

CHAPTER THIRTY-NINE

"Michael," Bua said, "it seems the Archbishop wishes to discuss our plans for the possible introduction of more and better qualified missionaries into our region. I have an appointment with the Archbishop and several members of major mission societies the day after tomorrow." Michael seemed pleased, very pleased.

After the clerical-collared secretary left, Michael briefed Bua on the meeting he had just had with General Wallace and his staff. He concluded by informing Bua that he was to be a part of the discussions from this time forward. Bua was delighted. "Michael, our plan, no make that God's plan, is coming together." Michael went on to mention the comments made about Colonel Ballentine. This simple factor confirmed that the plan actually had a chance to work. Bua then added, "Michael, do you think we might suggest that Colonel Ballentine be promoted to another positing and that our Major Somerset be promoted and moved into Ballentine' billet?"

"You know, Bua, that is not a bad idea, particularly if Somerset were to be made aware of our involvement is his promotion and transfer. Let's see if we can cautiously bring up the point about Somerset's handling of the Prince and his band of rogues."

Supi Yaw entered the room, being pulled by the small, rambunctious bulldog. Both men rose as she entered the room. Both men were anxious to tell her the news of the recent meeting with General Wallace; however, the expression on her face suggested that there was something which took priority. Supi Yaw had a serene, faraway look on her beautiful face. There was a glow about her. Michael reached down and picked up Gunga, scratched his back, and asked, "So, Princess Supi Yaw, how was your afternoon?"

"Michael, Bua, I have met the most wonderful man I have ever encountered while walking Gunga in the park. For a moment a sharp bolt of jealousy shot thorough Michael's entire being. His face radiated the emotion. Bua felt Michael's pain as if he too had been shot in the belly with a bullet.

Supi Yaw realized Michael's emotion and smiled a soothing smile. "This man is a strange fellow, with a long beard and fiery eyes. He and his wife sat down with me on a park bench and we began to chat. The man was strong and bold in his approach, but utterly polite in his manner. He asked me if I knew God. I responded that I knew of Him and about Him, but as far as a personal relationship; no. He went on to ask me if I wanted to know Him. I replied that I had once been a religious person but found that the Christian religion was much like the caste systems of India. I suggested that Christianity was designed for the western world and only included people like us when it was expedient to the cause of conquest. This man and his wife apologized profusely for what they called 'church house religion'. The man then went on to explain the essence of what he called the 'true gospel', that is to say, the gospel of loving a fallen and suffering world. He referred me to the Book of Matthew wherein it defines the true acts of divinely mandated love."

Bua entered the conversation. "I believe you are talking about the story of the Final Judgment where the entire world will be divided into two groups, those who loved with their mouth and those who loved with their actions."

Supi Yaw smiled, "Yes, brother, that is the portion of scripture he was talking about."

Both Bua and Michael realized that something, something very profound had happened to Supi Yaw in that park.

Michael asked, "Who was this man you met in the park?"

She answered, "William Booth and his wife, Catherine Booth. Booth mentioned that he had been thrown out of most 'respectable' churches because of his focus on doing the will of God rather than investing in all the rituals and trappings of princes and kings. Michael, this is first time I have seen the true message of Christ as it was meant to be taught and implemented."

While Michael was not a religious man, he was overjoyed that Supi Yaw had found what she had been looking for. Bua embraced his sister and whispered into her ear, "Sister, I have prayed for this moment for many years."

Supi Yaw smiled and replied, "Please brother, don't assume that I will be singing in the choir or playing dress-up on Sunday mornings. I would prefer to worship God in bamboo huts and mountain clinics. This Mr. Booth suggested that I use my God-given talents to heal the sick, give comfort to the dying, and give life where no one else wishes to go. He said, every time I extend my hand to heal the sick, I am to visualize the hand of God being extended. He further suggested that when I look into the face of a suffering human being, I consider that to be the face of God's own son. I then asked Mr. Booth why God had created so many hurting and ugly people. His reply was, "To see if you, Supi Yaw, would love them. An answer like that could only come from a true man of God. What religion could be more beautiful than that, Michael? Michael looked at Bua, not knowing what to say.

Bua then asked, "Did this Booth fellow by chance ask if you were willing to accept God's spirit and become an instrument of healing?"

Supi Yaw smiled a broadly. "Yes. He and his wife placed their hands on my head and prayed that God's spirit and power would come into me and work through my frail hands."

Tears filled Supi Yaw's eyes. For the first time since encountering the woman, Michael embraced her in a warm but respectful manner. As she wiped her eyes, the moment was broken. The American ambassador's man entered the room. "Madam, I must be getting back to the Embassy. Do you have a reply to the Ambassador's invitation for lunch tomorrow?" It was obvious that the man was not happy at being kept waiting for over four hours for her answer.

"Yes, we would be delighted to accept the Ambassador's kind invitation."

With that, the man bowed and left the barracks.

Michael commented, "We have much to talk about before that luncheon. I suggest we meet back here in an hour and go over our agenda and the possible expectations of the Ambassador's agenda. General Wallace tells me that the Yanks might be using this party to get their little toes into Burma's back door."

Back in Supi Yaw's room, she found herself gazing at her reflection in the ornate mirror. Several times she held up her hands as if there were something new and different about them. She realized that she needed to get back to her people and bring healing to sick and hurting people. She felt a new enthusiasm, no a sense of power, coursing through veins. Again the tears came.

Michael lay on his bed playing with Gunga while he formulated the next few moves in this ever-growing chess game. He was careful to mentally check every move he would be making by asking himself if this were truly in the best interest of the Empire. After all, he was above all, a British soldier and loyal to the Queen unto death.

Bua sat at the small desk in his room, making notes. In particular, he made a list of every cause and every effect; every action and every reaction. Bua was above all, methodical and cautious. He knew that the long term well-being of his people and ultimately his country could very well rest on his shoulders. While Bua was well into his third list, there was a knock on the door. Upon opening it, he found one of the barrack's chefs standing fully arrayed in a cook's uniform. This particular cook was a tall Sikh complete with heavy beard and a turban. "Sir," the man said in the most perfect English, "do you and your party wish to have an evening meal before retiring?"

Bua thought for a moment. "My good man," he replied, "would you happen to know of a decent eatery where a starving pilgrim would find a bowl of curry and rice? This English food is about to kill me."

The bearded man looked perplexed. "My superior won't allow the use of curries in the building. He says it smells of the gutters of Calcutta." He smiled and said, "If you don't mind a brief ride into the 'Indian neighborhoods, I can take you to a small food shop which I find quite good. How about your friends? Would they prefer a tray of sandwiches and tea or would they like to accompany us?"

Bua left the turbaned man standing as he ran down to Michael's room. "Michael, we are going to eat native tonight." He then dashed to Supi Yaw's room and announced the same message.

∾

CHAPTER FORTY

Within minutes, the four were in the back of one of the Queen's carriages heading off into the night. The conversation in the carriage was familiar and friendly, unlike most of the recent conversations where every word had to be measured before leaving the mouth and reaching the ear. Amerjit was both intelligent and articulate in his thoughts. While he asked questions related to the backgrounds of each of his party, there was no sense of intrusion, simply polite curiosity. As the conversation continued, it was found that Amerjit owned a string of seven tailor shops around London. His position as a chef in the junior officers' barracks allowed him access to potential clients among the military community. Without appearing too pretentious, Amerjit suggested that he was, in fact, quite wealthy for an Indian.

The cold, dank smell of London's streets soon gave way to the pungent fragrance of curry and roasting goat. The carriage stopped in front of a small eatery with a sign reading, "Taj Mahal of London." The four were escorted inside to a slightly dingy, but clean dining room. The walls were covered with tapestries depicting the Taj Mahal and other Indian structures.

Another man in a turban greeted the Sikh cook. "Amerjit, you have put on weight. Cooking for those English officers seems to suit you well. Introductions were made as if all were old friends. Amerjit then asked if he could make the order for the party.

Bua smiled, "As long as I have my bowl of rice and curry, I am a happy man." Amerjit also whispered to the owner that the Englishman was, in fact, the "Hero of the Irrawaddy" and winner of the Victoria Cross. Thirty minutes later, two dozen plates, bowls, and basins of exotic food adorned the ever-growing table. As the party began to attack the feast like hungry dogs, an Indian music ensemble began to play on familiar instruments. The music was enhanced by the movements of a heavily made-up and scantily clad Indian dancer. Bua noticed Supi Yaw giving a disapproving look at Michael as he watched the woman's body undulate to the music. "*This is good,*" Bua thought to himself, "*she is jealous.*" Bua then beckoned the owner to the table. "Sir, would you be so kind as to invite our carriage driver to join us for dinner. The poor chap must be starving."

Shortly, the owner returned, offering the driver's gratitude and polite refusal to join the party. "He says Indian food is toxic to his intestines," the owner said. "I will take him a plate of bread and gravy to prevent the poor chap from dying where he sits."

The meal was perfect as was the company. After weeks of bland English food, finally something that actually had taste. The meal concluded with cardamom and cinnamon-flavored Indian tea. A lavish platter of fruit completed the feast.

During the course of the meal, Michael, Bua, and Supi Yaw discussed the events of a most significant day. With the utmost diligence, they carefully planned the conversation for the luncheon at the U.S. ambassador's residence. Michael suggested that the ambassador might offer some sort of development assistance for tribal support. On the other hand, he might offer scholarships for key figures within the Christian communities. In any case, it was decided that no firm decisions or commitments would be made at the meeting. It was agreed that a full report of the luncheon would be handed over to the High Command for an analysis of the American's intentions.

The carriage driver was awakened and drove the party back to the barracks. It was a wonderful evening as each passenger pondered their private thoughts.

CHAPTER FORTY-ONE

The following morning, the carriage ride to the American ambassador's residence was yet another image out of a child's storybook. The carriage, top down, was escorted by two mounted horsemen giving the impression that its occupants were on a royal mission. Michael was wearing one of his new full- dress uniforms; complete with medals, and of course, his Victoria Cross. Supi Yaw was adorned in a magnificent blue and gold silk sari with gold embroidered sandals. Bua simply wore one of his white suits and a Panama hat. The carriage entered the gilded wrought-iron gates surrounding the ostentatious compound and was guided to the front portico. It was precisely twelve o'clock. The ambassador and his wife were waiting on the steps as the carriage rolled to a halt. A United States Marine, in full-dress uniform opened the door of the carriage and assisted Supi Yaw to the pavement. Bua then descended followed by Sergeant Major Michael St. John. The Marine offered a smart salute as he carefully eyed the small red and bronze item on the Brit's chest. Michael returned the salute.

The party was escorted through the main hall of the embassy to the dining room. Covering the wall were life-sized portraits of each of America's presidents. The portrait of Abraham Lincoln hung on the wall at the high end of the dining room table. "Michael looked at Bua with a raise eyebrow as if to say, *"We must be very important indeed."* Bua returned the look. The ambassador's wife then directed the party to the table. St. John was shocked to see Captain John Carter seated in a wheel chair already at the table. "*So, this is the ruse to give the good captain another chance at Supi Yaw,"* he thought to himself. Within minutes, St. John's mind was set at ease. Standing behind the Captain was a very attractive, full-bosomed nurse. Captain Carter blurted out, "I would stand up but your lady friend cut off my leg." At that, he laughed hysterically. He then turned sideways to address the nurse standing behind him. "And this angel of light is my personal nurse, Miss Opal Alston, from Queen's Gate Hospital. As soon as the white-clad woman opened her mouth, it was clear that she was Cockney and not terribly bright. While her comments were silly, Captain Carter was enchanted by her simple beauty. Before the ambassador could intervene, Captain Carter had unbuttoned his jacket exposing a recently performed tattoo bearing the image of a naked female with the name "Opal" beneath the image. The woman giggled profusely as Carter gushed openly over the lady's attributes. "I am trying to convince Miss Opal to marry me and run away to Boston with me. Again, she giggled.

The Ambassador, clearly embarrassed by his compatriot's crude behavior, attempted to redirect the conversation back to something more serious. Michael smiled inwardly at the American's behavior and the comments about marrying the nurse.

For the next hour, over platters of roasted turkey and mashed potatoes, the ambassador carefully directed the conversation back to Burma, India, and French Indochina. There was no question that he was fishing for information regarding the status of the peace and order situation, the economy, and the levels of insurgency in and around Burma. He then mentioned that he had heard something about a plan to bring the Christian tribal groups together into some sort of confederation.

Bua suggested that he too had heard of such an effort, but to his knowledge, nothing had transpired. The ambassador then asked if there might be any way the American government might be of assistance in bringing technology to some of these Christian groups.

Bua again replied, "That is a thought for serious consideration. I would be happy to discuss this issue with the members of my tribal group."

The Ambassador then directed his attention to Supi Yaw. I understand that you are sufficiently educated in the medical arts and that you might qualify to sit for a physician's examination."

Supi Yaw immediately picked up on the ambassador's drift. "Yes, Mr. Ambassador, I believe I would stand a chance of passing the exams, if I were allowed to. But, as you no doubt know, women and in particular native women, would not be permitted to sit for the exams. Unfortunate but true."

The ambassador acknowledged the unfortunate fact. "You know, my dear, we in America have had to deal with this same issue of women being qualified to become medical doctors. Fortunately, several highly motivated women have broken that barrier."

Supi Yaw indicated that she had read where several American women had become licensed physicians.

The ambassador continued, "Have you ever considered applying for a scholarship to one of our medical schools and sitting for the exam?"

"No sir, I have not had that thought," she replied, knowing full well that an offer was imminent.

The ambassador smiled, "If I were to offer you such a scholarship, would you consider it?"

Supi Yaw looked at Michael for a response. "I might," she said.

The ambassador continued, "And if you were to obtain the status of medical doctor, you would most certainly be in a position to aid your people in the possible development of native hospitals and clinics."

She replied, "I shall give it some serious thought and give you my response shortly." Before the conversation could continue, Supi Yaw asked if she and Captain Carter might be excused. She indicated that with Carter's permission, she would like to examine the stump of his leg to see if her procedures on the high seas were sufficient in maintaining the future treatment of the limb. "I took great care to see that all muscles and vessels were properly addressed and that the skin flaps were sufficient to make for a comfortable cushion. Please excuse my professional intrusion but much of the long-term success of a medical procedure is in the follow-up."

The ambassador looked at Carter who simply shrugged his shoulders in agreement. "Nurse Opal, if you would be so kind as to bring your patent into the next room, this shouldn't take a minute."

As soon as Supi Yaw was out of earshot, the ambassador said, "Very impressive, very impressive indeed."

The examination was completed, the stump redressed and gratitude extended for a delicious and cordial lunch. "I have one last favor to ask," the ambassador said. "Would you be kind enough to stand for a photograph? It is not every day we have guests of your prominence dropping by the residence."

A camera had been set up in one of the adjoining rooms complete with a waiting photographer. Two flashes and they were part of history. As the three mounted the carriage, the ambassador reiterated his offer for a full scholarship to an American medical school.

CHAPTER FORTY-TWO

As they drove off toward the barracks, Supi Yaw's head was spinning. *"A girl from the hills of Burma; a girl with little formal education being offered a full scholarship to an American medical school when her sovereign would not even suggest a woman be allowed into the world of medicine."* Michael and Bua could see her thoughts.

Things were happening fast; too fast. The trio from Burma felt as if they had been collectively swept up by a tropical cyclone and spun round and round. As the carriage came to a halt in front of the barracks, Bua spoke, "Michael, tomorrow we must draft a telegram to our people in Chittagong. There has been so much happening; we must make dead certain that those in the conclave are aware of our progress. And too, if those elders in the conclave have not been persuaded by my father's arguments, we must know that as well. Things are much too complicated to lose control of the chess board at this point." Michael agreed completely.

The rest of the afternoon was spent with Michael and Bua compiling notes and then drafting them into a form which could be telegraphed with some degree of security. As a secondary objective, Michael drafted another set of notes indicating points of discussion made between himself, Bua, and the generals. This set of notes was intended to be handed over to General Wallace for his confirmation and action. The topics of discussion included the concept of a Gurkhas-style unit being created within the supportive tribal groups, supplemental development support from missionary agencies and the possibility of Major Somerset's promotion to Lieutenant Colonel and regional commander.

Finally, St. John penned a brief outline of the luncheon with the American ambassador. The points of concern included an invitation for Supi Yaw to be given a full scholarship at an American university, possible technical assistance for tribal entities, and other bits of light intelligence which General Wallace might find of interest.

Dinner was announced. Several other guests were seated at the barracks' dining room table. Dinner conversation consisted of idle chit-chat and polite politics. The other guests, all officers of lower rank, eventually found their way to the subject of Sergeant Major Michael St. John's newly acquired notoriety. For the one hundredth time, Michael was politely compelled to give a description of the infamous "Battle of the Irrawaddy." And for the one hundredth time, the narrative ended with an introduction of Bua Tan Bo, infamous pirate, neatly attired in a linen suit and silk cravat. While the audience was well entertained with the blood-curdling story, Michael and Bua were becoming very tired of the routine.

Throughout dinner, Supi Yaw remained quiet, only speaking when spoken to. With dinner over, the dining room steward invited all present to the drawing room for tea and cakes. It was in the corner of the small, well-appointed drawing room that Michael asked Supi Yaw why she seemed so somber.

Supi Yaw replied, "Michael, I have spent the afternoon reading much of the Bible. Passages which I never considered important all of the sudden became quite relevant. This Mr. Booth and his wife I met in the park focused my attention on the true significance of Christ's mission to this world." Supi Yaw turned toward Michael and said, "Michael, for the first time in my life I know why I am here and what I am supposed to be doing. I know why I have been obsessed with healing from the time I was a child." Then with the utmost of sincerity she said, "Michael, I am called to be an instrument of God's plan in healing a broken and sick world."

Michael tried to speak but no words came. While he was inwardly elated with Supi Yaw's realization, he also realized it elevated her even further away from a common soldier's world.

For Michael, Bua, and Supi Yaw, sleep never came that night. The events of the past few days continued to swirl like dancers on a ballroom floor. Meeting the Queen, lunch with an ambassador, a small dog named Gunga, and so on.

Morning mercifully arrived with the announcement of breakfast. Boiled porridge and weak tea were served. Conversation was limited to the headlines of he TIMES. Michael picked up the copy of the LONDON TIMES which had been placed at his plate. The pages had been folded back revealing a photograph of the trio from Burma and the American ambassador. Michael's blood froze in his veins. The story below the black and white image related how the United States ambassador was eternally grateful for a British subject who had saved the life of an American sea captain on the high seas. The story went on to tell of the ambassador's keen interest in promoting aid and development to the Burmese people. He likewise acknowledged Sergeant Major Michael St. John's extreme bravery and wisdom in the face of adverse conditions. And last but not least, he lauded Bua Tan Bo for "seeing the light of civilization" and opting for a better life for him and his people.

Shortly after breakfast, a courier from General Wallace arrived with noted responses to Michael and Bua's memos sent the previous day. One particular item caught Michael's attention. "I have taken it upon your advice to promote Major Winston James Somerset to the rank of Lieutenant Colonel and transferred him from Chittagong to the regional command post in Rangoon. His predecessor shall be promoted to full Colonel and reassigned to a new posting in Ceylon."

Michael handed the documents over to Bua and pointed to the comments about Somerset.

"Bua, let's play a little game. Can you get a telegram off to Somerset, before this information reaches him? I would like to simply say, 'Congratulations, St. John." I don't want to mention why he is being congratulated, but I would like him to know that we had something to do with his promotion."

By mid-afternoon, several other telegrams were drafted informing those in the Banderban Hills of the progress in London. While some of the information was cryptic, most was much too complicated to disguise in clever verbiage.

∾

CHAPTER FORTY-THREE

CHITTAGONG BARRACKS

Major Winston Somerset had received a series of telegrams from London. One of the telegrams simply stated, "Congratulations." Signed, St. John.

"*Congratulations for what he pondered? This Sergeant Major St. John is up to something,*" he thought to himself. Other telegrams were to be forwarded on to the Baum village, either by horse courier or by heliograph. Major Somerset, however, decided to take a small mounted party and deliver the telegrams personally, and in so doing, see firsthand what was going on. He ordered a group of six men and horses to be ready to march at first light the following morning. Somerset had been to the village a year or so before, but managed to avoid visiting since the Prince had become an issue. He simply did not want to force a confrontation.

The ride into the Banderban Hills was pleasant and without incident. Within a kilometer of the main village, Somerset heard the sound of the big drum. As his party approached, the tempo of the drum increased. One hundred meters from the village arch, Somerset found both sides of the red-brick road lined with Baum villagers dressed in their most colorful finery. Women and children waved hibiscus blossoms and bougainvillea sprigs. At the far end of the line of people, he could make out Sergeants McMillan and Roberts in partial uniform. Nowhere in his region of responsibility were he and his men received like this. In the lowlands, men would hide the women folk and children whenever a military procession of any kind passed. This was different; these people were different.

On second glance he noticed a number of different tribal costumes in the group. Not all of these people were Baum. Some he recognized were Karen and Shaun. Something was happening here which he did not fully understand. He was warmly but cautiously pleased.

Elder Simon greeted the Major with a small garland of flowers. Sergeants McMillan and Roberts saluted and remained at attention until Major Somerset put them "at ease." Elder Simon spoke, "You are just in time for our evening meal. We would be most honored if you were to join us in our simple fare."

Somerset nodded. "I and my men would be honored."

Within minutes a huge feast was planned. Chickens and pigs were quickly killed and placed on spits. Pumpkins and sweet potatoes were prepared along with huge kettles of rice. The large drum again began to beat to a slow cadence with smaller drums adding counterpoints. A female voice began a chant echoed by other singers. This choir seemed to fill the valley already splendid with flowers and fruit trees. Major Somerset thought to himself, "*This is the most tranquil place I have ever encountered in my entire military career.*"

Somerset ordered his men to set up shelters and prepare a suitable camp. He ordered Roberts to take charge of the men and assign specific duties. He then ordered McMillan to accompany him on a brief "walk about." "Tell me, Sergeant McMillan, exactly what is going on here," he whispered.

Sergeant McMillan sucked in a large quantity of air. "Well sir, I am in a bit of a bind. Much of what is happening here is, well, secret."

Major Somerset then stopped short and handed McMillan the telegrams from St. John. McMillan read through each of the two pages and smiled. "Major, I would be delighted to give you the full details of what has transpired and what is hoped to happen in this region. I would, however, like to bring Sergeant Roberts into the conversation in the event I might have forgotten something." Somerset agreed to have Roberts join in.

Somerset then said, "What say we meet in my tent in thirty minutes for a full briefing?"

"Very well, sir. I shall inform Sergeant Roberts immediately." The briefing went on for hours. Somerset was particularly consumed by the battle against the Prince and his forces. Every detail of the battle was discussed in strategic language as if a full report were being issued for a military history class. The details of the Ballentine Doctrine were then offered–each component being defined in terms of cause and effect. In conclusion, each of the telegrams was interpreted as to its impact on the overall plan. Somerset was profoundly impressed at the depth of understanding offered by the two sergeants making the report. With most of the report concluded, Major Somerset then posed specific questions regarding the economic development issues discussed in theory. "Exactly what sort of economic project are you suggesting in this particular area?" Somerset asked.

Roberts responded, "Sir, Sergeant McMillan and I noticed a number of indigenous plants in these mountain and determined to capitalize on them. For example, coffee trees and cashew trees are prolific in this climate. While the local people have used these crops as a part of their barter system, their true market value is far beyond a few pence a kilo. Sergeant McMillan and I have identified a German merchant in Rangoon who is willing to buy all of the cashew nuts and coffee beans we can produce for a price one hundred times that of what the people were receiving in local markets. In order to make this work, we have established a regional cooperative whereby all beans and nuts are sold collectively. This means one price for all growers. It also eliminates middlemen and cheats."

McMillan went on to add, "Members of the cooperative have further agreed to tax themselves ten percent on all proceeds. This money will go toward building schools, clinics, and roads."

Somerset was elated at the report. Silently, he considered what the High Command would say after reports were sent regarding these developments. After all, this region was under his command and area of responsibility.

"Now," Major Somerset said, "tell me about this conclave you mentioned. I didn't notice any significant assemblies in the village. What has happened with the meetings?"

Roberts spoke. "It's like this, Major; these people like to consider themselves 'spirit led.' Rather than hold large meetings with one speaker after another trying to make his point, the delegates prefer to discuss and pray about issues in small groups of two and three men. If there is disagreement or conflict, it is discussed. Once agreement or understanding is achieved, they move on to another issue. From time-to-time, several groups will assemble to discuss their conclusions. For those who have a contrary opinion, they move off to another group with the same opinion. From early morning to late at night, you will find small groups of men, walking in the hills, sitting by a stream, or simply lounging on a bamboo mat discussing singular issues to be considered later in larger assembly. There is no arguing or offensive language, only polite reasoning. Every issue is discussed in terms of the immediate and eventual consequences on their people and the culture. I only wish our government would operate in the same way."

McMillan added, "Every few days, the senior elders will call for a consensus on a given issue. Eventually, all issues will be addressed and, for the most part, everyone will be happy with the outcome. Those who are not happy with the outcome of a particular item will sit quietly and say nothing more if they are in the minority.

It has been agreed that when the conclave has concluded, the elders should return to their respective villages and then travel to Rangoon and meet with British officials regarding the formal implementation of the plan. Major, these people are taking this issue very seriously indeed."

Major Somerset asked, "What will happen when the Buddhist and the Mohammedans get wind of this little plan?"

Roberts answered, "Sir, we strongly suspect they will not be happy, not happy at all."

Somerset continued, "Has Colonel Ballentine made any provision for a possible negative reaction from the Buddhist and Mohammedan sectors?"

Somerset said, "Perhaps we need to consider some sort of concessions for that sector as well. I would suggest that this Ballentine Doctrine be amended to include a number of concessions for the Buddhists and Mohammedans."

McMillan spoke, "Sir, if we were to ask the Buddhist and Mohammedan leaders for a list of concessions that could take years."

Somerset smiled, "Exactly!" McMillan and Roberts smiled at each other, realizing the wisdom of Major Somerset's comment.

The meeting was interrupted by a messenger from Chittagong. The courier had ridden his horse at fast gallop to arrive at the Baum village before nightfall. He snapped to attention and handed Major Somerset an envelope. Somerset opened the envelope, read the telegram inside and smiled broadly. "Gentlemen, I have just received word that I have been promoted to the rank of Lieutenant Colonel and been transferred to Rangoon to take command of that billet. It looks like our friend, Colonel Ballentine, has been transferred to Ceylon. Hmm."

Both Roberts and McMillan congratulated Somerset profusely. Roberts stepped aside and called over to a Baum villager, "Please go and fetch Elder Simon. I have good news to tell him."

Within minutes the villager was back with Elder Simon. The news of Somerset's promotion was relayed to Elder Simon who immediately ordered preparation for yet another feast of celebration.

Somerset went back to reading the telegram messages. He spoke, "It appears that I am to oversee the preliminary discussion for what the High Command calls, the Victorian Doctrine. Details to follow.

Roberts spoke up. "Sounds as if the Ballentine Doctrine was not to the High Command's liking. The Victorian Doctrine sounds a bit more in keeping with government's thinking."

Lieutenant Colonel Somerset then asked, "How much do you suppose Sergeant Major St. John had to do with this turn of events?"

Roberts replied, "Most, if not all of it."

Somerset smiled at the response. "I suspect you might be correct, Sergeant Roberts. Oh, by the way, I will have both of you transferred to my new command in Rangoon. You appear to have earned the confidence of the locals. That will be a significant asset in our further discussions." Roberts requested permission to speak freely and it was granted. He suggested that both he and McMillan be assigned as technical advisors to the tribal groups in the Banderban Hills. This would allow for more first hand implementation of the program once it had been confirmed.

Somerset thought for a moment, "Good thought! Good thought indeed!"

Elder Simon saw the significance of Somerset's promotion as it related to the overall pacification of Burma and his people. He was fully aware that the relationship between his people and the British Empire would be directly impacted by how the two parties got along. In light of the contrary attitudes of the Buddhists and the Mohammedans, the British needed all the friends they could find. This was an opportunity to build a personal bridge between themselves and the British regional commander.

A feast, complete with the drums and songs, went on well into the early morning. The remaining pigs, chickens, and goats were butchered and roasted. Virtually every jar of jungle berry juice was consumed by even the most temperance-minded member of the conclave. Toasts were made to every royal personality of the British Empire. Lieutenant Colonel Winston J. Somerset was toasted by every clan leader in the group. Dancers and singers kept the valley alive with music and motion as the copious platters of rice, fruit, and meat were consumed. Somerset's small host of soldiers was warmly included in the evening's events. There was no question but that a wonderful time was being had by all. Elder Simon was convinced that a sincere relationship now existed between his people and their new overseer, Lieutenant Colonel Somerset.

The following morning, the pounding of the drums had given way to the pounding in many British heads. Somerset ordered the bugler to stand down and allow for morning to come without the benefit of the infernal brass horn. By mid- morning most members of the British contingent were able to stand erect without leaning too heavily on their rifles.

Lt. Col. Somerset sent Sergeant Roberts to Elder Simon indicating that he would appreciate meeting with representatives of the members of the conclave to get an update on their deliberations. Elder Simon obliged and set a time of high noon.

The meeting was cordial and comfortable. There seemed to be no serious points of contention or controversy. Somerset asked many questions which were answered with clear meaning. Without specific instructions from his superiors, Somerset could not affirm any points nor make any commitments on behalf of the British government. It was his intention to simply gain an understanding of the business which had transpired under his nose, but without his knowledge. He liked what he had heard. The concept seemed to be in full accord with the best intentions of both the captors and the captives.

As the meeting began to draw to a conclusion, Somerset then asked the critical question, "What will happen when the Buddhists and the Mohammedans get wind of this plan?"

A cold wind seemed to descend on the meeting with the speaking of that question. Elder Simon spoke for the group. "Sir, we strongly suspect there will be problems. Our brothers, the Buddhists and Mohammedans, will not support any efforts to comply with or encourage British rule and domination of Burma. With these people it is not only a political conquest, but a religious conquest. With the Christian tribes, we at least have a common faith in a common God. But I would say this, Colonel Somerset, if we can demonstrate the advantages of this Victorian Doctrine to the opposition, they may eventually realize the benefits of full cooperation and the futility of continued opposition. If they see schools and clinics in Christian regions, they may wish to have schools and clinics in their communities as well. Likewise, economic development is something every man wants to see and prosper from. They must be made to realize that they surrender none of their religious tenets in order to enter into a reasonable relationship with the British government. They have nothing to lose and much to gain."

Lt. Col. Somerset saw the wisdom in this man's words and acknowledged his comments.

One of the other elders raised his hand and asked to speak. "Lieutenant Colonel Somerset, Elder Simon, Brothers in Christ, might I suggest that we invite the leaders of the main Buddhist and Mohammedan groups to our meeting in Rangoon. In this manner, we can present our concepts directly to them. Any opposition can be discussed in direct confrontation. This would allow for clarity of intent and avoidance of confusion and misinterpretation. In an open meeting, any opposition could be noted and acknowledged. On the other hand, if we were to hold a closed meeting, the opposition would create false rumors and ferment falsehoods."

Lt. Colonel Somerset nodded in agreement. "Gentlemen, at this point in time, I am unaware of the full intent of my government and must therefore defer comment on your recommendation. However, I would state that I concur with your reason and will attempt to implement your suggestion at the highest levels. I must, however, add that my government does not intend to rule by consent of the people. It is our mandate that rule is to be carried out by edict of the Monarch and intent of her government. If, however, we are able to rule with the humble cooperation of the people, so much the better for all concerned. Confirmation to British rule will be met with benevolence; contradiction will be met with force."

Somerset's comments were taken seriously by all present. He again thanked the elders for their efforts to bring a working peace between his people and theirs. He then took great effort to greet and shake the hands of each and every delegate to the conclave. Personal comments were passed back and forth between Somerset and the elders. The sincerity was felt by all.

The following morning, Lt. Col. Somerset and his party left the Banderban Hills. Roberts and McMillan remained behind for another week. For the next few days, members of the conclave began moving off toward their respective villages. Elder Simon drafted a telegram to his son, Bua Tan Bo. The men who had been trained to use the heliograph sent the message to the Chittagong Barracks and then on the telegraph office. The telegram read:

The conclave has concluded. All points were considered and agree to. Lt. Col. Winston J. Somerset will be hosting another meeting next month in Rangoon to officially ratify and define the agreement. I wish you to return home in order that you might represent our interests. I would expect Supi Yaw Lat to accompany you home. Our prayers are with you both.
Warmest regards,
Father

~

CHAPTER FORTY-FOUR

LONDON

The meeting with the Archbishop of Canterbury had been set, canceled and reset. As Bua's coach passed the magnificent Westminster Cathedral, he couldn't help but notice the cold, unfriendly stature of the building dedicated to God by his created beings. It seemed more like a palace in which an earthly ruler might reside and not the humble dwelling of the Christ of the New Testament. Bua Tan Bo was greeted by the Archbishop's secretary at the rear entry of the great Westminster Cathedral. While he was exactly on time and dressed in a fashionable dark suit, a dozen or so other clerics, fully attired in their clerical costumes were seated on "thrones" situated around a thick wooden table in an oak-paneled meeting room. The stained-glass windows cast an eerie light and blended into the smoke from dozens of wax candles. The room smelled of moth balls and camphor. In the distance an organ practice could be heard. For a moment, Bua considered the beauty of his village drums and the friendly chanting of the village women. These sights, sounds, and smells were foreign and most uncomfortable to him.

The Archbishop acknowledged Bua Tan Bo as an emissary from the "brothers and sisters in Christ from the far reaches of Imperial Burma." Immediately, Bua realized that he was in the wrong place at the wrong time. These men were not servants of Jesus the Christ but rather servants of the Church of England and ultimately, it's Queen.

The Archbishop politely offered Bua a chair at one end of the long wooden table. With all the piety he could muster, the Archbishop made formal introduction of the ancient men sitting on their thrones around the table. Each introduction included lofty and regal titles; "the Most Reverend So-And –So, Bishop of Such-And-Such." Then there were several "unrobed" individual from various mission societies. Those men carried titles such as "Sir" and "Lord." If ever there were a force of complete intimidation, this was it. Bua Tan Bo was a simple mountain man, educated well beyond his station. He did not even carry the title of tribal elder much less a title issued by the church. He was not so much intimidated as he was insulted. These men were more like associates of Christ than servants of Christ.

With the introductions completed, the Archbishop announced that Her Imperial Majesty, Queen Victoria had mandated a meeting between Bua Tan Bo and the "administration of the Church and its agencies." "Well, Mr. Bua Tan Bo, how can we serve you and our brothers and sisters in Burma?"

Bua tried to conceal his consternation by taking a sip of water from a crystal water glass in front of him. "Gentlemen," he began, "my mission in this instance is to bring to light the condition and plight of the Christian community in the country of Burma. As you well know, there exist numerous tribal groups which for several generations have embraced the Gospel of Jesus Christ and the entire content of the Holy Bible. I do not pretend to represent the members of these tribal groups, but will attempt to express certain of their mutual and combined concerns to this esteemed group of clerics and men of authority."

It was apparent that this little man's words and presentation impressed those sitting around the table. His command of the English language and the formation of his thoughts impressed them as a man to be seriously considered. For over an hour, Bua Tan Bo presented a verbal image of the living conditions of those calling themselves Christians. He particularly noted the desire for and the lack of formal education among the Christian communities. He likewise made note of the need for and the lack of medical facilities, agricultural programs, and so on. He subtly noted that the Buddhist and Mohammedan communities were not particularly interested in outside educational programs or "foreign influences."

One of the men sitting around the table then asked a question. "Sir, do we not currently send clerics to your region?"

Bua replied, "Sir, with all due respect, you do send vicars and a few missionaries. However, most of these men are in service to the British colonists in the major cities and towns. Very few, if any missionaries find their way into the hinterlands. I would add that most of the English churches actually discourage natives to participate in the regular church programs. Native Christians are encouraged to sit outside the church, near open windows on a Sunday morning or simply hold services in their own "special way."

Those sitting around the table acknowledged this unfortunate fact with a glance sideways or across the table. Rather than dispute Bua's comments, another cleric commented.

"Sir, would you suggest that we compel natives to sit among the British, thus making both natives and British uncomfortable during their time of worship?"

Bua felt the sting of this comment. "No sir, I realize that there is a place for the British and a place for the Burmese People, and sometimes that place is not the same place. I would, however, like to suggest that credible churches, complete with ordained clergy be arranged for Burmese people and that services be sanctioned under the authority of the Church."

Again there were side glances, raised eyebrows, and an occasional whisper. Bua continued, "If the current situation is left as it is, I fear that other denominations from other foreign influences will fill the void. I am told that in the eastern regions of Burma, several American denominations have already 'planted' churches and persuaded converts to follow a more liberal form of Christianity."

He knew that the mention of foreign mission agencies would strike fear in the heart of every man in the room and it did! The Archbishop spoke, "Tell me Mr. Bua Tan Bo, who are some of these foreign elements who dare to enter into our sheep fold?"

Bua realized he had struck a nerve. "Well to begin with, there are the French Catholics who visit from Indochina. Then there are the Baptists who find their way in from Siam. Each group brings with it incentives such as medical supplies, garden tools, and books. I would add that there are some villages where a headman is actually ordained after only a few days of ecclesiastical instruction."

That comment brought gasps and expressions of outrage from the ancients sitting around the table.

"Now," Bua continued, "if this situation is left unabated, the Church of England will gradually find itself without a single Burmese parishioner. They will have all sworn allegiance to the French and the Americans!" Bua emphasized this thought with a fist slammed down on the oak table. This thought of religious insurgency stirred the urgency of these men to chat among themselves for a few minutes. Bua thought to himself that it was truly unfortunate that the thought of foreign interference in their ecclesiastical sheep pen prompted these holy men to act when the true cause of the Gospel had been totally set aside.

One Bishop barked out, "Damn the Americans and their apostate church!"

Another added, "And damn the French with their Pope-kissing priests!"

Bua smiled silently as the holy men vented their contempt for their opponents in the business of soul saving.

After another hour of discussion, Bua had a list of concessions and programs which would be considered by the Church of England and its affiliated agencies. Bua felt good in a bad way. He realized that he had used trickery and human weakness to gain an advantage. The true cause of Christ and His ministry had become secondary to the political whims of these silly men. He consoled himself by saying, "*All things work together for good to them that love God.*" Perhaps in spite of the misguided intentions of these high holy men, the Gospel would find its way through the projects and programs of contrived and political generosity.

∾

CHAPTER FORTY-FIVE

Bua returned to the barracks where he spent the remaining hours of the day making notes on his meeting.

An hour after Bua Tan Bo had departed the barracks for his meeting with the Archbishop of Canterbury, Michael, still reading his copy of the TIMES and sipping his tea, was summoned to General Wallace's office. The note was neither polite nor was it cordial:

Your immediate presence is required at the office of General Wallace.

Signed, General W.C.R. Wallace

Sergeant Major Michael St. John acknowledged the courier who had brought the note and indicated that he would change into a dress uniform and return within five minutes. The courier waited as Michael changed.

Twenty minutes later, Sergeant Major St. John was ushered into General Wallace's office. This time there was not hand shaking, no glass of brandy, and no familiar chit-chat.

Wallace looked up from his papers and spoke. "Sergeant Major St. John, we have a problem. Wallace slapped down a copy of the TIMES OF LONDON on his desk. The photo showing St. John, Supi Yaw Lat, Bua Tan Bo and the American ambassador was face up. St. John's blood froze. He remained at attention and said nothing.

Wallace continued, "It says here that the American government offered certain concessions and scholarships to certain of Her Majesty's subjects. It also indicated that the United States government suggests possible involvement in certain educational and developmental programs within the context of Burma."

Again, St. John remained at attention and utterly silent. He knew full well that any comment on his part would only serve to worsen the situation. Wallace went on. "Sergeant Major St. John, these are not necessarily my thoughts, but opinions from high-ranking members of Her Majesty's Government who have indicated that they are not at all pleased by this infringement of American generosity into one of Great Britain's areas of responsibility. As we discussed in our briefing prior to the luncheon with the American ambassador, they are looking for opportunities to invest resources into numerous areas of Southeast Asia. Burma is and shall remain within the confines of the British Empire and not the American Empire. Is that clearly understood?"

At last St. John spoke. "Yes, General, it is clearly understood."

Wallace sat down, "Sergeant Major St. John, now that that nasty bit of business has been officially taken care of, let's you and I discuss what actually transpired during that infamous encounter with our misguided cousins, the Americans." Wallace continued, "Please Sergeant Major, take a seat. Sorry for the tongue lashing, but when the politicians get their knickers in a knot, someone has to bear the lashing. Unfortunately, it was you. Now then, off the record, take me through the events of the day with the ambassador."

For the next hour St. John, still stinging from the chastisement, presented every subject, every passive suggestion, and every direct inference to American participation in Burma's internal affairs. St. John was firm to note that every offer made to Bua, Supi Yaw, or himself was met with a deferral to consider rather than an open acceptance. There were no deals made, no loyalties exchanged, no promises promised. St. John made quite certain to note that the business with the photographer was a complete surprise and done without prior permission. It was simply one of those things which happened in complete innocence and without consideration of consequence."

Wallace replied, "I suspected as much. I know you well enough to realize that you would never compromise your position to benefit the Yanks. Bloody Yanks!

One more thing, the article mentions that the ambassador offered your friend Supi Yaw Lat a scholarship to an American medical school. This was, of course, meant to slam our medical system for not allowing women to become doctors. Did you sense any possible acceptance of this offer on the part of your lady friend?"

St. John was slightly offended at Wallace's reference to Supi Yaw Lat as "his lady friend." "I really can't say, General. Supi Yaw Lat is fully qualified to sit for the physician's exam and once having passed it, to perform the duties of a fully accredited doctor. Because of the traditional British thinking of most in positions of authority, a woman is not welcome in the world of medicine, no matter how well qualified. It seems to be a travesty that someone qualified to heal and save lives should be prevented simply because of her gender. Take, for example, the American sea captain. There is little question that he would now be floating at the bottom of the sea stitched in his hammock, had it not been for Supi Yaw and her knowledge of medicine. How many more people could be saved from unnecessary suffering and death if we had more physicians, even female physicians?"

Wallace replied, "Quite right, but you know how things are these days?"

It was now St. John who uttered, "Hmm."

With the perfunctory flogging complete and the friendly chat between friends out of the way, Wallace turned the conversation to St. John's future.

"So, Sergeant Major, now that we have that unpleasantness out of the way, let's get on with your career. Several members of the general staff have suggested that you remain here in London for a few months and assist our efforts in recruiting for the army. With your recent notoriety, young English lads would flock to hear of your exploits in the military. Then perhaps after a few months, we could send you back to Burma or somewhere else to your liking. What do you think about that?"

While this "suggestion" was more in the form of an informal order, Michael simply said, "I shall give it some thought." Michael was in no frame of mind to either debate the idea or to accept it. He was not all pleased by the way he had been lauded one minute and condemned the next by situations not of his doing. Michael simply wanted to be alone, with his new friend Gunga.

∾

CHAPTER FORTY-SIX

After being dismissed by General Wallace, he returned to the barracks. He located Gunga in the kitchen with Amerjit who had filled a bowl with cream and placed it on the floor. Gunga's happy face was deep in the cream with his stubbed tail wagging frantically from side to side.

Amerjit could clearly see that Sergeant Major St. John was not happy. He did, however, smile at seeing his dog pushing the bowl around the kitchen floor. "Sir," Amerjit said, "I am told by your friend, Mr. Bua, that you are a master chess player."

St. John looked slightly shocked. "I play chess but I am by no means a master."

Amerjit replied, "Sir, I have a chess board in my closet, and I would be honored to match wits with you over a friendly game. And too, I can make a pot of 'Indian tea' which you seemed to appreciate in our excursion into the Indian neighborhood." Amerjit looked at St. John hoping to see a change in his countenance.

A smile crossed his face. "You are on! But I must warn you. I do fall asleep on occasion during a chess game."

Amerjit was delighted. Seeing that Gunga had emptied the bowl of cream and was now begging for attention, Amerjit went to a pantry, found a large ham hock bone and tossed to Gunga. "This should keep him busy for a time," Amerjit said.

An hour into the third chess game was enough to clear the clouds from Michael's mind. The several cups of strong, heavily spiced Indian tea seemed to clear the clog in his bloodstream.

Amerjit noticed the clock on the wall and excused himself. "Sorry sir, I must begin preparing the evening meal. Tonight it will be kidney pie and turnips." Michael winced at the thought.

Michael put Gunga on a leash and took him for a brief walk outside before going to his room. For the next hour or so, he lay on his bed reflecting on the events of the day and of the past few months. He then focused his thoughts on his future. General Wallace's "suggestions" that he remain in England and promote recruitment did not feel good in any way. The thought of another posting was also uncomfortable. Even though Burma was wrought with every conceivable discomfort known to man, he was comfortable with those discomforts. He also gave serious consideration to Supi Yaw. His fondness had grown far beyond that of a friend and well into the foggy realm of true affection. He could not bring himself to use the word "love," but he knew that was the true emotion here and none else. He again wrestled with the thought of marriage, but convinced himself that her marriage to him would bring her down to an unacceptable station. And, he a career soldier would not have the time or resources to truly satisfy a wife of Supi Yaw's quality. The thought of letting her go and possibly finding another husband also plagued his mind. "*She is much too wonderful to allow just any man to take her. Perhaps she could find her way into British society in Rangoon.*" He thought, "*No, she would always be considered a 'native woman' no matter how well educated and cultured. She would always be considered second class. This would not do. She was far better than most of the simple-headed British women who make up polite society in Rangoon and other colonial enclaves."*

The thoughts were rudely interrupted by the gentle knock on the door. "Dinner is served."

Both Bua and Supi Yaw were already at table when Michael entered the room. The expressions on each of their faces were unanimous. Small grey clouds seem to float over each head as Michael sat down. Several other junior officers were seated at two other tables in the dining room. "Well, let's have it," Michael said. "It seems there are issues afoot."

Bua was first to tell of his meeting with the Archbishop and his gaggle of clerics. Michael seemed pleased with the apparent concessions discussed in the meeting. He too was disturbed, though, by the lack of Christian concern for the spiritual welfare of the Burmese People.

Then Supi Yaw voiced her frustration with the prevailing attitude about women entering into the medical profession. She mentioned one conversation she had had with a local medical profession where he suggested that she become a nursing sister and be done with her aspirations to become a doctor. She was absolutely furious at the thought of becoming a nurse. "How dare he?" she uttered with the utmost contempt. "A nurse!"

It was now Michael's turn to regurgitate the full content of his meeting with General Wallace. Both Bua and Supi Yaw were openly sympathetic with Michael as he related his ordeal. They too expressed exasperation with the High Command's "recommendation" that Michael become a recruiting symbol for the military. After all, he was referred to as being, "a soldier's soldier" not a recruiting image.

It was Bua who uttered, "I am appalled at the shallowness of their depth."

Michael replied, "Actually, I am appalled at the depth of their shallowness."

Realizing the truth in these comments, all three laughed aloud so that those at the two other tables looked over to see what was happening.

Supi Yaw then added, "The depth of their shallowness and the shallowness of their depth." They continued to laugh at the true irony of these words.

After tea had been served, Michael suggested that he should take Gunga for a walk. He invited both Bua and Supi Yaw to join him. Bua saw the need for Michael and Supi Yaw to be alone and declined. Michael said, "Bua, you certainly can't allow your sister to go out alone with a rascal like me."

Bua replied, "I have instructed Gunga to take off your leg if you should get out of line with my sister. And don't forget, she does take off legs as well!"

The three laughed at the unfortunate joke.

The London night air was cold and damp. The smells of the night were smoky and musty. It was not a pleasant place compared to the Banderban Hills that is. The small English Bulldog tugged at the leash and stopped at virtually every light post along the sidewalk. With the exception of comments about the weather, the smells, and the dog, very little was said between Michael St. John and Supi Yaw. Supi Yaw spotted a park bench and suggested they sit a while. Michael took out a handkerchief and dusted off the bench before Supi Yaw could sit.

"Michael, Bua and I didn't want to tell you until tomorrow, but we have news from father. The conclave has concluded successfully and will reconvene in Rangoon in two months for ratification. Father wants Bua to be there. He also asks that I not remain alone here in London. I must therefore return with my brother." These words seemed to empty Michael's blood from every vein. He felt as if he had been hit in the belly with a very firm fist. Michael opened his mouth to speak but no word came. For the first time, Supi Yaw placed her hand on Michael's hand. The terrifying empty feeling was immediately replaced by a surge of warmth and excitement. This was the first overt expression of affection expressed by either since they first met in the "Valley of the Pigs."

At long last, Michael found the words, "Supi Yaw, I think you know how much I respect and admire you both as a physician and as a woman. While I do not know what it means to love other than to love my country and my meager estate in life, I truly believe that I am deeply in love with you."

Supi Yaw moved closer to Michael and put her head on his shoulder. At this, Michael became almost totally incoherent. His mind and his mouth could not seem to connect with one another. Words and feelings seemed to collide in his chest and his head before they could find their way to his mouth. Supi Yaw began to laugh at his consternation.

"Oh Michael, you are no different than any other man, and I am no different than any other woman. We are made of the same cloth as our parents and their parents. Just because you are a rough and tumble soldier, barking orders all day, and I pretend to be some sort of magic healer, doesn't mean that we are simply made from the same clay as all others on this planet. I was attracted to you the very minute I saw you in the Prince's camp. I was also aware that any formal or informal relationship between us would lead to your condemnation for having taken up with a native woman. I know what they say about British soldiers and colonials who take native women as wives or mistresses. You are branded a leper and excommunicated from your society. Likewise, I would be considered an outcast for taking up with a Brit. Michael, I love you much too much to allow this to happen to a true hero of the realm. You might not agree to this now, but in years to come, you will see the wisdom in my feelings. Respect is the highest form of love. You told me this yourself. We must respect our stations if this life and do what we must do. I will forever hold you in the highest respect in my heart, and I trust that you will do the same of me. Unless things change drastically, I see no other way."

Michael thoughts circled and collided like confused and frightened birds caught in a fowler's net. He felt utter disgust for the social rules which prevented men and women from doing what men and women want to do. He was angry that he was compelled to remain in London to play soldier and entice others to join his fraternity. He felt enormous loss at the thought of Supi Yaw, his beautiful Supi Yaw going back to Burma.

Finally, Michael was able to focus on one thought. "Supi Yaw, will you do me a favor? Please take Gunga back to Rangoon with you. If nothing else, he will remind you of me from time-to-time. It will also give me a reason to come back to collect him."

Supi Yaw realized the enormity of the gesture and kissed Michael on the cheek. Michael could not speak. He was totally paralyzed with a warm beautiful emotion. Never in his life had he been kissed by a woman other than his mother. It was a feeling like none other – ever.

Supi Yaw spoke, "Michael, I think we had better be getting back. Gunga might decide to bite off your leg any minute now."

The walk back to the barracks was like a dream. Supi Yaw had taken Michael's arm as if they were husband and wife out for an evening walk. As they entered the barracks compound, Bua looked out the window and saw his sister and his friend, arm-in-arm with a small dog in a leash. *"How wonderful!"* he thought to himself.

The following morning breakfast was served as usual. Michael came to the table looking like he had floated down the hallway. Supi Yaw had on one of her most beautiful Indian style saris. Bua spoke, "Michael, my sister has informed you that we must be leaving London as soon as possible for Rangoon. With things progressing as well as they seem to be on both ends of this issue, we can't allow time to erode the progress we have made. I would like to ask that you attempt to contact General Wallace and obtain first-hand documents which I might hand carry to the general meeting. I would ask that they issue a formal document of intent and issues of consideration. This would serve to give them direct voice in the discussions. Then, after all is said and done, all memos and documents would be sent back to London for final approval. I see in this morning's TIMES that a passenger ship will be leaving for Rangoon the day after tomorrow. Supi Yaw and I will book passage on that ship. Hopefully, you will soon follow." Michael smiled at the comment about "soon following."

"I will make every attempt to see General Wallace today. I am afraid that I will also be compelled to give him a positive response to his 'suggestion' that I spend a few months working on a recruiting campaign here in London. Then," looking directly at Supi Yaw, he added, "I promise you I shall come to collect my dog." Supi Yaw responded with a warm glowing smile.

Michael was given a brief appointment with General Wallace who agreed to have a list of documents ready by the following day. Wallace also informed St. John of the decision that Lieutenant Colonel Winston Somerset had been put in command of the Rangoon billet. St. John was pleased. As if exchanging one favor for another, Wallace then asked if St. John had agreed to participate in a military recruitment campaign.

"Yes General, I think it might enjoyable for a month or two. Let's give it a try. After all, I do owe my Queen and country a debt for this little expression of their gratitude," he said, pointing to the little red ribbon and medal on his chest.

CHAPTER FORTY-SEVEN

Two of the Queen's carriages transported Bua Tan Bo, Supi Yaw and Michael to the London docks. One carriage was piled high with boxes and cartons filled with books, medical supplies and presents for family members back home. The small English Bulldog sat on Michael's lap, leaving large quantities of dog hair stuck to his trousers. Porters carried the boxes and suitcases aboard the waiting ship as Michael bid farewell to his friend and his lovely Supi Yaw. As Michael transferred Gunga from his arms to Supi Yaw's, they exchanged a brief embrace. "You take good care of my dog. After all, he was a gift from the Queen."

Bua and Supi Yaw boarded the ship and within minutes, the ship had loosed its moorings and slipped away. In the distance Michael could see Supi Yaw gently kiss the squirming little pup in her arms, as if to say, "This one is for you, Michael."

The journey back to the barracks was cold and empty. There was an ache he had never felt before. He looked over at the medal on his chest. "*So much to do about nothing,*" he thought. *"All this silliness for one little piece of ribbon and gun metal."*

Arriving back at the barracks, he spotted Amerjit coming out of the dining room. Amerjit sensed Michael's mood and simply nodded. "Amerjit," Michael said, "what do you say that you and I sneak out after hours and get a little Indian curry and a mug or two of ale?"

"Sir, the curry sounds appetizing but I must humbly decline the ale. My religion forbids me to indulge in spirits of any kind."

Michael said, "Ten o'clock, Amerjit. And bring your chess board. We are going to play for blood this evening."

Amerjit replied, "For blood? Oh my goodness gracious. This sounds serious."

"As serious as it gets, my friend. As serious as it gets!" Michael said as he disappeared down the hall toward his quarters. In all his life, Michael had never been alone until now. As a soldier, there were always other soldiers. Here in the junior officers' barracks, he could not find a single man who had ever spent a day in battle or on a march or even in a barroom brawl. The best he could do was an Indian cook who played a good game of chess and knew the whereabouts of exotic Indian eateries in this God-forsaken place called London.

It required three members of the London constabulary and Amerjit to put Sergeant Major Michael St. John to bed at five-thirty the following morning. While the constables were fully aware of their charge's identity and notoriety, they were not happy with his frequent reference to Queen Victoria as his old buddy "Queen Vicki." The dozen or so pints of ale had loosened his tongue and scrambled his reason to where he no longer felt the pain of watching Supi Yaw disappear down the Thames. Within minutes of resigning himself to bed, Michael found himself on his knees head down in his porcelain water basin. He was now examining the copious amounts of curry and rice, mixed with the dozen or so pints of ale he had consumed over the past few hours. While his stomach seemed a bit relieved, his head pounded beyond belief. After several hours of in and out sleep, there came a gentle knocking on the door. Without needing an answer, Amerjit opened the door, holding a silver tray of tea and other items.

"And that, sir, is one of the many reasons my religion does not approve of taking strong drink," Amerjit said as he placed the tray on the small dressing table. "I have a few herbs and potions which should serve to relieve the pain in your head and the queasiness in your tummy." A cup of some sort of purple tea, a raw egg, and several pieces of dry bread were placed before Michael. "Please, sir, eat. You will feel much better if you do and much worse if you don't," Amerjit pleaded.

"Amerjit, I will consume this manna on one condition."

"Yes sir, anything you wish, sir," Amerjit replied.

"Amerjit, fetch me one of those silly turbans you wear doused in cold water. I will for a brief moment pretend that I too am a Sikh."

Amerjit dashed from the room, found a lengthy table cloth, doused it in water and returned. He proceeded to wrap the table cloth round and round Michael's aching head. "There, sir, you truly resemble one of our maharajas. All that is missing is a jewel between the eyes."

Michael laughed and felt the pain subside slightly. Michael thought to himself, "*No, all that is missing is my Supi Yaw, and no raw egg or herbal potion can take away the pain of that loss.*"

By noon, Michael was able leave his room without fear of vomiting on some junior officer's shiny boots. "God bless that Amerjit and his potions," Michael uttered on several occasions. "Just like my old friend Gunga Din; always there when you needed him."

Another courier interrupted the after-lunch tea. A dispatch from General Wallace indicated the calendar of events for the forthcoming recruiting campaign. Michael read the four pages of times, places, and events where Sergeant Major Michael St. John, Hero of the Irrawaddy, was to appear. On some days there were three and four events! On Sundays, Michael was to attend various churches in and around London. He checked to see if his brother's church was on the list. It was not. To add insult to injury, he was assigned to a newly commissioned junior grade lieutenant. Just the thought of this twenty-three year old son of an aristocrat left him feeling ill. Michael again regarded the list of events to see when the first public viewing of the "Hero of the Irrawaddy" was to take place. Tomorrow, ten o'clock. As the thought of the event began to sink in, a slight shadow moved over Sergeant Major St. John. It was that of Sub-Lieutenant William Victor Page, son of the Earl of Something-or-Another. Sub-Lieutenant Page clad in his unit's finest dress uniform stood at the end of the dining table where Michael was pretending not to notice the very junior officer. Page cleared his throat and raised his eyebrow, suggesting that Sergeant Major St. John needed to stand at attention and offer a proper salute to a fully commissioned officer of Her Majesty's Welsh Guards. Michael slowly rose to his feet and made a weighted but nonetheless proper salute to his superior officer. The young pup in all his finery returned the salute and instructed Sergeant Major St. John to "stand at ease." This was the ultimate insult to an old and seasoned soldier. The pompous young pup smiled politely and spoke, "Well Sergeant Major St. John, it looks as if you and I shall be working together and I shall be your commanding officer for the next few months. With a bit of luck we can encourage a few lads to join our little brotherhood of men-at-arms. I trust you are up for the job."

Sergeant Major St. John replied, “Sir, I am indeed up for the job.”

“Very well Sergeant Major, I have commandeered a coach from my father’s stable to make our travel throughout London a bit more comfortable. I shall have the coach collect you tomorrow morning at eight o’clock. You shall then pass by my residence, and we can be off to our first encounter with the public. I trust you will have prepared a brief speech and perhaps an account of the famous Battle of the Irrawaddy. Until then, good day.” With that, the junior officer placed his feathered hat on his pointy little head and left the room.

Michael plunked down in his chair as if someone had hit him squarely in the stomach. One final violent convulsion of anger, frustration, and remnants of the previous night’s events erupted on to the floor. From the kitchen Amerjit heard the violent sounds and came running. “Oh my goodness gracious, sir, you appear to have vomited,” he said.

Michael could only shake his head and utter, “So it would appear.”

Immediately, Amerjit fetched a bucket and a mop. Michael lumbered back to his quarters and fell face first on the bed.

Somewhere well after dark, Amerjit appeared at Michael’s door with a bowl of split pea soup. “Sir, you need to have something in your stomach. To vomit on an empty stomach is none too pleasant. Please take the soup and perhaps you will feel better.” The bearded Indian man politely left the room, whereupon Michael tasted the warm thick soup. It was welcome. No further vomiting occurred.

In light of tomorrow’s events, Michael began to make notes on what he would say regarding service in Her Majesty’s Military Forces. He considered mentioning the food. Anything he said in favor of military cuisine would be a lie as would positive comments regarding living accommodations, pay, benefits or virtually anything else one could mention. After several hours of trying to invent some sort of encouraging incentives for young men to join up with the military, he was completely without a single thought. For the young sons of aristocratic families, yes, there were many incentives. In fact, for the aristocratic military service was almost mandatory if one ever considered a career in politics or business. But military service as an officer was not even similar to service as an enlisted man. After giving his speech a great deal of thought, he concluded that enlistment was not at all a good thing unless a young man had absolutely no trade or family business. He then focused on the primary driving force of the enlisted soldier; service to his country and Queen regardless of the downside. Honor, duty, tradition, and other noble characteristics soon filled his note paper. Hopefully these same values of the English race would cause hapless lads to sign documents of enlistments and serve Queen and country regardless of the cost to their personal aspirations.

Sleep did not come until early in the morning as Michael attempted to recite his brief speech over and over again.

CHAPTER FORTY-EIGHT

At exactly eight o'clock, after several cups of tea and breakfast cakes, Sub-Lieutenant Page's carriage arrived at the front gate. Sergeant Major St. John dressed in his Burma Police uniform dusted off any remaining crumbs and entered the carriage. Oh, how he wished for a single horse and saddle. An hour later, Page was collected at his officer's quarters on the far side of town. Page was regaled in one of the Welsh Guard's full-dress uniforms. Michael noticed two medals on Page's chest, neither of which he could recognize. At ten o'clock the carriage arrived at a town square near the London docks. A small brass band had been playing and twenty or thirty people had assembled to see, "the Hero of the Irrawaddy." Someone had painted a banner which had been hung across the street reading, "Welcome home Hero of the Irrawaddy."

Sub-Lieutenant William Victor Page was quite eloquent in his introduction of St. John, mentioning his long and faithful service to the Queen. After a painfully long speech regarding the welfare of the empire and its possessions, Page finally introduced St. John. There was mild applause as Sergeant Major St. John recited his comments related to honor, duty, Queen and country. Someone then yelled out, "Tell us about the battle, you know, the Battle of the Irrawaddy."

Michael then went on, like an actor, recalling the distant event. He tried with all his skills to bring the brief encounter with the notorious river pirate Bua Tan Bo to life. In his mind, it was like telling a group of children a fairytale. At the end of the event, there was more mild applause. Several young men came around to ask specific questions regarding enlistment. They seemed genuinely interested. One young man asked about serving in faraway places where the natives speak foreign languages. Michael asked the lad if he wished to spend the rest of his life working as a carter on the London docks, or would he prefer to see what it was like in one of these faraway places. With that, the young man signed enlistment papers on the spot. "Anything is better than this," he said. With that, two more lads signed on.

Sub-Lieutenant Page was ecstatic. Three enlistments in one morning! The following day, there were two events and eight more enlistments. By week's end Page had collected a total of twenty-two British recruits. While Page loved every minute of this duty, St. John hated every second. He felt like an actor, when his true calling was that of a soldier.

With the first month behind him, Michael felt totally numb inside. One afternoon he arrived at the barracks to find a letter from Burma waiting on his door plate. His heart jumped almost out of his mouth. Because Amerjit had placed the letter on the door plate, he made certain that he was standing in the hallway when Michael opened the letter. Michael looked down the hall at Amerjit and said, "What, haven't you ever seen a letter before?"

"Not one from Burma," Amerjit replied with a broad smile. "And not one from a beautiful lady friend."

Michael frowned, "You rascal. What do you know of lady friends?"Without opening the door, Michael carefully opened the red wax seal on the envelope. Michael's eyes began to tear.

My Dear Michael.

Out trip home to Burma went without incident. This time there were no American sea captains requiring my services. There were, however, several bouts of seasickness and several cases of food poisoning. Nothing too serious. Both Brother Bua and I spent most of our time reading and digesting our new books and journals. I was thrilled to find so many new advancements in medical science in the past few years. I am more determined than ever to follow my calling to help heal the sick.

Bua has spent many hours writing project proposals for village agriculture programs as well educational programs. I only hope and pray that the church leader with whom he spoke will honor their intentions to fulfill Bua's dreams.

Next week Father will travel to Rangoon for the preliminary meetings with the new regional commanding officer, Lieutenant Colonel Somerset. Both Bua and I met Colonel Somerset and find him extremely agreeable. He did ask Bua if you had anything to do with his promotions and reassignment. Bua, of course, said that you did. Michael, you have a friend for life. On the other hand, Colonel Ballentine is reported to be quite unhappy with you. He blames you for renaming 'his Ballentine Doctrine.' Oh well, he is now in Ceylon and poses no problems.

Michael, the only one who misses you more than Gunga is me. After our little chat in the park near the barracks, I find myself wondering if my calling to medicine is more selfish than my other instincts. As you know, I am not a religious person, but I have spent hours on my knees asking God for guidance in these matters of the heart. I can only ask that you do the same. There are pains which are caused by natural infirmity and unseen germs. The pain I feel is not one related to either of those causes. My pain is due to a strong sense of loss. I continue in prayer to deal with this pain.

Bua sends his best regards as do I.
Your most respectful friend,
Supi Yaw

Amerjit remained motionless as he watched Michael read and re-read the letter. "My friend, you radiate pain like a kitchen stove radiates heat in the wintertime." Michael simply looked at this bearded friend and forced a smile.

Amerjit, spoke, "Sir, this lady friend of yours; do not lose her." With that, he left Michael standing at his door.

Michael re-read the letter over and over again, trying to visualize Supi Yaw sitting at a candlelit table writing it. He could visualize Gunga sitting at her feet possibly begging for a cup of warm milk. Michael realized he was trapped. Even if he wanted to return to Burma and take Supi Yaw as his wife, he had no money to even buy a house. His income would allow for a few extra coins each month but not nearly enough live a proper life. If he were to remain in England, he would feel like a foreigner; a man without a country. Finally, he considered Supi Yaw's words, "continue to pray." For the first time in many years, Michael found his way to his knees. With his head on his bed, he prayed for a solution to his dilemma. Somewhere in the middle of the night Michael found his way into bed, feeling somewhat better for having laid his issues at the feet of God.

The next morning, as Michael was taking breakfast, Amerjit escorted a large unpleasant-looking man, wearing a clerical collar to his table. "Sir," said Amerjit, "this man has been waiting to see you. He tells me that he has unfortunate news."

The large man extended his hand toward Michael. "Sergeant Major St. John, my name is Bishop Henry Alton. I was your brother's bishop."

"Was?" Michael said.

"Yes, 'was.' It is my unfortunate duty to inform you that your brother Arthur St. John passed away yesterday in his home. I had the privilege of being present with my friend and fellow vicar as he passed." Michael took the news hard. Even though he was not close to his brother, he felt yet another enormous sense of loss.

Michael asked, "Was my brother ill? I saw him only a few weeks ago and he seemed in good health."

"Michael, your brother has suffered from an aliment for many years. Every so often the problem manifests in fainting spells and periods where he must be sent to bed. His housekeeper had the good sense to summon me to his side. This time, he simply went to sleep and passed on," the Bishop said.

Again Amerjit stood back and watched the pain radiate through Michael's being. Seeing the nature of the problem, Amerjit informed Michael that he would tell the coachmen that Sergeant Major St. John has suffered the loss of a family member and humbly begs a brief leave from duty. The coachmen relayed the message on to Sub-Lieutenant Page who cursed quietly at the news.

Bishop Alton suggested that Michael pack a bag and accompany him to his brother's church where the final rights would be conducted and his brother's estate settled.

CHAPTER FORTY-NINE

The ride to the outskirts of London was long and painful. When Michael was not thinking of his brother, he was thinking of Supi Yaw. In both cases, he was not happy.

The Bishop's single-horse carriage arrived at the familiar church. The small stone cottage at the rear wore a black bunting around the door. The Bishop suggested that they first visit the church where Vicar Arthur St. John lay in his small wooden box. Enormous amounts of grief and guilt flooded Michael's soul as he stood looking down on his brother's body. This man was of the same blood and bone as he yet he regarded the dead man as a stranger. The guilt on not loving this little man or attempting to be a part of his life pounded in his mind. "He was my brother, yet I did not know him," he whispered to the Bishop standing next to him. "God forgive me for not loving him as a brother should love a bother."

"Michael, I have many things to tell you about your brother that will bring joy to your heart. Although you two were far apart, he was closer to you than you think." Michael looked at the Bishop and wondered about his comments. "Michael, with your permission, I have scheduled Arthur's funeral for tomorrow morning. I have taken it upon myself to ask several ladies of the parish to prepare an evening meal tonight and a luncheon tomorrow. After we complete the formalities, you and I can get down to some serious business of the estate.

If you are willing, this afternoon we can go through your brother's possessions and determine their disposition. Michael, I think you will be surprised at some of the things your brother has collected."

Michael cleared his mind as best he could. "Bishop, I can't thank you enough for taking charge of this dreadful event. As you know, Arthur and I have no other living relatives and I have no friends in this community to give assistance."

"Come, Michael, let's begin to get to know your dear brother," the Bishop said as he led the way to the cottage. "First of all, Michael, I what to show you where Arthur spent most of his time." The Bishop pulled out boxes of letters, all tied in neat bundles and arranged according to date. "These are letters received from all over the empire. This box contains letters from your parents while they served in India and while he was in seminary. This carton contains letters sent by you from your various postings in Indian and Burma. Those boxes over there contain letters received from British soldiers and sailors from the towns and villages in this part of England. Michael, your brother spent hours each day writing to soldiers and sailors all over the globe. Many, if not most, would reply to his every letter. Over the years he became friends with many of his correspondents. In fact, quite a few paid him a visit upon returning to England for home leave or retirement. Arthur made it well known that he prayed for each and every one of his soldiers and sailors and offered up prayers for their safety during his church services."

Michael picked up the packet of letters he had sent to his brother. The bundle of papers represented an entire lifetime of soldiering in faraway places. Michael had never realized the number of letters he and his brother had exchanged. In Michael's case, he simply discarded a letter after receiving it and replying to it. He never considered saving it for some sort of posterity.

The Bishop took the bundle of letters from Michael's hand and flipped to one particular letter which had been sent from northern India. The letter mentioned the extremely difficult duty of having to participate in the hanging of a young British soldier for the murder of a sleeping comrade in arms. Michael gasped as he relived the writing of that letter just hours after the young man had been cut down. "Michael, your brother located the hometown of this soldier's family somewhere in Wales and personally went to offer his prayers and condolences for the loss of their son. As I recall, his name was Daniel Deever. Poor soul!" Michael turned away as tears began to flow down his face. The Bishop continued, "Michael, each time a report of a soldier or sailor's death was reported in a local newspaper, Arthur would either make a personal visit to the family or at least write a letter of condolence. In spite of the fact he was not fit to serve Queen and country in the military, he nonetheless gave his all for England's fighting men wherever they served."

An enormous sense of pride filled Michael's heart upon hearing about his brother's ministry to soldiers and sailors. Here was a man who truly deserved the gratitude of Queen and country more than he, Michael thought. Michael spoke, "Bishop, I only regret that I did not know my brother better."

"Now, Sergeant Major St. John, I have some good news for you. As a result of your brother's passion for writing, he has managed to collect thousands of postage stamps which you will find in those boxes on the shelf. Both Arthur and I spent many hours cataloging his stamps and mine. On occasion, he and I would travel to meetings of stamp collectors and show off our respective collections. It appears that your brother's collection is quite valuable. In fact, he is in possession of three postage stamps which have unusual value. Now, these items are yours along with a bank balance of several hundred pounds. While this is not a great deal of money, I would suggest that the stamp collection is quite valuable; possibly in the neighborhood of twenty thousand pounds. If you should wish to sell the collection, there is a shop in London which would happily purchase the entire collection; that is unless you would wish to continue the collection."

"No Bishop, I have never been fond of collecting anything. Anything a soldier collects must fit into his travel pack."

A knock on the door announced the arrival of several women carrying covered baskets of stew, buns, and boiled potatoes. A table was set and the two men availed themselves of the meager offerings. After the meal the Bishop suggested that they indulge in a slight glass of Irish whiskey which Andrew kept in a cupboard. Michael, recalling his last bout of intoxication, politely declined and used his recent bout of malaria as his excuse. The Bishop took a full water glass of the amber liquid. "To Arthur, brother and friend." Michael simply nodded in agreement.

The following morning, the church bells announced the funeral services for Vicar Arthur St. John. A goodly number of parishioners and friends arrived to pay their respects and send a godly man on to his reward. After the small wooden box had been properly buried in the English soil, one person after another came to Michael and shook his hand. "Your brother often spoke of you and your exploits in India and Burma," they would say. Others suggested that Arthur's soldier brother was, in fact, his hero. As the last of the mourners left, Bishop

Alton spoke, "Michael, we need to get on to sorting out your brother's things. Being that you are considerably larger than Arthur, I would suggest that his clothes be given to the poor. As for his letters and stamps, they need to be boxed and made ready to move to your quarters. Once again, I would suggest that you consider selling the stamp collection, unless you have other plans. After all, as you yourself said, "A soldier can only collect what he can pack in his travel pack."

As the thought of twenty, or so, thousand pounds in his pocket became more of a reality, his thoughts turned to Supi Yaw. With that amount of money, he could both buy his way out of the military and have sufficient resources to marry. He then recalled his recent prayers asking for a resolution to his quandary. Perhaps this was the answer to those prayers. In spite of the sadness surrounding his brother's death, he realized that this might be his entry into a new life.

By the following day, Michael and the Bishop had boxed the letters, the stamps and a few personal items and placed them at the rear of the carriage. The ride back to London was less strained than the ride to the church.

The Bishop bid Michael farewell and bestowed upon him a formal blessing. "May the Lord God bless your efforts in finding new life in a new place."

CHAPTER FIFTY

Michael took note of these comments; "a new life in a new place?"

Amerjit appeared at the door and assisted Michael in bringing the boxes to his room. Amerjit could see a sense of joy in his friend's face as he removed his tunic and asked for a cup of tea. Michael went to the dresser where he had placed Supi Yaw's letter and again read the wonderful words.

Amerjit returned to the room, knocking before entering with a tray of tea and cakes. "Sir," he said in his way, "there is a note from your Lieutenant."

Michael opened the note and read:

My Dear Sergeant Major St. John,

On behalf of myself and my regiment, I wish to express my sincere condolences on the death of your brother. As your commanding officer, I would like to extend seven days of personal leave in order that you are able to settle all affairs related to this unfortunate event.

Our levels of success have not gone unnoticed by our superiors. It is therefore imperative that you and I continue with our campaign of recruitment as soon as possible.
Warmest regards,
Sub-Lieutenant William Victor Page

Michael was totally repulsed at the thought of any more recruiting circus. The thought of bowing and scraping to any more costumed twenty-something- year-old officers was also repulsive. Something had to change and change fast.

The following morning Michael summoned a carriage and went directly to the address of the stamp shop the Bishop had given him. The little man behind the dimly lit desk immediately recognized the collection. "So, my friend Arthur has passed? I will miss him. He was one of the truest collectors ever."

Michael asked politely as to the value of the collection. The little man suggested that it would take him a day or two to determine a value and then another day or two to find a buyer. The stamp man smiled, "Sir, your bother's collection is well known throughout Europe. There are collectors who would jump at the chance to bid on this collection, particularly these three stamps right here." The three stamps were in wax paper envelopes and labeled "very special."

Michael then asked, "Sir, can you give an approximate value of this collection?"

The stamp man rubbed his balding head and thought for a minute, "I would say somewhere in the neighborhood of thirty thousand pounds." He continued, "If I were to make an open offer and auction the collection, I would be asking a commission of five percent of the total price."

"Done!" said Michael. "Do what you need to do and do it fairly fast. My clock is ticking."

The stamp man smiled at the thought of a large commission. Michael also smiled at the thought of breaking the bonds of his present incarceration. No more a dancing monkey held on a string by Sub-Lieutenant What's-His-Name.

CHAPTER FIFTY-ONE

Hours later, Michael arrived back at the junior officers' barracks and found his few belongings packed and waiting in the kitchen. Amerjit was there to explain that a large contingent of junior officers had just arrived from Egypt and required immediate lodging. It was noted that Sergeant Major St. John was indeed not a junior officer and therefore needed to be relocated to another barracks specifically for senior non-commissioned officers. While this was not totally unexpected, it was yet another slap in the face of a career soldier whose only wish was to serve Queen and country. Amerjit apologized profusely. Michael smiled and patted the shoulder of his Indian friend. "Do not worry, my friend; things are beginning to change. I will keep you informed as to my whereabouts. I will expect our usual game of chess and perhaps a curry dinner from time-to-time."

Michael was driven to his new quarters near the horse stables of the Cold Stream Guards. It was not the smell of horses that he first noticed, but rather the dank frigid air which seemed to hang over the neighborhood like an unseen fog.

Two days later, Sub-Lieutenant Page's carriage driver managed to find Michael's new quarters. Three more days of play acting and trying to collect more enlistments than the previous day. Michael looked at Page as if he were a circus clown holding a monkey on a string. *"Dance monkey, collect more names on my little papers. Bring more pats on my head from my feather-hatted superiors. Perhaps I shall receive yet another medal for my uniform."*

Michael smiled inwardly knowing that this would soon end.

At the end of a particularly taxing day, Michael returned to his barracks to find the stamp man waiting. "Sir, I have extraordinary news. I have sold your brother's stamp collection for a grand sum of forty-two thousand, one hundred and sixty-one pounds. Minus my five percent, that leaves a sum total of . . ."

"Never mind, man, this is fantastic. It is beyond fantastic!" Michael chimed.

The stamp man presented two bank drafts, one for Michael and one for himself. Now, if you will simply sign this document indicating that the sale was satisfactory and that my services were sufficient, I can be off."

Michael was euphoric as he continued to examine his bank draft. This coupled with the one hundred and twenty-two pounds left in his brother's account made him a reasonably wealthy man, by some accounts. He began to figure. It would require several hundred pounds to buy out his enlistment from the military. Then what? He could catch a ship back to Burma, then what? If he should marry Supi Yaw, then what? If he took up residence in Rangoon, he would fall into the social ranks of "Brits gone native." He would not be seen as a proper Englishman nor would he be considered as Burmese. He would be someone in between. He needed a plan.

CHAPTER FIFTY-TWO

The following morning was a Sunday. He was again scheduled to appear in church and "wave the flag" as Page put it. He walked to a church near the London docks near where he had bid farewell to Supi Yaw. After the church service and sufficient "flag waving," he strolled toward the fog-shrouded Thames. The thought of finding one of these ships bound for Burma occupied his thoughts to the point he was ready to desert and catch the first ship to anywhere east of Suez. But he realized that would not be the way to end a distinguished career and particularly a soldier with the Victoria Cross.

As he walked through the streets toward his barracks, he felt the fever coming on him. It was the same fever he had felt each time he was about to be hit by the insidious malaria creatures in his blood. He made it back to the barracks as his eyes began to blur and his head began to ache beyond description. Within an hour, the cold sweats followed by the burning fever shook his body almost to pieces. St. John managed to find his way to his bed before he entered into a painfully muddled state of unconsciousness. Once again, the demons and devils which had plagued him in other malarial attacks returned.

After several painful attempts, he managed to focus on the alarm clock on the small table standing near his bed. At almost the same moment he was able to focus on the face of the clock, he heard the dull thuds of Big Ben in the distance announcing that it was noon in the City of London. For an instant his mind raced back to his last and most-beloved posting, Burma. He reckoned that it was the middle of the night in the small riverside village in the outskirts of Rangoon and that his Supi Yaw, his lovely Supi Yaw Lat, would be in her little bamboo bed, with several joss sticks burning near the door of her bamboo hut. He visualized Gunga, the small English Bulldog, lying across the doorway in order to protect his mistress from intruders or snakes.

The brief reverie was rudely interrupted by a pounding on the wooden door of his non-commissioned officers' barracks room. "Sergeant Major St. John, are you up and about?" a syrupy sweet voice called. "It's time to change your bed linen; and who knows what else!" the stout, pudgy woman at the door whined. Sergeant Major St. John managed to move his bare feet onto the cold, hard slate floor. It required every ounce of strength the ailing soldier could muster to place his suspenders over his aching shoulders and stand reasonably erect. He took a long drink from a glass of stale water and coughed. The mirror across the room confirmed how Sergeant Major Michael Oliver St. John truly felt. Again the pounding and again the voice, "Michael, please open up. We can't be sleeping all day now, can we?" she mewed like a cat in heat.

"No, I guess we can't," the Sergeant Major uttered as he moved toward the protective wooden barrier which kept the world and this bothersome woman out of his temporary sanctuary. He took hold of the cold brass door knob and forced his mouth into a smile. "Good morning, Mrs. O'Brien, and how are you this fine English morning?" he said sarcastically.

"Well, Sergeant Major for one thing, it's no longer morning; you have slept most of the day," she said in a scolding tone.

"Actually, Mrs. O'Brien, I have not been feeling too well these past few days. I believe I have had a touch of the jungle fever."

The meddlesome woman pushed her way into the small room holding a pile of bed linens and towels. She sniffed the air and surveyed the room looking for signs or smells of rum. "No, Mrs. O'Brian, I do my drinking at the pub, not in my room. I do not break the rules of the barracks." St. John said courteously.

Realizing that she had briefly offended the gentleman, she began to apologize profusely. "Michael, please call me Katherine. My late husband, Clancy, God rest his soul, was taken by the rum. His last days were horrible. I don't want to see another of God's most glorious creatures tortured to death by the 'Devil's drink'."

The apology was politely accepted knowing that as soon as she changed the bed and replaced the towels, she would be gone until next week, much like a recurring nightmare.

As the large lady was moving toward the door, she stopped in front of Michael's dress uniform neatly hanging on a hanger. She carefully examined the dozen or so collection of medals hanging from the left breast. She also took occasion to notice the small red and gun-metal grey symbol of extreme valor and its framed citation reading:

"The Victoria Cross, presented to Sergeant Major Michael St. John;

For gallantry above and beyond the call of duty."

As the woman stood looking at the medal, the weary middle-aged man glanced at the mirror and wondered for a moment, "*Am I the same man who received the Victoria Cross from my queen only a few weeks ago?*" The blurry-eyed man pulled in his bulging stomach and attempted to stand a little taller. "*Yes, I am that same man, just a bit under weather. This lousy London weather is enough to bring an early demise to any man.*"

The lady once again moved toward the door. She stopped. "Michael," she mewed, "perhaps you would like to take a walk with me later this afternoon. Perhaps we could have tea in a cozy little tea shop I recently discovered." Her cheeks reddened as she waited for the soldier's answer. She coyly continued, "and perhaps we could find some mischief to take our minds off the weather."

St. John remembered back, a few days ago when she managed to cross his path as he was going for a brief walk. She sidled up to the poor man and affixed herself like a stray pup. Before Michael could break free from the woman, she almost proposed marriage! The woman was clearly smitten and desperate for someone, anyone, to keep her company on cold English nights.

"Perhaps another time, Mrs. O'Brian, this afternoon I have an appointment with my tailor. We have matters of a spiritual nature to discuss."

Mrs. O'Brian, openly rejected, curtsied and left the room, moving on to the next soldier in the next barracks cubicle.

The brief confrontation and proposition on the compromise of his virtue with Mrs. O'Brian combined with weakness in his limbs from the malaria left Michael confused and somewhat hungry. There was a small tea house with a pleasant sign inviting him to 'Have a Cup of Tea and a Fresh Made Cake'. For the next hour, he pondered his present and immediate future. With his newly acquired inheritance he would be able to buy his way out of the military and do exactly what he wanted. Here was the problem; he needed a plan on what to do, how to do it, and with whom. After a cup of tea and several cakes he decided to walk to the London docks and inquire about ships going to Burma within the next few days or at the latest, the next few weeks. He inquired at several shipping offices and found that no ships were scheduled for Burma directly until sometime late next month. He could take several ships from one point to another and eventually arrived in Rangoon, but this could prove to be unreliable and perhaps even dangerous. After numerous failed attempts to obtain some sort of intelligent direction, he pounded his fist on the desk of one agent and barked, "Perhaps I will need to purchase my own vessel to get me to Rangoon."

The clerk sarcastically pointed to a ship moored directly across the street form the shipping office. "You might wish to start with that one, sir," he said sarcastically.

Michael turned and looked at the one hundred and six foot Baltic Trader tethered to a pier across the street. "Is it for sale?" he quipped.

"Yes sir, its captain-owner was taken by the fever a few weeks back, and now it belongs to the money lenders."

For a moment Michael took the thought seriously. *"Why not buy my own ship. It is probably within my means. But, what do I know about sailing a ship?"*

As he left the booking agent's shop, he wandered over to the double-masted ship and gave it a good look-over. "Perhaps I could learn to sail it. Ridiculous!" he whispered, "I am a soldier, not a seaman."

"On the other hand, I would not object to becoming a seaman." The internal argument went on for some time as he found

his way to the harbor master's kiosk. The harbor master was taking a nap, with his feet on his desk and his chair tilted back against the wall.

After several feigned coughs, the old man woke up. "Sir, what can I do for you?" he asked.

Michael spoke, "I was informed that that black and white hulled ship over there might be for sale."

The old man looked toward the ship. "Yes sir, its captain-owner died from the fever and left it to the money lenders. The last time I heard, it was for sale."

Michael continued, "And what sort of price would a craft like that fetch?"

The old man scratched his silver beard and thought for a moment. "In better times, it might fetch twenty-five to thirty thousand pounds. Under today's circumstances, with the money lenders being tight on money, I would say that a person could have it for twenty thousand."

Michael was beginning to feel a warm sensation course through his body. "Thank you very much, Harbor Master. Thank you very much." An idea slammed into his mind like a runaway horse, *"Captain Carter, the American sea captain!"*

As the cab driver asked him for directions, he tried to recall the name of the hospital where Carter was convalescing. "Take me to Queen's Gate Hospital on the double."

~

CHAPTER FIFTY-THREE

An hour later, Michael was escorted into Captain John Carter's room. Carter was sitting in a wheel chair as Nurse Opal Alston was strapping on his newly acquired wooden peg leg. With the affectionate assistance of Nurse Opal, Carter rose to his "feet." "Ah, if it isn't my old friend Sergeant-Major St. John! And what brings you to this side of London?" Carter asked as he extended his hand toward Michael. For the first time since laying eyes on the American, he felt absolutely no animosity toward him as he did when Supi Yaw was present. He also realized that his full intentions and affections were directed toward Nurse Opal, who continued to gush over his attentions.

"Captain, I have a large favor to ask of you."

"Certainly, anything for an English cousin," Carter replied.

"I have recently come into some money. It is my intention to resign my position in the military and return to Burma as soon as possible for personal reasons."

Carter laughed out loud. "Those personal reasons wouldn't have anything to do with that little lady friend of yours, would they?"

Michael's face reddened. "As a matter of fact, it has everything to do with her. I have never wanted someone so much in all my life. I love this woman and I believe she loves me." Michael was shocked at what he had just said.

Nurse Opal smiled broadly and added, "Isn't love just wonderful!" as she patted Carter on the shoulder.

"Now then," he continued, "I have spotted this little sailing ship down at the docks. I am told that it is for sale. I have no idea of its value, or for that fact, its seaworthiness. I would appreciate a professional opinion on both. If you and I could take a ride to the docks, you might give me your professional opinion. After all, you do wear four gold stripes on your sleeve."

"Sergeant Major St. John, I would be honored to examine this ship of yours," Carter said.

Before Michael could respond, he found himself flat on the floor, completely dazed. Nurse Opal yelled for orderlies to come double quick. Minutes later Michael opened his eyes in an examining room surrounded by several doctors and nurses. He felt a large bump on the back of his head from where he had collided with the floor. "Sergeant Major," one of the doctors said, "I believe you are suffering from an active case of malaria. Your blood chemistry shows positive signs of the organism not to mention symptoms of some liver damage."

One of the other doctors then asked, "Sir, are you the Sergeant Major who recently received the Victoria Cross?" Michael nodded that he was.

"We are honored to be of service," he said.

Michael confirmed that he was indeed suffering from frequent bouts of malaria. A thought then occurred to him, "Doctor, in your professional opinion, would you say that this condition is sufficient to call for a medical discharge from my current military posting?"

The doctor conferred with two other doctors standing around the examining table. "Why, yes, we would lend our professional support to a request for a medical discharge."

Michael smiled, "Then, I would like to request a written document requesting an immediate medical discharge. I was actually planning to retire in the near future, but this would expedite the process considerably."

Within a few minutes, Michael was feeling much improved. Nurse Opal provided him with a strong cup of tea heavily laced with honey. "Much better!" he said as he walked Carter back to his room. "John, what do you say we take that little ride down to the docks?"

Carter replied, "Only if I can take my favorite nurse in case you fall on your head again."

CHAPTER FIFTY-FOUR

Captain John Carter took seriously his evaluation of the small ship. With the considerable help of his nurse, he managed to walk the gangplank leading to the ship's main deck. He began to thump his wooden leg against the deck board, sideboards, and any other object of wood. "The decking sounds good, there are no cracks in the masts, and all the brass work seems to be in good order."

Carter then descended the stairway leading below to the six small cabins, galley and the main holds. Thirty minutes later he returned to the main deck. "This little boat is in prime condition. It is my opinion that she can get you to Burma and quite possibly beyond."

Michael smiled. "How many men will it require to sail her?"

"No more than ten, no less than eight," Carter replied.

"I would have to hire a crew and a captain," Michael said.

"That you will; that you will," Carter said with a slight smile moving across his face.

Michael noticed the grin forming on Carter's face. "Captain Carter, could I interest you and your nurse in an Indian dinner? I think we might have a few things to talk about."

"Sergeant Major St. John, after almost two months of hospital food, English hospital food at that, Indian food sounds wonderful."

Michael ordered a huge amount of food; far more than the three of them could ever consume. After completing his order, Michael asked the proprietor if he might send word to the junior offices' barracks and invite Amerjit to join them when his shift has finished.

It was obvious that Nurse Opal had never been in an Indian eatery before. The smells reflected on her pretty face. Michael, seeing her consternation, quietly ordered a bowl of split pea soup and a lamb chop for her.

With the ordering taken care of, Captain John Carter fixed his gaze directly on Sergeant Major Michael St. John, soon-to-be Sergeant Major Michael St. John, retired. "Now my friend, tell me about this fantasy of yours to buy this ship and sail off to fetch your lady fair."

Michael laughed out loud. "John, it is a fantasy. There's no question about it. This little plan is nothing more than a wild fantasy. But, what's wrong with a fantasy? All my life I have lived by taking orders from parents, officers, and idiots. Now for the first time in my life, I will be free to make any decision I like. I will be free to follow any fantasy that comes my way. I could end up like most retired soldiers where life becomes something you do while you are waiting to die. John, I inherited a substantial sum of money from my late brother. This gives me an opportunity seldom realized by most retired soldiers to actually pursue a fantasy rather than simply dream about one. I will be free to sail wherever I want."

Carter interrupted, "But Burma, Michael, Burma is just an extension of England. You will still be Sergeant Major Michael St. John, retired. Your social status was dictated at the time of your birth. Even though you are smarter and wiser than those Englishmen who were born with titles and family crests, you will never be able to move in their circles. You will always be a common man with an uncommon medal hanging on your tunic. You will become a relic to be venerated but not considered as a member of the social set."

Michael looked long and hard at Carter. "Michael, why don't you snatch up your lady love and flee to America where your place in the social structure is what you make it to be?"

Michael looked as if he had just been slapped. "You mean desert my country? Leave all that I hold dear?" Michael said.

"Michael, your country has deserted you. You have given your life for your Queen and country. Now, as you put it, you dance like a trained monkey on a string in town squares, with a feather-hatted fool calling the tune." Michael looked deep into his plate of lentils and curry. "Michael, let's take your little ship and make a run for it," Carter said.

"Let's?" Michael whispered. "Are you suggesting that you and I sail this ship to Burma and then on to America?"

Carter moved his face as close as he could to Michael's face. "No, you flaming fool, I am suggesting that you, I, Opal, and Supi Yaw make a run for America."

Michael was overwhelmed at both the audacity and the honesty of this man. He sat, looking completely stunned at the thought.

Just then Amerjit entered the dining room. "I was able to discharge my duties early this evening. Sergeant Major, it so good to see you again. The barracks seems so much colder now that you and you little doggie are gone.

Michael introduced Captain Carter and Nurse Opal to Amerjit who bowed low at the introduction of the lady. Nurse Opal giggled.

Michael's head was still spinning from Carter's comments about running away.

John Carter then opened the conversation to include Amerjit. "Mr. Amerjit, I was trying to persuade your friend here that he should buy a ship, fetch his lady love and sail away to American with Nurse Opal and myself."

Amerjit's reply was, "Oh, my goodness gracious. Might you be needing a good cook for your journey?"

Michael looked at Amerjit. "Amerjit, Carter is not joking. He is crazy serious!"

Amerjit replied, "So what's wrong with crazy serious? I, for one, am totally fed up with this silly country of yours. No matter what I do or where I go, I am treated as a third-class person. You Brits have taken over my country where I am also treated as less than a third-class person. I would truly like to find a place where I do not have to jump off the footpath every time I see an Englishman coming my way."

This was the first time Michael had seen the true feelings of his Indian friend. Amerjit looked at Carter for some sort of affirmation. Carter gave it. Carter then looked at Nurse Opal, "Opal, how would you like to sail to America?"

Without giving it a second thought, she said, "Captain, we would have to be man and wife before I could make such a move. After all, I am a proper lady."

Carter looked at Michael. "Consider it done," Carter said. Again Nurse Opal simply giggled. Michael was dumbfounded. While he in no way rejected the idea, he was unable to place one thought in line with another. Carter then began to make an outline.

"First, you procure full title to the ship. Then, to defray expenses, we find a cargo we can haul to Rangoon. Something sufficiently heavy to keep the ship firm in the water but not heavy enough to slow our progress. After all, we want to get you to your lady love as fast as your little ship can run. I will then have to order up supplies sufficient for a three-to-four-legged journey. I figure we can put in at Capetown, South Africa; Colombo, Ceylon; and possibly somewhere in between."

Michael was still stunned. "Forget Ceylon, I don't want to put in at Ceylon."

"Why not Ceylon, Michael?"

Michael simply said, "Not Ceylon!"

"Alright, we will skip Ceylon. Whatever you say 'Master of the Ship'."

Michael, still somewhat baffled by the whole turn of events, said, "It's still Sergeant Major St. John."

Carter acknowledged the rebuff before turning to Amerjit. "Mr. Amerjit, are you serious about signing on to cook for us? If not, I need to know right now. Even more important than the ship's captain is the ship's cook. A rotten cook will bring about a mutiny, for certain."

Amerjit said, "Sir, I am not a man to fool around. Silly talk is not in my nature. I too would like to enjoy the freedom you talk about. I am not afraid to take a chance in this America of yours, and sir, I am an excellent cook to be certain! And besides, I am anxious to see these people you Americans call 'Indians'."

Michael then asked, "John, why should you, a successful sea captain throw in with a worn-out British soldier about to sail off the edge of the world? If what you are serious about marrying this lady, and I assume you are, why would you want to sail off to who knows what?"

"Michael, when I lost my leg, I lost my chances of ever commanding a serious ship again. In the old days, sea captains with peg legs and patched eyes were part of the system. Today, there are hundreds of highly qualified sea captains, all with working parts and more experience than I ever hope to have. I received a letter from my company informing me that I was being relieved of command due to my injuries. I am to receive a moderate compensation for my injuries and a modest pension for my service. Not even a gold watch! Just a thank you note and a few dollars each month. Now, Sergeant Major Michael St. John, if I can find a way to build my own small fleet of cargo ships, I am fairly confident that I can eventually build a significant business."

Michael looked at the man across the table and pondered his comments. "John, I perceive you to be quite serious about this concept."

"As serious as I can get!" he replied. The two men sat looking at each other for what seemed like an eternity. Ideas, possibilities, consequences, and a thousand 'what ifs' races around each man's mind.

"Michael, I have a savings of around thirteen thousand American dollars. I am willing to put most, if not all of that money on the table if you are willing to enter into a partnership. We can begin with a single one hundred and six foot Baltic Trader and add to our fleet as our profits enable us. I would suggest that we locate our home port in San Francisco. From there, we can provide shipping to and from Asia as well as Alaska and South America."

Michael soon visualized the picture. He stopped dead in his tracks. "What about Supi Yaw? Where would she fit into this picture?"

John smiled broadly. "Michael, as I recall from our conversations with your lovely Supi Yaw, her only desire in life was to become a *bona fide* medical doctor. Here in Britain or for that fact in British Burma, she will never be able to realize that dream. You heard the American ambassador yourself offer her a full scholarship to an American medical university. Michael, there are medical universities all over the San Francisco area. Once she has qualified, she can practice medicine anywhere she wants in the United States! If she remains in Burma, the only thing she will be allowed to do is carry bed pans in British hospitals and deliver the babies of native women."

As Michael looked at John Carter, tears filled his eyes. "By Almighty God, I like the idea. I like the idea a lot!" Michael thrust his hand toward Carter. "Let's do it! By Almighty God, let's do it!" They shook hands and embraced.

Amerjit then spoke up. "Sirs, where do I fit in this little adventure? I too believe this plan will prosper. Now, gentlemen, I have a significant amount of money that I would be willing to invest in your adventure, if you would be willing to consider me as a faithful investor."

Carter spoke, "Significant amount?"

"Yes, sirs, I can contribute, perhaps ten thousand pounds. It is my life's savings from my employment with the British military and my tailor shops. I would be happy to place my assets at your disposal. In so doing, sirs, I would be receiving a portion from the profits of your enterprise. I could remain, as you say, a silent partner."

Carter looked at Michael and raises his eyebrow. "Why not? If he cheats us, we can simply throw him overboard to the sharks."

Michael replied, "Or, as our cook, he could simply poison us and take our ship and run."

Amerjit, shocked at the comments, said, "Oh no! I would never poison anyone intentionally. Never, sirs!" Carter and

St. John extended their hands toward Amerjit and welcomed him into the enterprise.

Now it was Nurse Opal's turn to speak. "John my love, when shall we plan to get married. I shall need to inform my mum and dad and find a preacher. We must do this all prim and proper you know. After all, if you are to become a proper gentleman, you will require a proper wedding." She giggled again.

Michael looked at his pocket watch. "Twelve-thirty in the morning. I suggest that we call it good for the day. With all this talk of ships and cargo and weddings, we will need to be moving and moving fast. John, when you return to the hospital, will you do everything possible to expedite the letter from the doctors? If I can get this document submitted to General Wallace, I can likely have my release within a week. Tomorrow, I shall track down the owners of the ship and arrange to make purchase. Once that is completed, John, you and I can begin arrangements to sail."

John interrupted Michael's comments. My dear friend, aren't you forgetting one very important issue? I might suggest that you send a telegram to your dear Supi Yaw and see what she thinks about this plan. What happens if she had found some native head hunter and married up with him? You would be up a creek with nothing but a long, black and white boat. You might ask her what she thinks about going to America and becoming a full-fledged medical doctor. She might have changed her mind. After all, you know women do change their minds. And too, if she does agree to run away to American with you, you might have to have her father's permission."

Michael stopped short. "You are right, John. Perhaps I need to send a telegram and ask if she is willing to marry me. If she were to decline, my life would take a different direction altogether."

Good old Nurse Opal then added, "And if she agrees and I am certain she will, she will want an elaborate wedding with all the ribbons and bows," she giggled.

Michael was now fully consumed with the grand plan. "John, I shall contact you at the hospital as soon as I have any news on the ship. Nurse Opal, will you be good enough to remind John to obtain the medial release papers. Amerjit, I would suggest that you submit your intent to resign from your employment at the barracks. And I shall spend some time drafting a telegram to Supi Yaw."

For John Carter and Nurse Opal, the ride back to the hospital was extremely amorous to say the least. Amerjit chose to walk to mile or so back to his lodgings, smiling all the way at the thought of traveling to America's Wild West and seeing first-hand these people with feathers in their hair who dare to call themselves "Indians."

CHAPTER FIFTY-FIVE

Michael was fully occupied until three o'clock in the morning with drafting a telegram complete with expressions of his love and his intentions. He weighted every word, every thought. He tried to visualize Supi Yaw actually reading the telegram and wondered if she would laugh at his proposal and plans to run away to the far side of the earth. He was quick to make mention of the scholarship offered by the American ambassador and the fact that a woman, even a foreign woman, could practice medicine in America and he mentioned his plan to partner with Carter and Amerjit in building a shipping business. Michael concluded with a bit of humor. *"My Dearest Supi Yaw, in conclusion I would ask you to consider the welfare of our little dog, Gunga. Without both a master and a mistress, the poor little fellow could not have a proper upbringing. So in that regard, I would again ask that you agree to become my wife and lifelong partner. I anxiously await your reply.*
Lovingly, Michael St. John, Sergeant Major, retired.
P.S. Letter to follow.

Several times between completion of the telegram and the morning call for breakfast, Michael played with the words of his message. Finally, at eight o'clock he handed the lengthy message to a telegraph operator who read the document and politely smiled. While he said nothing, he smiled at St. John. In her last letter, Supi Yaw indicated that she would be residing at Joseph's compound on the outskirts of Rangoon. The telegram was therefore addressed to the Green Frog Tea Shop, Central Market, Rangoon, Burma.

Michael St. John felt an enormous weight, being both lifted and replaced on his shoulders. "*What happens if Supi Yaw rejects my offer of marriage? Or what happens if she agrees and her father does not? What happens if she agrees to marriage but not to travel to America?*" These and dozens of others filled his mind as he hailed a cab.

∾

CHAPTER FIFTY-SIX

The Baltic Trader was still waiting idle at the docks. Michael went again to the harbor master's kiosk and inquired as to the address of its temporary owner. From there, Michael took a cab to the financial district where he was introduced to the "owner of title." Within an hour, a deal for twenty-two thousand pounds had been signed, sealed and handed over. Michael St. John was now the owner of a ship.

His next stop was the Queen's Gate Hospital where he found Carter sitting on the terrace holding an envelope. Carter's smile was broad and telling as he waved the envelope back and forth. "Sergeant Major St. John, here are your freedom papers. The doctors told me that they would personally vouch for your condition if any military doctor should wish to contest their opinions." Michael read the document which suggested that he be immediately relieved of duty and of any further active military service and any ancillary services" Carter said, "I had them throw in the last part about ancillary services just in case they might wish to keep you on as a circus monkey."

Michael was delighted. "I shall have this on General Wallace's desk by the end of the day. Hopefully, my discharge will come within a few days. For the first time in my life, I will be free. It will be a strange feeling, John. Most military men don't know what it's like to be free. Most old soldiers simply gravitate to some home for old soldiers and refight old battles and tell old stories until there is no one left to listen."

Carter added, "If Supi Yaw agrees to marry you, your freedom won't last for long; that along with the responsibility of overseeing a fleet of sailing ships." Michael smiled at the thought. He was completely overwhelmed at the way things were falling into place. "By the way Michael, did you send your telegram to Supi Yaw or did you have too many other things on your mind?"

"I sent the telegram, John Carter! Don't be worrying yourself about that. You need to be worrying yourself about your getting married."

"John, one more thing I would appreciate."

"Name it," John said.

"Contact your ambassador and inform him that Supi Yaw is considering his offer of a full scholarship. If she agrees to my proposal, I want to let her know that a scholarship is a reality. You might also wish to inform the ambassador of our mutual intent as well. You never know when we might need a friendly face."

"Consider it done, Michael."

"John, I have been thinking. Handshakes over bowls of Indian curry are all well and good, but we will need a formal agreement between you and me and Amerjit if we are to make this thing work properly. I would like to suggest that we bring in an attorney-at-law to draw up a formal agreement creating a partnership."

John replied, "I fully agree. I suggest that we arrange this as soon as possible. I would also strongly suggest we use a maritime lawyer."

"Good thought," Michael replied.

For the next two hours John and Michael discussed everything from tidal charts to teacups. They concluded by agreeing to meet with Amerjit the following day at the ship. From there, they could work the details of the first journey. "One last thing," Carter requested, "I would like permission to take up residence aboard our ship as soon as possible. I really need to get out of this hospital. My abilities to restrain my lustful nature toward Opal are running thin. I would also suggest that we get Amerjit on board so I won't starve to death, and he can become accustomed to living aboard ship."

Michael replied, "Good idea. In fact, as soon as I receive my formal discharge papers, I too shall join you aboard our ship."

"By the way, John, did you notice the name of the vessel? "Highland Heather?" Can't we change the name to something a bit more adventurous? How about the Burma Tiger?"

Carter smiled, "The Burma Tiger it is. Our next ship we can call the English Lion and the third, the American Puma. Before you know it, we will have a complete collection of cats. I will see to the name change and the paperwork."

Another night of making mental lists was often interrupted by thoughts of what would happen if Supi Yaw spurns his proposal. Excitement and agony blended along with fatigue. Never had Michael St. John experienced this much anxiety or excitement. Even before a battle in India, he was generally calm and collected. All this new business of shipping, marriages, and running off to America had him quite well stirred.

By noon, the three partners had arrived at the ship. At one o'clock a black-coated lawyer arrived and was shown by Amerjit to the main cabin. By four o'clock, documents had been drawn up and signed. All was well. By six o'clock, Amerjit had prepared a full-course dinner, complete with a bottle of wine. By nine o'clock all three partners were being rocked to sleep by the gentle motion of the river.

At nine o'clock the following morning a courier from the telegraph office tied off his horse and moved across the gangway. "Telegram for Sergeant Major Michael St. John," he called.

Michael almost broke his leg as he flew up the step from the cabin below. He grabbed the envelope as a hungry dog would grab a meaty bone. Without any pretense at politeness, he tore the envelope open and gasped for a moment. His eyes exploded. The telegram simply read,

"YES! YES! YES! Come soon!

Gunga misses you.

Your loving Supi Yaw.

John and Amerjit heard the yells of joy as Michael proceeded up the rope ladder to the top of the mast. "She said, yes!" he yelled as loud as his lungs would allow.

"John, I want to move out as soon as possible. How fast can we be ready to sail?"

John smiled, "Michael, your Supi Yaw will be waiting no matter when we sail. We can't be going off half-cocked on our first effort. I will have to find a crew, locate a cargo, and, let's not forget, I have to get married as well." John turned to Amerjit who was standing near with a huge smile on his thickly bearded face. "Amerjit, get this poor man a strong cup of tea. His head is in the clouds and he is thinking about only one thing." Amerjit complied.

As Amerjit brought two cups of strong "Indian" tea, he spoke. "Gentlemen, last evening I mentioned my newfound opportunity with my cousins who staff my tailor shops. They begged and pleaded for me to bring them along on the journey. They even offered to work for free simply to gain passage to America. They convinced me that they had sufficient resources to open a tailor shop or perhaps a sail-making shop in California." Amerjit stood silent, waiting for any sort of reply.

Carter asked, "Do any of them have seaman's papers?"

"No sir, but they all speak and read English quite well. I am certain they could learn to sail our ship perhaps even better than your regular English seamen."

Carter looked at St. John. Michael, still euphoric over his telegram, simply shrugged his shoulders. Carter then said, "I will have to have at least one licensed first mate. The rest can obtain regular seaman's papers. For certain, no one will insure us or the cargo, but we might make it in spite of our crew. Alright Amerjit, let's give it a try. But," he interjected, "Indian food for the Indians and western food for the rest of us."

Amerjit beamed and proceeded to violently shake hands with his partners. "Please, sir, give me two days to accomplish the ultimate disposition of my tailor shops." Carter nodded.

As for Michael, his mind was wandering the compound in Rangoon with Supi Yaw and Gunga. Michael had submitted his formal request for a medical discharge. Two days later, a mounted courier delivered the official discharge papers and an extraordinary commendation from General Wallace, extolling St. John's virtues as a soldier and a gentleman. There was a personal note attached to the documents, a note from General Wallace.

Sergeant Major St. John,

Her Majesty's secretary has informed me that he has obtained information regarding your family's position in the English hierarchy. It appears that you are indeed an heir to a formal title.

If you should wish to avail yourself of this opportunity to pursue the matter, please inform my office, and we shall make every effort to invest you into your proper position within the British list of titles. If you were to successfully achieve your rightful title, we might be able to consider a full commission to the position of 'Officer in Her Majesty's Military Forces'. Give it your careful consideration.

Warmest regards,

General W.C.R. Wallace

Immediately, Michael thought of himself dressed in one of those silly feathered hats and gold-festooned uniforms. He then thought of Supi Yaw standing on the deck of his ship, heading for America. "No thank you, General Wallace. No thank you, Queen Victoria. I much prefer 'Doctor' Supi Yaw," he said aloud.

Captain Carter saw fit to visit a nearby maritime supply business. There, he purchased all the navigation instruments necessary to navigate a ship across the seas. He also purchased virtually every book on the subject of seamanship including basic celestial navigation, knots, weights and balances, and so on. His intent was to turn the Burma Tiger into a floating university for nautical sciences. He also determined that his new partner, Michael St. John, would be able to pass the examination for his captain's papers by the time they reached San Francisco. He also determined that each of his crewmen would be able to, at least obtain able seaman's credentials if not higher. As for his wife-to-be, he selected a copy of The Maritime Medical Manual. If nothing else, it would give her something to do during the long days at sea. He then reckoned that she might profit from time spent studying with Supi Yaw once they departed Burma for San Francisco.

The week flew past with work lists and shopping lists being checked off. The Indian crew was well into "evening classes" memorizing the names of each mast, rope, and wench aboard the Burma Tiger. One member of the crew located a large piece of oak. He then found a set of wood chisels in the carpenter's locker and began to pound and cut. Within a few days, a magnificent wooden tiger emerged from within the small log. The tiger's mouth was wide open, as if it were leaping toward its prey. After some paint, the bow figure for the newly named ship was ready to be affixed along with a plaque bearing its new name; THE BURMA TIGER. Michael smiled at the leaping tiger and shook his head slightly. He picked up the small wooden mallet from the deck and tapped one of the tiger's wooden fangs, breaking it off. He commented to the surprised wood carver, "This is the tiger I remember."

The day arrived for Captain John Carter's wedding to Miss Opal Alston. The bride's family was a typical working-class family, complete with a dozen or so cousins, uncles and aunties. Michael served as best man along with Amerjit as a groomsman. The presiding vicar was somewhat perplexed at the fact a Sikh, in fact eight Sikhs, were present in a Christian sanctuary. After some conversation about speaking God's precious word to the unsaved, the vicar relented and the issue was dropped. By midnight, Nurse Opal Alston was now Mrs. Captain John Carter. By one o'clock Captain John Carter was well into his honeymoon aboard the small black and white ship.

The following morning, Captain Carter emerged from his cabin and ordered the crew to "stand by." The crew, now including one English (actually Irish) first mate, stood at attention on the deck. Even Michael stood at attention as Captain Carter, "inspected" the crew. As he passed in front of Michael, he winked. Michael winked back. "Master of the Ship St. John, are we prepared to cast off?"

"Aye, Captain Carter, I believe we are prepared," Michael replied.

"Mr. Ryan," he said to the first mate, "cast off lines and hoist the foresail."

"Aye, aye, Captain," the Irishman replied.

First mate Timothy Ryan ordered the Indian crew, one man at a time, to pull a line or cast off a line. Things went remarkably for a first-time cruise consisting mostly of people who had never been on a ship, much less out to sea. Before the Burma Tiger left the Thames and entered into the open sea, Mrs. Carter made her first appearance on the deck. Dressed in a bright yellow frock and parasol, she simply smiled at Captain Carter and with a gentle smile suggested that he come below. Carter flushed violently. "Michael, take the wheel. Keep the compass course exactly on 182 degrees. Mr. Ryan, come to the wheel and assist Mr. St. John in his first lesson in navigation." Ryan smiled a knowing smile and ordered full sails be set.

CHAPTER FIFTY-SEVEN

The Indian crew dashed and darted pulling ropes and tying off knots they had learned in their nightly courses in seamanship. Everyone was truly excited as they watched England disappear into the fog behind them.

An hour later Carter emerged from his cabin to "check the watch." He seemed extremely content with the operation of the ship. Michael was ecstatic with his performance as helmsman. Mr. Ryan was careful to see that the compass needle remained exactly on the 182-degree mark. Several more times that day, Carter disappeared into his cabin. No comments were made nor any required.

Ryan then spilt the crew into a day watch and a night watch. Those on the night watch were ordered below to get some sleep. Ryan knew that, under the circumstances, he would be standing a full watch, since Captain Carter was preoccupied.

The ship cut through the water with amazing speed. With each mile, Michael could only think about moving closer and closer to his beloved Supi Yaw. Each hour was one hour closer to his new life as a husband. On occasion, he thought of John Carter below decks and his new wife.

One of the few items Michael kept from his brother's estate was the family Bible. The huge book was well bound and colorfully illustrated. In reading through the Psalms, he recognized many of the passages he had remembered as a child. In Proverbs, he again recognized many of the admonitions his mother used to utter. Michael was particularly keen on the Song of Solomon and the references to husbands and wives. Before long, Michael had focused his attention on reading the book from beginning to end. John was little help in difficult passages or heavy questions. Mr. Ryan, on the other hand, appeared to be a godly man and knew his scriptures quite well. Quite often, while on watch Michael and Mr. Ryan would discuss specific passages of scripture. With each passage came reflections on their respective lives and careers. As Michael progressed through the various books of the Bible, he soon found himself on his knees in his cabin praying that his beloved Supi Yaw would come to love him as much as he had grown to love her. He also prayed that he might become the best and most honorable husband in the world. Many times his private prayer sessions would last for hours. Mr. Ryan was aware of this new relationship with God and offered his personal prayers that Michael would be granted the success he so earnestly desired.

Days turned into weeks. The Indian crew soon became sufficient to guide the ship around the tip of Africa and into a port stop at Cape Town. With added provisions and a bit more cargo, it was off across the Indian Ocean toward Burma. In light of usual monsoon predictions in the northern regions of the Indian Ocean, Michael reluctantly agreed to a stop at Colombo, Ceylon for provisions.

Early one morning Captain Carter arrived early for his watch at the wheel. Michael reported the course and events of the night. Carter rubbed his forehead with his fingers. "Michael, there is a storm brewing. Whenever my forehead begins to throb, there's trouble in the making." Carter then checked the brass-mounted barometer. "Yep, we had better batten down for a blow."

By high noon, nothing of the sun could be seen. Great waves were tossing the ship from side to side rocking back and forth. The sails had been furled to prevent tearing while sufficient to maintain a forward movement. Every man and woman eventually found themselves vomiting heavily. Even Carter who seldom showed any sign of sea sickness contributed his portion to the sea. Michael noticed Mr. Ryan folded on his knees while holding on to the side rail. Without warning, Ryan jumped overboard into the raging water. Michael immediately tied the ship's wheel and dashed to where he could see Ryan bobbing in the water. "Man overboard!" he yelled. Three of the Indian crew heard the call and ran to where Michael stood. Michael had thrown a cork-filled life ring to Ryan, but Ryan failed to take hold of it. One-by-one the three Indian crew members jumped into the raging waters and made their way to the desperate man. Carter was now on deck calling out orders to two other crew members. Carter untied the wheel and brought the ship about. St. John located a free rope and tossed it to the crew members in the water. One man caught hold of the rope and attached it to the cork life ring. Ryan was limp, but nonetheless alive. One-by-one, each of the soggy men was hoisted aboard the Burma Tiger, Ryan being the first.

Ryan was carried to his small cabin below. He was exhausted but alive. Michael ordered a cup of hot tea be brought. Carter poked his head in the cabin door, "Ryan, what happened?"

Ryan replied, "I slipped and fell overboard, Captain. I promise it won't happen again."

Carter resumed his station at the wheel while St. John remained below with Ryan. "Mr. Ryan, you did not slip and fall overboard. I was watching you. You jumped."

Timothy Ryan put his face in his shaking hands and began to cry.

"Mr. St. John, I presume that you know the story of Jonah and the whale."

St. John acknowledged that he indeed knew the story.

"Well Mr. St. John, I am Jonah. Your ship and your crew were in grave danger of being drowned in the sea because of me. You see, I too am running away from God."

St. John said nothing, but simply looked as if he were asking for the whole story. "Mr. St. John, for most of my adult life I was a priest in Northern Ireland. I was a good priest at that. Unfortunately, like many in my profession, I became involved with a lady, an extremely beautiful lady, perhaps something like this lady you are going to marry. But unlike you, I was not permitted to enjoy any sort of relationship with a woman, or for that fact, to marry. And, like many in my situation, I succumbed to temptation. The result of this little indiscretion was a child. To make matters worse, she compelled me to pay her money in order to keep the matter quiet and out of the ears of my superiors. I was forced to rob from the church in order to maintain my horrible little secret. Shortly after the child was born, it died. This too was my fault; like David and his child with Bathsheba. My sins were far too great to confess to my confessor or to take to my superiors. My only recourse was to remove my collar and robes and run. Like Jonah, I am running away. Through Captain Carter and yourself, I have seen what a wonderful thing a loving relationship with a woman can be; unfortunately, I am still bound by my oath of poverty and chastity. Even though I violated that oath, God still holds me accountable. My death would have ended that oath, and final judgment would have been dealt. And too, I did not want the deaths of this crew to be added to my account. So, Mr. St John, I jumped."

Michael smiled. "It was a noble, but foolish thing you did, Mr. Ryan. After you have had a bit of rest, we can talk about this little problem. There is an answer. If you will promise me that you won't attempt to take your life again, I will try to help you find it." Ryan nodded.

Amerjit tapped on the door. "A warm cup of tea for Mr. Ryan," he said.

The storm abated and moved on to the northeast. The seas had calmed but still carried the foam generated by the turbulence. As the sun set behind the Burma Tiger, Mr. St. John took the watch from Carter. Michael asked Carter as he left the wheel, "John, could you ask Mr. Ryan to come up on deck?"

Ryan looked like a whipped pup. He lit a pipe and spoke in his thick Irish brogue, "Captain Carter said that you wanted to see me."

Michael nodded, trying to find an opening into what was to be a long and difficult evening. "Mr. Ryan, I have read and re-read the story of Jonah and nowhere did I find any reference to you. God did not order you to go to Nineveh, or for that fact, Northern Ireland. It was your choice, not God's. As for the vows you took, again they were your choice to take or not to take. If you will carefully examine the scriptures, nowhere does God require his ministers to remain unmarried or for that fact to disown their wives for the sake of the church. This business about celibacy is purely a man-made regulation and subject to the whims of man. It is my guess that God would much rather see His ministers happily married much like Captain Carter is and I soon hope to be. So in that respect, Mr. Ryan, your sin is actually against the rules of the church and not against God.

As far as your sin with the woman and taking of the money, that was a sin against God. The death of the child had nothing to do with you. If it was God's will to take the child as He did with David's son, so be it. That is His concern. Mr. Ryan, there are thousands of children born out of wedlock, and they are not killed by some unseen hand of an angry God, are they?" Ryan simply shook his head.

"Likewise, every man or woman since Adam and Eve has committed sins, some great, some small. Does God send violent storms to end their stinking lives?" Again Ryan shook his head. Ryan blew a plume of smoke into the wind as he processed St. John's comments.

St. John continued, "Now, as for dealing with the guilt of your sins, you are guilty! There is no way to lessen the gravity of that guilt except to confess these sins, express true contrition, and ask for full and complete forgiveness."

Ryan spoke, "But you see Mr. St. John, I have no confessor. When I ran away from the church, I left my confessor behind. And too, if I had made confessions of these sins, I would have been severely disciplined or excommunicated altogether. So, to whom am I to confess?"

"Mr. Ryan, you have already confessed your sins to me!" St. John said with a smile. "Likewise you have expressed your contrition and desire for forgiveness to me."

Ryan looked confused. "Mr. St. John, with all due respect, you are not an ordained priest. How can you forgive another man's sins and announce absolution?"

"Mr. Ryan, I am not well versed in the Holy Scriptures, but nowhere do I find that confessions be spoken to an ordained priest, rabbi, or preacher. Because Christ considers all believers to be members of a royal priesthood, any person who believes in Christ and His teachings has not only the right, but obligation to forgive sins."

"But think about it, Mr. St. John; my sins are much too great to ever expect forgiveness without paying a price on my part."

"Mr. Ryan, if that were the case, Christ's death on the cross was only meant for the minor sins of mankind leaving the larger sins to be handled in some other way. Consider for a moment the event of the crucifixion. Without question, the most horrible sin ever committed against God Himself was the murder of His Son. Did Jesus condemn those who participated in this murder? No, while hanging on the cross, He pleaded with His Father that these people and all people be forgiven. Now, Mr. Ryan, are your sins any greater than those who murdered the Son of God? I think not." Ryan was dead silent as St. John's words seemed to melt away the pain of the sins this man deemed eternally fatal.

Finally, after a long silence, Michael St. John placed his face directly in front of Timothy Ryan's face and spoke, "Mr. Ryan, your sins are forgiven, man! Let's start over. And while we are at it, please consider for a minutes those three heathen lads who jumped into the ocean to save your life. Perhaps you should consider investing time in the saving their lives, their eternal lives. I would suggest that you consider the lost of this world as a new and valuable life ministry. For many years you comforted the believers in Ireland. You might wish to redirect your efforts toward those who are not believers, like Mr. Amerjit and his cousins and beyond."

Ryan looked puzzled. "Mr. St. John, I was trained as a priest, not a missionary."

"Mr. Ryan, I am not suggesting that you become a missionary. I am merely suggesting that you reach out your hand to those in need of a hand and allow God's Spirit to do the rest. Look at Christ's example. He fed the hungry; He gave water to the thirsty, and listened to the broken. Through these simple acts, God's Spirit was manifested. Mr. Ryan, I have known this Jesus only a short time now, but I am anxious to share His power and comfort with the rest of the world. You too can use your God-given gifts, perhaps aboard ships, to share the gifts God has given to you." Ryan said nothing, he simply nodded. "Mr. Ryan, will you check to sails?" St. John said, as if to end the session. Ryan complied.

The following morning St. John noticed Mr. Ryan talking with the three Indian men who had saved him from yesterday's storm. They were sitting casually on the forecastle laughing at something Ryan was telling them. Ryan looked up at St. John standing on the afterdeck and smiled.

Over the next week, Mr. Ryan asked to borrow Mr. St. John's family Bible for a time of "story telling" as he put it. He had invited the Indian men to an informal reading of stories from the Bible. Soon, this became a daily ritual. Even those Indian fellows with all-night duty came to the event. St. John happened by the "story tellings" one evening to hear Mr. Ryan's somewhat comical interpretation of the events of the Bible. However, when he discussed some of the events in the New Testament, he became very solemn. On one particular evening, Michael noticed Amerjit sitting among his cousins, listening to the stories.

CHAPTER FIFTY-EIGHT

Arriving in Colombo, Michael decided to send a note to the Commander of British Forces in Ceylon, Colonel Joseph Ballentine. Much his surprise, Ballentine acknowledged his note and invited Michael and his party for tea.

Michael was less than enthusiastic about accepting an invitation to have tea, or anything else for that fact, with his former commanding officer. This was particularly true in light of the misunderstanding which seemed to have been generated by senior officers in London. In any case, after seven weeks as sea, a cup of tea with a gentleman, even if he was a British Colonel, did not seem too unpleasant.

Michael extended the invitation to Captain and Mrs. Carter. Opal was clearly delighted for an opportunity to put on one of her frilly frocks and silly hats and show herself off as a sea captain's wife. Michael and the Carters hailed a carriage while Amerjit opted to remain behind to load on water barrels and food baskets. Colombo seemed much like Rangoon and other Indian cities Michael had visited. The smells of all sorts of spices mixed with the stench of raw sewage in the streets only whetted his desire to return to Rangoon all the sooner.

The carriage arrived at the headquarters building. A sentry met the carriage and escorted the party into the main reception room. A few minutes later, Colonel Ballentine entered the room dressed in a less than formal uniform. It was clear that this was meant to suggest that St. John and his party were not sufficiently significant to warrant a full-dress uniform. "Ah, Sergeant Major St. John, how good to see you again," he said in his most pompous tone.

"Actually Colonel, it is now simply Mr. St. John. I am retired from Her Majesty's Military Service," Michael said casually.

"Not so, St. John," he corrected. "Once a Sergeant Major, always a Sergeant Major."

"If you like, Colonel Ballentine, but for my purposes, I prefer Mr. St. John." To end the verbal duel, Michael took charge. In an obvious attempt to show his brief indignation, Michael introduced Captain and Mrs. John Carter. Correct protocol dictates that the senior person is to be introduced to the junior person. In this case, Michael prevailed on Carter's rank of captain which, in many circles, exceeds that of a colonel.

Ballentine gushed over Opal Carter. It was obvious that she was something of a novelty in this part of the world. Opal made certain that she presented her feminine qualities as well as she could.

Tea was served, complete with all the trappings of an English gentleman. Finally, after much frivolous chit-chat, Ballentine, in a plaintive voice, asked the question, "St. John, what went wrong with our plan? We were so confident that all points had been addressed. We allowed for ample adjustments. It seemed so perfect! I had my career staked on the blasted thing."

"Simply put, Sir, several men at White Hall and the government had their own agendas. The plan changed. As much as I tried to maintain the overall integrity of the original plan, the politicians ran away with it. Simple as that, Sir."

Michael made no mention of the comments made about Ballentine's career transfer and subsequent fall from grace. The air was cleared between the two men. Handshakes were sincerely given and respectful farewells extended.

A coach delivered the trio to the Burma Tiger whereupon they weighed anchor and moved off toward Rangoon and Supi Yaw.

CHAPTER FIFTY-NINE

Two days out from Colombo, at the evening "story telling" time something quite unique occurred. As Ryan ended his "story" about Jesus healing the blind man, Amerjit stood up and announced, "Sir, I wish to follow this Jesus of yours. My religion is wonderful, but none of my gods are able to do the things this God of yours can do. Sir, may I be allowed to become, as you call it, a Christian?"

Ryan looked absolutely shocked. This was the first time anyone had ever converted to Christianity in his presence. Ryan did not have any idea as to what to do next. "Yes Brother Amerjit, you are most welcome to become a believer in the true God."

Without warning, one-by-one each of Amerjit's cousins rose from their places and asked if they too could become followers of this Jesus person?" Ryan acknowledged each man with a handshake and an affirmation of entry into the brotherhood of Christians.

Amerjit then did something which shocked all those present; he took out a small knife from his waist band, unwrapped his turban and cut off his long, dark hair. He then proceeded to chop at his beard. His cousins were clearly amazed that a Sikh man, who had never cut his hair or beard, would remove both in an instant of emotion. One-by-one, each of them followed suit. All thought the men looked ragged and poorly clipped, but they looked to be new men. Ryan raised his hands and began to pray loudly–loudly enough to attract the attention of Michael St. John and John Carter who were standing at the wheel. Carter tied off the wheel and accompanied St. John to the forecastle where the Indians and the Irishman were lost in prayer. Carter looked at St. John, "What in the name of heaven is going on here? Our crew is going bald and going mad."

St. John recognized what was happening. "No Mr. Carter, God is at work here. Perhaps we need to get back to the helm and let God and Mr. Ryan do their work.

From that time, the regular story tellings become prayer sessions and story tellings. From that time, God began to work through the outstretched hand of Mr. Ryan. Before long, Christian songs and simple hymns were being sung as the ship's business was going on. Christ had come aboard the Burma Tiger.

The last leg from Colombo to Rangoon seemed like an eternity. Every few hours Michael looked at his pocket watch and calculated the hours until they would catch sight of Rangoon. He consulted the navigation chart, measuring each mile that passed. Every hour, he would take a sun reading with the sextant to determine exactly where the Burma Tiger was.

He then plotted how he would grab the first cab he could find along the Rangoon docks and race to James's compound and

Supi Yaw. He fantasized how he would hold her and how she would respond to him. He tried to formulate the words he would use when he once again asked her to become his wife. When he wasn't daydreaming about Supi Yaw, he had his face buried in one of the many books on seamanship Carter had insisted he read. By now, Michael had virtually memorized every rule of the sea, every point of the compass, every knot needed on a ship, and every detail of cargo stowage. He even memorized the semaphore and Morse codes methods of communications. Michael could navigate with a sextant almost as well as Captain Carter. When he wasn't engrossed in one of his seamanship volumes, he was reading the Bible. In fact, by the time they had reached Colombo, Michael announced one evening at dinner, that he had completed the entire book from Genesis to Revelations.

At the approximate time expected to have the first sighting of Rangoon, Michael turned the wheel over to Mr. Ryan. Michael climbed the rope ladder to the top mast. There, he perched himself in what might be called the crow's nest. From thirty feet in the air, he could see nothing but ocean in all directions. As hard as he tried to see land in the distance, none came. After about an hour, he did sight a handful of seagulls circling the ship. "Gulls!" he yelled. Seagulls always indicate land. "Garbage!" he then yelled, "Garbage in the water; we must be getting close to land!"

As Michael continued to watch the garbage and seagulls overhead, someone on the bow sprint yelled, "Land ho!" Michael rushed below, changed into a clean suit and cap, washed his face and combed his shoulder-length hair.

CHAPTER SIXTY

Two hours later, the Burma Tiger tied up at one of the many piers along the Rangoon waterfront. Michael handed Captain Carter a map he had drawn up showing the way to James's compound on the outskirts of Rangoon. You can find me there as soon as you get settled with the customs business. I have someone I very much need to talk to."

As Michael jumped over the side of the ship, John Carter yelled out, "Permission to leave the ship granted."

Michael found a rickshaw and ordered the driver to run, double quick to the compound. He stated the price would be doubled if he truly hurried.

The poor rickshaw puller managed to find every short cut in Rangoon and had Michael at James's main gate in under an hour. Michael pounded on the large wooden gate until a servant opened it. Bua Tan Bo recognized Michael's yell. "I am here at last!" Bua and Michael embraced like long-lost brothers.

"Where is she? Where is Supi Yaw?" Michael demanded. Bua and James laughed as Michael looked for his woman.

James spoke, "Supi Yaw has told us of your proposal and intentions. While we are pleased with your intentions regarding our beloved Supi Yaw, you must follow our traditions for engagement and marriage. After all, you are once again in Burma."

Michael took a very deep breath. "I am sorry Elder James, but I have come a long ways, not only from England, but from being a soldier. My life is more than half over, and I am anxious to get on with the rest of my life, with Supi Yaw."

James again spoke, "Michael, Supi Yaw's parents are here at my home. We have been expecting you. Before you will be allowed to speak with Supi Yaw, you must first observe our primary courtship custom. I will arrange for a 'cup of ginger tea' with her parents. You will sit at their table and discuss the weather. If her father finds you acceptable as a son-in-law, he will offer you a second cup of tea. If he has reservations, he will not. If that were to happen, you would simply leave and be done with it. On the other hand, if you are offered a second cup of tea, you may proceed to Supi Yaw's cottage at the rear of my compound. She knows that you are here. When you go to Supi Yaw's cottage, you will go with Bua. He will hand you a hibiscus flower which you will then offer to Supi Yaw when she opens the door. If she takes the flower, she will then open the door and you may enter. At that point the engagement is confirmed. If for some reason, she should reject the flower and close the door, you will leave and not return–ever.

A sharp pain shot through Michael's heart at James's last comments. Seeing the brief look of concern, Bua whispered, "My sister will grab both the flower and you and slam the door behind." Michael smiled at Bua's comment.

James said, "Come Brother Michael, let us meet the parents. Elder Simon and his wife were sitting at a small round teak table in a teakwood pavilion surrounded by bamboo and hibiscus bushes. They were both dressed in traditional Baum attire and keenly aware of the events about to happen. Michael greeted the pair with a low bow expressing his ultimate respect for them as well as their positions in the Baum community. He then, careful not to turn his back on the two, took as seat next to Bua.

Elder Simon offered Michael a cup of ginger tea. Michael took a sip of tea only when he saw Simon take a sip. For the next hour they talked about the weather, the size of the mango crop this season and even the events of Michael's journey from England. The seemingly meaningless conversation appeared to last for hours. At last, all of the tea cups on the table were empty. Michael's heart began to pound. *What happens if he doesn't offer me a second cup? Do I simply get up and go away? Do I take Supi Yaw in spite of his opposition? What do I do if…?"*

At that point, the old man, seeing the consternation on Michael's face, picked up the teapot and poured a second cup of tea for all those around the table. Bua smiled directly at Michael. "Welcome to my family," Bua whispered.

Michael smiled. "Not so fast. I still have to see what your sister does with my flower."

James, smiling from ear-to-ear stood nearby, plucked a crimson hibiscus flower from a nearby bush and held it up for Michael to see. He beckoned Michael and Bua to follow him. The red-brick path led the way to a small bungalow at the rear of the compound. Flower pots filled with brilliant red bougainvillea covered much of the front of the bungalow. James then handed the flower to Michael. Bua stood beside Michael as Michael nervously tapped on the wooden door. A long thirty seconds passed before the door opened and Supi Yaw stood facing Michael St. John. Before anyone could move, Michael slowly extended the flower toward Supi Yaw. She smiled and took the flower. She then stood aside and invited Michael inside. Michael's heart was pounding so violently, he thought for a minute that he might faint. Supi Yaw slowly closed the door, leaving Bua and James outside, smiling. Supi Yaw simply melted into Michael's arms. The feelings, the pent-up emotions surged for what seemed like hours. The magnificent rush of love from one to another was briefly interrupted by a small English Bulldog scratching at Michael's boot. Gunga was demanding to be recognized. Both Michael and Supi Yaw laughed as the little dog danced on his hind legs and yipped to be held. The physical affection soon gave way to questions–good questions. "When can we be married? What sort of ceremony shall we have? Shall we have a Christian wedding or a traditional Baum wedding? Who will do what and where?

Michael responded as most husbands-to-be respond, "Anything you wish my dear; anything you wish."

Supi Yaw said, "Michael since your first proposal, I have given our wedding a great deal of thought. I am not one of those silly girls who want all sorts of flowers and dancing and the like. I simply want to be united in a way which is pleasing to my family and your people. I would suggest that we hold the wedding here in James's compound with one of our tribal pastors officiating. If you prefer, we could include a vicar from the local church."

Michael thought for a moment. "My dearest, Supi Yaw, my ship, the Burma Tiger, is probably one of the only ships on the high seas with its own chaplain. He is an Irish gentleman who was fully ordained and well suited to perform a marriage. If that is to your liking, I could prevail on him to perform the deed."

Supi Yaw smiled at the thought of Michael's mention of having a "ship's chaplain." "Yes Michael, I believe even an Irishman would suit me well."

Several hours passed as Michael and Supi Yaw considered the future together. Supi Yaw had hundreds of questions about how they would live, where they would live and so on. Michael strongly insisted that he and his new partners would make a successful business of their new shipping venture. He also reaffirmed the issue of a full scholarship to an American medical school and the right to sit the examination for the position of physician. Michael could clearly see that this was a significant part of her willingness to immigrate to a foreign land.

The conversation was abruptly interrupted by a knock on Supi Yaw's door. It was Bua. "Michael, you are not married yet. It is time we all went to bed. You can either spend the night here in my quarters, or you may return to your ship." Michael opened the door. Bua held up his pocket watch–12:30.

"Bua, I shall accept your kind offer to spend the night near your beloved sister. I wouldn't want anyone sneaking in the middle of the night and carrying her off to the mountains. I will remain close."

Michael bid Supi Yaw a fond "good night" and left with Bua. Michael put his arm around Bua's shoulder. "Just think, I am about to become the brother-in-law of a famous river pirate," he laughed.

"And I am about to become the brother-in-law of the Hero of the Irrawaddy," Bua replied.

The following morning, the gong at the front gate of the compound announced visitors. Both Bua and Michael were still asleep, as they had talked well into the night. Michael recognized Carter's voice and the occasional giggle of his new wife. A knock on the door caused St. John to jump for his trousers. One of James' servants announced that a Captain and Mrs. Carter had arrived to speak with a Mr. St. John. "It's only John and Opal."

Michael and Bua entered the garden area where they found Supi Yaw and the Carters about to have a cup of ginger tea. "Good morning, Michael," Supi Yaw purred. Michael simply smiled, unable to speak.

John also said, "Good morning, Michael" in a mocking way.

Michael replied, "Up a bit earlier than usual, aren't you, John? You are usually not out of bed until noon."

John smiled at the jab. John spoke, "So, this is the very same woman you have blubbered about, day and night since we left England. I must admit, she is worth the trip."

Opal nudged her husband in the ribs. "Hush," she whispered. "Be nice."

Several platters of fresh fruit along with a plate of sweet sticky rice were set on the table. Supi Yaw presided over the pouring of tea and the distribution of plates of fruit and sweet sticky rice. Bird songs in the background, along with the gentle tinkle of brass "temple bells," added to the beauty of the moment.

Opal began asking all the questions about the wedding. What would Supi Yaw be wearing, who would be acting as attendants and so on? Supi Yaw then asked if Opal Carter would do her the honor of standing as her matron of honor. Opal was overwhelmed with joy at the invitation.

Michael then looked over to Bua, "Best man?" Bua nodded in agreement.

Michael then looked at Carter, "Groomsman?" Carter nodded.

Before the Burmese sun had risen to its high noon position in the hot blue sky, the news of Michael St. John and Supi Yaw's engagement had reached almost every Baum in the realm. Many older people, particularly the older women, shook their heads in mild disagreement that one of their own would blend with a foreigner. But after the usual market talk, most were satisfied that the lady "medicine man" would be, at last a respectable married woman. Now she could stay home in her bamboo hut and make babies for her husband and her parents to gloat over.

Unbeknownst to Michael, and prior to his rising from his bed, Supi Yaw and her parents had set the date for the wedding and subsequent celebration. Supi Yaw's parents were adamant that one month's time be allowed to provide sufficient time for every Baum in the entire universe to make their way to Rangoon. After considerable discussion, two weeks were agreed upon. This would allow for those who seriously wanted to attend a three, four, or even five-day feast to attend. Even though the Baum people were Spartan and conservative, they nonetheless liked to throw long and expensive wedding feasts.

By the time the same Burmese sun had reached its course, Colonel Winston Somerset, the new commanding officer, had received a personal note from Sergeant Major Michael St. John, retired, requesting his presence at the wedding. Michael also noted that most of the Baum tribal leaders would be attending the event. He subtly suggested that this would present an extraordinary opportunity for the Colonel to meet these dignitaries on an informal level.

Like all women since Eve, Supi Yaw created great long lists of things to be done, who would be doing them, where people would sit, where people would stand and where Michael would be at any given moment. At breakfast on the second day of their engagement, Supi Yaw and her mother began to unravel the great long list which seemed to have no end. Michael and Bua simply looked at each other and exchanged expressions of befuddlement. All the while Michael's thoughts were focused on what provisions he would need for the crossing of the Pacific and what cargo he might procure. The wedding was something which had to be gotten through; something like going through a typhoon.

After a week of the engagement and one week prior to the actual wedding, Michael received a note, delivered by a British soldier inviting him to a bachelor party hosted by Colonel Somerset. In Colonel Somerset's note he indicated that the American ambassador would also be attending. The mention of the American ambassador's participation in the event caused more than mild concern when the story reached Carter's ears. "There's something going on here, Michael. Brits and Yanks simply don't mix on a social level unless there's something afoot. If I were you, Mike, I would stay close to your pals and watch your wallet."

Michael grinned and spoke, "John, the Ambassador simply wants to reaffirm the scholarship commitment his government has given to Supi Yaw. The Yanks want another woman doctor before the Brits can catch up. If they can Shanghai a former British subject and make her a doctor, so much the better.

The day of the bachelor party had been set two days prior to the wedding. Colonel Somerset had managed to schedule the event at one of the more prominent British clubs, providing that any non-British attendees enter by way of the servant's door at the rear of the club, and they not be seen using any of the facilities, including the restrooms. To add to the mix, all non-British attendees were to be attired in proper evening suits, complete with cravats and polished shoes. Bua Tan Bo had opted not to attend the bachelor party, but Supi Yaw reminded him that the first responsibility of a best man, in the Baum tradition, was to prevent the groom from falling into any sort of debauchery prior to promising his vows. She had heard about some of the bachelor parties for British soldiers where the groom was rendered intoxicated and enticed into illicit activities with ladies other than his intended bride. Supi Yaw made it perfectly clear that her husband-to-be would not be allowed to fall into anyone's trap of enticement or poor judgment. She made it perfectly clear to her brother that any abnormal consumption of alcoholic beverages would most likely bring on an unfortunate bout of malaria.

Michael, John and Bua arrived well after most of the guests were well into their second gin and tonic. This was the first significant event where Michael did not wear any sort of military uniform. A new suit which had been commissioned by his bride-to-be felt different and almost uncomfortable. John sported a newly tailored sea captain's uniform, complete with four gold stripes on its coat sleeves. Again, a formal "request" issued by his new wife. His neatly trimmed beard and wooden peg leg rounded out the image of a storybook sea captain. Bua wore a tailored, white evening suit complete with stylish Panama hat.

Colonel Somerset raised his glass as Michael entered the room. Michael noted the obvious consternation among several Brits who quietly commented that Bua had not entered by way of the servant's door. Most of those in attendance opted to ignore the indiscretion and lifted their glasses in a mutual salute to the groom. Aside from the usual British merchants, civil servants, and those who make a living out of attending every party in Rangoon, there were several of Michael's former fellow sergeants from the Rangoon barracks. Michael also noticed both Roberts and McMillan standing near the rear of the room. He broke into a broad smile as they raised their glasses.

Shortly after Michael made the rounds and shook hands with all in attendance, Richard Lowen, the American ambassador entered the room. With all of the countenance of a Roman emperor, Ambassador Lowen made straight for Colonel Somerset who was talking with St. John, Roberts and McMillan. "Ah! Mr. St. John, what a pleasure to meet you at last. There has been so much said about you and your exploits in the local press, I feel that I know you quite well. You have become quite a legend in these parts, with all that business about the 'Battle on the Irrawaddy'."

Michael then introduced Bua Tan Bo, the infamous pirate of the infamous battle. The ambassador seemed duly impressed with both men. Michael beckoned to John Carter who was talking with several merchants and summoned him to the small group. Michael introduced John Carter, the American sea captain whose life was saved by Michael's bride-to-be. The ambassador reached for a glass of brandy from a passing waiter and loudly announced another toast to the three notables, Michael, John and Bua Tan Bo. With all eyes focused on the ambassador, he slowly took a note from his coat pocket. As if it were a religious relic, he ever so carefully unfolded it and began to read:

"From the desk of Abraham Lincoln, President of the United States of America. On behalf of my fellow Americans, I wish to extend my profound gratitude to Miss Supi Yaw for having saved the life of American sea captain, John Carter. It is obvious that the skills of this talented medical practitioner should not go unnoticed or unperfected. As a result of her extraordinary actions on the high seas, I wish to extend to her a full scholarship to an American medical institution of her selection. Subsequent to her course of studies, I further extend the right to sit for the examinations required to confirm her as a bona fide medical doctor with all rights and privileges incumbent in that title.

Respectfully submitted,
Abraham Lincoln

Ambassador Lowen then handed the note to Michael and asked him to present it to his bride-to-be. Michael looked the ambassador directly in the eye and replied, "Sir, with all due respect to your and your President, I would ask that you personally present this note to Supi Yaw yourself. That way, if she doesn't like the idea, it will be you who will receive her answer and not me." At that the entire room broke into laughter. Michael continued, "This means, sir, that you will be required to attending our wedding." The ambassador agreed. Michael added, "You may bring your wife along as well."

Again more laughter. As soon as the laughter died down, Ambassador Lowen removed another document from his other breast pocket, unfolded it and began to read:

From the desk of Secretary of War, Edwin M. Stanton to Sergeant Major Michael Oliver St. John.

Sir, it has come to my attention that you may be considering visiting our shores with the intent of becoming a part of our great nation. In light of your possible and most welcome inclination to immigrate to the United States of America, and in consideration of your lengthy and distinguished military career, I would humbly offer you a commission in the Union Army of the United States of America. Said commission would be at the rank of Lieutenant Colonel.

As you are well aware, the United States of America is engaged in an unfortunate conflict with the Confederate States of America. Men like you would prove to be extremely valuable in our righteous conflict to re-establish the American Constitution over all states and territories of the United States of America. If you are willing to accept this most generous offer of commission, please inform Ambassador Lowen.

Most sincerely,

Edwin M. Stanton, Secretary of War

United States of America

The ambassador smiled as he handed the note to Michael. Michael did not extend his hand to receive the note. "Mr. Ambassador," he said quietly, "I could never serve in a conflict where brother was expected to kill brother or cousin to kill cousin. To my simple way of thinking, this sort of conflict is unthinkable. It reminds me of Cain killing his brother Abel. Perhaps the cause both warring factions deem worthy, brothers killing brothers can never be justified. Please extend my gratitude to your Secretary of War for his generous offer. You may wish to include in your conveyance that I would make myself and my resources available in the defense of the United States in the event of foreign aggression, but I cannot abide brothers killing brothers.

Realizing what St. John had just said, Ambassador Lowen folded the note and replaced it back in his breast pocket. Lowen looked St. John straight in the eye and gave him a silent affirmation of the words he had just spoken. Lowen realized that this was one of the very few truly honorable men he had met.

By the stroke of midnight on the club's wall, John Carter had procured more than a dozen cargo consignments for transport to Singapore, Manila, Hong Kong and San Francisco. If all went well, the profits from the voyage would add considerable weight to the slowly depleting resources of the ship's company.

Bua rose to the occasion of a militant best man. Each time someone would hand Michael a new glass of brandy or gin and tonic, Bua would snatch it away and replace it with a glass of chilled pineapple juice or coconut water. One of Supi Yaw's warnings indicated that consumption of even moderate amounts of liquor might bring on another bout of malaria. She added that a malaria bout would most certainly call for the postponement of the wedding or at least the honeymoon. Needless to say, Michael heeded the warning.

Somewhere well after midnight, Colonel Somerset, now quite intoxicated, declared the party over. Sergeants Roberts and McMillan both suggested that they accompany Michael home in order to protect him from any further high jinx. While Bua found no problem with this suggestion, Carter recalled several pre-wedding events where grooms-to-be were "baptized" in a nearby body of river, and usually left naked to find their way home. He strongly suspected that this was the intent of these two Scots and suggested that he too accompany Michael back to his ship. As the group prepared to mount a waiting carriage, Michael stopped dead in his tracks. His blood froze in his veins as he found himself staring into the dark beyond the carriage. He immediately recognized a face which permeated every cell in his body with absolute terror. Bua notice that Michael stood like a marble statue. After a few seconds, he then saw the familiar face smiling back through the thick evening haze. It was the Prince. His highly exaggerated eyes and toothy smile shown like a masquerade mask beneath his black turban. "Noble sirs," the turbaned spirit said, "Allah has been most generous in allowing us to once again meet, but this time, on more hospitable terms."

Although slightly intoxicated, both Roberts and McMillan realized that this was the rogue they had conquered at the "Valley of the Pigs" some months back. Both men moved themselves forward to provide cover for St. John in the event the sinister little man attempted any sort of threatening gesture or provocative act.

The Prince went on the offensive by extending his hand toward McMillan and Roberts. "You two gentlemen must be Sergeants Roberts and McMillan. Word of your magnificent humanitarian works among the Baum has reached my humble ears. I am told that your efforts have resulted in numerous agricultural cooperatives and educational programs among children and young women. Gentlemen, you are to be congratulated on your work. I have prayed many times that God will continue to bless you and your endeavors." All those listening to the little man's words realized that he was attempting to calm the water before crossing the bridge.

The Prince opted to continue with his introduction before arriving at his main point. "And you, Mr. Bua Tan Bo, you have become the subject of a thousand stories. Your manifestation of godly power at our camp along the river, still leaves me wondering. Was it indeed some sort of a trick, or was it truly an act of your God?"

At that point, Bua interrupted the monologue. "Sir, perhaps it was a trick of God."

The Prince threw back his head and laughed. "Well answered, my friend, well answered."

Michael then entered the conversation. "Perhaps I should know your true name; the moniker 'Prince' seems to be a bit out of place here."

The Prince replied, "You are quite right, sir. As a matter of fact, all but a few of my subjects deserted me after that most terrible day when they were showered with pig entrails. Almost of my former associates were told by a local Hindu priest that, in order to cleanse themselves of the sinful filth of the pig blood, they must bathe in the headwaters of the sacred Ganges River. So, most of my little flock of faithful are somewhere between Chittagong and the Himalayas. I, on the other hand, felt it sufficient to simply bathe in the Bay of Bengal. Now, as for my proper name, I was called by my father, Akkmed Abdul Abass. You may call me Akkmed if it pleases you.

Again he smiled broadly. "Now to the point of my visit. In our first meeting, you indicated that a railroad line would be built from Chittagong inland and possibly on to Rangoon. You also mentioned that concessions would be issued for support facilities along the way. During our conversation, you suggested that someone like my humble self might avail of one of these concessions, perhaps at the same location where we first met. I would humbly beg your good offices to be considered for such a concession."

Before Akkmed could utter another word, Colonel Somerset stumbled, literally stumbled into the group. Recognizing the little man at the crosshairs of everyone's gaze, Colonel Somerset blurted, "You stinking pig thief, I don't know what you are doing here, but I can assume it is not good. If you are not out of my area of responsibility by morning, I will personally hang you, using your rotting turban as a hangman's noose."

Both McMillan and Roberts grabbed the Colonel as his knees crumbled beneath him. "Good night, Mr. St. John. Our first duty is to our colonel. You will have to see yourself home."

The Prince's face looked as if he had been slapped. "Well gentlemen, he sighed, it looks like my suit for a concession has been denied before it had been presented."

Not wanting to lose any more face than already lost, Akkmed extended his hand toward Michael. "So, again we part. Who knows, perhaps Allah will bring us together another time and in more friendly circumstances."

While Michael shook the man's hand, Bua did not. Instead he replied, "I seriously doubt you and he will be meeting ever again. Mr. St. John will be sailing for the United States the morning after his wedding to my sister. There is little chance you will be meeting after his ship departs Rangoon."

Akkmed retorted, "His ship?"

"Yes," Carter replied, "Mr. St. John is the owner of a one hundred and six foot sailing ship bound for San Francisco."

"So," Akkmed replied, "you have become a man of means. Congratulations!" With that, Akkmed bowed slowly and disappeared into the thick Rangoon mist. Carter ordered the carriage driver to take the three men to the ship.

The following morning, a brunch was held at Elder James's compound. Each of the crew members including Mr. Ryan had been invited. Opal Carter was once again properly attired in one of her London frocks, complete with lace parasol. There were at least thirty people standing around a table heavy laden with fruits, cakes, and sweet rice. Supi Yaw emerged from her cottage, dressed in a traditional costume for a bribe-to-be. As she entered the pavilion, every eye was focused on the magnificent woman. She moved directly toward Michael who beamed with delight. To demonstrate her respect for the man, she lowered her head and bowed from the waist. Michael reached out his hand and lifted her chin and spoke, "Most honorable lady, do not ever bow or lower your head to me again. It is I who stand in awe of you. You are more than my equal; you are my reason for being."

Supi Yaw Yat realized what Michael was saying and why, but her father and mother did not. Supi Yaw moved to quell any conflict of cultures by saying, "My beloved Michael, as you once said to me, 'respect is the highest form of love.' If this be the case, for me not to show you my respect, even by bowing my head, could be seen as a termite in the fabric of our mutual love. Besides, my dear husband-to-be, it costs me nothing to bend my body in order to demonstrate my outward affection. It also allows others to see the level of my affection toward you." Michael smiled in agreement as did Elder Simon and his wife.

Michael then began to make formal introductions. First was Captain John Carter. Carter looked brighter and more fit than Supi Yaw had ever seen him. She commented on this fact. Carter then presented his, still blushing bride. "This is the reason for my fantastic state of health and state of mind. This little lady, Nurse Opal Carter, nursed me back to health, and then insisted that I marry her."

Opal poked her husband in the ribs playfully and extended her hand toward Supi Yaw. In her thick cockney accent said, "Your Mr. St. John talked about you day and night during our sea voyage, but you are far more beautiful than his words expressed. I would also have to say that you are getting quite a gentleman."

Timothy Ryan was then introduced as the "clergyman" who would be presiding over the holy service of matrimony.

Amerjit was then introduced along with his cousins. Supi Yaw did not recognize Amerjit without his turban and thick beard. Then she warmly recalled Amerjit's frequent services during her stay at the bachelor officers barracks. As Amerjit shook Supi Yaw's hand, he leaned forward, close to her ear, "I am one of you now. I am a Christian," he said proudly.

Supi Yaw looked at Michael as if to ask, *"Amerjit a Christian? What is going on here?"*

It took almost an hour to greet all those in attendance. Michael noticed that someone was missing. Brother James, would you be so kind as to step outside the compound and invite our carriage driver, Mr. Gabriel."

CHAPTER SIXTY-ONE

THE WEDDING

The following morning, Michael St. John accompanied by Bua Tan Bo, Captain John Carter, and Mr. Gabriel rode though the streets of Rangoon much like a king going to his coronation. The alley leading to James' compound was crammed with carriages parked on both sides. Michael recognized the emblems and standards of Colonel Somerset and Ambassador Lowen. There were many others with company emblems or simply flags on the doors. Like the Queen's personal coachman, Gabriel sat high on his seat with his head held high. Somewhere he had found an almost new silk top hat and a bright red feather to place in the hatband. The door to the compound was festooned with orchids of every description. Bua Tan Bo led the way as Michael and Carter followed through the one hundred or so seated guests. Before taking his place at a beautifully bedecked altar, Michael St. John moved from his designated place and went to where Supi Yaw's parents were seated. He bowed low to Elder Simon and took the slightly weeping woman's hand and kissed it politely. Supi Yaw's mother's smile expressed a thousand words–all of them good.

Timothy Ryan emerged from behind a drape of bougainvillea dressed in a simple but handsome robe. Around his neck was a pectoral cross made from rough wood.

A soft, deep thud of a distant drum brought the entire assembly to silence. A woman's voice began a ritual chant which was echoed by a chorus of unseen singers. Soon, a descant voice added to the three-part harmony. Many of those seated had never heard such a magnificent canticle in any cathedral or in any palace in the world. The simple symphony stopped. Then, another drum, a much smaller drum, began a slow cadence followed by the unfortunate drone of a bagpipe. Sergeant Roberts with his bagpipes followed Sergeant McMillan with a tenor drum into the compound. Ryan then gave a gesture for all to stand. Behind the two sergeants came Opal Carter looking more like an angel than an angel. Behind her stood two other Baum women dressed in hand-woven native skirts and blouses. While Michael St. John's eyes were entirely focused on the entry, Bua Tan Bo's gaze never left the face of his friend and brother-in-law to be. Bua wanted to capture the expression on Michael's face when his new bride appeared. Everyone in the assembly was wondering if the bride would be wearing a traditional Baum costume or a European-style gown. As Supi Yaw entered the compound, she was wearing an ivory dress made from pure silk. With hand-embroidered flowers along the bottom of the skirt and blouse, it was the perfect blend of the most tasteful European styling with strong but subtle Asian accents. There was an audible gasp as the beautiful woman, bedecked in an indescribably beautifully marriage costume began her slow march toward her husband-to-be.

Michael was absolutely dumbfounded. Never in his entire life had he seen some one so beautiful, so completely perfect. Bua Tan Bo smiled as he saw the expression on Michael's face.

Bua thought to himself, "Perhaps I need to find a good woman and settle into a marriage."

Mr. Ryan motioned for the assembly to be seated whereupon, he began the ceremony which Supi Yaw and her mother had woven together. The ceremony included symbolic actions which were taken from both British and Baum tradition. Timothy Ryan had spent two short days and two long nights creating a message which constituted more than a simple marriage homily, soon forgotten by all involved. The Reverend Timothy Ryan began:

"Dearly beloved, in the very beginning, Almighty God saw that man was not intended to be alone. While man, in the form of Adam, was given authority over all of the animals of the land, the birds of the air, and the fish in the sea, he sorely needed someone with whom he could abide. God could have given Adam a creation which would become subservient to Him in every respect and attend to His every need. God could have even created a being which would worship this Adam as if he were himself a god. But, God opted to create a creature, which like Adam, had a free will. This new creation, which He called woman was ordained to be a 'helpmate' to this creation He called man, but not a servant or a slave. Actually, it would have been easier to have created whole legions of slaves and servants, much like the army of angels which surround the Almighty. Woman was created with the freedom of choice to either complement her mate or to conflict with him.

Isn't it odd that some men prefer to demand respect at the point of a gun or spear rather than to earn it through honorable actions? Isn't it strange how some men strive to put themselves in a position where they are worshiped and given lofty titles usually reserved for deities? Isn't it peculiar how some men demand that people love them when they are clearly unlovable? All of these situations are a result of free will gone awry. During the preparation for this wonderful event Supi Yaw mentioned something that she was told by Michael. He said, 'Respect is the highest form of love.' If we think deeply about this statement, we find the true essence of God's commandment that we are to love one another. There are thousands of books and hundreds of thousands of sermons which attempt to define what that love truly looks like. Love is quite often a result of biological conditions necessary for the continuation of the species or even worse, economic necessities. Unfortunately, love has all too often been relegated to a philosophical concept and left to be defined by those who least understand it. If we are to fully understand the concept of respect for another person as the highest form of love, we can see how a husband and wife can bond together as one and truly live a God-pleasing life. Michael, Supi Yaw, always give more than you take. Always build rather than tear down. Always hold your spouse in higher esteem than you hold yourself. In other word, respect one another."

Mr. Ryan then asked for the rings. Both Bua and Opal placed the two symbols on a silver plate whereupon Mr. Ryan uttered a litany of symbolic words. He then asked Michael to place the smaller ring on Supi Yaw's finger. Then it was Supi Yaw's turn to place the larger ring on Michael's sweating finger. "By this simple act, I declare you to be husband and wife. I further admonish you to live in the brilliant shadow of God's love and His covenant."

Mr. Ryan then turned the couple toward those assembled in Simon's garden and said, "From this day forth, they are known as Mr. and Mrs. St. John, husband and wife."

The planned recessional almost immediately dissolved into frenzy of congratulations, huggings, and all-purpose happiness. In order to bring some semblance of order to the situation,

Sergeant Roberts began *Amazing Grace* on his bagpipes, accompanied by Sergeant McMillan's drum. Shortly, the Baum singers entered the concert for a seemingly never ending singing and playing of the hymn.

Soon, every hand had been shaken and cheek kissed. Now, it was Colonel Somerset's turn to make an official proclamation of congratulations on behalf of the British government. Before Somerset could bring an end to the event, Ambassador Lowen took the floor. With his hand held up slightly, there was absolute silence. "Ladies and gentlemen, it is my delightful duty to present Mrs. Michael St. John an invitation to attend any American medical school of her selection and subsequent to a course of study, to sit for the examination for medical doctor." The ambassador removed the note from President Lincoln and, after clearing his throat, read the invitation aloud. This bit of theater was in part to show his high regard for the lady, but moreover to poke the British in the eye for failing to allow women to enter into the world of medicine.

While there was general applause at the announcement, most of the Englishmen, including Colonel Somerset, were a bit restrained in their response. In fact, Colonel Somerset whispered to one of those standing next to him, "Grandstanding."

Supi Yaw took the document from the ambassador and said, "I shall have to confer with my husband before I can give your President an answer."

She then looked at Michael who grinned and nodded his head. "Yes, I believe you would make an excellent doctor, perhaps even a surgeon."

She then turned to the ambassador, "Yes, I believe I will accept your kind offer."

Another cheer went up, mainly from the Baum and Burmese people. The ambassador then handed her another document instructing her to contact a certain, Army Doctor Hitchcock at the Presidio in San Francisco, California. He would serve as Supi Yaw's liaison, and hopefully, mentor.

Elder James, again regaled in his 'lord chancellor's garb, announced that a luncheon would be served as soon as the chairs could be replaced with tables. For the next few hours, there was feasting on every sort of fruit and meat. Well before afternoon, James ordered several large jars of jungle berry juice to be brought to the tables. Many of those familiar with the toxic purple liquid were first to the table. Others like Mr. Ryan and Captain Carter were soon made aware of the wine's ability to lighten one's mood considerably. Michael saw that Ryan and Carter were well into their second or third cup of the wine. He then called out, "Enough of that potion, we are sailing tomorrow morning. One more cup and you won't be ready to sail for a week." Captain Carter saluted as did Mr. Ryan.

Michael took his gold pocket watch from his vest pocket and considered the hour. He knew that if he didn't cast off tomorrow morning, Supi Yaw might have second thoughts about leaving her beloved homeland. In fact, he even considered remaining in Asia and forgetting the whole business about going to America. After all, he could make as much money hauling cargo between Asian ports as American ports.

Michael noticed his wife talking with her parents on the far side of the garden. He made his way to her and attempted to gently enter the conversation. Elder Simon then handed his daughter a small box wrapped in a colorful hand-woven cloth. "This is soil from our village, the village in which you were born. Treasure it. If you are blessed with children, allow them to touch this soil. When you die, ask that this soil be placed in your grave. You should always retain a small piece of your past with your present and your future. Now my daughter, go with your husband and do not look back." With that, the old man kissed Supi Yaw on the forehead and turned away. There were tears in Supi Yaw's eyes as there were in Michael's.

Michael took his wife by the hand and led her toward the compound's main gate. Bua Tan Bo was standing, waiting for the couple's departure. "Michael, we shall say good bye tomorrow before you cast off. I have everything in good order regarding the business between the tribes and the British government. The council of elders has granted me the authority to act on their behalf in attempting to formulate a working relationship. I will keep you posted by mail on our progress. Pray for me. I will need all the wisdom God can spare."

Michael nodded in confidence that his new brother-in-law already possessed sufficient wisdom to bring the plan to fruition.

Gabriel was found sleeping in the rear of his carriage. His orders were to take the new bride and groom to the ship. Unfortunately, some of Gabriel's friends had provided him with ample amounts of the jungle berry juice, whereupon he found himself unable to conduct the business of a coachman. Michael simply laughed, hoisted his bride into the driver's seat next to him, cracked the whip, released the foot brake and trotted off into the Rangoon evening.

The Indian crew had made an arch over the gangway complete with flowers. Amerjit had prepared several dishes of food for the bride and groom, to be eaten at their leisure. Amerjit had diplomatically arranged that all crew members, including Captain and Mrs. Carter, be lodged somewhere off the ship. Amerjit even took the responsibility for seeing that Gunga was comfortably caged and sent to stay the night with his cousins. Amerjit and his cousins applauded as the bride and groom dismounted the carriage. Michael picked up his wife in his arms and carried her cautiously across the gangplank and kissed her passionately as he stood on the deck. "Welcome to our first home, my beloved wife."

"Thank you, my dear husband, for coming for me in this way. I know of no other man who would do what you have done. There are no words to express the absolute joy I feel right now. You are more wonderful than I could have ever imagined. You are worthy of my utmost love and respect."

Amerjit could clearly see that things were beginning to become a bit too personal for the eyes and ears of him and his cousins. "Alright crew, we have things to do. Let us allow Mister and Mrs. St. John to tidy up the ship and make ready for tomorrow's sailing."

"Tidy up the ship, indeed!" Michael whispered to his wife as he again picked her up in his arms and moved toward the rear cabin. "Tidy up indeed!"

Morning came with all the noise customary to the busy Rangoon port. Michael awoke to the sounds of a dozen or so different languages all moving ships, cargo, and people. From the cacophony of voices outside his porthole, he heard Captain John Carter ordering the loading of twenty earthen jars filled with Baum jungle berry juice. Simon had agreed to allow the use of his compound for the wedding if Michael and John would attempt to explore potential markets for this purple elixir. Michael noticed that his new wife was not beside him in the bed. Realizing where he was, what had happened, Michael leapt from his bed and dressed. Within seconds, he was on deck looking for his bride. Mrs. Michael St. John was sitting on a rope locker with the small English Bulldog on her lap, talking with Mrs. John Carter. The two ladies were deeply involved in a book on general biology. Supi Yaw St. John acknowledged her husband with a broad smile and a gentle wave. Michael immediately made his way to where the two women were sitting. Gunga yipped playfully to be picked up and scratched by his master. "Michael," Supi Yaw purred, "I didn't want to wake you. I thought you might be tired from all the events of yesterday."

Michael blushed violently as Opal attempted to hide a knowing smile. Opal, still stifling a giggle, went off to find her husband, leaving the newlyweds to discuss things newlyweds discuss.

The Burma Tiger had missed the morning tide and would have to wait for the afternoon tide to sail. While Michael was anxious to be under way and begin a new life, there were dozens of last-minute details to attend to. Somewhere around ten o'clock, Bua came dashing up the gangplank. "Michael, I was hoping you were still here. I have great news. But you must keep it absolutely secret. The American ambassador has quietly given me his support for our development plan; that is, if the British government fails to act or acts too slowly. He indicated that he would personally see to it that we would receive several dozen American missionary groups. I don't know how he received the information about the plan, but he seemed very well informed. In any case, we should have the support needed to bring our various tribal groups into the modern day. I would give anything to see the expression on the face of the Archbishop of Canterbury if all of the sudden, the back hills of Burma are crawling with American missionaries."

Michael laughed out loud at Bua's comment.

Bua continued, "And Michael, the council of elders has granted me the authority to act as their spokesman during the discussions with the British government. One of the elders quietly suggested that I find a suitable wife soon so that I might be considered for a position as an elder. I am not certain that I am ready for a wife or a seat on the council of elders. I am having too much fun the way things are now. And think of it, Michael–what woman in her right mind would want to marry a notorious river pirate?"

Michael spoke, "Dear brother-in-law, I highly suggest marriage. Even after twenty-four hours of being married, I believe even you would find it quite pleasant."

Now it was Bua who laughed out loud. "I shall give it strong consideration. Michael, as soon as the meetings with the tribal groups and the British government begin, I will send you details of our progress. I truly hope that within a year's time, we will begin to see some specific progress in our efforts. Pray for us daily, brother-in-law."

Supi Yaw saw Michael and Bua talking near the gangplank and came to Michael's side. Bua spoke, "My dear sister, my brother-in-law tells me that he is well satisfied with his new position as a husband."

She smiled and glanced at Michael who returned the smile. Bua handed Supi Yaw a small silk bag. "You forgot your banjo."

By four o'clock all of the last-minute items had been purchased from dock-side shops, including several bags of hard candy. Captain John Carter took hold of the Burma Tiger's wheel and commanded that the two holding lines be freed and the jib sail set. The Indian crew followed his instructions like a well-oiled machine. Final good-byes were shouted between those who were embarking on a new life and those who remained on the dock. Within minutes the Burma Tiger was divorced from the land. Carter pointed the broken-toothed tiger southward toward its next port of call, Singapore. Opal Carter took a stand beside her husband at the wheel while Michael O. St. John and Mrs. St. John stood on the foredeck gazing off into the future.

∾

CHAPTER SIXTY-TWO

Well into the second day out of Rangoon, Amerjit became hysterical. As if he had seen a ghost, he came running frantically from the galley storage locker. "Oh my goodness, we have a person hiding in the pantry!" he yelled. "There is a frightening man hiding in the galley pantry. I thought Gunga was attempting to flush out a rodent from behind several rice sacks when I noticed the rodent was not a rodent, but a man."

Captain Carter handed off the ship's wheel to one of the Indian crew members and barked out a compass bearing as he dashed toward the weapons locker. Carter grabbed two rifles and two bandoleers of cartridges, and then ran toward the galley storage pantry. He nearly collided with Michael as the two entered the passageway outside the small chamber. Carter tossed Michael one of the rifles and a bandoleer. Both immediately crammed a cartridge into the chamber and prepared to enter the tiny room. The English Bulldog was standing at point, trying his best to resemble an Irish setter. His small tail was twitching back and forth like the baton of a conductor at a band concert. Before either Michael or John could move, a familiar voice came forth from the pantry. "Please do not shoot me, my friends; it is only me Akkmed, your friend. I mean you no harm. I will be coming out with my hands above my shameful head."

The small, dark man, covered with his black cloak and turban, emerged from the cell with a broad smile across his face. "Sirs, your Colonel Somerset ordered me out of his area of responsibility or he would hang me. It appeared to me that my only recourse to meet his deadline was to find a ship leaving Burma. When I discovered that your ship would be sailing, I decided that this would allow me to comply with Colonel Somerset's order and leave this cursed land of Burma. Then, I thought to myself that I might even decide to continue on to the United States of America with you and your party and begin a new life."

Michael and Carter looked at each other in total disbelief. By this time, Amerjit and several of the crew had assembled in the passageway behind Michael. Carter barked an order, "Amerjit, find a rope and tie a hanging knot. We are going to hang this pirate from the bow sprint."

Michael interrupted, "There will be no hanging on my ship. I have seen all the hangings I ever want to see."

John looked at Michael and winked letting him know that he was jesting. The little man in the black cloak and turban fell to his knees. "In the name of Jesus the Holy Christ, His Holy Mother Mary, His Holy Father and all the holy saints of heaven, please do not hang me. Cut my head off, yes, but do not hang me by a rope. It is a horrible sin to be hanged by a rope."

By this time Supi Yaw arrived in the tightly cramped passageway. Demanding to know what was going on, Amerjit gave a minute-by-minute account of the discovery and capture of this stowaway. He was quick to announce the death sentence which had been pronounced on the quivering little man on the floor. Before she could enter into the situation, Michael gave her a smile and indicated that the death sentence was only a ruse to drive the severity of the situation deep into the man's soul.

Carter took charge. "Mr. Ryan, lock the prisoner's hands behind him and take him to the afterdeck. Things are getting a bit too tight down here." Ryan complied and marched the bound man up to the main deck.

Akkmed, the dethroned prince, was babbling incantations in an unknown language. His eyes were rolled back in their sockets as he groaned his prayers, curses, or whatever he was groaning. All those on the ship, including Gunga seemed to enjoy the drama being played out on the afterdeck of the Burma Tiger. Finally, Mr. Ryan entered the ruse. "Captain Carter, Mr. St. John, I would appeal to your sense of Christian justice and allow this man to remain on this side of eternity for a bit longer. Hanging him would only end his earthly suffering. I suggest that we allow him to live on the intestines of some of the sharks which escort our ship."

Again, the black-robed man began to cry out, "Please show this poor misguided man some Christian mercy you followers of the Holy Christ are always proclaiming. Allow me to live. I promise I will convert to your religion and serve you as a slave all the days of my miserable life."

Amerjit, not realizing that the event had become a macabre ruse, jumped to the defense of the little man in the dirty black robe and turban. "Good sirs," he pleaded, "I recall once having visited my uncle in the city of Bangkok. On the occasion of that visit, I was witness to an unforgettable event which I believe you will find relevant to this situation. A criminal was to be beheaded in the Royal parade grounds, near the Grand Palace of the King. The King's judge read the indictment and the death sentence. The King's judge then ordered the executioner to stand ready to cut the poor man's head off. Before the executioner could strike his sword against the neck of the condemned man, the King's Chief Minister held up his hand and spoke. He ordered the executioner to stand down. He then read a confession and statement of contrition the guilty man had signed several days prior to his execution. In that statement, the poor man acknowledged his crime against the King and his law. He further acknowledged that he was deserving of the death penalty. He did, however, pray for clemency from the King and promised, if granted, he would gladly submit to a life of servitude. The King showed mercy and allowed the poor man to keep his miserable head, but insisted that he suffer the consequences of his transgressions. So, Sergeant Major St. John and Captain, I would plead on behalf of this degenerate scoundrel that you grant him the same clemency the King of Siam granted that condemned man of whom I spoke. I would further support my petition in light of this new and wonderful religion you have introduced me and my cousins to. If our God can forgive us, we must certainly forgive this poor miserable man standing before us now. With that, I rest my case."

Carter and St. John looked at each other in complete fascination of Amerjit's defense speech and his comprehension of Christian justice and mercy.

Carter and St. John whispered back and forth between themselves. Finally, St. John spoke, "Captain Carter, I suppose we could use a ship's slave. I suggest that we let him live, at least until we put in at Singapore. By then, we can determine if his is worth his feed."

"Agreed Mr. St. John."

The little man once again fell to his knees and attempted to kiss the boots of the two. While Opal was getting quite a laugh out of the goings-on, Supi Yaw regarded the act as an extreme insult to the soul and dignity of a fellow human being. Michael could see from her expression that she was not amused at the kangaroo court being held. He could also see that he would have to rectify this injustice soon or find himself sleeping with Gunga in the rope locker.

Captain Carter ordered Akkmed to be unshackled, with the condition that he not make any attempt to escape or do harm to any member of the crew. The pathetic little man then began swearing one oath after another promising to comply with every wish and order of his captors.

Michael's first order of business was to clear the air with Supi Yaw. He suggested that they go below to their cabin for a cup of tea. Supi Yaw's face was not smiling. Michael called out to Amerjit to bring a pot of tea and some biscuits. "Now," he began, "I intended to let this villain fully understand that we are not fools to be played with and that his little comedy act was not amusing. He needed to understand the severity of his actions and the consequences of our system of law and order. We have every right to hang a stowaway, pirate, or insurrectionist. We also have the right to counter those consequences if we determine that more good can come from our actions than bad. In the case of Akkamed, or the Prince as he likes to call himself, Carter and I decided to exercise our Christian prerogative and grant him grace for his transgressions. But, he needed to realize the true consequences of his actions if that grace had not been granted." Michael had spoken with all of the authority he could find under the circumstances. He did not want wish to create an argument or an adversarial situation between himself and his new wife. Apparently, his comments resolved the consternation within Supi Yaw's mind. She wrapped her arms around Michael's neck and entered into an embrace which was to last for several hours. When Amerjit knocked on the door with the pot of tea, he was informed to place the tray on the floor and get back to his duties in the kitchen. Eventually, Gunga discovered the locked cabin door and the biscuits on the tea tray.

Two days out from Singapore, one of the crew members shouted, "Ship on the starboard bow." While a goodly number of merchant vessels had been seen going to and from ports in the area, this ship seemed to be different. It was an Arabian dhow. It was riding high out of the water and moving toward the Burma Tiger at a high rate of speed. Carter focused his telescopic glass on the dhow's mast. "I was afraid of this he muttered. Pirates."

Just as he uttered the poisonous word, Michael St. John came up beside Carter. "Did you say, 'pirates'?"

"I did indeed, Mr. St. John. Pirates."

It was obvious the heavy laden Burma Tiger could not outrun the smaller craft. Michael then asked, "John, do we have any cannons aboard the ship?"

Carter smiled, "Michael, our artillery consists of a dozen rifles and a few pistols. From what I can see, they have at least a dozen medium-range cannons. They could easily blow our ship to splinters within minutes."

Michael continued, "So I assume that our only recourse is to lower our flag and trust that these criminals will be satisfied by stealing our cargo and leaving our ship to continue."

Carter attempted to maintain his sense of courage in the face of abject danger. "Michael, my primary fear is that these savages will not only confiscate our cargo, but our wives as well. The slave trade in this area is quite lucrative. Opal, being a white woman, would fetch a handsome price in an Arab slave market. Supi Yaw would likewise bring a substantial bounty." He then ordered Mr. Ryan to insist that the women remain below decks in order that the pirates not get a glimpse of their comely feminine attributes.

Standing immediately behind the two men, like a dismal shadow was Akkmed, newly ordained, "Prince of the Privy." Akkmed smiled. "I know these pirates. They have often put in at Chittagong under the flag of some Arabian potentate. If you gentlemen will allow me to save your stinking little lives, I will resolve this matter, hopefully without any of the consequences which, by Allah, should befall you."

Michael shot back, "What on earth are you talking about?"

"Sergeant Major St. John," he said with a wry grin, "if you will be so good as to set me adrift on one of your lifeboats, I will offer my humble self as a ransom for your degenerate lives–and those of your respective wives. These rascals know me and my family history. I will be of far more value than you, your cargo, or your respective wives."

Carter looked at St. John, "What choice do we have?" Carter then shouted an order to the crew. "Make ready a lifeboat on the starboard side." Within seconds, Akkmed was stroking the oars of the lifeboat toward the *dhow*. As he neared the craft, he began shouting, "*Allah Akkabar!*" A stream of sounds flowed from the little man's mouth as he was brought aboard the dhow. Through the telescope, both Carter and St. John could see the animated conversation being held on the deck of the pirate ship.

Carter's primary fear was that Akkmed would align with the pirates and take revenge for the humiliation he had received during the kangaroo court. As the pirate ship continued to run parallel to the Burma Tiger, Akkmed could be seen at the rail raising his arms and waving. The *dhow* then changed its sail and veered off in another direction. Michael spoke, "I am beginning to feel that I am destined to be plagued by pirates in some form or another for the rest of my life."

Long after the *dhow* was out of sight, Michael and John told their wives of the confrontation as if it had been nothing more than a bump in the road.

In the port of Singapore, several items of cargo were off loaded and several others taken on. Carter planned only one full day in port. Unfortunately, Supi Yaw and Opal decided to go shopping. Several articles of clothing as well as items for the galley were purchased. Michael took the opportunity to pay a visit to a wine and spirits vendor near the main docks. The proprietor required only one cup of Simon's jungle berry juice to initiate an order for several large containers of the substance. An order was written and sent back to Rangoon by postal service.

Halfway between Singapore and Hong Kong, Supi Yaw found Opal Carter hanging over the railing of the poop deck. She was vomiting profusely. Supi Yaw placed her hand on Opal's forehead to determine if there was an abnormal temperature. She then suggested that the two women go to Opal's cabin for a brief consultation. Twenty minutes later, Opal Carter whispered into the ear of her husband who was standing at the ship's wheel. The expression on his face went from stoic to ecstatic. He almost yelled, "A baby? Are you certain?"

Opal smiled and replied, "Supi Yaw is positive. You are going to be a father." Carter turned the wheel over to Mr. Ryan and ran to find Michael. Within minutes, every person on the small ship was offering Captain and Mrs. Carter their congratulations.

In Hong Kong, more cargo was exchanged and more jungle berry juice orders were sent back to Rangoon. Several merchants sampled the product and saw fit to place the elixir into glass bottles labeling it as a health tonic. This seemed more palatable to the Chinese than simply selling foreign-produced liquor. To the Chinese mind, becoming intoxicated by means of a health tonic was far preferable to suffering the aftermath of a drunken binge. By all accounts, St. John surmised that Elder James' new enterprise related to jungle berry juice promised to become quite lucrative.

Somehow, the two days planned for Hong Kong became four days. Amerjit managed to locate several "cousins" who were able to procure last-minute supplies for the long crossing of the Pacific Ocean. First on Supi Yaw's shopping list were Bibles for each member of the ship's company, including one for her. Not surprisingly, Opal and Supi Yaw managed to find items they would need in their new situation in America. They also managed to find several dresses which would accommodate Opal's eventual increase in girth. Supi Yaw considered the fact that most, if not all of Amerjit's cousins, were accomplished tailors. This, of course, necessitated several meters of fine Chinese silk and brocade cloth. She rationalized to Opal, "If people in America were going to stare at this strange lady from another land, they should at least have something beautiful at which to stare."

The morning of the fourth day, the Burma Tiger slipped its moorings and sailed east toward San Francisco, California, United States of America. All those aboard were excited, while at the same time, fearful. It was a long voyage and full of potential hazards. Even for John Carter, beginning a new life with a new wife and child was a daunting thought. As Hong Kong slipped slowly into the ocean behind the Burma Tiger, Mr. Ryan moved to the forward-most point of the deck and spread his arms wide open. In a loud voice he called out, "Almighty God, protect us on our way so that we might serve you in this land where You have ordained that we go. Place Your hands on Mrs. Carter and the new life in her body. Amen." Ryan turned and noticed Michael and John looking directly at him. Ryan nodded as if to say, *"There, now we have nothing to worry about."*

CHAPTER SIXTY-THREE

THE CROSSING OF THE PACIFIC

After the first day out of Hong Kong, the ship's company settled into a well-structured routine. With little to do, except to tend the sails occasionally and correct the course, disciplined activities were necessary to prevent boredom from festering into more negative states of mind. Mr. Ryan held his daily classes on subjects related to the Bible and the new faith of the "Indian lads" as they were affectionately called. Ryan also presided over classes in basic seamanship, proper English language, and an assortment of other subjects. On more than one occasion, the Indian lads asked Mr. Ryan to teach them about the subject of women. Mr. Ryan cautiously deferred the subject to Supi Yaw who with all the tenacity of a medical doctor in a lecture hall gave them the full account–A to Z. For days after the infamous lecture on the nature and features of women, the Indian lads found it difficult to confront Supi Yaw without issuing a bashful grin.

John Carter spent hours drilling St. John on the intricate details of sailing ships, their cargo, international laws, and the like. When things became too tight below decks, Carter would send Michael to the forecastle of the ship while he remained on the afterdeck. For hours they would send semaphore back and forth. After several weeks of this little game, Michael could send and receive faster than most signalmen. Then, they both turned their attention to the newly created Morse code. Within days, both could send and receive almost as fast as they could talk. As the two men played with their "signal language," most of the Indian lads watched and learned the signaling skills as well.

Opal Carter had determined to learn everything she could about the fine art of nursing. Supi Yaw had agreed to tutor Opal for as far as she wanted to go. Each morning and afternoon, the two women had set aside time for study. For the first time in her life, Supi Yaw became focused on the study of the Scripture, particularly those passages dealing with healing. As soon as she had fully understood the implications of these passages, she would pass them on to Opal as a part of her medical curriculum. Supi Yaw dug deeply into the assortment of medical books she had brought with her. Likewise, Opal read and re-read the books on nursing they had procured. Often times, Opal would interrupt Supi Yaw and ask a simple question which ultimately turned into a lengthy and informative lecture. Like their husbands, the two women formed a bond of mutual emotional and intellectual support.

Below decks in the galley, Amerjit and Gunga became almost inseparable companions. This was in part due to Amerjit's propensity to drop morsels of food from time to time.

Almost every evening, after dinner, someone would suggest that Supi Yaw fetch her little Baum banjo and sing a few native songs. Eventually, the Indian lads began to request Christian songs Mr. Ryan had taught them.

The crossing was good with a few storms, but none severe. On several occasions, crew members came down with a stomach bug or head pain all of which Supi Yaw remedied with the pill and potions she had brought along. Opal Carter's pregnancy progressed with the usual issues of morning sickness, swelling of the legs, and unexplained grouchiness.

The charts were indicating that the Burma Tiger was a mere one hundred miles from the Bay of San Francisco. Captain Carter doubled the watch due to the many ships encountered heading to and from San Francisco. Most ships were magnificent cargo vessels with three and four masts and dozens of billowing sails. Both Michael and Carter felt a bit insignificant with their tiny one hundred and six foot Baltic Trader. It was Carter who pointed at one of the three-masted ships. "I want that one!" he said emphatically.

Michael replied, "Alright, let's plan on having either that one or one just like it in twenty-four months." The two men looked directly into each other's eyes knowing that, if it could be done, they could do it.

CHAPTER SIXTY-FOUR

CALIFORNIA

The California coastline appeared through the morning fog like a curtain being raised at a theater. Green mountains rose up out of the dark blue sea like great whales breaching in consort. The entire ship's company stood on the deck watching as the tiny vessel moved closer to the welcoming arms of San Francisco Bay. Carter commented that the scene before him reminded him of the Straits of Gibraltar.

Their reverie was interrupted by the sound of a ship's horn directly behind them. A large steamship was fast approaching from off the stern. Carter took the wheel and brought the Burma Tiger off to the starboard. The Indian lads all dashed below to tidy up and put on clothing more appropriate to the occasion of landing in this new place. Opal and Supi Yaw likewise decided to dress for the occasion complete with parasol.

As the Burma Tiger passed through the land gate leading to the famous San Francisco Bay, a small pilot boat came alongside. An official from the harbor master's staff requested to come aboard. Permission was granted whereupon two men climbed the rope ladder on the deck. Formalities were exchanged and a docking assignment was arranged for the Burma Tiger. Carter and St. John were informed that they, and particularly their Indian crew members, would be subject to a routine customs review. The official was polite but emphatic. An hour later, at a small out-of-the-way pier, the gangplank was extended and the ship's company moved toward a building marked, UNITED STATES CUSTOMS OFFICE. Over the office door was an American flag. For John Carter, it was like coming home to a familiar hearth. For the rest of those looking up at the red, white, and blue flag, it was like something both frightening yet at the same time, exhilarating. While they all felt totally committed to their respective countries, they felt an overwhelming excitement about becoming Americans. A customs officer politely opened the door for the group and tipped his hat as the two ladies, parasol in hand, entered. Captain Carter led the group to a desk marked, First Entry. The official behind the desk showed slight indifference when Carter handed over the ship's papers and manifest. "Sir," Carter asked in a polite way, "may I know your name?"

The official stiffened a bit, "My name is Benjamin Johnson."

Carter continued, "Allow me to introduce myself. I am Captain John Carter, captain of the Burma Tiger." Carter then summoned Michael to the desk.

Carter spoke again, "Mr. Johnson, allow me to introduce you to Sergeant Major Michael O. St. John retired, formerly of Her Imperial Majesty's Burma Police and Hero of the Irrawaddy." John whispered into Michael's ear whereupon Michael produced the letter from President Lincoln. Captain Carter pointed to the two names on the document; President Lincoln's name and Supi Yaw's name. "You see, sir, these words here," pointing to Supi Yaw Lat, "means in the Baum language, "princess." This lady is the daughter of His Highness, Prince Simon of Burma. And this gentleman," pointing to Michael, "is her consort, Sergeant Major Michael St. John. I assume that you read about Sergeant Major St. John's receipt of the Victoria Cross from Queen Victoria herself." The customs official looked bewildered as he nodded that he had indeed read about the event some time back.

Almost immediately, the customs official stood to his feet and became very attentive and somewhat confused as to how to handle the situation. After all, a presidential appointment is a very special issue. The customs official took particular note of the Indians, all neatly dressed in similar uniforms. He asked about the nature of these gentlemen and was informed by Captain Carter that these gentlemen were a part of Princess Supi Yaw's personal retinue. Carter looked directly at St. John as if to say, *"How's that for a sailor's tale?"* Within seconds, all documents were duly recorded in the logs and ledgers.

Carter quietly instructed two of the Indian lads to fetch the baggage cases from the ship. Mr. Ryan was instructed to set a rotating watch aboard the ship and see that the Indian lads were allowed to cautiously explore their new environment in pairs. Please see that Gunga does not leave the ship. I want him to go through a complete quarantine first. Carter then produced a roll of British pound notes and asked Mr. Ryan to see that each of the Indian lads was given a sufficient amount of money to convert at a money changer and have a reasonably good time.

"Mr. Ryan, please see that your lads do not find themselves behind bars or worse, caught in the embrace of some painted lady." Mr. Ryan smiled and saluted.

Carter continued, "We will return by noon tomorrow."

The customs official then went directly to Supi Yaw who was oblivious to the conversations between Carter, St. John, and the customs official. The uniformed man removed his hat, bowed low and said, "Princess, on behalf of the Government of the United States of America, I wish to welcome you to our country. I trust your stay with us will be of benefit to both our peoples."

Supi Yaw rose from her chair, curtsied and looked directly at Michael as if to say, *"Princess? What is going on here?"*

The group moved past the picket gate into the waiting arms of San Francisco. Just out of earshot, Supi Yaw whispered to Michael, "Princess?"

Michael whispered back, "I'll tell you later."

As soon as the group had left the building, the customs official slowly dashed to his superior's office and reported the entire event. His superior then contacted his superior who contacted his superior. By day's end, the word of an Asian princess and her war hero husband arriving in San Francisco, as a result of a presidential appointment, was all over town.

San Francisco embraced the newly arrived couples like a loving uncle. Immediately, the Carters and the St. Johns recognized a welcoming warmth as they stood on the great semi-circular road known as the Embarcadero. Hundreds of horse-drawn carts and wagons plied the cobblestone pavement heading to and from the hundreds of tethered sailing ships. Accordion and fiddle music could be heard coming from dozens of nearby cafes and watering holes. Over near the fishermen's wharf, countless seagulls filled the air hoping to find bits of fresh fish or shellfish which had fallen off a passing cart. From the direction of the water, unseen seals could be heard barking playfully as seamen taunted them with bits of bread. Looking across the bay, great waterfalls of crisp white fog could be seen cascading over the mountains toward the small town on the other side of the bay.

Carter then spoke, "Let's find a hotel and get settled. Hopefully as soon as tomorrow, we can present Princess Supi Yaw to the army people at the Presidio. From there, we have to plan our entire lives into something that is going to allow us to buy that three-masted ship we saw within the next twenty-four months." Michael simply smiled in agreement.

John hailed a passing carriage and ordered the driver to take them to the Imperial Hotel. "Tonight we celebrate; tomorrow we begin again."

The following morning, both couples arrived at their breakfast table to find the hotel's manager waiting. He and several waiters were obviously focused on the two couples. The manager then held up two copies of the major San Francisco newspapers. The headlines read, "Asian Royalty Graces S.F."

John Carter laughed out loud. Michael grabbed one of the papers and began to read. From what little was said to the customs official, several columns of print had been constructed, including details about the bloody Battle of the Irrawaddy. The St. Francis manager then offered his most sincere welcome. "I must warn you," he said, "there is quite a flock of reporters at the front door, including California's Emperor, Emperor Joshua Norton himself. Off the record, Emperor Norton is a self-proclaimed potentate who, while being a wonderful man, is a bit off in the head. I suggest that you go along with his antics. He is harmless and adds to the unique nature of the city."

A bevy of waiters began to display platter after platter of fruits, breakfast sweets, and sausages. The manager commented quietly, "Compliments of The Imperial.' The manager left as the brief morning banquet began. Supi Yaw looked Michael directly in the eye. "My dear husband, perhaps you would be good enough to tell me what is going on here."

John interrupted before things got out of control. "My dear Supi Yaw, sometimes it is necessary to create illusions. I do not mean lies; I mean fanciful images. Just like this chap waiting outside, this Emperor fellow. Everyone knows that he is not an emperor, but they enjoy a bit of theater now and then. So, the actor plays to his audience and the audience is happy. In our case, the customs official was more than likely locked into his routine of signing papers and pretending to be official. Then, you came along from an exotic place this little man only dreams about and like a storybook genie, I transform you into an Asian princess. Immediately, the day takes on a new sparkle. He is in the presence of royalty. That makes him significant. He can go home at the end of that day and tell his wife and kids that he met a real live princess from somewhere on the back side of the world." Supi Yaw looked at John and smiled reluctantly. Michael then went on to add, "After all, my love, you are the daughter of a tribal headman. In some communities, that would make you a princess–of sorts."

Opal laughed and bowed her head in mock adoration. John suggested that he and Opal return to the ship and deal with the cargo and the business of finding a proper berth for the Burma Tiger. He suggested that Michael and Princess Supi Yaw make their way to the Presidio and Dr. Hitchcock. Opal then spoke, "Before we do anything else, Princess Supi Yaw's adoring fans are waiting outside."

Michael went to the front desk and asked for the bill. The clerk behind the desk handed over a formal billing which had writing across it. It read:

'Compliments of the Imperial Hotel. In appreciation for your service to humanity.

Signed,

George Mitchell, General Manager, Imperial Hotel."

On the front steps of the St. Francis were three dozen reporters, photographers, and His Imperial Excellency, Emperor Joshua A. Norton. The two Imperial Hotel doormen, neatly attired in their uniforms, opened the huge double doors of the hotel. Like Queen Victoria herself, Supi Yaw and her consort, exited to the brief applause. The manager of the Imperial Hotel had made his way to the top step and made formal introduction. Photo flashes lit up the doorway as Norton issued an impromptu proclamation of welcome to the princess and her company. Carter almost immediately realized that this event afforded a major opportunity to advertise the soon-to-be established Burma Tiger Shipping Company. After Norton had completed his rather lengthy speech and Supi Yaw gave a brief reply, John grabbed the opportunity to make his comments. For a few minutes, Carter related his own personal experience with Princess Supi Yaw saving his life by amputating his mangled leg while on the high seas. The reporters quickly scribbled the words, and in some cases, added journalistic embellishments. Carter then concluded his comments by announcing the new shipping company. Not to stop there, John went on to include a sail-making company and general shipping services company. Michael glanced sideways, not knowing what to expect next. Before the group could free themselves from the reporters, one young woman reporter with a strong Irish accent, approached Supi Yaw and began to ask her about her village, her childhood, and her family back in Asia. Seeing that Michael was beginning to show some impatience, Supi Yaw asked the young lady for her card. "I will contact you when time allows and we can chat about these questions you have." The young reporter seemed pleased with the response as he passed her card to Supi Yaw.

The crowd began to disperse with several reporters remaining behind to garner more information on the Battle of the Irrawaddy, the Victoria Cross and the amputation at sea. Somehow in the conversation, the point of Queen Victoria presenting Michael with a dog came up. Norton immediately grabbed onto the comment. "Sergeant Major St. John, I would consider it an honor to introduce my two canines to yours." Both men shook hands and smiled at the thought of dogs creating a bond between men of rank.

CHAPTER SIXTY-FIVE

THE ARMY PRESIDIO AT SAN FRANCISCO

After collecting their belongings, John and Opal took a carriage back to the ship while Michael and Supi Yaw went to the Presidio.

Dr. Charles Hitchcock, who carried the insignia of a lieutenant colonel, was expecting them. He too had a copy of the morning newspaper on his desk. After a short introduction and general chit-chat, Michael felt conscience bound to give Dr. Charles Hitchcock the back story of the news articles. Hitchcock laughed. "The newspaper people are tired of news from the Civil War in the east. Any bit of news they can find, or for that fact create, keeps them in business. I know first-hand how these jackals can find a drop of blood in the water, and like sharks, form a feeding frenzy. Unfortunately, I have a daughter who attracts the presses' attention all too often."

Just as Dr. Hitchcock was completing his comment, a young woman, looking to be around twenty to twenty-two, burst into his office. A young corporal came after her in a futile attempt to stop her from entering the office. The corporal apologized and retreated.

"Speaking of the devil," he uttered.

Before anyone could speak or make formal introductions, the young lady thrust her hand toward Supi Yaw and spoke. "Hi, I am Lilly; you must be the princess from Burma everyone is talking about."

Then addressing Michael, she said, "And you must be the 'hero of the Big Muddy'."

Michael shook her hand and said, "Let's make that the Irrawaddy, and I am not really a hero. I just happened to be at the right place at the right time."

The young lady continued, "Daddy, can we invite the princess and the hero to our house for dinner. I'll bet they have some fantastic stories to tell."

Dr. Hitchcock frowned sufficiently to let his daughter know that she needed to back off a bit. "Sorry, Daddy," she uttered.

Dr. Hitchcock continued, "Mrs. St. John and I will be working together during her time in San Francisco. As soon as you folks get settled into a house, I will take you to meet with several members of the local medical establishment. We are quite certain that we will find a suitable medical institution in this immediate area. I would add that we are all extremely pleased to see more qualified women enter the American medical profession. In fact, most physicians in my circles are pleased to see the United States take the lead in this new concept." This was an obvious jab at the British medical system.

Again the young lady interrupted, "Daddy, do you mean that the Princess is going to become a doctor, a doctor like you?"

Her father nodded. "Yes, Lilly a doctor just like me."

She continued, "Well, if a woman can become a doctor, why do you object to my wanting to become a firefighter?"

"Lilly, we shall discuss that later when you and I are alone," the poor man said.

Seeing Dr. Hitchcock's immediate dilemma, Supi Yaw spoke, "Lilly, I wonder if you would be good enough to show me around San Francisco this afternoon? That is if your father agrees. Perhaps we could pass by our ship and collect Captain Carter's wife, and we could make it a bit of a shopping trip. After all, the Captain's wife and I have been closed in aboard a ship for some time now."

Dr. Hitchcock smiled and agreed to the plan. "Please, take my carriage and driver. After all, you are here at the behest of President Lincoln." Michael then passed a small bundle of American dollars to his wife and suggested that they have a good time."

The two women left the doctor's office leaving the two men alone. Dr. Hitchcock then spoke, "Now then, Mr. St. John, how may I be of service to you?

Michael replied, "Sir, it is my wife who is here under the auspices of the President."

Hitchcock replied, "That is true, sir, but any man who holds the Victoria Cross is, in my opinion, worthy of utmost consideration. As a military man myself, I believe it is an honor to serve a true hero and you, sir, are a true hero."

Michael held up his hand and attempted to refute his status.

Hitchcock interrupted, "Sergeant Major St. John, as well as being a doctor, I am also a student of history–military history. I am quite familiar with the various honors for extreme gallantry, and I know that no one receives the Victoria Cross by mistake. So, let's be done with this argument." Michael leaned back in his chair and conceded the issue. Hitchcock again asked, "How may I be of assistance to you, sir?"

Michael thought for a moment, "Doctor, my partner, Captain John Carter, and I will need to locate a large building sufficient to contain cargos and a sail factory. If such a structure exists, it must be near the docks. Once we have established our operational center, we can begin contracting for cargos and taking orders for sails."

Hitchcock asked, "What about living quarters for you and your wife?"

Michael replied, "We can live aboard our ship until we find suitable accommodations for my wife and me and Captain Carter and his wife. By the way Doctor, Captain Carter's wife is expecting. She will require some looking after as her time draws closer."

Hitchcock thought for a minute. "Mr. St. John, under the circumstances, I believe that I can offer both you and Captain Carter temporary quarters here on the Presidio until you establish your own homes."

St. John pondered the offer and nodded. "I would gladly accept your offer, but I feel that we should remain close to our point of operation."

Hitchcock then added, "I have one condition; however, I would ask that your wife attempt to instill some sense of grace and manners into my daughter. My wife and I have tried and failed. Lilly insists on chasing fire engines, dressing in men's pants and finding her way into gambling dens. I was told that she even smokes cigars."

Again, Michael nodded. "We will do our best."

Dr. Hitchcock stood and said, "Now, if it is not too much trouble, I would like to see this ship of yours and see if we can find you a building." Hitchcock ordered two riding horses brought to his office door. This was the first time since leaving Burma that Michael had ridden a saddle horse and the only time he had ridden through the streets of a real city. It was fun.

As the two men passed a police constable's box, Hitchcock reined his horse to a stop. The constable, seeing the officer's insignia of Lieutenant Colonel, saluted smartly. "Constable, could you send word out that I would appreciate a meeting with Emperor Norton. We shall be found at the south pier aboard the Burma Tiger. If we could impose upon the Emperor's valuable time, I would gladly provide him with a substantial lunch."

The constable again saluted, "I shall see that His Excellency is located and your message delivered."

Hitchcock then turned to St. John and said, "Norton knows every building, vacant or occupied, in the city. If anyone can find you a property, it is our beloved Emperor Norton."

CHAPTER SIXTY-SIX

The cargo of the Burma Tiger had been off loaded into a temporary warehouse leaving the ship almost vacant. The Indian lads were occupied with scrubbing the decks, polishing the brass, and examining the sails. Captain Carter came to the gangplank and welcomed the two men aboard. The huge clock in the ferry tower terminal at the opposite end of the embarcadero struck eleven o'clock. Michael spoke, "Dr. Hitchcock, would you be our guest for lunch? Among our ship's company we have a world class chef."

Hitchcock replied, "We may have an Emperor arriving any minute now. Can you accommodate his palate as well?"

Michael nodded, "If he can provide suitable fare for a princess, I am quite certain that he can please a mere emperor." Michael called out for Amerjit and instructed him to prepare a meal fit for an emperor. Amerjit barked orders to several of the Indian lads who scurried off in several directions. Within an hour, the wonderful aromas emerging from Amerjit's galley were being noticed by all those within a two-block radius.

At twelve-thirty Emperor Joshua A. Norton was announced by one of the dock guards. The old man, dressed in a badly faded military uniform and high-top silk hat, adorned with bird feathers stood on the deck of the Burma Tiger. All the proper courtesies were offered, including being piped aboard by Mr. Ryan's boatswain's whistle. At the old man's heels were two dogs who he introduced as Bummer and Lazarus. Gunga, standing behind Carter, regarded the two intruders with a quiet growl. As if to incite the small bulldog, Lazarus lifted his leg on one of the deck rails.

Neither Carter nor St. John knew exactly how to play this act, so they silently deferred to Hitchcock. Hitchcock then suggested the group go below for luncheon. Amerjit had truly outdone himself this time. A plank table complete with table cloth had been arranged in the main cabin area. A complete set of fine china had been set on the table. Michael looked at Amerjit as if to say, *"Where did you find this?"*

Amerjit whispered, "My wedding gift to Mrs. St. John."

Dr. Hitchcock seated Norton at the head of the table while the others took seats around the table. Amerjit and his Indian lads began bringing platter after platter of steamed vegetables, curry sauces, rice, and several assortments of chicken. Norton ate with dignity, but also like a man who had not had a decent meal for some time.

A dessert of fried bananas with a brandy sauce was served with a cup of coffee. The Emperor finished off his coffee and then spoke, "Colonel Hitchcock, I am quite certain that you did not summon me there simply to enjoy this fantastic meal. What is it that you would request of me?"

"Your Excellency," Hitchcock began in a most diplomatic tone, "it is well known that you are familiar with almost every street, sidewalk, and building in San Francisco. In that regard, sir, I would like to solicit your insights as to the availability of a building large enough to contain cargo, a sail-making shop, and perhaps several small apartments."

Norton leaned back in his chair and pondered the ceiling of the room. After some scratching of his beard, his eyebrows raised by an inch. "Yes, I know of such a building. In fact, it is within walking distance from where we sit at this moment. For many years it served as a warehouse for jute binding used in the cotton industry. Unfortunately with the great war in the south, the cotton industry is in decline, leaving this jute warehouse empty and in default." St. John, Carter, and Hitchcock all exchanged glances.

Norton went on, "The owner of this building is a widow somewhat down on her luck. I believe that an offer consisting of adequate living expenses may be sufficient to procure the property."

Amerjit, God bless him, entered the room with a tray on which was one of the final bottles of jungle berry juice and four glasses. He poured the purple liquid into each glass and presented one to each of the four men sitting around the table. Carter then raised his glass, "A toast to Emperor Norton and to President Lincoln." Norton looked at Carter as if he had been slapped.

Hitchcock saved the moment by restating the toast, "To Emperor Norton and his two noble consorts, Lazarus and Bummer." Both Norton and Hitchcock remarked about the excellent bouquet of the foreign brandy.

Back on deck, Michael mentioned to Hitchcock that he wanted to re-register his ship under an American flag. Norton then announced that he would be delighted to provide registration under his personal flag. He then suggested that the Burma Tiger become his personal flagship.

Michael replied that he would give the thought some consideration, but it first needed to be re-flagged and its new home port designated as San Francisco.

Norton called his dogs to his side and bid the group farewell. As he made his way down the gangplank, he called out, "When

I procure this building of yours, I will expect it to carry the seal of my personal patronage."

Michael called out, "Consider it done."

For the next hour, St. John, Carter, and Hitchcock walked around the ancient warehouse Norton had mentioned. While it was by no means dilapidated, it was in need of considerable cosmetic attention. Michael felt the strongest urge to do something he had seldom done before. He knelt and folded his hands. John Carter saw what he was doing and knelt beside him as did Dr. Charles Hitchcock. Michael then began, "Father, you have said in your book that if we will commit our ways unto You, You will give us the desires of our hearts. There is no question in my mind and heart that all of the events of the past year have been directed by You for some divine purpose. There is no doubt that You have brought Bua Tan Bo into my life so that I might meet Supi Yaw. You brought Supi Yaw into the picture so that she could save the life of my good friend and brother, John Carter. If it were not for John Carter's successful recovery, Opal Alston would still be tending to bedpans in a London hospital. You brought Amerjit into our lives so that he could change the lives of his seven cousins. And then there is Mr. Ryan who managed to drown the demons from his past through entering our little circle. Father God, there are simply too many vital events in this little drama to consider the crossing of so many lives to be an accident. I truly believe that You have ordained a divine drama, where all characters of the play will eventually lead to some great and wonderful conclusion. In this respect, Almighty Father, I would ask that you intervene and '...give us the desires of our hearts'."

Michael hesitated in his prayer whereupon John Carter, not prone to open prayer, began. "Lord, when I was a youth, I behaved as a youth. I am now a man and soon to be a father, and I would ask for your wisdom to behave as a man and a father. I would also ask that you forgive the sins of my youth, of which there are many. Father, we ask your direct involvement in our enterprise. Give us the wisdom and courage to become true men of God in all that we do and say. Compel us to be honest and true with our clients no matter what should happen. Father, this building before us appears to be suitable for our immediate requirements. If it is Your will, please let it become ours."

Before the men could continue with their prayer, Emperor Joshua A. Norton, accompanied by his two dogs approached from behind and cleared his throat. "Gentlemen, the building is yours, providing you can meet the simple requirements of its owner. I met with her just moments ago, and she has expressed her willingness to quit the property. This poor lady's husband has passed on and left her with a large house, this building, and almost no financial income. It seems that most of their resources have been lost as a result of the war in the east. The dear lady did read the story about you and your wife in the morning's papers and feels that you would be suitable occupants. In light of your situation, her conditions appear to be more than generous. She is willing to accept one hundred dollars a month to be applied to the purchase of the building. Upon the occasion of her death, the balance owed on the property would be directed to a charity of her choosing."

Michael and John looked at each other in total astonishment. Michael spoke, "I find that more than generous. As soon as we can have a written agreement drawn up, we can begin to rehabilitate the building and open for business." Dr. Hitchcock seemed absolutely amazed at what had just happened.

John Carter simply smiled and said to Hitchcock, "You commit your ways unto the Lord, and He will give you the desires of your heart."

While Dr. Hitchcock was not a particularly religious man, this event penetrated any and all rational explanations which he would have otherwise considered.

St. John invited Emperor Norton back to the ship for a cup of coffee. Norton and his two dogs accompanied St. John, Carter, Hitchcock and Gunga back to the Burma Tiger. Just as they arrived, a black carriage pulled up carrying Supi Yaw, Opal Carter, and Lilly Hitchcock. They were giggling like a bunch of school girls at a sleep-over party. Each of the ladies had purchased numerous bits of clothing, bonnets or shoes. Supi Yaw noticed Michael and waved a handful of newspapers over her head. “Michael, they have written all sorts of things about us,” she called out.

Michael reached for the papers as Carter introduced Norton to the ladies.

Emperor Norton removed his top hat and bowed low as he shook the hand of each of the women.

As he shook the hand of Lilly Hitchcock, he commented, “I believe I have seen you at numerous fires here in the city. If my memory serves me correctly, you are the mascot of the Knickerbocker Fire Company, Number 5.”

Lilly replied, “That is correct, sir. And if my memory serves me correctly you are the Emperor of California and Protector of Mexico.”

“At your service,” the old man replied in a most dignified manner.

Lilly also acknowledged Norton’s two dogs by name.

Norton looked at his pocket watch and regarded the setting sun. “Ladies, gentlemen, as much as I would enjoy taking a cup of coffee with you, my duties here in the city summon me. There is so much to do and so little time in which to do it. I am told that there may be a problem with our Chinese brothers somewhere over in Chinatown. I will keep you informed as to the progress on your building." With that, the strange old man disappeared into the late afternoon fog.

Supi Yaw spoke, "Your building?"

"Yes, my love, our building," Michael said as he related the events of the afternoon and the details of the transaction to his astonished wife.

Michael became deeply engrossed in the bundle of afternoon newspapers, each with a banner headline referring to him and those aboard his ship. "Let's get below where we can talk. This afternoon fog will soon have us bumping into walls," Carter said.

Below deck, in the main cabin, St. John laid out the various newspapers. Almost all of the publications carried photographs of the group, standing on the steps of the Imperial Hotel. Norton's proclamation was printed, word for word as well as a number of quotes from those pictured in the articles. One publication went so far as to suggest that the group had fled the tyrannies of British-occupied Burma in favor of freedom-loving America.

Carter was openly delighted with all of the "free publicity" as he called it. "They will know that we are here and what we want to do," he said time and time again.

Carter turned to St. John and spoke in a most emphatic tone. "Michael, we must get our building refurbished and our business moving as soon as possible. We must strike while the iron is hot if we are going to have another ship in our fleet within twenty-four months."

Michael was again impressed with Carter's zeal for his dream. Michael replied, "The very day we sign the papers, we will begin remodeling."

The conversation at dinner was animated and excited. Topics ranged from the kind of wood needed to panel the walls to sewing machines for the sail-making project. No one aboard the Burma Tiger slept that night.

At a few minutes past ten o'clock the following morning, a carriage pulled up to the pier occupied by the Burma Tiger. Emperor Joshua Norton and an elderly lady stepped down from the carriage. Carter concluded at once that the old woman must be the owner of the building two blocks away. He was correct.

The elderly woman, dressed in black mourning attire, was assisted aboard the ship, as Mr. Ryan again piped the visitors aboard with his boatswain's pipe. All of the Indian lads snapped to attention as a sign of respect for both the pretend potentate and the elderly woman. Carter and St. John laid aside their current work and graciously acknowledged the two visitors. Norton then introduced the gentle lady as Mrs. Alice Worthington formerly of Savannah, Georgia.

Overhead, the sun was shining and the seagulls were performing for the unfortunate wingless creatures below. Over the side and unseen, several seals were barking, begging for scraps from the galley. Amerjit called for several of his crew to fetch a table and chairs. Mrs. Worthington was seated, followed by the Carters, and the St. Johns. Norton chose to stand, at least until he had concluded his oratory. For the next thirty minutes, Norton summarized the careers of all those around the table. He then suggested that God Himself had ordained this meeting and that everything to be done from this time forth, would be done to achieve His divine agenda. While the slightly crazed man's comments seemed a bit comical, they nonetheless carried the weight of profound truth. Norton had obviously overheard Carter and St. John's prayer to the Almighty and decided to improve on it. At long last, the old man in the tattered uniform sat down.

Mrs. Worthington then spoke. "My good friend and confidant, Emperor Norton has informed me that you have shown an interest in my late husband's jute warehouse several blocks over." All those around the table nodded in silent agreement. She continued, "I will save the rhetoric related to this sort of business. I am an old woman and hopefully will join my late husband very soon. I am also very broke. I own a huge house on Telegraph Hill, which I can't afford to maintain, and the old warehouse. The weather keeps me sick in bed most of the time. Because of the awful war going on in the South, I am prevented from returning to my home and my family. I have no children to care for me nor do I have a maid to cook and clean for me. So, life has become something I do while I am waiting to die; nothing more, nothing less.

Opal Carter began to cry. "Mrs. Worthington, I would consider it a great privilege if you would allow me to help you with some of your personal and household needs. After all, I am a licensed nursing sister; it is my calling you know."

The old woman smiled. "I would consider it an even greater privilege to accept your kind offer."

"Now then," the elderly lady said in a formal tone of voice, "shall we get on with the business at hand? My financial requirements do not exceed one hundred dollars a month. The price of my building is five thousand dollars. If you will pay me one hundred dollars each month, you may purchase my building. Upon my death, you shall continue to pay the balance to the San Francisco Home for Children."

Again, there was a silent nod of agreement. The elderly lady then placed a document on the table for signature. Michael St. John signed, then John Carter. Michael then called for Amerjit. "Amerjit, you are into this as well. Your signature is also required." With that, Mrs. Worthington handed over a set of keys.

Amerjit beamed as he scratched his signature on the piece of paper. "This calls for a banquet of celebration," Amerjit said.

Opal responded, "I agree; we should celebrate with those who have brought us to this point. Just think, a year ago, none of us would have ever imagined that we would be on a ship in San Francisco Bay starting a new business and a new life."

Michael spoke, "I concur, but our primary objective is to get the building in order. Amerjit, if you and our wives will see to a small dinner party in our new quarters, the rest of us can cut and nail timber until we have a building worthy of our calling."

Amerjit seemed ecstatic. "I shall prepare a banquet fit for a queen, or at least a princess, an Asian princess. None of that nasty English food; no sir, only fine Asian food."

∾

CHAPTER SIXTY-SEVEN

The Emperor and Mrs. Worthington left the ship. Within minutes, every last man and woman in the ship's company was standing, lanterns in hand, inside the vast empty building two blocks from the dock. It was huge! One single room was separated by a loft above. Raw timber beams and unfinished boards existed throughout. The smell of jute still permeated the dusty air. An occasional rat the size of a house cat could be seen dashing from one pile of rubble to another. For the longest time, no one said a word. Imaginations were running wild; a wall here, a platform there, an office over there. Michael found a large roll of binders twine and began pacing off where walls might be placed. Supi Yaw and Opal focused their attention on the upper deck of the building. They both concluded that several apartments could be constructed, complete with indoor toilets. They even suggested a dormitory-style complex for the Indian lads, with separate quarters for Amerjit. After determining the necessary space for cargo storage, a portion was lined out for a sail-making shop. As a sea captain, Carter was familiar with sail-making facilities and made several sketches of lofts and sewing tables which needed to be made or purchased. By four-thirty in the morning, reams of notes, sketches, and long lists of materials had been compiled. It was Carter who announced that it was time he got his very pregnant wife to bed. Tired but elated, the group walked back through the thick, cold San Francisco fog to the Burma Tiger. Gunga was the only living thing aboard the ship to greet them as they found their way to their beds. It was good!

Norton had managed to conscript a dozen or so Chinese workers to assist with the building. Within five days, all walls had been put in place, all doors hung, and all carpet laid. Bathtubs, stoves, and gas lamps had been duly installed and found to be working properly. One of the Indian lads had found a large piece of lumber and set about to carve a company sign. The sign read: BURMA TIGER SHIPPING AND TRADING COMPANY. Beneath the large letters were the words, Under Patronage of Emperor J.A. Norton. The letters were painted in gold guild paint with a black background. By anyone's standards, it was a handsome sign. It took four men, a block and tackle, and plenty of advice from Opal and Supi Yaw standing below. It was nailed into place just above the main entrance. Another sizable log soon became a replica of the original broken-toothed tiger which was placed above the sign. Two extremely well-appointed apartments, each with its own picture window looking out over the rooftops of nearby buildings, provided a clear view of San Francisco Bay.

Each day, while the crew and hired helpers worked at the warehouse, Opal and Supi Yaw took a carriage to the home of Mrs. Worthington. The house was one of the largest and most palatial on the high bank overlooking the Pacific Ocean. Mrs. Worthington explained that her husband had built the mansion with the intent of filling it with children and grandchildren. With a tear in her eye, she quietly mentioned that their four children had all died in a whooping cough epidemic some years back. Since the recent death of her husband and ultimate loss of their vast fortune, she had not visited any of the dozens of bedrooms, sitting rooms, private suites, or even been to the top of the bell tower- style turret which overlooked San Francisco Bay and much of the city. She had become a prisoner in her own house, unable to afford servants or simple upkeep. So rich, yet so poor. When the weather was good, Opal and Supi Yaw insisted that the elderly woman take a carriage ride through the city to see the flowers. On several occasions, they would visit the San Francisco Home for Children and perform simple medical examinations for the children. Each time the two women would visit Mrs. Worthington, they would bring along one of Amerjit's recent creations; sometimes a prune cake doused with brandy, sometimes a half of a chicken sautéed in an exotic sauce. On more than one occasion, Supi Yaw would ask if they could simply read aloud books of the Bible. Mrs. Worthington who was, by her own admission, not a religious woman began to ask questions about God and what to expect after death. One particular afternoon, after remaining silent during the reading, Mrs. Worthington began to sob into her handkerchief. Opal put her arms around the whimpering woman and asked, "What troubles you, my dear?" She tearfully relied, "I know about this Jesus you talk about, but I am afraid that He and I are not on speaking terms at the moment. You see, He took my late husband after a long and miserable fight to simply stay alive. I have said some things to Him and about Him that I believe He would not approve."

Opal then asked, "Are you sorry for your thoughts and actions?"

The old woman nodded, "Yes, but they were said all the same. I cannot take back a bullet that has already been shot from the barrel of a gun. What's done is done."

For the next hour, Opal then related the story of how the Prince, a hardened Asian criminal was granted a complete reprieve from a well-deserved punishment upon his admission of guilt and repentance. The illustration seemed to find its mark. The old lady barked, "I am truly sorry for my wickedness and my attitude toward God, but there's nothing I can do about it." She then turned her tear-filled eyes toward Opal. "Opal, to the best of my recollection, I have never even been baptized, and if what you say in Bible reading is correct, I should be baptized in order to get into this heaven you read about." Then turning to Supi Yaw, the old woman said, "I am too old to go to a church and get dunked or splashed or whatever they do these days."

Supi Yaw let the comment hang in the air like a circling seagull before asking in a sarcastic way, "Do you really want to get baptized and make confession of your sins?"

"Yes!" the old lady yelled. "Yes, I want to get rid of these stinking ulcerous sins so I can feel better about dying. Every night I go to bed wondering if I am going to die in my sleep and be found rotting in a week or two. Or what happens if I fall down and lay there for who knows how long until I die of starvation. And all this talk about the devil and hell–why it's enough to cause a person to die of fright. And just look at that silly prayer our parents taught us to say at bedtime, 'Now I lay me down to sleep, I pray the Lord my soul to keep. If I should die before I wake, I pray the Lord my soul to take.' Now if that doesn't scare the daylights out of a kid, I don't know what does."

Supi Yaw then grabbed a nearby water basin and pitcher and said, "Lean over."

The old woman, shocked at Supi Yaw's rough tone, leaned over toward the basin. With that Supi Yaw scooped out three handfuls of cold water. "In the Name of Jesus Christ, I baptize you in the name of the Father, the Son and the Holy Spirit. There, now you are ready to go."

Mrs. Worthington, still dripping and totally shocked said, "You can't do that; you're not a preacher.

Supi Yaw replied almost jokingly, "I am a princess; I can do anything I want."

For the next fifteen minutes, Mrs. Worthington continued to cry, wail, laugh, and even make a few profane and inappropriate remarks to her dead husband. She then took a deep breath, stood up and said, "You're darn right, sister, and I'm ready to go. I'm ready to go shopping. I need to spend some of that money your husbands are paying me. I am a free woman now, and I want to have some fun before they close the box on me."

Opal and Supi Yaw looked at each other knowing that another soul had just been rescued from a state of physical and emotional bondage not to mention an eternal prison.

Ten days from after signing the sales contract, the building was complete inside and out. Amerjit was given the order to prepare for the inaugural banquet he talked about all during the construction.

Supi Yaw had taken it upon herself to compile a list of those she would like to invite. It was an odd list which simply included those who had personally helped bring their dream to reality. First, there was the customs official and his wife, who first welcomed us to this great country. Then, there is the manager of the Imperial Hotel who presided over our "coming-out party." Our guests of honor will, of course, be Emperor Norton and Mrs. Worthington. Then, we will invite Dr. and Mrs. Hitchcock and their daughter, Lilly. And then, I would like to get to know this young lady newspaper reporter we met. And finally, I feel that we have neglected our Mr. Ryan; he too should be seated at the table.

Invitations were written and hand delivered by the Indian lads to their respective recipients. Amerjit hired a carriage, drove to the Imperial Hotel, and personally delivered George Mitchell's invitation. Mitchell was delighted.

CHAPTER SIXTY-EIGHT

Anne Brier, reporter for the San Francisco Call Newspaper and, correspondent for the TIMES OF LONDON, was especially pleased to receive her invitation. So was the well-dressed gentleman sitting across from her desk, Mr. Stanley Ribbon, Queen's Council General for the British government, San Francisco Consulate. After reading the hand-delivered note, Miss Brier handed the invitation to Mr. Ribbon who, upon reading it, became openly agitated. Ribbon, looking directly at Anne, barked, "Accept the bloody thing. Who does this simple soldier think he is?"

Anne scribbled out a short reply including a request for a personal interview of Supi Yaw prior to the dinner event. The message was received and a time for the interview was set for the following morning at ten o'clock at the office of the BURMA TIGER SHIPPING COMPANY.

At ten o'clock the following morning, Anne Brier arrived at the newly renovated building. Supi Yaw was standing in the doorway with a bright smile and a parasol. Extending her hand toward the attractive, red-haired lady, Supi Yaw suggested that they walk two blocks to the Burma Tiger and begin their interview. En route to the ship, Supi Yaw was acknowledged by dozens of stevedores, carters, and policemen she had come to know. Each had a polite comment to make as the two women made their way to the dock.

Mr. Ryan had just completed final maintenance on the ship and was about to leave for several errands. As the two women approached, he pulled his boatswain's pipe from his shirt pocket and piped them aboard as if they were visiting dignities. Anne Briar was openly impressed at the gesture. Supi Yaw noticed that Mr. Ryan was a bit more attentive to the attractive woman than usual and in her introduction, emphasized, 'Miss' Anne Briar correspondent for the SAN FRANCISCO CALL NEWS and the TIMES OF LONDON. Within seconds of opening their respective mouths, both Briar and Ryan realized that they were both Irish. Then, it came down to where in Ireland each came from and which side of the "fence" each stood. Several comments in Gaelic were exchanged leading to broad smiles on both faces.

Mr. Ryan spoke, "Princess Supi Yaw, it seems that Miss Briar and I come from a similar part of Ireland and have similar feelings about your husband's queen and her band of bully boys. We shall, however, attempt to maintain as much civility as is possible for an Irishman; but only when sober." The three laughed at Ryan's comments.

Supi Yaw then explained to Mr. Ryan that Miss Briar would be doing an interview which could very well impact their new enterprise. Supi Yaw then asked Mr. Ryan if he would show the young lady the ship while she arranged a pot of tea and some biscuits. Ryan then picked up Gunga and again spoke in Gaelic, "Little doggie, let's show this charming

Irish lass our little boat." The lady stroked the dog affectionately. She also noticed the royal monogram on the dog's collar.

Thirty minutes later, Ryan and Briar emerged from one of the passage doors onto the main deck. One of the Indian lads had prepared a table, chairs and a sun shade. For the next two hours, Supi Yaw answered questions about her home, her family, and her aspirations as a female doctor and as a newly landed immigrant. Then cautiously, very cautiously, Annie began to probe into the life and legend of Michael St. John, Hero of the Irrawaddy. An hour later, Amerjit brought forth a lunch consisting of baked salmon, fresh vegetables, and an assortment of cakes and coffee. Briar was overwhelmed with the hospitality shown to her. Mr. Ryan had just arrived with a wagonload of supplies for the ship. Seeing that Miss Briar was just about to leave the ship, he offered to escort the lady to her destination. In Gaelic, Briar accepted the offer from one Irishman to another.

Supi Yaw noticed the unmistakable signs of mutual attraction between a very lonely man and a very attractive woman. Several of the Indian lads standing at the rail also took note of Ryan standing a bit straighter and pulling in his mid-section a few inches. It was two hours later that Ryan returned to the ship with a firm grin on his face. He immediately went to his cabin and trimmed his somewhat shaggy beard. He likewise had one of the Indian lads trim off a few inches of his hair. Mr. Ryan was clearly smitten.

The following morning, the San Francisco Call newspaper carried a front-page photograph of Princess Supi Yaw and her husband Sergeant Major Michael St. John. It was a photo taken on the steps of the Imperial Hotel some weeks prior. The brief headline read, "Ranking refugees find a home in America." Ryan had purchased several copies from a street corner newsboy and practically ran to the Burma Tiger building. The St. Johns and the Carters were having breakfast in the Carter's apartment. It was Opal who practically yelled out, "Refugees! What's this about refugees? We are most certainly not refugees. We might be immigrants, but we are not seeking refuge from anyone." Those around the table read and re-read the article several times, noting the quotes from Supi Yaw indicating that she, a woman and a woman of color at that, was not allowed to pursue a medical career under the oppressive British medical system. The article went on to indicate that her husband and national hero was unable to achieve his true place in the business world or the military system unless he could establish some sort of formal family pedigree. The writer then suggested that Michael abandoned his calling and his country in favor of the classless society of America. Those around the table sat silent ruminating on the unkind words printed about them. The article had little to say about the new shipping company they had formed; nor did it attempt to promote any good will among the company and the community. The article caused a dark, grey fog to fill the room.

Mr. Ryan broke the deafening silence. "I can't understand why this woman would write such a hurtful article. I thought she was friendly toward us." Ryan felt confused because of the "relationship" which seemed to have developed between the two. He felt horribly abused and questioned his judgment in regards to women, Irish women in particular.

Supi Yaw's face turned hard. "Mr. Ryan, I would appreciate very much if you would accompany me to Miss. Briar's office. I believe that she has an ulterior motive in her essay. It is clear that she has not represented my comments correctly; nor has she conveyed many of the positive personal views I openly expressed. What she had written in this article is not what we discussed. Something is wrong."

Two hours later Supi Yaw and Mr. Ryan were ushered into the office of the assistant editor of the paper. Politely but firmly, he indicated that his newspaper only prints "the truth, the whole truth and nothing but the truth." He failed to add, "so help me God!" The editor dismissed his guests after refusing to allow them to confront Miss. Brier directly. "I must protect my reporters and the truth, the whole truth and nothing but the truth at all costs," he blathered.

An hour later, Mr. Ryan, along with Supi Yaw, retraced his steps back to the small stark apartment Miss Briar called home. Miss. Briar was at home, still in her house coat. At first, the Irish woman refused to allow Ryan and Supi Yaw to enter. She feigned a touch of the flu and suggested that they meet sometime next week. Ryan then addressed her in Gaelic. Whatever he said got the door opened, and the two entered the small cramped room. As with any English or for that fact Irish person, there was the obligatory offer of a cup of tea. Supi Yaw politely declined.

"I suppose you are here about the article," Briar whimpered.

Supi Yaw simply nodded her head. "Miss Briar, I allowed you to enter into the privacy of my world and my personal thoughts. I trusted you. For some reason, you have chosen to betray that trust and fabricate a story which I did not tell. As a result, my husband and I are made to look like we have abandoned our country and our people. This is simply not true. Both my husband and I love our countries, and in spite of certain political differences, we still hold our queen in extremely high regard. And I would add that my husband is still considered a national hero by virtue of his receipt of the Victoria Cross."

Ryan then added that he too still considered himself a distant, but nonetheless, loyal subject of the queen. He went on to add that this "band of refugees," including the

Indian lads came to America, not to escape the tyranny of the British system, but rather to contribute to the American system.

At this point, Anne Briar broke into tears. For the next ten minutes she cried, blubbered, and filled her handkerchief. "Please take a seat," she finally moaned.

For the next hour interspersed with crying fits, the lady unfolded the story of her destitute parents coming to America to work on the railroad. She told how her mother died after working in a railroad wash house for twelve hours a day and how her father dropped dead of a heart attack while pounding spikes into railroad ties somewhere in the middle of the Utah desert. She went on to tell how she eventually found her way to San Francisco and began to work as a housekeeper for the British Council General for San Francisco. Her story went on to tell how she learned to write and write well, well enough to write for the San Francisco Call News. Through the influence of her employer, the Council General, she soon became a credentialed reporter for the TIMES OF LONDON. Because she was a woman, and an Irish woman at that, the TIMES required her to write under a pseudonym, Edward Prescott. Then, all the emotions a woman could muster broke loose. The tears flowed like Victoria Falls. Anne Briar then recounted how Council General Ribbon used her to obtain information about subjects which had a direct impact on the British Empire. Many of her news reports to the TIMES were slanted to give a strong negative impression of the American government and the American political system. There was a heavy emphasis on the issue of slavery, the plight of the American Indians, and other unsavory topics. She confessed that she held the American president, Mr. Lincoln, in the highest regard, but was persuaded into making him look like a bumbling fool. Then came the subject of Sergeant Major St. John and Supi Yaw. She told how

Mr. Ribbon has specifically ordered her to write a story which portrayed them both as traitors to the Empire. In fact, she blathered, the story sent to the TIMES was far more vitriolic than the one published in the San Francisco Call News. After more than an hour of tearful catharsis, Anne Briar blew her sorely reddened nose, took a deep breath, and smiled as if the weight of the world had been taken off her delicate shoulders. "So there you have it. The whole dirty little story," she said.

Mr. Ryan and Supi Yaw sat silent for several minutes attempting to assess the situation.

Anne then said, "It sounds to me like you need to keep your distance from our Council General, Mr. Ribbon."

Supi Yaw looked Anne directly in the eye and said, "Quite the contrary, my dear. We shall confront this man and his issues directly. If you run from a bully, you will spend the rest of your life running from every bully you encounter. Mr. Ryan, we must find a way to put this fellow in his place."

Ryan smiled and winked at Briar. He spoke, "Thou preparest a banquet in the presence of mine enemies...' Perhaps we should invite the honorable gentleman to our little dinner party. As the old saying goes, 'you can't fight a bear while he is hiding in the bushes; you must bring him out in the open'."

Supi Yaw thought for a minutes and smiled, "Mr. Ryan, you may have something there. Let's see if we can bring this bear out from his hiding place and see if he is as fierce as he pretends to be. After all, he can't be much of a bear if he insists on hiding behind a woman newspaper reporter, now can he?"

Anne spoke, "Perhaps you can get Mr. Ribbon to say something about your President Lincoln and his war with the South. He truly hates Mr. Lincoln and has great sympathy for the southern cause. He has even asked me to interview people who share his distain for the President and report their comments in the British press."

Supi Yaw again smiled, "Yes, Mr. Ryan, let's invite our beloved Council General to our little party. Perhaps with a bit of luck, we can bait the bear into saying something which will show his true colors."

By late afternoon, a personal, handwritten, and hand-delivered invitation was in the hands of Queen's Council General of San Francisco, Mr. Stanley Ribbon. Mr. Ribbon smile as he considered the invitation. His butler, who had received the invitation, said, "Sir, what shall I tell the gentleman who delivered the message? He is awaiting your response in the entry hall. Ribbon sucked in a deep breath, "Tell the gentleman that the Queen's Council General would be honored to participate in this celebration of British hospitality."

∾

CHAPTER SIXTY-NINE

With two days until the dinner party, Supi Yaw had managed to conscript many of the Chinese day laborers her husband had employed to renovate the new premises. Unlike many of those who hired Chinese workers, she managed to learn each of their names and was able to employ a few phrases in Chinese. Throughout the work day, Supi Yaw would offer the workers a cup of tea or a glass of cold water. Between her efforts and Amerjit's, they managed to erect temporary walls in the back corner of the great warehouse, near the makeshift kitchen. Within hours the empty space had been transformed into an elegant, but not ostentatious, dining room complete with borrowed portraits of President Lincoln at one end and a painting of Queen Victoria at the other. The final touch was a proper swinging door separating the kitchen from the dining room. The Indian lads had washed and ironed their newly created uniforms with the finishing touch being turbans fashioned from old discarded drapery material Opal found in Mr. Worthington's home. Supi Yaw collected Michael and

John's most recent uniforms and had them pressed and buttons polished. From Michael's personal armoire, she took the Victoria Cross from its small wooden case and pinned it respectfully to the upper left panel of the Sergeant Majors tunic. A tear filled her eye as she vividly recalled the morning when Queen Victoria handed the small object to her man.

Amerjit had received a note from his new friend, Mr. George Mitchell, manager of the Imperial Hotel, asking if he might be in need of any fine dinner china or silverware for the occasion. Amerjit gladly accepted the generous offer. Mitchell dispatched a delivery wagon with all sorts of china, serving utensils, candelabras and table cloths. Amerjit was beyond elated.

Not being particularly familiar with dinner parties, Opal Carter opted to spend most of her free time visiting Mr. Worthington; cleaning and taking the elderly lady for carriage rides in local parks.

In the front of the BURMA TIGER building John Carter and Michael St. John were deeply involved in bringing the books of account up to date. John spoke in a somber tone. "Michael, we are slowly running out of money. We must find clients and fast. The article in the newspaper did not help matters as we had hoped." Michael simply nodded in agreement.

A man in a blue courier's uniform entered the front door. "I have a dispatch for a Mr. Michael St. John," he said.

Michael took the packet and handed the courier a coin. "It's from Bua Tan Bo," he said as he examined the various papers contained in the heavy brown envelope. Among the items was a sealed envelope addressed to Supi Yaw St. John. Bua had written a lengthy dissertation regarding the "Ballentine Doctrine," now labeled the "Victoria Doctrine." He went into each aspect of the tentative agreement and the complications affixed to each. What had seemed so simple had been complicated by political jargon and racial innuendo. While the British government appeared to support the broad objectives of the concept, they wanted every facet to be in their favor, with few, if any concessions being given to the Burmese supporters of the doctrine. It was all "take" and very little "give." There was no question that Bua Tan Bo was not very optimistic about the initial outcome of the plan. He did mention that the new British Governor of Burma had appointed him to the position of Vice-Chairman of Council of Indigenous Concerns. Bua suggested that this was the British government's way of placating him and the Baum people and keeping him busy with numerous meetings and meaningless paperwork. On a positive note, he mentioned that several dozen missionaries, make that American missionaries, had been assigned to serve the Christian tribal groups in Burma and Nagaland. The Archbishop of Canterbury had sent two clerics to augment the paltry contingent of Church of England clergymen serving the Burmese people–that is, after they had served the requirements of the British expatriates.

Another noteworthy comment dealt with Michael's old "friend" The Prince. It seems that the Prince had managed to commandeer control of a small armada of *dhows* marauding off the coast of eastern India and western Burma. After several encounters with British patrol boats, the Prince was captured, tried, and hanged for all to see. The assorted notes went on to cover a wide range of informational items. Sergeants Roberts and McMillan were still working in the Banderban Hills setting up agricultural cooperatives among the various hill tribes. According to Bua, Roberts had fallen madly in love with one of the local Baum ladies and expected to retire among the Baum. A pang of melancholy shot through Michael as he reflected on the time he spent among the Baum people and how he had come to know and love Supi Yaw. He silently promised himself that, someday, he and his wonderful wife would return to the Banderban Hills—at least for a visit.

On a final note, Bua mentioned that James had become quite wealthy due to the demand for his jungle berry wine. Because of the high demand from the Chinese in Hong Kong, he had hired more than two dozen men to collect and process the fruit, bottle it, and send it on its way. According to Bua, the Baum people were planting jungle berry bushes on every piece of ground not currently covered by coffee or cashew trees. That seemed to put a broad smile on Michael's face. He excused himself from John and found Supi Yaw in the kitchen. After a brief but affectionate embrace, he handed her the envelope from Burma.

Supi Yaw took a seat at the table and reverently opened the red wax seal. It was from her father. The letter was brief but carried enormous content.

It read:

God's richest blessings to you, our loving daughter, Supi Yaw St. John.

After your wedding, your mother and I returned home to the tranquility of our hills and trees. We are ever grateful to our loving God for having given us the awesome privilege of participating in your marriage to your wonderful husband. Both your mother and I truly believe that Michael St. John was divinely appointed to become your husband. No other man in our realm could have fulfilled the enormous expectations you have for your calling.

Unfortunately at the time of your wedding, neither I nor your mother had an opportunity to express our deepest feelings toward you and your husband. The Baum people are a small and insignificant group of human beings hidden away in a remote corner of the earth. Very few in the world outside of the Banderban Hills even know we exist. Thanks to your husband's brave deeds, the world has had a brief look into the small world known as Burma. Thanks to our beloved son, Bua Tan

Bo, even the Queen herself knows of our existence in this insignificant spot on the globe. Now, Supi Yaw St. John, the people of America are looking at you. God willing, you will become the first Baum physician to be accredited. Not only will you be the first Baum woman to achieve this high and noble position, but you will be the first female from the British Empire to carry the title, Doctor of Medicine. I can only hope and pray that every person my Baum daughter touches will come to know our people as good and God-fearing people. I can only hope that every person that my precious daughter touches will feel the divine power that comes from God and no other. Supi Yaw St. John, I speak for every Baum person who ever lived and who will come to live; we are enormously proud of you."

As his wife read the letter, Michael stood behind her. Tears were flooding from her eyes. She stood and embraced Michael. "The weight of my calling is almost too much. If I fail..."

Michael placed his hand over her mouth before she could say more. "My dear wife, you have not failed thus far; why should you start failing now?"

She smiled and wiped away the tears. "Michael, by the Grace of God, I shall become the first Baum physician and the first female physician from the British Empire!" she said as she looked directly at the portrait of Queen Victoria.

∾

CHAPTER SEVENTY

At precisely eight o'clock, Emperor Joshua Norton, Emperor of California and Protector of Mexico, accompanied by Mrs. Worthington, arrived at the BURMA TIGER Shipping Company. They were escorted by two of the handsomely attired Indian lads through the great warehouse, as it had come to be called, and into the makeshift dining room at the rear. They were greeted by Sergeant Major Michael and Mrs. Supi Yaw St. John, Captain and Mrs. John Carter, Mr. Timothy Ryan and Mr. Amerjit Singh. Within minutes, Queen's Council General for San Francisco, Mr. Stanley Ribbon, and Miss Anne Briar arrived in a coach bearing the British Royal Seal on its door. At almost the same moment, Mr. George Mitchell arrived in a carriage bearing the seal of the Imperial Hotel. Then a small public taxi, carrying Mr. and Mrs. Benjamin Johnson of the United States Customs Department arrived, as did Colonel and Mrs. Hitchcock and daughter Lillian. As each invited guest arrived, a private photographer politely called for a pose for each of the guests. It was Carter's suggestion that a photographer be included so as to provide "appropriate" images of the guests for local newspapers. These photos, along with a proper commentary of the event written by Anne Briar, would be issued to the newspapers in the area and to the TIMES OF LONDON.

Inside the dining room, the Indian lads distributed an assortment of exotic delicacies personally created by Amerjit. Each item emphasized a particular spice or flavor unique to Asia. The crystal wine glasses, complete with the Imperial Hotel's monogram, were filled with the last remaining supply of Burmese jungle berry juice. Without exception all those in attendance commented on the delightful flavors and unique quality of the "wine." Even Council General Ribbon was complimentary. In fact, after his third glass of the ruby liquid, C.G. Ribbon became overly complimentary, offering several toasts to Queen Victoria. At last, Colonel Hitchcock offered a toast to President Lincoln, whereupon Ribbon simply raised his glass an inch or two and grunted quietly. The gesture was noted by all present. Supi Yaw then invited the guests to be seated. Each place was designated by a hand-inscribed name card. John Carter then asked if Mr. Ryan would offer a blessing for the meal. All bowed their heads and gave thanks–even Council General Ribbon.

With Michael at one end of the table and John Carter at the other, Amerjit gave the order to begin serving. The waiters then began a ritual whereby each guest was being presented with a culinary object of art. The fine china, the monogrammed silver service, combined with the magnificent presentation of each tureen of soup, platter of salad, or plate of fresh bread introduced the meal as an event rather than simply a meal. Amerjit watched each face around the table as his waiters presented his creations. Supi Yaw watched Amerjit's face as he quietly beamed with artistic delight at the response to his art. Of particular interest were the facial expressions from Mr. Mitchell. On several occasions, Mitchell silently acknowledged his pleasure with a nod and a smile. Amerjit was bursting with quiet pride.

Captain Carter managed to keep the conversation moving around the table. He would direct a question to each of the guests and allow that person time to respond. He would then solicit responses from others on the topic of the moment. Carter was careful to avoid difficult or delicate issues such as the war in the South and the unfortunate political events of the day. He then addressed Supi Yaw and asked about her progress toward a medical diploma. Before she could respond, Dr. Hitchcock entered the conversation. "Captain Carter, I apologize for not having discussed this with Mrs. St. John prior to this event, but I have taken the initiative with my colleagues in the local medical community to assess Mrs. St. John's qualifications for becoming a licensed physician. From what I and my fellow physicians conclude, Mrs. St. John needs only to sit for the medical licensing examination, and I would add, pass it with a sufficiently high score to convince the examination board that she is indeed qualified to assume the title Doctor of Medicine. This would be followed by an internship at a local hospital for two years. Under the circumstances, I would offer my hospital at the Presidio and my personal attention in regards to the internship. I wish to add that Mrs. St. John will not be afforded any extraordinary consideration because of her gender or attention of the President. If she is deemed not to be fully qualified in every aspect of the profession, she will not be granted the title of Doctor of Medicine. On this you have my professional word. I would further add that there are many American women who have achieved the rank of medical doctor in spite of those opposed to the idea."

This last comment seemed to hit C.G. Ribbon right between the eyes. He retorted, "Colonel, it appears that you Americans are not only interested in inventing new and better systems of government and of social orders, but now, you wish to destroy the ancient and noble profession of medicine. A woman's place in is the home, not in a surgery. The next thing you know, you will be permitting women lawyers, women politicians, and God forbid, women military officers."

The room was silent as Hitchcock and Ribbon glared at each other. Captain Carter opened his mouth to speak. Before he could formulate some sort of pacification, Ribbon blew again. "Just like your idiot President, wanting to free the slaves in the South. If change is needed, change will come, but not through the insane antics of some Illinois log splitter."

Again, there was absolute silence in the room. Even the waiters froze in their tracks. Finally after a long cold silence, Colonel Hitchcock rose from his chair and whispered, "Sir, you are no longer welcome in my country. I shall be making a full report to my commanding general in the morning. I will expect that you will vacate your posting shortly thereafter. Is that clear?"

Queen's Council General Ribbon slowly rose from his chair, turned, and staggered quickly toward the door. Before reaching the door, the little man turned and said, "And while we are at it, Sergeant Major St. John, your queen awarded you the highest military medal in the realm and you have opted to desert Her Majesty's empire in favor of this pagan frontier the Americans have chosen to call, the United States. In my humble opinion, this is treason at its worst." Michael St. John rose from his seat as if to challenge the pompous little man. Ribbon, seeing the possibility of a physical conflict, turned and bolted for the door. Again there was stunned silence.

After what seemed like an eternity, Opal Carter almost like a naive child, spoke, "Mr. Amerjit, I don't think I have ever tasted such a magnificent meal in all my life. Sir, you are to be congratulated." The warm words seemed to melt the cold harsh words which had spoiled the evening.

There was a round of applause followed by a brief comment from Mr. Mitchell. "Mr. Amerjit, I would offer you two propositions; first, I would like to invite you as a guest chef in my main kitchen for special occasions. Secondly, I would strongly suggest that you consider opening a dining house of your own. I might even be persuaded to go into partnership with you." Again there was a round of applause.

Amerjit rose from his chair and began to speak. "My friends, this is the first time in my life when I have been able to present culinary fantasies which have been cooking in my mind for years. Because a chef must appeal to the palates of his consumers, I have been limited to preparing food for the stomach, not for the palate. Tonight, I prepared each dish not knowing if it would be appreciated or rejected. It was my intent, however, to create and present dishes which might serve to go beyond the expectations of a daily meal. Having said all of that, I wish to serve you a very special dessert." Amerjit nodded at one of the waiters who proceeded to begin the dessert ritual with slightly baked bananas, covered with a rich chocolate sauce, sprinkled with walnuts, and sprayed with exotic liquor. As each plate was being served, another waiter lit the liquor afire. A strong South American coffee was served with thick cream.

It was Anne Briar who spoke. "Poor Mr. Ribbon; I am certain he would have enjoyed this lovely banana." Those around the table laughed, partially because her comment was funny and partially to break the tension of the unfortunate incident with Mr. Ribbon.

Seeing the need to lessen the formality of the evening, Supi Yaw suggested that the gentlemen retreat to the front office or perhaps the sidewalk in front of the office and partake in a good cigar and a glass of after-dinner brandy.

Outside, on the front steps of the Burma Tiger Shipping Building, Michael St. John offered cigars all round. John Carter spoke, “Colonel Hitchcock, I can’t help but admire your direct comment to Mr. Ribbon. While he does have certain diplomatic privileges in this country of ours, he does not have the right to openly criticize it or its President.”

St. John added, “I can assure you, gentlemen, he does not necessarily reflect the opinions of the British people. Granted, we are a stodgy bunch, but we are not generally rude and boorish.” Blowing a plume of smoke into the fog, he continued, “My wife tells me that Mr. Ribbon was actually inciting Miss. Briar to create negative images of the American people in the British press. In my opinion, this smells of bad business on Ribbon’s part.”

Emperor Norton had remained unusually quiet during most of the evening. Now he spoke, “By tomorrow morning, I will have issued a public proclamation declaring Mr. Ribbon *persona non grata* in my realm. I will afford the gentleman thirty days to vacate his post and depart. I might suggest that he present his credentials to Jefferson Davis and possibly gain employment as a council general for the Confederacy.” That brought another well-needed round of laughter. St. John noticed two of the waiting carriage drivers and the photographer sitting in the rear of one of the carriages. He walked over to them and offered each of them a cigar and a light. The gesture was noted by the group. Mitchell had moved to where Amerjit was standing and began to follow up on his proposition to become a guest chef at the Imperial. An hour or so later, the two shook hands on a deal of some sort. St. John engaged Colonel Hitchcock in conversation regarding his wife and her situation with the medical profession. Captain Carter discussed the possibility of Benjamin Johnson coming to work for the Burma Tiger Shipping Company–as soon as they began to turn a profit. And Mr. Ryan simply puffed quietly on his pipe and considered the young lady journalist inside talking with the other women.

Inside, the ladies were focused on Opal Carter's maternal condition. Plans were made for an anticipatory event the Americans called a "baby shower." While Anne Briar was engrossed in the conversation, her thoughts were on Timothy Ryan, standing just outside the building. While he was somewhat older than she, he was after all Irish.

A gentle rain began to leak out of the thickening San Francisco fog. Those standing outside opted to enter the building and thank the hostesses for the wonderful evening. Emperor Norton took Mrs. Worthington by the arm and led the way to the waiting carriage. Colonel and Mrs. Hitchcock signaled for their carriage. Lilly had managed to convince Anne Briar to come with her to the Knickerbocker firehouse to see the magnificent fire pumpers and to meet "the fire laddies," as she called them. Mr. Ryan had hoped to escort Miss Briar home, seeing that her escort, Mr. Ribbon had left unexpectedly. After gaining reluctant permission from her parents to visit the firehouse, Anne whispered into Lily's ear. Lilly called out, "Mr. Ryan, why don't your join us?" Ryan blushed violently as he smiled and nodded his agreement.

Michael whispered as Ryan moved toward the door, "Try to be home by dawn, Timothy."

Ryan gave Michael a look which was meant to say, *"Mind your own business, young fella."*

Michael looked at his wife who had also noticed the budding relationship. She too smiled knowingly.

Somewhere around three o'clock and after two fire calls, Timothy Ryan delivered Miss Anne Briar to her front door. Thirty minutes later, Mr. Ryan floated aboard the Burma Tiger. One of the Indian lads noticed the silly grin on his first mate's face. He also noticed several prominent lipstick imprints on various parts of the same face. Before the morning tide had ebbed, news of Mr. Ryan's night out had been embellished by the Indian lads and passed on to Amerjit who added his two pennies worth and passed it on to Mrs. St. John. Over coffee and fresh biscuits, Opal informed her husband of Mr. Ryan's night on the town with Miss Briar.

Michael St. John spoke, "I think it's time that Mr. Ryan and I had a father- and-son talk. The man clearly needs to be informed as to the true nature of women."

Supi Yaw frowned at Michael and replied, "And just what do you know about women, Sergeant Major St. John?" Michael simply smiled and said nothing.

CHAPTER SEVENTY-ONE

Michael and Carter spent the morning in the office writing letter after letter to companies involved in the commercial shipping trade. They offered special freight rates for new clients as well as promises of better service. Around noon, Timothy Ryan came into the main office of the Burma Tiger Shipping Company. Ryan's demeanor clearly suggested that he was perplexed about something. Lighting his familiar pipe, he spoke, "Michael, could you and I take a walk down to the ship? There is something I need to talk to you about."

Michael looked at Carter as if to say, "*This must be important.*" Half way to the pier, Timothy spoke, "Michael, of all the men on this earth, I consider you to be the finest man I have ever known. Out there on the Indian Ocean, you set me straight on the course of my life. I had planned to spend the rest of my life sailing around in ships, ministering to those whose religion is the same as mine and attempting to convert those whose religion is misdirected. Everything was fine, until last night."

Michael spoke, actually knowing what had happened last night, "Tell me Timothy, what happened last night?"

"Michael, I. . ."

Ryan couldn't continue. His speech stammered to a full stop.

Michael, with a broad smile on his face said, "Mr. Ryan, you fell madly in love with this Miss Anne Briar woman. Is that correct?"

Ryan simply smiled, showing every tooth in his mouth, and nodded. At that point, Michael put his arm around Timothy Ryan. "Congratulations, my friend. Harpoon this lass before she gets away."

At that comment, Ryan stopped, causing several fish carts to barely avoid missing the two men standing on the walkway.

"Michael, I once took an oath of celibacy before my bishop. How can I break a second oath? We simply can't go around breaking every oath we feel like just because we are in love, can we?" Michael realized his friend's problem.

"Mr. Ryan, at your age and position in life, you truly need a wife to keep you in order. This little Irish lady seems to fit that order to perfection. Timothy, you are not a young man any more; nor is Anne a young lady. If you are going to move, you have to determine that this is the woman you want to spend the rest of your life with and make it happen. As far as your vows are concerned, I would suggest that you and I take a coach over to the Catholic Church and have a chat with the priest regarding this matter. I am fairly certain that there are reasonable provisions for issues of this sort."

Ryan replied, "What happens if the priest refuses? What happens if he reports me to the cardinal or even higher?"

Michael thought for a moment. "You tell me, Timothy. What happens? They toss you out of the church on your ear and you become a Protestant."

Timothy thought for a moment, "You are right, Michael. Let's make an appointment to visit with a priest."

Michael replied, "No, my friend, let's catch a cab and go now. Let's get this thing over with so you can get on with Miss What's-Her-Name."

"It's Miss Briar," Ryan replied as Michael hailed a passing coach.

Father William O'Riley, an old and wizened priest, realized the true nature of the penitent priest's dilemma. Two difficult hours later, Father Timothy Ryan was officially Mr. Timothy Ryan. He had confessed his transgressions to the old priest who assured him that his sins would not result in his eternal damnation nor would any member of the Catholic clergy be hunting him down like a common criminal. With the waving of his ancient hand, in the form of the cross, the deed was done. He was completely absolved from his sins, removed from his office as a priest, and committed to remaining a loyal member of the Catholic Church. While the priest did not actually have the authority to release Ryan from his oaths, he did so nonetheless. Timothy Ryan felt as if a huge millstone had been lifted from his shoulders as he left the red-brick church. Michael hailed a cab and suggested they stop off at the Imperial for lunch. Timothy smiled broadly and indicated that he preferred to go over to the San Francisco Call newspaper building. There was something he needed to take care of. Michael grinned, "Sharpen your harpoon and make certain your rope doesn't tangle." Ryan saluted and hailed another passing carriage.

CHAPTER SEVENTY-TWO

St. John reconsidered having lunch at the Imperial in light of the recent events. He instructed the cab driver to take him home. Over a bowl of split pea soup and sourdough French bread, Michael related the whole history of his quiet friend, Timothy Ryan, to his wife. Michael then suggested that Mr. Ryan and Miss Brier might be making some sort of an announcement sometime soon.

Supi Yaw shook her head. "Of course, they will be making an announcement soon. The poor man was clearly hooked by the woman. My guess is that they are just now planning the nuptials."

Supi Yaw plunked herself down in Michael's lap and gave him a long and adoring kiss followed by a long and well-needed nap—of sorts.

Amerjit had prepared a dinner consisting mainly of leftovers from the dinner party. The improvised dining room was still in place in the lower "great room." The table flowers were still somewhat fresh and the table cloths had been washed and ironed. The Carters and the St. Johns took their places around the table. Opal Carter asked, "Where is Mr. Ryan?"

At that exact moment, Timothy Ryan and Anne Briar entered the room. Both were beaming.

Supi Yaw boldly spoke up and asked, "Well, Mr. Ryan, did you propose marriage to Miss Briar?"

He shook his head ruefully, "No, Mrs. St. John, I did not. There was a long and uncomfortable pause. "She proposed to me."

Those in the room went wild. Hands were shook, cheeks were kissed, and congratulations were offered–an abundance of congratulations.

To add to the festiveness of the moment, Mr. Ryan plunked down an afternoon copy of the San Francisco Call newspaper. Opening to the business page, Mr. Ryan proudly pointed to a headline, "New Shipping Company Receives Notables at Banquet. Michael picked up the paper and began to read aloud. "The most recent investment in the American shipping world comes in the form of a boat loaded with a British war hero, a Burmese princess, a one-legged American sea captain, an Indian gourmet chef, and a wild-eyed Irishman. If that mix of personalities doesn't spark the imagination, nothing will. Seeing the potential for vastly expanding trade with Asia, South America and regions to the north, these unusual entrepreneurs have set up shop at the south end of the embarcadero. Their primary vessel, the Burma Tiger, will soon be booking cargo for all points around the Pacific. To mark the occasion of their entry into the American shipping market, the new owners hosted a banquet at their new facility, fit for a king, or at least a princess, and an emperor. The guest of honor was none other than HE Joshua Norton, Emperor of California and Protector of Mexico. Other guests included Mrs. Alice Worthington, widow of former San Francisco businessman Arthur Worthington, Colonel and

Mrs. Charles Hitchcock, their daughter Lillian Hitchcock, Managing Director of the Imperial Hotel, Mr. and Mrs. Benjamin Johnson of the U.S. Customs Service and Mr. Stanley Ribbon, British Council General for San Francisco. Plans for expansion of the Burma Tiger's shipping fleet were noted along with continued financial support of the San Francisco Children's Home. A good time was had by all."

Ryan then pointed to the byline; Anne Briar. Then, as if to add frosting to the cake, he turned to page two of the paper and pointed to a photograph of Council General Stanley Ribbon. The caption read, "British diplomat insults American President." The story went on to read:

> *"In a recent public event, British Council General, Mr. Stanley Ribbon was heard to offer scurrilous comments regarding President Lincoln and his handling of the ongoing conflict between the United States of America and the Confederate States. He likewise suggested that American women, like their British counterparts, should not be afforded the same educational and professional opportunities as American men. Council General Ribbon's open and antagonistic comments were met with rebuttal based on the American concept of equality for all. It was strongly suggested, by an attending member of the United States government, that Mr. Ribbon may wish to consider a foreign posting more suited to his personal preferences."*

There was no 'byline' attached to his article, but judging from the grin on Anne's face, she had written the article.

The euphoria of the evening was heightened by a second round of gourmet delights left over from the previous evening's dinner party. With dinner concluded, the men excused themselves to smoke a "stogie" in the street, as Captain Carter put it. The conversations inside focused on an engagement and a wedding. Outside, the conversation was directed toward more practical matters such as professional issues. Carter strongly suggested that Ryan take the first opportunity to achieve his captain's papers. He concurred. Ryan then mentioned that his bride-to-be had expressed her serious desire to become a writer of fiction. She had several partially completed manuscripts, but needed an entry into a publishing house before she could devote any more energy toward her writing.

Michael nodded, "Timothy, I will have a chat with our friend George Mitchell from the Imperial. He might have a contact or two."

Then a wide smile crossed Michael's face, "She could become the author of "The Battle of the Irrawaddy." Several people have suggested that I take time to write an account of the skirmish. Perhaps Anne would like to take the opportunity." The evening ended with another round of congratulations and comments about poor Mr. Ribbon.

∾

CHAPTER SEVENTY-THREE

Once again, the breakfast ritual was interrupted by the ringing of the front doorbell. Michael put on his coat and answered the door. It was Mrs. Worthington and another gentleman who was dressed in a sea captain's uniform. The grey-bearded man was introduced as Captain Andrew Iverson, owner of a sailing ship. Subsequently, the guests were invited to take a seat in the main office of the Burma Tiger Shipping Company.

Supi Yaw served coffee and took a chair next to her husband. Shortly, John Carter entered the room.

Finally, after a few comments about the grand evening and the weather, Mrs. Worthington came to the point of her visit. "Over the past few weeks, we have become more than friends; you are, in fact, more like my family than my actual family. You have comforted me in my time of emotional distress and assisted me with my physical issues. And more importantly, you have brought me to a new relationship with my God and Savior. For this, I am eternally grateful. Now, as to the nature of my visit. For many years, Captain Iverson has been a close friend and confidant of my late husband and me. We have been through a great deal together since we arrived here in San Francisco. It was Captain Iverson who helped my late husband develop a successful business and establish our place here in San Francisco. This past week, Captain Iverson has indicated his intention to retire and, along with his wife, purchase a house here in San Francisco. In order to facilitate the purchase of a suitable house, overlooking the ocean Captain will be selling his sailing ship. After some thought, I made the Captain an offer. I would exchange my house overlooking the ocean for his ship and the small house in the Napa Valley where his wife lives while he is at sea. I would then take up residence in the Napa Valley, and he would occupy my house. This leaves me with a ship to sail and manage."

At this point, John Carter was beginning to see the plan. Carter then interrupted the conversation. "Captain, tell me about your ship. What is its payload, how long is it, what sort of a crew does it require and what sort of revenues have you realized?"

For the next few minutes Captain Iverson went into every detail of the ship's creation, its maintenance schedules, concluding with a detail of the past five years of its revenues. Iverson concluded his comments by indicating that the ship was still quite seaworthy and capable of generating a substantial income for anyone willing to run a tight operation. Carter smiled at St. John and offered Captain Iverson a cigar from a teak humidor with the head of a one-fanged tiger carved into the lid.

Carter and St. John sat silently waiting for Mrs. Worthington to speak. Savoring the moment, Mrs. Worthington took a long sip of coffee and spoke. "Now then, here's my offer. I will exchange my house for Captain Iverson's ship and house in the Napa Valley. I will then enter into partnership with the Burma

Tiger Shipping Company. You will manage my ship and its cargos. I will continue to receive a share of the profits from the combined resources of the company until the time of my death. At that time, the ship will revert, in full to the Burma Tiger Shipping Company, with one provision." Mrs. Worthington then lifted her coffee cup and took a long exaggerated sip in order to add a bit of drama to her offer.

St. John raised his eyebrow as if to say, "*State your provision, woman.*"

Mrs. Worthington continued, "With the addition of another ship to your infant fleet, your business should increase considerably, particularly if Captain Iverson asks his current clients to retain their relationship with the ship. So, here's my provision; the Burma Tiger Shipping Company and its affiliated interests will donate a full ten percent of its net profits to the San Francisco Children's Home. This goes for the sail making and any other enterprises owned by the company." Again St. John and Carter looked at each other, blowing plumes of cigar smoke toward the ceiling.

Supi Yaw spoke, "We will have to discuss this with Amerjit, but your offer sounds most generous." Michael and John looked at each other as if to say, "*Why not?*" Supi Yaw then excused herself to find Amerjit.

After hearing the details of the proposition, Amerjit joyfully agreed to the deal and suggested that the circumstances called for another gala banquet.

Within a week, dozens of documents had been drawn up by Mrs. Worthington's attorney. A second round of hand-written invitations was completed, this time including the mayor of San Francisco, the commanding officer of the Presidio, and several prominent businessmen. The expansion of the invitation list required that the temporary walls of the improvised "dinning room" be expanded. This time, a fabric canopy, resembling a tent, fashioned from sail cloth, served as a ceiling. Several of the Indian lads spent many hours decorating the canopy with painted images of sailing ships, whales, and scenes from far-away islands. With the expansion of the dining room, came an expansion of the temporary kitchen. For the final touch, Amerjit convinced Michael and Carter that there need to be a door cut into the wall so that the guests would not have to enter the empty cargo room on their way to the dining room. Actually, it was Supi Yaw who did the convincing after Amerjit whispered his dream into her ear. Amerjit, with tears running down his face, informed Supi Yaw that his dream was to open a luxury dining facility. He suggested that this dream might have begun with the first formal dinner party. A second and a third would certainly give a great boost to his reputation in the city. Supi Yaw smiled as she listened to the dream unfold. Amerjit continued, "Madam, once my reputation as a great chef has reached every corner of this city, I would be forced to find larger and more adequate quarters for my dining house. In the meantime, I could open my dining room here in this unused portion of the cargo warehouse. I would naturally remain as a partner of the Burma Tiger Shipping Company and share a portion of my profits with all parties concerned. I would name my dining house, The Burma Tiger Dining House."

Supi Yaw shared Amerjit's vision with Michael and John. They both smiled and nodded. By the end of the day, a door, leading to a seldom-used alley had been constructed, complete with a striped canopy and a hand-painted sign reading "BURMA TIGER FINE DINING HOUSE."

CHAPTER SEVENTY-FOUR

The same day the final documents were signed, transferring title from Captain Iverson to Mrs. Worthington and creating Mrs. Alice Worthington as a partner in the Burma Tiger Shipping Company, Captain Iverson arranged for a short cruise on their newly acquired vessel, to the Farallon Island twenty-seven miles outside the San Francisco Bay. Mrs. Worthington invited all of her new partners, new friends, Mr. Ryan and Miss Brier, and of course, Emperor Norton and his two dogs. While Norton's dogs were a bit skittish about the ship, Gunga raced around the deck as if owned the boat. Even though Opal Carter was the size of a whale and according to Supi Yaw, very close to her day, she insisted on making the one-day trip around the rocks known as the Farallons. Within minutes of leaving the dock, and much to the chagrin of her parents, Lilly Hitchcock found her way to the crow's nest at the top of the main mast of the one hundred and ninety-two foot China Clipper class ship.

The thick fog had lifted just as Captain Iverson ordered the mooring lines be loosed on the ship he called, the KING'S RANSOM. Both Captain Carter and Michael St. John stood at his side as the great ship pulled silently past the sleeping BURMA TIGER. John Carter quietly whispered to the TIGER, "See your new sister? You and she will have great fun running the Pacific."

As the ship glided past the two great arms of what was called the Golden Gate, Emperor Norton was describing to Mrs. Worthington how he envisioned a great bridge connecting the opposite shores. Because the KING'S RANSOM was empty of a cargo, she rode fast and high out of the water. With all sails fully set and a strong wind coming off her starboard, the magnificent ship moved across the water like the dozen or so dolphins which accompanied most of the ships entering or leaving the Golden Gate.

Iverson saw the delight on Carter's face and turned the wheel over to him. Like a kid with a new pony, Carter spun the huge wheel to the starboard and then to the port. The ship responded like a well-trained riding horse. Within the first few moments of leaving San Francisco Bay, several inbound ships passed with their captains calling out, greeting Captain Iverson. On several occasions, Captain Iverson was heard to whisper, "I will miss this, Oh, God, how I will miss this life."

Two hours out from San Francisco Bay, Opal Carter announced with a shrill scream, "My baby is coming!" Supi Yaw was on the forecastle with Amerjit watching the dolphin play their little games when she heard the yell. Supi Yaw asked, no make that ordered, Amerjit to locate Dr. Hitchcock who was somewhere below decks and bring him to the captain's quarters immediately. John Carter, still holding the great wheel, saw Supi Yaw running toward his wife who was lying prone on the wooden deck. He handed off the wheel to Captain Iverson and ran to his wife's side. Carter ordered several crewmen to bring a stretcher. He gently lifted Opal Carter onto the stretcher and carefully supervised her transport to the captain's cabin. Dr. Hitchcock was waiting next to the long wooden dining table. Dr. Hitchcock asked Supi Yaw to remain with him as he ordered all others including John Carter out of the cabin. After several long minutes, Supi Yaw opened the captain's cabin door and spoke, "John, Opal has gone into labor. The baby is coming fast, but I believe everything will be fine. We won't have time to return to San Francisco, and most certainly, we will not have time to get her to a proper hospital. So, just like unfortunate day when I placed you on your captain's table in the Atlantic and cut your leg off, Dr. Hitchcock and I will be once again turning this ship into a sea-going surgery. Only this time, I expect the outcome to be more pleasing." With that, she smiled and closed the door.

Amerjit came down the gangway carrying a large kettle of boiling water, an armful of towels and a porcelain basin. He pushed his way past the two anxious men standing at the door and entered. "I suggest that you gentlemen fall on your knees and petition the Almighty God to bring this child into the world without blemish or malady."

Mr. Ryan found Michael St. John and Captain John Carter both on their knees deep in prayer as the pathetic screams of a woman in heavy labor could be heard from the other side of the carved-oak door. Timothy Ryan too dropped to his knees and joined the men who he now considered as brothers. Soon, two cries were heard, one from the crow's next announcing "Farallon Islands off the port bow"; the second was the cry of a newborn infant announcing that it was hungry and not at all happy with being disturbed at this time of day. The door to the captain's cabin opened and Supi Yaw, holding a newly born baby wrapped in a towel, smiled and spoke to Captain John Carter. "John I would like to introduce you to your new daughter. What do you plan to call her?"

Again the call from the crow's nest came, "Farallons off the port side."

Carter, stunned as he held his new child, grinned broadly, "I think I would like to call her Farallon; that is if her mother agrees."

Amerjit then commented, "It is fortunate for the young child that she was not delivered in San Francisco Bay; you might have decided to call her San Francisco." This bit of Indian humor broke the stress of the moment, causing everyone to laugh loudly. Within minutes of the birth, everyone aboard the one hundred and ninety-one foot sailing vessel was celebrating the unusual entry into the world of this child now called Farallon. Before the KING'S RANSOM had returned to its berth on the Embarcadero, John Carter had used the semaphore flags to signal virtually every passing ship. Virtually every passing ship then returned, by semaphore flags, "Congratulations and God bless this new mariner."

As the ship passed the watchtower of the Presidio, Carter signaled the watchman on duty to have an ambulance carriage waiting at the dock. He "signed" the message from Colonel Charles Hitchcock.

The following day, The San Francisco Call News carried the story of the unusual event aboard the newly transferred ship. This resulted in dozens of congratulatory notes being delivered from sea captains, cargo brokers, and one from the Mayor of San Francisco.

Within the next three days, the Burma Tiger Shipping Company had a full calendar of shipping contracts including several to South America and one to Alaska. In fact, they had more business than they could handle. Added to their contracts for shipping, they received three orders for complete sails. Unfortunately, all three clients wanted their sails to be finished by yesterday. In order to keep their clients reasonably happy and have the sails completed within a reasonable time frame,

Amerjit, through Joshua Norton, hired two dozen Chinese gentlemen from over on Grant Avenue. The sail making went on at a frantic pace, virtually twenty-four hours each day. The newly acquired Singer sewing machines did not stop, except to change a belt or change the person falling asleep on the job. Each sail was completed to perfection and bore a small image of a single-fanged tiger in the lower corner.

Between cooking fresh batches of "Chinese soup" for the sail makers, Amerjit prepared platter after platter of exotic delicacies for the next great dinner party. He had managed to acquire a large icebox from a ship chandler wherein he could keep his culinary creations. In the office of the Burma Tiger Shipping Company, Michael St. John Captain John Carter, and Timothy Ryan, newly promoted business manager, sailed their way through bills of lading, insurance forms, crew contracts, and dozens of other bits of paper required to run a shipping company. No more simple handshakes and a glass of brandy to seal the deal.

Not to be outdone, Amerjit submitted several packets of paper related to food costs, labor costs, and potential income figures. Along with this, he broke down the costs for each sail and the profit on each sail. The numbers all looked good, very good.

When John Carter was not pouring over loading schedules, he would dash over to the hospital to visit with Opal and Farallon. When Supi Yaw was not sitting in an anatomy lecture or pouring fluids into test tubes in a chemistry lab, she was making final arrangements for the forthcoming formal dinner. When Timothy Ryan was not interviewing potential seamen for forthcoming cruises, he was at the offices of the San Francisco Call News talking to or simply staring at his bride-to-be while she filled her "out" box with copy.

~

CHAPTER SEVENTY-FIVE

The evening of the second dinner party arrived with quiet anxiety on everyone's part. The Mayor of San Francisco and his wife arrived after most of the lower ranking had arrived. Aside from those members of the Burma Tiger Shipping Company, there were twenty-five guests seated at the U-shaped table. Once again George Mitchell from the Imperial Hotel had loaned Amerjit sufficient table service and serving utensils necessary to create the ambiance suitable for the evening. Mr. Ryan had invited Father William O'Riley, the priest from St. Mary's Catholic Church. Michael welcomed those present and asked Father O'Riley to offer a blessing. Those of a Catholic persuasion crossed themselves as Father O'Riley delivered a brief prayer; first in Gaelic then in English. As the priest took his seat, Amerjit began his presentation of the meal. His Indian lads, pressed into service as waiters and elegantly costumed as Oriental courtiers, began serving one magnificently prepared platter of food after another. Emperor Norton held up his empty wine glass and demanded to know if there was any more of the "jungle berry" wine. Michael replied that there was none, but a shipment would be ordered from his source in Rangoon as soon as possible. Meanwhile, a wine from the nearby Napa Valley was poured into each glass. Toasts, toasts, and more toasts were made from one end of the table to the other. Several significant comments related to possible business ventures were couched in toasts offered by those from the business community. Without seeming too obvious, Anne Briar took notes and recorded comments made by those at the table. Mrs. Worthington, usually silent, rose to her feet and made a brief statement. "I would like to inform the community that the Burma Tiger Shipping Company has generously offered to commit a full ten percent of its profits to the San Francisco Home for Children." She looked directly at Father O'Riley and continued, "Father O'Riley, I believe this charity is one of your church's programs, is it not?" Mrs. Worthington knew full well that it was, but asked the question all the same. The priest nodded in agreement. She continued, "Father O'Riley, I think this rises to the occasion of a blessing of the two ships from the Bishop of San Francisco himself."

O'Riley again nodded. "I will see what I can do," he muttered through the wine impacted speech center of his brain.

John Carter, likewise a bit foggy from the abundance of toasts, added, "And perhaps you can toss in a free wedding for our friends, Mr. Ryan and Miss Briar."

There was a round of laughter and applause. The old priest, seeing the levity and the gravity of the moment, spoke, "I think that could be arranged. Give me a date and a time."

Timothy and Anne, both blushing profusely, went along with the comment. Timothy Ryan then looked Anne Brier straight in the face and asked, "Well, give me a date and a time!"

Anne again blushed, "Here and now," she replied. Ryan's face went blank, absolutely blank.

Ryan whispered, "Here and now?" The suspense in the room was absolutely electric. No one moved or spoke. Ryan looked at the old priest who was smiling from ear to Irish ear.

Anne continued, "We have our guests here, you have your best man and groomsmen, and I have my matron of honor and bridesmaids. We have had a wedding banquet before the actual event, but who cares. Why not here and now?"

Mrs. Worthington blurted out, "Yes, Timothy, why not here and now?"

Timothy Ryan looked as if he were about to pass out. Finally, Father O'Riley spoke, "I will concede to this unprecedented bit of Irish passion on one condition. This is not a sanctified church. If we could all simply load up our respective carriages and go to my humble church, we can get the deed done proper like. And then after the deed is done, we can all go out and get thoroughly drunk as would befit any proper Irish wedding party."

The party exploded in laughter and joyful emotion. Amerjit had not yet served his dessert but that could wait until another day; a wedding could not.

The coachmen were summoned, carriages loaded, and a parade of cheering celebrants drove off into the San Francisco night toward St. Mary's Catholic Church.

Within minutes, candles were lit, sacred vestments were put in place and a nuptial mass was underway. The sermon was brief and the blessing was in Gaelic. What could be better than that?

As the bride and groom moved toward the door of the church and the unknown, Mr. Mitchell came over to Timothy Ryan and whispered into his ear, "Mr. Ryan, I am putting the Imperial Hotel honeymoon suite at your disposal for the rest of the evening and tomorrow as well." The entire party, including Father O'Riley, then loaded into the carriages and headed toward the Imperial to continue the festivities. Mr. Mitchell served a round of brandy, coffee and cakes before bidding the bride and groom good night. What an evening!

The following morning's papers, with the exception of the San Francisco Call News, had the full details of the gala party and wedding at the Burma Tiger. The event was well on the way of being the most significant social phenomena of the San Francisco high-society calendar. Most of the information came from carriage drivers and the Indian lads who had been paid a few dollars for the details. One of the Indian lads had mentioned to a reporter that Maharaja Amerjit had planned to open a very private and exclusive dinner house limited to the most discerning connoisseurs of exotic cuisine. This comment led to the flood of inquiries from prominent socialites and businessmen. By mid-afternoon, the day following the gala and wedding, Supi Yaw returned from her class at the medical institute. She was exhausted; yet there seemed to be a glow about her. Supi Yaw slowly entered Michael's office, sat down and spoke, "Michael, according to Dr. Hitchcock, I am with child. He says that I am about two months pregnant."

Michael rose slowly from his chair unable to speak. He scooped up his wife in his arms and held her. Tears began to flow from his eyes. Just then, the front door opened and John and Opal Carter entered the office. Opal was holding their new daughter in a tight bundle of blankets. John looked at Michael and spoke, "What's the matter? Is she ill?"

Michael answered, "No, she's next." Michael put Supi Yaw gently on her feet as the congratulations began. Minutes later, Amerjit entered the office. He was told the wonderful news and in his own Indian way, expressed his joy and congratulations.

There was a look of consternation on Amerjit's face which could not go unnoticed.

Carter spoke, "Well, what is it? Something has you upset. Come on, man, get it out."

Amerjit took a deep breath and began his discourse. "My dear friends, when we embarked on this great adventure, some of us did not anticipate the total isolation from our people. You Europeans have other Europeans with whom you can interact. Likewise, you Americans have other Americans with whom you may socialize and perhaps even marry. My Indian boys and I would add, myself, have no one with whom we might. . . " he paused as he attempted to find the right words.

John interrupted, "What you are trying to say is that you and your boys would like to get married. Is that correct?"

Amerjit raised his eyebrows and nodded rapidly. "Yes, we would enjoy the companionship of a woman from our culture. Here in San Francisco there are no Indian women. Well, actually there are Indian women, but they are American Indians, not true Indians from India. My boys have talked about this to the Chinese gentlemen and find that there are no Chinese women for them to marry and to make families. We are somewhat frustrated with this situation. We have discussed this problem in great detail and have concluded that if proper Indian women could be found to come to America and for the purpose of marriage, they would more than likely be Sikhs or Hindu believers as we once were. I would say that there are few, if any, female Indian Christians to be found. So there you have our dilemma. Just like yourselves and now our brother, Mr. Ryan, you enjoy the joys of matrimony while we must suffer the pangs of loneliness. My boys are talking about returning to Asia if something cannot be done."

Supi Yaw listened to Amerjit and smiled. "Amerjit, I would like you to have your boys write brief letters describing what they would like to see in a wife. And I would like you to do the same. If you are willing, and we can work through the immigration regulations regarding bringing foreigners to the United States, I might have a solution to your issue."

Amerjit looked intently at Supi Yaw as did the others in the room. "It is a tradition that Baum women be attended by their mothers or grandmothers at the birth of their first child. A blessing then passes between the mother and the new child. With my husband's permission, I would like to invite my parents and perhaps my brother to sail to San Francisco for the event. Now, if my parents could persuade our elders to allow a number of young, unmarried girls to accompany them, perhaps marriages could be arranged. While Baum people are not truly Indians, they are nonetheless, cousins. And too, Baum people are Christians."

Amerjit broke into a huge smile as the thought raced around in his mind. The thought of a wife for himself took priority. "*She must be able to cook and cook well,*" he thought.

"I will announce this to my boys at once. They will be delighted with the thought of having a wife to delight them as your wives have delighted you," Amerjit prattled.

John Carter then added, "Supi Yaw, I would ask that you also request as many barrels of jungle berry wine as your man in Rangoon can send. I truly believe we have a major market here."

Michael spent the rest of the day making arrangements to bring his father and mother-in-law from Burma to San Francisco. He also wrote a brief letter to Mr. Johnson over at the customs house, asking for his assistance in bringing seven or eight Burmese girls to San Francisco.

Supi Yaw and Opal spent the day between the Carter baby's nursery and the storage room that would soon become the nursery for the St. John baby. That evening while Supi Yaw sat in Michael's lap studying Pharmaceutical Chemistry, Michael finished reading the final chapter of *Maritime Cargo Management*. Life was full and full of promise.

The following morning, Mr. and Mrs. Timothy Ryan arrived at the front office of the Burma Tiger Shipping Company, both looking delighted with their new status. Ryan smiled and spoke, "Nothing like a good Irish wedding to get the old heart pumping again."

Carter replied, "Perhaps you need a good cup of South American coffee to get the old brain pumping again. Too much of a good thing can bring a man to his knees, if he's not careful."

Michael suggested that Anne go upstairs and catch up on the news of the day, and there is some great news. "After all," he said, "you are in the business of reporting the news." Ann scampered off like a dog chasing a bone.

It seemed to strike all three men in the room at the same time. Within the past year, all three of them had gone from being bachelors to husbands. Likewise, all three had gone from one life to something completely different. All three had been brought together by some divine plan which seemed to culminate in this small, insignificant spot on the world map. It was Ryan who spoke. "In the past few hours God has given me a wife. In the past few months He has given me a new relationship with Himself. Nothing could be better."

Amerjit entered the office with a pot of coffee and four cups. He poured coffee and handed a cup to each, taking one for himself. Plunking down in a chair, Amerjit spoke, "I am the only unmarried man among you. I pray to the God that Mrs. St John can arrange for me to have a wife, a good wife; one who will tolerate my somewhat strange and unusual idiosyncrasies. Michael then offered his friend Amerjit and his brother Timothy a cigar. As he lit the black Cuban cigars, he informed them of the new life discovered in his wife's wonderful body. Timothy

Ryan totally lost all composure. He burst into prayer, with his eyes closed and his hands raised toward heaven. Not knowing exactly what to do, Michael, John, and Amerjit stood and followed suit. After what seemed like an eternity, Timothy stopped. There was silence as the four men remained standing with eyes closed and hands raised. Somewhere from deep inside Michael, rivers of prayers flowed outward and upward. Prayers for forgiveness, prayers for his brother, and prayers for his shortcomings and prayers of gratitude for granting him the woman he now called his wife. Then John Carter, moved by others, added his long list of transgressions to the pile along with expressions of affection toward his wife and new daughter. Amerjit, with tears streaming down his face, then began his time at this private altar. His prayers, in the most pronounced and correct King's English, went on and on. His final petition included copious details regarding the size, shape, and disposition of his long wished for wife. As far as Amerjit was concerned, he was addressing God directly in listing the intimate details of this bride-to-be. While Michael, John, and Timothy were slightly amused at Amerjit's prayer, they nonetheless added their support to the petition being delivered to the Almighty.

The Indian lads preformed their daily tasks of sail making, but with a strange expression on each of their faces. While trying to concentrate fully on the needles going back and forth in the sail cloth, they would on occasion poke a needle into a finger. Someone would giggle and suggest that the wounded party keep his mind on the business at hand and not a beautiful, young girl.

Meanwhile, Supi Yaw had written a lengthy letter to her parents inviting them to come to America for the birth of her first child. She included the letters from the Indian lads describing their desired brides, and of course, describing their manly attributes as well. To give support to her petition, she emphasized the wonderful life they had found in San Francisco and the many opportunities for a Baum wife in this open society.

Also in her letter, she mentioned that her American medical mentors had suggested that she would be ready to take a formal examination within the next six months. If she were to pass this examination, she would be the first Baum doctor in their people's history. Not only would she be the first Baum doctor, but she would be the first British woman to adorn her name with the title, medical doctor. She asked that all the Baum people petition God for her success in this noble effort. She further added that Michael would be taking his examination for full captain-of-the-seas status within two months. As a certified captain, he would then be recognized as a commissioned officer; no longer a non-commissioned officer. For this too she asked for the Baum people to pray.

CHAPTER SEVENTY-SIX

The next few months passed with enormous anticipation. A letter from Supi Yaw's parents agreeing to travel to the United States was received. They also indicated that Bua Tan Bo would take a brief recess from his work with the Christian tribes and foreign missionary groups and join them. A second envelope contained seven letters from Baum ladies willing to consider a marriage to one of the Indian lads. An eighth letter addressed to Mr. Amerjit Singh written by a young Baum widow indicated that she would be delighted to consider a marriage, providing Mr. Amerjit would beat her only when she transgressed mightily and never about the head or face. She indicated that she was well suited to working in the kitchen and was particularly fond of growing her own herbs and preparing her own spices. This mention of fresh herbs and spices seemed to seal the deal for Amerjit. "Just imagine it. A woman who grows her own herbs! What could be better than that?" he note aloud.

For Michael and John, business was beginning to pile up to the point where they contracted with other ships to transport cargo under the flag of the Burma Tiger Shipping Company. Orders for sails were likewise coming in faster than those orders could be filled. The Indian lads were required to hire several shifts of Chinese employees who worked twenty-four hours each day. The number of Singer sewing machines had grown from three to ten. Amerjit had to hire on three full-time cooks to keep the Chinese soup, as he called it, cooking. Amerjit was adamant about the proper feeding and treatment of these unfortunate Chinese folks. At one point, he hired a group of Chinese musicians to play during the long work sessions. On many occasions, Emperor Norton visited the sail-making shop to ensure that "his Chinese subjects" as he called them, were well taken care of.

As for the Burma Tiger Dining Room, reservations for private parties filled the calendar almost every night. On one occasion, the Governor of California hosted a dinner for the Japanese ambassador. Although many of these private events had been held at the Imperial Hotel, John Mitchell was happy to share in the success of Amerjit's newly developing clientele. In fact, four months after the first gala dinner, Mitchell invited Amerjit to have lunch at a small French café near the famous Union Square. There, he proposed a formal business partnership between Amerjit and himself as a silent partner. Mitchell indicated that he knew of an empty building near Union Square which would be an ideal location for an exclusive dining house. As Amerjit paused to consider the offer, Mitchell interrupted, "I would expect you to maintain your relationship with your partners at the Burma Tiger Shipping Company, and I would agree to commit ten percent or our net profits to the San Francisco Children's Home."

Amerjit was much too overwhelmed to speak. Mitchell continued, "It is my dream to open the finest dinner house in the city and someday to retire here in San Francisco. I have the funds to buy the vacant location I mentioned, but I must maintain my position at the Imperial for a few more years. If a chef with your skills were to take charge of the kitchen and the menu, I know we could both prosper." Unable to speak, Amerjit simply nodded as tears ran down his dark brown cheeks.

Supi Yaw spent every waking hour memorizing medical charts, medicines and symptoms. Between attending lectures, studying, and attending to her wifely duties, she held an informal clinic for dozens of Chinese people who feared white doctors and their needles. On several occasions, she invited a Chinese herb doctor to participate in her consultations. While the herb doctor learned bits and pieces of western medicine, she gained insights into the Chinese medical world.

As for Mr. Ryan and his new bride, Timothy assumed full responsibility for the hiring and welfare of the crews of both the BURMA TIGER and KING'S RANSOM, recently re-named THE AMERICAN PUMA. Many of Ryan's visits to the ships included brief Bible studies and impromptu homilies. He became well respected and unlike many "ship bosses" he was well liked. "Princess" Anne, as he liked to call his new wife continued to write for the San Francisco Call News. When she was not writing copy, she was adding pages to her slowly growing novels about California, the Wild West. After considerable begging, she convinced Timothy to allow her to sail to Seattle on the AMERICAN PUMA. This resulted in a major manuscript about life on the high seas. After several rejections, a New York publishing company purchased one of her three completed novels, <u>The Battle of the Irrawaddy</u>. Within two months of signing the first contract, the second and the third were placed under contract. Ann Ryan was at last a nationally known author. Timothy was enormously proud of his little Irish Princess, as were the rest of the Burma Tiger "family."

CHAPTER SEVENTY-SEVEN

The scheduled date for the arrival of the China Clipper carrying the precious cargo from Rangoon was one of three dates, "depending on the winds, the currents and the will of God," as the sailors say. John Carter asked Dr. Hitchcock if the duty guard on the Presidio watch tower could make a special effort to watch for the China Clipper, GREAT BARRIOR REEF when she entered San Francisco Bay. Hitchcock agreed to notify those anxiously waiting at the Burma Tiger office.

Michael dressed in his newly tailored captain's uniform, complete with four gold stripes on the sleeve and a captain's hat on his desk, nervously pretended to do paperwork. Doctor Supi Yaw, now greatly expanded across her mid-section likewise pretended to file documents in wooden file cabinets. Amerjit pretended to cook Chinese soup and he anticipated the features of his bride-to-be. The Indian lads pretended to sew sails, pricking fingers and leaving bloody stains on clean white sail cloth as they went. Gunga pretended to nap in his basket on the floor next to Michael's desk.

Early in the morning on the second day, an army orderly, riding a bicycle arrived at the office of the Burma Tiger Shipping Company and announced that the GREAT BARRIOR REEF had just cleared the lighthouse and would be docking within the hour. Everyone in the building dropped what they were doing and dashed for the street. Three carriages were summoned and the race began to Pier 27, at the far end of the embarcadero. The great ship was about twenty meters from the pier as the company of the Burma Tiger Company raced toward the awaiting gangway. Michael immediately recognized his brother-in-law, Bua Tan Bo. Supi Yaw recognized her parents and the Indian lads recognized a bevy of sari-clad Asian beauties, each adorned as if it were her wedding day. The young men stood gaping and wondering which of these handsome creatures would be his. A slightly older Asian lady, also adorned in a sari, smiled as she saw Amerjit standing, with his mouth slightly open. Because Asians are somewhat reserved when it comes to the show of emotion and affection, greetings were formal without the hugging and kissing common to westerners. Elder Simon could clearly see the expressions of excitement on the faces of the young Indian men, who stood wondering about who would be matched with whom. He motioned the seven young ladies to form a line in front of where he was standing. Taking a sheet of paper from his breast pocket, he began a brief speech. "In the wonderful book of Genesis, God has made clear that "... a man shall leave his father and his mother and cleave unto his wife, and the two shall become one flesh." He further declares that "It is not good for a man to live alone." So, in this respect, we have mutually determined that these young ladies from our community would be prayerfully suited to these young gentlemen standing here before us. Judging from the letters we have received from these gentlemen and the response made by these charming young ladies also standing here, my beloved wife and

I have determined that that the following lady is best suited for the following gentleman. Then, Elder Simon called each of the Indian men by name and introduced him to one of the young ladies. One by one, each man came forward and greeted his chosen lady with a bashful grin and a polite handshake. He then took the young lady by the arm and led her back to the group. Nothing in their respective lives could compare with the glowing emotions contained within these newly appointed couples. The girls would shyly peaked out from behind their head coverings to try to get a look at their new consorts while the young men would, without seeming too forward, attempt to assess the beauty of his new partner.

Then Elder Simon spoke, "I would caution each of you to consider this event as a mere introduction and not an engagement. If anyone of you should be uncomfortable with the arrangement, we can make adjustment. If, after several weeks, it is determined that each of you is content with our selections, we will make provisions for a brief term of engagement. Take note, that I said brief term of engagement. Then, once you feel comfortable with the person we have chosen for you, we shall consummate the relationships with a formal wedding. Until that event, I would expect you to conduct yourselves in a manner well pleasing to God."

During Elder Simon's comments, Amerjit focused on the slightly older lady standing next to Elder Simon's wife. The gentle breeze caused her head covering to flutter away from her face giving Amerjit a peek. A definite smile moved across his face. As the lady noticed Amerjit's smile, she too began to smile. There was no question; both were pleased with their respective outward appearances. The butterflies in Amerjit's stomach began to feel like eagles. Finally, Elder Simon asked Amerjit to come forward and introduced him to his impending partner in the kitchen–and elsewhere. Amerjit was openly excited as he took the lady by the arm and led her back to the group.

As the group moved back toward the embarcadero, a dozen carriages were conscripted for the brief journey back to the office of the Burma Tiger Shipping Company. Amerjit and Rani, his new "friend," immediately disappeared into the kitchen where they prepared a lunch for the entire group. Opal Carter announced the young ladies would be accommodated at a nearby boarding house and that all young ladies needed to be indoors no later than nine o'clock. She went on to inform the ladies that they would be given a tour of San Francisco the following day in the company of famous author, Anne Ryan. They would then be treated to a picnic in a local park. Elder Simon and his wife opted to remain behind and visit with their daughter.

Unfortunately for Michael, his business was growing so rapidly that his social time was extremely limited. Likewise, John Carter and Timothy Ryan were up well before dawn and often times, worked until well after nightfall. With the help of Mrs. Worthington, now living in the nearby Napa Valley, Carter found a vintner who would take the sixty barrels of "jungle berry juice" and bottle it under the label, "BURMA TIGER, Asian wine." Many of the bottles were purchased by George Mitchell and Amerjit. The price was kept sufficiently high so as to create a "legend" as to its creation.

Within weeks of arriving the young Burmese ladies had settled into their new accommodations. Likewise, they had become familiar with their respective partners and were well satisfied with the relationship. Each of the young ladies was more than willing to participate in the daily occupation of sail making. On several occasions, several of the ladies would ask permission to design and create a dress they had seen using discarded scrap materials. Amerjit and Rani realized the potential for this sort of entrepreneurial endeavor and asked Carter if he might consider allowing the ladies to perhaps, look into opening a dress shop, perhaps in a year or so. While Carter was not particularly enthused about the idea, Opal was ecstatic. Soon, a dozen or so ladies' frocks were sold to a nearby dress shop. Within a month, two dozen more dresses were created and sold.

As for Amerjit, he moved his entire operation to the newly renovated space near the Union Square. He likewise prepared an apartment in the attic above the dining room and kitchen where he and his new bride might live until they were able to afford a house.

Timothy Ryan and Anne Ryan spent as much time as possible sailing from Seattle to San Francisco and then down to South America. With royalties from Anne's three books, she purchased diaries and ship's logs as resource materials for several new books she was working on. Timothy's passion for shipboard Bible studies gave him the moniker, Reverend Tim. Timothy, with the help of Anne did manage to arrange that they would be in San Francisco near the appointed time of Supi Yaw's delivery date.

One foggy San Francisco day, Dr. Supi Yaw announced while having dinner that it was time for her to make a visit to the local hospital. While she remained calm and reserved, her husband and father were not. Michael barked an order for one of the Indian lads to fetch a carriage and fast. The following morning, William, Michael, Simon, St. John was born. All of the Burma Tiger family was at the hospital following the wonderful event. By noon, flowers from every shipping company in San Francisco, not to mention the mayor, adorned Supi Yaw's room. But best of all, Dr. Supi Yaw managed to convince the attending physician that her mother needed to be present at the actual delivery in order that she might pass on an extremely important blessing to the child as it took its first breath of life.

The week following William Michael Simon's entry into the world, Elder Simon announced that a wedding would be held the following day. Any present wishing to become man and wife should make their intentions known immediately. One by one, the Indian lads and their respective partners sheepishly raised their hands. Without exception, everyone, including Amerjit and Rani raised their hands. "Good!" Simon barked, "Make yourselves ready. I have asked my good friend, Mr. Ryan, to make arrangements at his friend's church. A certain Father O'Riley has agreed to allow me, a minister in my community, to conduct the ceremony. While I am not of his persuasion, he nonetheless will acknowledge the validity of the marriages and see that all necessary procedures are adhered to. I have also asked Mr. Ryan to have a "special talk" with the gentlemen about to me married, and Dr. St. John with have a "special talk" with the ladies. This should serve to eliminate some questions you might have regarding your newly acquired status as husbands and wives." These comments brought giggles and red faces among the young people.

Rani whispered to Amerjit, "Perhaps you might go along with Mr. Ryan, to make certain he gets everything correct."

Amerjit looked at Rani and whispered back, "And perhaps you should be looking in on Dr. St. John's lecture."

If love could grow between a boatload of strangers and a flock of sail makers, it had grown to its fullest. The unseen forces of the need to love and be loved had become manifest in each and every couple. There were no strangers in the church that morning, except for Emperor Joshua A. Norton, Emperor California and Protector of Mexico. Gunga properly sniffed his two friends, Bummer and Lazarus, as Norton entered the church. The words *making two people one* were spoken. Father

O'Riley then added his blessings along with a few comments about married life. Michael quietly whispered to his wife, "What would he know about married life?" Supi Yaw simply smiled as she admired the baby in her arms.

A small but enthusiastic reception and lunch was held at Amerjit's, no make that Amerjit and Rani's dinner house. Following the meal and subsequent activities, the newly married couples were dispatched to various hotels in the neighborhood where they might enjoy a peaceful night's rest. It had been agreed that, once married, the boarding facilities and the newly abandoned dining and kitchen areas would be made into small, very small, apartments for the Indian lads and their new wives.

CHAPTER SEVENTY-EIGHT

Less than a month had passed since the birth of William and the marriage of fourteen Asians. The transitions had taken place with little or no negative impact on the operations of the Burma Tiger Shipping Company. One morning, a uniformed delivery man from the British Council entered the office and asked to speak to Michael St. John. "Sir, I have a personal note from our new Council General to San Francisco." The man handed the note to Michael who had just been joined by John. The message read, *"Her Majesty Queen Victoria has requested that I invite you and the members of your company to a dinner to be hosted by my most recently appointed Council General to San Francisco. The event is to take place at the Burma Tiger Dinning House, with the following persons to be invited;*

Sergeant Major (ret) Michael Oliver St. John
Doctor Supi Yaw St. John
Mr. Amerjit Singh
Mr. Bua Tan Bo

Others to be invited are at the discretion of the Council General and yourselves. It is our intention to duly recognize you for your significant accomplishments.

Respectfully,

Walter R. Smith–Morton,

Her Majesty's Council General of San Francisco.

Amerjit prepared a banquet as if Queen Victoria would be personally present. A dozen invitations went out under the seal of the Council General. Numerous socialites got wind of the event and attempted to have their names placed on the invitation list, but given the limited seating capacity of the new Burma Tiger Dining room, total capacity was limited to thirty-five guests.

As the guests arrived, photographers and reporters cluttered the sidewalk. Anne Ryan stopped to chat with a few of her former colleagues and promised an inside story sometime tomorrow. Mrs. Worthington and Emperor Norton (and his two dogs) arrived by carriage, as did the Mayor of San Francisco, the ranking Bishop of the Anglican Church, and other dignitaries. George Mitchell had loaned Amerjit his very best silver service and table settings. In fact, Mitchell could be seen peaking from behind the kitchen door from time to time as the guests assembled in the room. All of the Indian lads and several Chinese kitchen staff had been re-uniformed especially for this occasion. The ambiance in the new Burma Tiger was beyond anything else found in the City of San Francisco. Mitchell was quietly pleased at his newest creation.

The Council General beckoned each guest to their places around the U-shaped table. He then asked the Anglican Bishop to offer an invocation for the evening and for the meal. He did in the most eloquent and lengthy of terms. The meal was unlike anything Amerjit or any guest in the room had ever imagined. Glasses of Burma Tiger Asian wine were consumed, refilled, and consumed again. As dessert was being slowly savored, the Council General rose from his seat, slightly impaired from the wine. He began a brief speech. "Her Majesty, Queen Victoria, Queen of Great Britain, Empress of India, (so on and so on), has graciously requested that I act on her behalf in giving proper recognition to certain of her loyal subjects, now present with us here this evening. Captain Michael Oliver St. John, would you please come forward and receive this token of Her Majesty's appreciation for your accomplishments both as a mariner and as a businessman. Her Majesty has asked that I personally present to you this sword as a symbol of your rank of captain and as a recognized officer. We have further requested that your name appear on the official listing of British sea captains and afford you all considerations of that rank."

The Council General placed a long wooden box on the table in front of him and slowly removed the magnificent sword from its housing. On the pommel of the sword was the seal of Victoria, Queen of Great Britain. Slowly, the Council General pulled the gleaming silver object from its scabbard. "Here on one side of the blade was inscribed, "Presented to Captain Michael Oliver St. John, 'Hero of the Irrawaddy'." On the other side the inscription had the words, "In Hoc Signo Vinces." The Council General went on to read from a letter, personally written by the Queen, "*My good friend Michael, I shall always treasure the brief time we spent together here in London. You are one of the few heroes I have had the good fortune to encounter who did not equate his valiant deeds or noble behavior to being himself, valiant or noble. True greatness is manifest in humility rather than the false trappings of greatness. You will notice the inscription on the sword 'In Hoc Signo Vinces' is a quote from the first Christian Emperor, Constantine in 312 A.D. Our reason for selecting this inscription comes directly from the design of the sword itself. Unlike many weapons of war, your sword is constructed in the shape of a cross. It is therefore this symbolic image of Our Savior's Cross and the Latin words, "By This Sign I shall Conquer" that we ask you to use this symbol and its true meaning to make the world a better place for mankind. I have asked both my God and my representative in America to keep a special watch on you and your career until we once again meet."*

Warmest and most sincere regards,

Victoria, Regina Britannia

Tears flooded Michael's face as he received the sword. Like Constantine the Great, he held the object high over his head and uttered the words, "By this sign I shall conquer." Totally without any further words, Michael took his place as his wife politely embraced him.

The Council General then requested Dr. St. John rise. An attendant handed him another hand-crafted wooden box. He began reading, "*Doctor Supi Yaw St. John, while my domain is not yet ready to accept women in the world of medicine, you have by your own tenacity and tact found your way into this mystical world of healers. For this we laud you and your accomplishments. I can only assume that one day, persons of your race and gender will be universally welcomed into this world of healers.*

In recalling your visit to Buckingham Palace I am compelled to revisit our little consultation regarding matters of an extremely personal nature. If you will recall, you suggested that I make use of a particular herb in the treatment of a particularly uncomfortable ailment. I discreetly availed myself of this potion and within a fortnight, my condition had greatly improved. I regret to say that none of my personal physicians had any knowledge of this cure. While I am not in a position to recognize your newly acquired position as a medical doctor under the American system, I wish to acknowledge your service to your queen with this small token of my great esteem for you and for your accomplishments."

With that, the Council General opened the black ebony box in front of him and lifted out a stethoscope. The earpieces were made from ivory and the hard tubes were made of silver. The cup piece was carved deer horn. At the juncture of the two ear tubes and the chest tube, there was affixed Queen Victoria's Royal seal. Supi Yaw likewise broke into tears as she acknowledged the gift and its extreme significance to her.

Bua Tan Bo was then summoned, whereupon he stood, shocked that his name would be called. The Council General was handed yet another box. "Mr. Bua Tan Bo, Her Majesty the Queen has invested in me the privilege of presenting you with credentials elevating you to the rank of diplomat with special portfolio, specifically to the tribal groups in Burma. Walter Smith-Morton handed Bua Tan Bo a document bearing a royal seal affixed to the bottom. Then, Smith-Morton opened the ebony box and brought out an extremely handsome royal decoration. The item was a collar to be placed around the neck of its recipient. At the center of the chain was an emblem with the images of St. Michael and St. George. With the help of the Consul General's assistant, the chain was placed around Bua Tan Bo's neck. "It is my profound pleasure to award you the Most Distinguished Order of Saint Michael and Saint George. Speaking on behalf of my sovereign, I present this for what you have done and what you are yet to do. Please accept my sincere congratulations for having been presented with this high royal honor."

Bua could not utter a word. He simply nodded and smiled a cautious smile. He looked at Michael who returned the smile. He then looked at his father and mother who sat motionless exuding quiet expressions of the most profound pride a parent could imagine. Both of their children honored by the Queen. Nothing in the history of the Baum people could compare with this. All those present rose to their feet as Bua Tan Bo returned to his chair, savoring the weight of the high honor he had just received. Then, the Consul General reached for one final wooden box. "Mr. Amerjit Singh, please come forward. Amerjit was standing at the rear of the dining room, totally enthralled with the events of the evening. "Mr. Singh, it has come to our attention that you have achieved the levels of a master chef and restaurateur. While this brings well-deserved attention of the general public, as a British subject it also brings notoriety to your culture and your country. In holding with British tradition, we hereby accredit your place of business as being under Royal Patronage. We make provision for this patronage in the event that we, or others from our family, might enjoy the pleasure of dining in your establishment. We therefore award you and your establishment this symbol of Royal Patronage and authorize you to display the seal of Royal Patronage within your establishment and upon documents relating to your business. With that, the CG removed a carved gilded royal crest and notice of appointment. The CG called for his assistant to place a nail in the wall behind the head table and hung the plaque for all to see. Amerjit called for his wife to join him from the kitchen. The sense of pride she exhibited toward her new husband brought him to tears.

That evening in San Francisco was like none other. It seemed that every life that had been touched by the Burma Tiger had changed and changed dramatically. Like dozens of shooting stars all colliding in a single place, in a single point in time, every life, from that of a small English Bulldog to those newly married Indian lads, to an obscure English nurse, to a British soldier had melded into a single wonderful community, no make that a family.

EPILOGUE:

The profits from the Burma Tiger Shipping & Trading Company allowed for the addition of one new ship each year for the next ten years. After the fifth addition, steamships were included in the fleet. Likewise, Anne Ryan added a new book to her growing list of best sellers along with two children, both born on the high seas.

Amerjit's fame as a restaurateur and gourmet chef compelled him, Rani, and George Mitchell to expand their dining room and kitchen facilities into two adjacent buildings facing the very exclusive, Union Square.

As the success of the Burma Tiger enterprises increased, so did the San Francisco Children's Home. As a matter of fact, Mr. Ryan recruited a number of older boys from the home to serve on the ships as seamen.

The Indian lads expanded their activities from sail making to clothing enterprises. There wives were particularly innovative in creating well-made and well-designed women's fashions for a number of exclusive dress shops. As their businesses grew, so did their families. Oddly enough, all of their first children were born within weeks of each other.

Lilly Hitchcock married a wealthy man by the name of Coit and moved rapidly up the social and economic scale; perhaps too fast.

Emperor Joshua A. Norton passed away as did Mrs. Alice Worthington. In fact, Lilly Hitchcock Coit, as she was now called after her marriage, purchased Mrs. Worthington's home in the Napa Valley and turned it into a personal private gambling establishment for her and her friends.

Captain Michael St. John and Captain John Carter were sufficiently successful to be invited to join the prestigious Pacific Union Club. Both declined the invitations in favor of spending more time with their growing families and the families of what had become called the Burma Tiger Family.

Dr. Supi Yaw St. John was invited to become a member of a small but prominent medical school in the San Francisco area. She too declined the generous offer in preference of working with a group of followers of a General William Booth from England and an organization calling itself, The Salvation Army. Supi Yaw recalled meeting this General Booth while in London and was strongly attracted to the work being done by these members of this new "army." It had become her passion to stand with these "soldiers of God" on the street corners in the darker parts of town and offer medical services to those who could not afford a general clinic. And while she was not looking after her three children, she looked after the well being of the children in the San Francisco Children's Home.

As for Gunga, he made regular visits to kennels where he would meet special lady friends who ultimately bore dozens of prodigy whose pedigree papers bore the title, "Gunga, of Queen Victoria."

Bua Tan Bo, along with his parents, returned to Burma where he continued his efforts to bring the benefits of the western world to the hinterlands of Burma. Unfortunately, the stated intentions of the British holy men in London never fully materialized. On the other hand, the heads of certain American mission societies had been persuaded to take the challenge Bua had placed before them during his brief meetings in San Francisco. Within two years of his visit, much to the chagrin of the British clergy, over twenty American missionary units had entered Burma and found their way into where they were needed and welcome.

Sergeants Roberts and McMillan were both granted honorable release from the military, complete with handsome pensions. Sergeant Roberts married a beautiful Baum woman and was commissioned as a full-fledged missionary with the American Baptist Mission. McMillan signed on with the British government as a full-time agricultural development inspector under the direct supervision of Bua Tan Bo. While McMillan opted to make his home in Chittagong, he and Roberts held regularly scheduled rock-tossing contests and sword-dance events in the Banderban Hills.

As a result of the fabled jungle berry juice, Bother James had become wealthy beyond his wildest dreams. In his compound, nothing had changed with the exception of a few new trinkets for his wife. Almost every penny of his profits were used to fund schools, books, medicines, and the like for poor Buddhist, Moslem and Christian villages in the mountains.

The old tiger with the broken fang continued to roam the mountains of Burma looking for a cool drink of water.

THE END